Praise for *Dreamland*:

'A beautiful book: thought-provoking, eerily prescient and very witty' **Brit Bennett, author of *The Vanishing Half***

'Rankin-Gee's novel is a triumph, being as much a love letter to the heady ups and crashing lows of youthful entanglements as it is a paean to the former grandeur of its stark coastal setting. Read this now' *GQ*

'A writer of a new time ... A writer we will all want to read again and again' **Monique Roffey, author of the Costa Book of The Year, *The Mermaid of Black Conch***

'Water courses through its pages, as rising sea levels heighten inequalities, buoy populist politicians and wash away every certainty of civilisation. But there's also the novel's prose – its liquid grace and glinting sparkle – and the sheer irresistibility of a narrative that sweeps along with a force that feels tidal in its pull' *The Observer*

'She vividly captures the balance between ferocity and vulnerability as the two girls explore their burgeoning desire; one minute they're greedy for each other, the next they're proceeding more gingerly. Theirs is a great first love, blazing bright and furious amid the poverty and the pain, the perfect counterweight that's needed to make the novel sing. Dreamland brings us face-to-face with much of what we're on the threshold of losing; nevertheless, it manages to convince us that its characters have everything still to live for' *Guardian*

'A great coming-of-age story, and a warning' *Evening Standard*

DREAMLAND

ROSA RANKIN-GEE

SCRIBNER

LONDON NEW YORK SYDNEY TORONTO NEW DELHI

First published in Great Britain by Scribner, an imprint of Simon & Schuster UK Ltd, 2021
This Paperback edition published in 2022

SCRIBNER and design are registered trademarks of The Gale Group, Inc.,
used under licence by Simon & Schuster Inc.

1 3 5 7 9 10 8 6 4 2

Simon & Schuster UK Ltd
1st Floor
222 Gray's Inn Road
London WC1X 8HB

Simon & Schuster Australia, Sydney
Simon & Schuster India, New Delhi

www.simonandschuster.co.uk
www.simonandschuster.com.au
www.simonandschuster.co.in

A CIP catalogue record for this book
is available from the British Library

PB ISBN: 978-1-4711-9384-2
EBOOK ISBN: 978-1-4711-9383-5
AUDIO ISBN: 978-1-3985-0157-7

Printed and bound in Great Britain by CPI Group (UK) Ltd, Croydon CR0 4YY

For Erinn, and my godson, baby Magnus.

And for Leah, always.

Today I watched a man walk into the sea. Not walk, he was running, the top half of his body moving faster than his legs through the water. He stumbled once, twice, then thrashed his way back to standing.

At first, from where I was, it looked like he was making his way to a box that was floating. Then I saw it was a piece of clothing. A jacket. A jacket filled with air, a soft dome puffing out above the water, the shape of a jellyfish back. When the man got closer, he took the jacket in his hands. He turned it over – it was heavier than it looked. There was a body zipped inside it.

The man started yelling. He yelled again and again. I jumped down from the broken tidal barrier where I was sitting and started to run over. When I got closer, I saw it was a child's body, small in his hands. The man lifted the body out of the water, held it up to his chest, then started to make his way back to land, waves crashing white against his shoulders. As he got closer, the sounds he was making got louder. When he hit sand, he dropped to his knees.

It was a boy he was holding. Four, five, thin. He held the boy's head in the palm of his hand, he touched his face. He put the boy down on the beach and started pushing at his chest. He tried mouth to mouth, but when I got to them, I saw water coming out of the boy's lips, more and more and more of it.

'My son,' he said. 'He's my boy.'

I started to say I could get help, that I could go and find someone, but it was too late. The kid's lips, his eyes, his fingertips were purple. 'Yesterday he went missing,' the man said, 'yesterday. But I had to work. I had to get work. I left him with his sister. I never should have left him.'

The man held the boy like I used to hold Blue, his arms like a hammock. The boy's limbs hung slack either side. A walnut filled my throat till it blocked it completely. I couldn't swallow. It felt like I couldn't breathe. The sea started to pool in the dipped sand around us.

'You have to get off the beach,' I said. Each wave brought the tide higher. 'Please.'

And finally, I got him to walk with me, his son in his arms, water dripping from both their clothes.

My legs felt heavy as I climbed the stairs back to our flat. My mum was lying on the sofa when I got there. She was stone asleep, her face tilted towards her shoulder. I went over, ran my fingertip under her left eye. When they're open, her eyes can look a bit soft now, like soap left in water. I made space next to her legs, and found a place for my body at her side.

You never once saw inside my house, did you?

Even when you came to the door, I blocked you looking in. I stood on my tiptoes to make myself bigger and pushed you back out into the corridor. Not that the corridor was any better.

I don't know exactly how long it's been since I last saw you. Standing right here in my doorway. Maybe a year and a bit, maybe longer, but it's hard to tell.

However long it's been, it's been long enough for me to have forgotten the details of what you look like. Sometimes I know the edges, how your skin met your hair. But the most important parts, how your face made sense in the middle, I lost that one day.

You said that you would come back. You looked me in the eye and said that. Well, if you had, this is what you would have seen: soft wood, black cracks, fridges in the road. The broken spines of old rides at Dreamland. Me and my mum, tangled silent on the sofa.

I didn't tell her what happened at the beach. We didn't speak. At some point, she fell back asleep. And then it came – the knock on the door. Her eyes shot open. Mine did, too.

Two heavy, dull beats, the gap between them slightly too long.

'That's not Davey,' she said. She turned to me. 'It isn't Davey, is it?'

I shook my head. I felt my body freeze. After the knock, a sound that shouldn't have been possible.

The sound of a key sliding into our lock.

Just the word Dreamland – it can't get much better than that, can it?

TRACEY EMIN, AS SHE TURNED ON THE
NEW DREAMLAND LIGHTS, JUNE 2017

Tane'tus, a small island of Albion. Ptolemy calls it Tolianis. It is now Thanet.

LEMPRIÈRE'S CLASSICAL DICTIONARY, 1788

I.

The plan was simple, once she'd decided it. Our mum wanted us to move to Margate before I remembered anything else. But it's never quite like that. There's always a before. Half-memories, and memories I made myself when someone else told me the story later.

The first thing I remember is being under a blanket with my brother, JD. The blanket was held up by his head, which he had shaved that day. He was nine years old, and I was four, and he was telling me we'd be famous. Not we, actually – he.

The blanket was because the room was cold, air conditioning flushed in like a storm all day, but also because the story made more sense in the dark. We were living in a hotel – we'd been living in hotels and B&Bs for as long as I could remember – and that particular one was directly in front of a

3

motorway. It didn't have a thirteenth floor because no one would have wanted to live on it. It went 12, then 14, which is where our room was. My hands were so cold they'd curled up. 'Gimme them seashells,' he said, and he put them under his armpits, right after he'd done press-ups, so my hands would warm up.

All across the hotel, there were notices on every door, even the ones inside, that said 'No dogs, no kids, no DSS'. We weren't allowed in the lobby in case 'actual' guests came, though there were never any signs of that. In our tiny room, JD would parkour around – soft bed to clanky side table, using drawer handles like the nobbles on climbing walls.

'Orbiting around you like some mad planet,' our mum Jas used to say. 'Always been obsessed with you. When you were a little baby he'd just look at you, like he was waiting for you to grow up and be able to talk.'

We had different dads, so he was my half-brother actually, though it never felt like that. The way she always said it, was that his dad was stupid and mine was Swedish – though I came out alright.

She had a job at a school on the other side of London, in the north, working as a TA in the art studio. It was in an area that was half-Jewish, half-gangs, so she called it Stabford Hill. Sometimes, if she couldn't find anyone to look after us, we went into work with her.

''Kin hell, look at the hat on him!' JD would say, pointing at an orthodox man, as Ma pulled us away down the street.

4

'Let me get one of them, then. One of them hats. Big-man style. That's class.'

There were always armed guards outside the front door of the school, guns like black shiny beetles against their chests, but it was okay, because Ma could tilt her voice one way to flirt with them, and then the other if we bumped into one of the other teachers in the corridor. That voice was a bit posh, frazzled and eye-rolling in the right way. 'Absolute nightmare,' she'd say, grouping our bodies together into the shape of a family photograph, 'their nanny's sick.'

She used to be good at reading a room, and changing her voice to meet it. JD wasn't. 'Oi, what's a nanny?' he'd say, before she could reach down. 'Oi, don't pinch me, no, get off.'

He and I sat on the bench in the corner while she helped the teacher with the lesson. One time, JD went and got us some of the crayons to play with, and she came over saying, 'No, no, no.'

'What?'

'They're for the children,' she said.

'She is a child,' he said, pointing at me, 'fucking look at her.'

'JD, your manners. Honestly, did you grow up in a barn or what?'

'Yeah, I did thanks. With you. Pigs and everyfink.'

'Thing not fink.'

She tried to take back the crayons but he managed to keep one, and I believe that was the time he drew a penis on the wall.

*   *   *

5

It was a barn, it wasn't a barn. She was pretty good when we were at home. JD had a school he was supposed to go to but he rarely went and they'd lost him on the system anyway because we'd changed school zones so many times. When Ma came home from her school she tried to teach him with stacks of books they didn't want any more, but he was the most restless child in existence. He'd flit from one wall to the other, like a trapped bat, and I remember her turning to me once and asking if I'd do it.

Every other Sunday, her phone would ding with a transfer of money from her parents. The reason for sending was always pointed; a 'to do' list of things she hadn't done. DENTAL CHECK 4 CNJD. FLAT DEPOSIT SAVE DNT SPEND!!

Judgement was the word she used. Judgement was the thing she couldn't bear. 'Honestly, they're your classic Surrey bigots,' she said to a friend in the corridor, their backs leaning against opposite walls, sharing wine from the bottle. 'They don't understand how life is now. They don't understand the lifestyle.'

'Lifestyle,' the friend said, reaching up to flick the switch that didn't work. 'Yup. Straight from the pages of *Town and Country*, this.'

Once or twice, JD took me on the train to see them. He'd ask to borrow someone's phone halfway, so Grandad could pick us up from the station. On the train, I practised reading on all of the adverts around the route map. There was one that was everywhere at that time. It said, 'I hate funerals so why would

I have my own?' The person in the photo was quite young, smiling, wearing a pork-pie hat. The tagline said, *Make space. Nembuta and cremation all-in-one End-Life packages.*

'What's Nembuta?' I asked JD.

'Dunno,' he said. 'Ask Nana when we get there. Not right away though, 'cos it's rude.'

I wish I could remember more about their house, but all that's left is flashes, a feeling more than anything. Two cars in the driveway, a separate dining room, a smell through all the corridors of flowers left in water. I remember that they didn't cook well. Grandad liked his potatoes burned and his chicken 'tender', which meant translucent closest to the bone. JD would hold a piece up on his fork to the light, then say I was vegetarian, so I didn't have to eat it. 'Look, yummy, potatoes are nice.' He'd cut them up into little bits for me, and pull off the blackest black. 'Trust me, the meat'll give you the squits.'

They still had a TV with a round back. It slid into a low antique cupboard to keep it out of sight. It would make JD crack up when Grandad would forget we were there and swear at the screen. 'Fucking *Windrush* still. Endless, endless. Endless kowtowing, endless apologies – it's enough!' His hand would swat like he was slamming an invisible door. 'Mo' hammed? I'd prefer to see less Hamid, thank you. Just fucking fuck off home, why don't you?' There was one politician he liked, a guy called Rex Winstable, and for him, he'd just say, 'Exactly, EXACTLY. A bit rough around the edges but he gets it. A sense of *order*. Just get rid of the *waste*.' But everyone else it would be back to FUCK off, or fucking fuck off, which was his preferred way of saying it.

'Proper potty-mouth for a posh boy,' JD would whisper to me, shaking his head. 'Can tell he's posh 'cos it sounds like he's speaking out his nose.' At certain points, when the swearing was really bad, JD would try to cover my ears with his hands, but he was laughing so much I could always hear through the gaps.

'It's the dementia,' Grandma told us in the kitchen.

'Him too?' JD asked.

'No, still mine. He says the hospital is overrun. Blames all those nurses who left and never came back. I don't know. He says I don't get the treatment I need. He's just upset. It's not an easy time.'

Her brain was a map with holes in it, quicksand, landslides, but there were moments she was on solid ground.

I asked her what Nembuta was, and she said it was a poison, then narrowed her eyes. 'Why?' she said. 'Is that supposed to be a hint?'

Before we left – they always built up to it, you could almost see them doing it, taking steps inside their chest – they asked how our mum was, and it was always a hard question to answer. JD would always get a little spiky, but try to swallow it down, because he knew what he was there for.

'Quallers!' he'd say, grinning like a light bulb when we left. 'Fucking fuck off bullseye!' They always gave him cash. He'd count it on the train, smell his fingers, get me to smell them too, and say they smelled of being rich.

Even though I was only six, he said I had to have a twenty on me at all times, just in case I had to buy my way out of trouble.

It wasn't a selfish thing, going to our grandparents to get money. It was for me as much as it was for him. We had a box. At that point it was a shoebox, but a small one because it was from shoes I'd had as a baby. To fasten it up, JD put Sellotape round his wrist and did circles and circles till the whole thing was shiny.

The money box was the first thing we packed whenever we moved – when the hotel we were in was sold, or the management changed the lock on our door. The last time, our stuff was left in a pile on the landing, in big bin bags, the dark green ones used for carrying wood. They'd slashed the sides with a Stanley knife, so we had no easy way to carry our clothes. They'd left a note with a fine on it too – for a lamp we'd apparently damaged. The fine was more than the lamp would have been new.

The hotel we were put in after that was the worst. There was one microwave to share between forty families, and the freezer and the oven had been taped shut. 'My God,' Ma said the first time we walked in, 'the land that hygiene forgot.' We kept a tall, plastic-wrapped stack of antibacterial wipes by our bedroom door. We brought in takeaway food from outside and ate with a chair as our table. Throughout the day, we could hear the out-of-time beeps of fire alarms with run-down batteries – the sound of a trainer sole squeaking against a polished floor. The lino in the bathroom was wet, always wet, thick wet with who knew what. If we had to wee in the night, Ma came with us. Checked the corners of the room, checked behind the shower curtain, checked everything, before she locked the door behind us.

She called Emergency Accommodation EA for short. 'EA Games, EA Sports. But this one's like a fricking point and shoot,' she said.

There was a man who walked up and down the corridor pausing outside our room. JD nicknamed him Tennis because of the ringworm that had drawn lines and circles on his head. He tried to talk to me when I was on my own once, trying to read this long mad graffiti someone had written on the corridor wall, but JD came back to find me just before Tennis got the words out.

There was only one bed in our room, a small double. Ma took the edge side, I was in the middle and JD had the wall, his feet sticking out the whole night so they could press into the cold wallpaper. None of us slept. It was the way the footsteps stopped at our door. The way the light from the corridor changed. It was the way he tried to turn the door handle – how we saw it move, how we heard it shake. And it was what came through the keyhole, hot from Tennis's mouth. It was the first time I smelled kem.

'Don't worry,' Ma said that night. 'I'll fix this.' I could hear her heartbeat in our pillow, and it was like a bird's heart. Too-quick, flickering.

The next day, she locked us in the room, both locks, and said if there was a fire, we should scream the place down, and worst case, fashion a rope. She came back, hours later, with a look of determination on her face. Determination, excitement – her hair was escaping from her ponytail. She was also a little bit drunk. I could tell because she had shiny-fresh lipgloss on, like she'd put it on outside the door to smarten up. 'I've done it,' she said. She looked at us. 'Five. Two. Two,' she said after that.

We looked back.

'Five hundred for me, two hundred for each of you.' She had cash in her hands. She dealt it like cards onto the bed. 'Upfront, my friends. Just like that.'

'Ain't your friend,' JD said.

'Well you stay here if you like, then. 'Cos me and Chance are going tomorrow.'

'Going where?'

'Does it matter?' she said. 'You wanna stay here with that freak Tennis, do you?'

He thought about it for a second, then shook this head.

'Anyway, I'm trying to tell you,' she said. 'I went down to the housing centre and told them everything. That we had one bed between three of us, and a grade A nutter outside the door.'

Surprise, surprise, she said, the council didn't have anything in all of London, but they sent her across town to a new foundation instead. 'Non-gov this time. Some Winstable project, that monster your grandad likes, *but* —' her but was as big as the sky ' — they said they could offer us a cash packet instead.'

'Cash for what?' JD said. It was all tens and twenties. He held one up to the light.

'To get gone,' she said. She said it happily. It sounded like a jingle. 'The whole system's been bare bones for ages, so I thought might as well seize the opportunity, carpe the diem.' She was definitely drunk, the lips and neck of a small bottle were sticking out of her pocket. She told us the payment was based on 'Reconnection Policies'. That you had to have somewhere to go. 'So I told them Margate,' she said. 'Which is where I had you, anyway.'

She said London was too expensive to be the future. She said it was a fourth world country now. A hotbed, a bomb waiting to go off. That, and an island for rich Russians. She told us she'd always believed in the power of a clean start.

'Look at all this,' she said pointing around the room, then she put her fingers over my eyelids, heavy, and held them there, and said, 'Pfff,' the sound of a file deleting on her old laptop, 'just like that, forget it. This is when life begins. From right now. No more waiting.'

When she woke up in the morning, her mouth doing a slow dry-clap from having drunk too much, she let us pack our own bags and I took all the wrong things. I even took one of her bras, one that she didn't seem to be taking with her, one I'd always liked. Green lace, underwires like smiles.

'Wasn't that the worst hotel on the entire planet,' she ask-told us as we walked. 'There are nice hotels out there, you know. In the real world, hotel's a good word. But that place? That place was a paedo per child. Seriously,' she said, 'you can tell from the eyes. Every other male in there was on a list.'

When we got to the train station, she and JD helped me jump the barrier. On the platform, she sat in an uncomfortable squat over a low metal bollard, pointy like a pyramid.

'Oi, stop though,' JD said. 'Why you doing that for?' Even I remember being aware of people looking.

'They put them to stop people sleeping here. "Urban furniture." So rude! So I like to sit.'

She took her wallet out from her backpack and opened it up for me when JD was walking back and forth along the platform practising smiling at two girls his age. The wallet was full of the cash she'd been given. 'Money money money,' she said, then she DJ'ed with her mouth to turn it into 'Mo Money Mo Problems', the *I'm – coming – out* chorus bit. We got on the first train that came, and she opened the door with a bow, then looked like she might vomit. 'Hangover,' she said. 'Look away, please. Avert your eyes.'

The train didn't take us far. We'd got on a commuter train, and there were too many people for the carriage. 'Hold your breath,' she said to us before we got on. 'Honestly, lads, ooof, a little bit of deodorant wouldn't go amiss.' It was mostly men. Men in dark suits pushed up against each other, their ties the only things that were loose. A couple had their faces covered, eyes peering hard at their phones above masks. Other people were reading the same paper, and the headline said SATURATION POINT. Everyone was double my height. I looked up at them and they looked down at me. I remember their faces, faces that said, Weird little kid, what are you doing here?

I remember half of the journey to Margate exactly, then the other half, I slept across Ma's lap. We didn't have a ticket, so we hid in the loo. One of the big ones, for disabled people.

It was JD's idea of torture, being locked in a small square like that. First, he tried to take apart the smoke detector with his hands, then he spent a long time turning the tap over the sink on again, then off again.

'Yes, JD,' she said. 'We get it. The magic of a tap.'

Still, she tried to make the trip fun. At one point, she used the assistance bar for balance and held one leg up like a ballerina. We washed our hands lots of times so the scent of the soap would stick. She snuck out for three minutes and bought something from the man who was bringing through snacks.

She came back with crisps – I remember them tasting of lemon but that must have been the hand soap mixing with salt – and she said buying the crisps was us paying our way. Even though all of us knew that the man with the snacks had nothing officially to do with the train, he was just a random guy with a scuffed Bag for Life full of multipacks.

Out of the windows, I remember rushing past yellow fields, razor-lines cut through them. I remember silver water, houseboats along its edge – 'Rochester!' she said. 'A number-one dump' – and that must have been when I fell asleep.

I woke up on a set of wooden seats, with glass behind us and the sea in front – a huge, hard, choppy blanket, blue mixing with orange because of the setting sun. We were about 100 metres away from Margate train station, under a shelter painted white and green. The tiles at our feet were like a red and black chessboard, and the roof of the shelter had a fringe of carved wood, and some bits were broken, which in that moment made me think of someone creating space between their hair to see.

There was a lot to see. In the distance, the gap between the sea and the sky was so blurred that tankers or trawlers looked like they were floating just above the water. Up close, they'd made the metal street light to look like it was held up by the thick, swirly tail of a giant fish. Ma said we should all breathe in deep, that sea air was cleansing and we had to get London out of our nostrils.

'There's a tidal pool somewhere down underneath there,' she said after that, pointing through the promenade's green railings at the seawater splashing beyond it, 'and over there, that's the harbour. When I lived here before, I always thought if you could see it from above, it would look like the arm of a record player going into the sea. And look, Chance,' she said to me, leaning back, 'a funfair.'

Not far away, on the seafront still, was the tall concrete sign of Dreamland, a shining square of windows next to it. Behind them I could see the top of the big wheel, folded in half like a taco. She finger-painted in the air for me back to the harbour. 'See that jaggy white building over there? Like waves crashing back into the sea? That's the Turner,' she told me. 'Art gallery. World class.'

JD did a handstand by the public toilet next to us and walked on his palms, his calves bending down in a curve towards his head for balance. 'Where are we, though?' he shouted from upside down, the sound somersaulting to us through the air.

'Home,' Ma said.

I was tired, the kind of tired that makes you feel like all the parts of your body are tied to the ground. I tried to nestle into her, the way that young puppies do, or cats, babies. Try to find space for themselves.

'T. S. Eliot wrote some poems here,' she said into my scalp. 'Very famous. Loved the place. A lot of clever people came

16

here. Were born here. Did things. This will be good for us.'
She made her mouth a hot O against my skin and her hand
made a basket for my head.

We stayed there until the sun slipped into the water. It
was the first time I had seen the sea, and it seemed to be all
around us.

'High these days,' she said, 'higher everywhere.'

I was seven years old. She was thirty-two. JD, who was
already walking away, calling down to a girl on the beach,
had just turned thirteen.

Blue wasn't born yet – he came afterwards – and you
came, too. But the three of us, we would never leave.

We found our first place to live through a handwritten advert in the window of a sweet shop. There were so many signs for rooms to rent that they were all piled on top of each other. 'So cheap they're practically giving it away!' Ma said. 'It's like a menu, all you can eat. Come on up, donkeyhead, help me pick.'

By the time we got to Margate, lots of people had already left. Not a few people – when it's that many, 'droves' is the word people use. 'It's a little bit rough again,' she told us, 'but it will pop back up. Always does. There was a second coming, but there'll be a third. Every time they say it has good bones . . . Bones!' She pinched my earlobe. 'I always liked that. Like the new people would be the flesh.'

She took us down Love Lane and King Street, cobbles and painted shop signs. 'Pastel, and that pink colour. Was like a magnet for the last lot. Was like a magnet for me. I'd walk like a zombie—' and she jerked forward with her hands out.

But, like she said, if there'd been a second coming, by the time we arrived, it had come and gone.

It was already nearly dark, so we chose a place to stay quickly and met a man in an empty pub so he could hand over keys. One key. A key that looked small enough to be for a padlock. The man had a tooth-gap that was slightly to the side, and he took Ma's earrings for a deposit. It wasn't his suggestion. She offered them to him. I remember her wiping the thin bit that goes through the ear on her jacket, half glad she'd done that, half wishing she hadn't.

There were left-behind mattresses in the flat and the first night, we used our bags as pillows. It was above a shop that was called Newsagents – not because it had any news to sell, but just because that was what it had always been called. They played music on a loudspeaker from breakfast till midnight. Bangla, hip-hop. Ma didn't mind. She'd found a tin of paint in the alleyway next door, and she danced as she painted two walls green the next morning, swapping to a make-up brush to do the edges around a fire blanket inside a red box that was nailed to the wall.

Her arms were thin; you could see exactly how muscles worked by asking her to flex. All of her was thin. The way she said it herself was that she had a kid's body, but with breasts. 'Look at them,' she'd say, 'like spaceships.' Low trousers, flat stomach. People would ask if she was my brother's sister. She wore her hair half-up half-down, or in a messy bun at the top of her head, and she wore a lot of baggy suit jackets at that time, sleeves rolled up, delicate silver and goldish bracelets that would glint on her wrist.

Me and JD knew it. Everyone did. She had something about her then. Something likeable. If you looked closely, one of her teeth had already gone a little bit grey, tea gone cold, but when she smiled it was like a light going on. I don't know if this is the right way to say it, but everything was in the right place on her face. Her cheekbones could look like the sides of a wine glass coming into the stem, these perfect curves. Apparently she'd even modelled for my dad a couple of times. That was how they'd met.

That was one of the things I wished for most, when Blue was born. That he could have known how she used to be. How funny she found things. The haircuts she gave JD based on – but always incredibly different to – pictures he found in magazines. How her arms would dance, do these kind of swimming stroke things, when she walked. Not to be annoying. Not because she thought someone might be watching. But because she couldn't help it. How happiness used to bubble up inside her and spill out onto you if you were close. How she'd put her hands on people's knees or their arms because she said she felt things so much she needed an earth wire.

'Come on,' she said that afternoon, 'we're not gonna be the type to literally watch paint dry. Get your coat, JD, you've pulled. We're going to the beach.'

We left the flat and I was desperate to see everything. It was the first place we'd ever had to ourselves, and I wanted it to count for something. As we stepped outside, the squawks of seagulls were like someone hammering on a doorbell. Up high in a bright window on the other side of the road, the word AMAZING was painted white on red on a thin slat of wood. I wanted us to stay here. JD walked taller than he was, and slightly separately from us too. I remember thinking, even then, you have to do it all differently because you're about to be an adult, because you'll be a man. I heard him call one guy boss, then another.

We went downhill towards the sea via the thin, curved high street. I remember shopkeepers standing in their doorways, as if looking up and down would make people come. I remember a woman smoking outside a hairdresser's with tinfoil folded all through her hair, the metal of it glinting in the sun. A man doing a scratch card with his thumb. A windsock made from half a pair of trousers. The orange flash on a seagull's beak. All these new things.

Old things, too. Shut-down shops and sun-faded For Sale signs. Someone sitting on the steps of a boarded-up bank, talking to the air. Ma nodded to a house that still had Christmas decorations up, and said, 'There it is! That unstoppable party spirit.' She pointed at the inflatable Santa that had flattened onto the road into a dirty red and white rug.

'My old stomping ground,' she said as she pulled me close to her hip when we passed a pub that was doing 3 p.m. karaoke, but the beach, when we got there, was a perfect scene.

21

The sand was stretched-out wide, the colour of beer, and if you followed the edge of the land you could see all the way to a castle. Some girls my age were talking in a huddle, and some older boys were cycling circles around them, leaving spirograph tyre marks in the sand.

The waves were low and long that day, the white froth pushed over them like fingers over piano keys. After we'd touched the sea, Ma used her wet fingers to bless herself with the sign of a cross. 'Spectacles, testicles, wallet and watch,' she said. 'Well, not testicles in my case, but you know what I mean. Your grandad taught me that.'

She said it was against the law not to take your shoes off when you walked on the sand. She stretched her toes out, dug them in, then pulled them out like she'd got a sand pedicure. She also used the sand to cover up the Frida Kahlo tattoo she had and hated on her ankle: eyebrows, flowers and the words, 'Feet, what do I need you for when I have wings to fly?'

I was so light I didn't leave any footprints. JD wrote his name in the sand, and was about to embark on his trademark – another penis – when Ma asked why my eyes were watering.

'Dunno,' I said. 'The wind.'

'Why were you scrunching up your nose before?'

'It smells a bit like . . .'

'Fish?'

I shook my head. Almost at that exact moment she sneezed so violently she jerked forward.

We'd just got to the top of the sea steps, not far from the road. A man in a van leaned out of his rolled-down window. 'That's it, love,' he said. 'It's the sewage!' He gave a thumbs-up and grinned. 'Smell Margate and die.'

That evening, we went with her for one of her meanders. Normally we weren't allowed to go, because it was 'adult time' and, as she liked to remind us, she wasn't just a mum, she had her own life too, but that night she broke the rules and we ended up with her on a terrace right bang-smack in front of the sea on Marine Drive. She'd seen people leaning over the edge of the terrace to ash, and shouted up.

'Okay, so the basic sitchoo,' she told us once she'd crafted us a little sitting spot on a couple of wooden pallets, 'is this. 1960s, Margz was more or less the Marbella of Britain. Then all these cheap flights came along – easyJet and that pikey Irish traveller one – and what we see before us—' she made her hand a table for the line of the beach '—died a death. Empty hotels, empty beach.' She'd pulled us close like she was trying to speak privately, although she kept accidentally shouting. 'Turns out they all wanted Costa del *actual* Sol.'

'I still don't get it,' JD said, as she cleaned off the lip of a beer can with her T-shirt. 'I was born here, or you was?'

'*Were*. You were born here. Not me. Not Margate born and inbred, no. I moved here from Surrey when I left home though. That was when it was *cool* again.' She rolled her eyes around the o's of cool. 'Shoreditch-on-Sea, the Kentish Riviera—' she was trying to be ironic but she kept smiling

23

'—whatever bollocks names the papers came up with. Honestly, it was so fun though. Around the time I got pregnant with you, it was ridiculous. On a Saturday, you can't even imagine. Club nights on the sand, or in the square. Proper sound systems. The harbour all full up with people watching the sunset like it was the cinema. Restaurants, coffee. Vintage shops. *Vin-ta-je*,' she said after that, like it was a kind of plush international designer. 'Think I even did yoga once.'

'You got your lame Vitamin Sea tattoo,' JD said. 'You got a nice free baby . . .'

'My future breadwinner,' she said, grabbing his head and kissing it before he could lurch away. 'Didn't pay for much, actually. When I was doing the art school thing, I once didn't pay rent for six months! My Nan Goldin days. The Goldin Girls.' She laughed, and knocked over her beer but managed to grab it before she spilled any. 'Always two worlds but I felt I sat kind of fatly in the middle. When one lot would go to bed, I'd hang out with the others. I liked them though, the ones who stayed. Stayed beyond the weekends I mean. They'd rip out double glazing and pay a million pounds to put the old wood windows back in. Painted everything dark blue. Named their kids Orca or whatever. They were nice.'

She crushed an empty can with two fingers, easy, like she was reaching to pluck a petal from a flower. 'In a way it was good it stopped though,' she said. 'It was great, it was great, it was great, and then it got too expensive.' She broke, for a

24

sentence, into her posh voice: 'Lovely Georgian housing stock, Oscar.' The crack of a new can. 'It's just that with so many new people coming, what were the original poor lot meant to do? They were being slowly edged out. Not even slowly. Lemmings shoved off a cliff.' She did a side-to-side waddle thing to make me laugh. She reached to release a strand of hair that had got caught in my mouth. 'Then after the corona whatever, even *more* fuckers came to escape the city. Sea breeze, get a garden. Jam-packed.'

'Not now,' I said. 'You were saying there's a lot of room here now.' I picked up the pull tab of her beer and put it on my finger, like a ring.

'Yeah,' she said, 'the seaside's a bit less fun when no one has a job. And anyway, people are funny. They always want out of the city, but then most of them want back in again. Bit of a boomerang. 'Cos whichever one you are – if you need money, or you have it – the city's where it's at, I guess. Anyway, it's good there's room here now.' She used a licked thumb to get salt off my cheek. 'Good for us, anyway.'

We were sitting on bare pallets, a little bit splintery on my legs, but other people had brought cushions and old pillows up to the terrace. They'd brought their own drinks, too – drinks clustered in plastic bags, in the middle of circles, where a fire would be. Not too far away, there was a man drinking a four-pinter of whole milk. Next to him, a woman was using her dog as an armrest. On the street below, a kid cycled by with no air in his tyres; we could hear the sound of his rims from all the way up where we were.

The sunset filled the whole sky. Gold clouds that looked like they'd been done with a mascara brush. 'Does bring me back,' she said, looking at the label of her beer. 'Tyskies, Karpackies. The Margate classics. Anything over eight.'

'Eight quid for one beer?' JD said, walking away. 'Fucking hell—'

'Don't swear!' she shouted after him, but it made her laugh. 'Not pounds. Percent. Alcohol content.'

Her eyes looked for JD as he emerged from the front door below and wandered off to do pull-ups on a bus stop. Ma looked at me, and the light bounced back at me off her face. 'I wasn't clever like you, but I wasn't bad.' She let out a burp through pursed lips. 'Feels so weird now, to think that could be real life, becoming a painter. Should have seen my paintings. You'd find them funny.' She smiled this smile that wasn't really a smile. 'I liked them though. They were good.' I turned to face the setting sun, and she stroked my face back to her. 'Never look at the sun, not right at it. It'll mess with your eyes.' She rested her hand on my hair and said, 'Better you had me when you did.'

'You had me.'

'We had each other. Have each other.' She got distracted for a second by a man across the terrace looking at her. She smiled at him then mouthed the word *What?* 'All have each other,' she finished. Her eyes floated back to where JD was, sitting on the bus stop roof now, blowing into a pool of green water that had collected in a dip. 'Gorgeous, isn't it,' she said after that. 'Look at all the angles of the lighthouse, like a tower of 50ps stacked up.' She reached for my hand. 'Do you like it here?'

I looked at the lighthouse, and up at the sky above my brother. The sun that night was a perfect coin as it slotted down into the sea. And way on the other side, the moon was a small white freckle. I nodded. Seems stupid to say it, but I remember hope feeling like glitter – tiny, small pieces, but so much of it, each one catching different bits of light.

Ma got a job at a pub called The Chipped Pearl, which had a sign above the door that said its chips were famous. She brought home the menu to show us. 'Look, peanut,' she said to me. '"Our Famous Chips, served with our Famous Gravy." It's basically a pub for celebs.'

It was only women who did the daytime shifts at the Pearl, and most of them had kids the same age as me. We played between the bar stools as our mums wiped down the wood and changed the kegs. In the morning, when the deliveries came, Ma would lift the keg above her head as she passed me. Her arms got stronger. She pulled pints like she was steering a ship. When she picked up empties, she'd have one on each finger, like a loose glass glove.

Of the other kids, there was a boy called Anthony, who touched his hair so much it was always greasy. He ate salt with his fingers, would put a pile in his hand and lick it off his palm. And there was Trix, a tiny girl with no pigment in her skin and the palest eyebrows. 'Both on the spec-trum,' Ma would say, in another one of her sing-whispered jingles.

Neither of those two matter, really. It's just to say that the Pearl was also how I first met Davey.

It was his legs I noticed first. Sharp knees that pushed at the denim of his jeans. A restlessness that reminded me of JD. He looked – unlike the other kids – aware of the situation he was in. Fast-eyed, able to think, rather than just letting life happen in front of him. His mum would drink in there all day, and so one lunchtime, when her head was already down on the table, my mum said Davey had better come and sit with us.

He wouldn't look at any of us at first. He just rubbed away at the little islands of eczema on his arms and tried to look bored. He said what Anthony was doing with the pickles was manky, and I decided, in less than one minute, that I wanted him to be my friend more than the other two. I could see in the way his eyes darted, darted away but always came back to me, that he felt the same.

We started off by being rude to each other. Davey taught me that. He said that being polite didn't really get you anywhere, particularly round here. 'Being a pussy is for gays,' he said. 'Fact.'

Our mums brought us food before anyone else came in to eat. Meat pie, with crisps. Pasta from the day before, with crisps. 'Nah, bruv, like this,' Davey would say, and taught me how to eat the crisps vertically, because of the bash when our teeth broke them in two and the knife-edges of the crisp hit the roofs of our mouths.

Ma would always present the food like we were at a restaurant, an imaginary silver presentation dome.

'You've seen the film *Hook*,' she said.

'No,' I said.

'I always forget you're younger than me.' She looked at me with this kind of vague expression, then took a sip from the pint of what she called 'disco water' that she kept nestled on the shelf of trinkets behind the bar. 'Anyway,' she went on, '*Hook*. Imaginary food fight. That's what I'm trying to say.' She looked at me expectantly. That was another thing: even when she was like this, I never had to feel worried in front of Davey, because his mum was always worse. 'It's all about imagination!' she said. 'The beach? It's paradise. This pub? The lap of luxury. The lap dance of luxury. It's just the way you think about it. You – got the power,' she said. Or sang, rather, using the broom handle as a microphone.

I looked at her. I looked at her drink.

'Oh, come on,' she said. 'You're supposed to be the clever one.'

We didn't live in the flat above Newsagents for very long. Ma restarted her number-one hobby: finding boyfriends. Which meant, in our first year, we moved around a lot. Dane Valley, Tivoli Park, and two different places on the Northdown Road, up in Cliftonville, or Ghettovilleshittown, as JD sometimes called it.

Each time we packed up our stuff, he seemed more and more scratchy in his skin. I woke up in a bed next to him one morning, somewhere with tiny windows on the Millmead estate, and he hadn't slept at all. He'd managed to pick off the little pads that made a dot pattern on the wallpaper of all four walls.

All of the men our mum went for had something wrong with them – graveyard teeth, birthmarks like splashes of wine, one guy with dandruff so bad Davey said he was making his own parmesan. They were problems anyone could see from across the street, if that was the way you looked at people. But she didn't look at people like that. Particularly men, and ones who liked her. She knew this about herself. 'What can I say but whoops?' I remember her saying to a random girl she was chatting to on the street.

Liam was the first one I thought was okay. The first one who let me pick out new pictures for his walls. He was a tiny bit shorter than Ma, had freckled forearms – sometimes he'd let me pluck a single hair off them if I asked – and his T-shirts always smelled of laundry powder. He worked nights and slept on the sofa in the daytime, and whenever we got back from the Pearl, Ma would sit on his ankles, and he'd tell her to get off, but nicely, and we'd talk to him like that. She called him a pint-sized princess, and he teased her for being posh.

'Er, excuse me. In what world am I posh?'

'Always banging on about being an artist. Or an ex-artist. Or a painter, sorry. Whatever you call it. Find me one poor person who would say that.'

'I am poor. Why else would I be mucking about on Athelstan Road?'

'Poor from birth! Who does that? Always the same. Artist types dipping low for the street cred.'

'Street cred, oh my God. Are you a hundred and five?'

He laughed at her, but in a way that was kind, not not-kind. 'I'm not even being mean!' He kissed her fingers. 'What I'm trying to say is, I'm honoured.'

'Believe you me,' she said, 'I've burned all my bridges.' She turned her hands into an inferno, fingers as fire, then made an explosion sound with her mouth. 'Why would I ever be in this shithole if I could be anywhere else?'

'You said it was for the money,' JD cut in. 'The getaway cash. She sold us down the river for a tenner, Lee.'

Which was the first time I'd ever thought of it like that. What it meant that we'd been paid to come here. Paid to leave. That in some ways it was a last resort, rather than the type you'd go to for a holiday.

Ma sent me to the same school as the other kids from the pub. Tracey Emin Academy, or TEA, though everyone called it Tracey's. There were posters of her work in clip frames. Neon writing, blurred ink. *She Lay Down Deep Beneath The Sea. I Followed You To The Sun.* Tracey on a horse, Tracey dancing. Tracey writing her name on the beach. I could spend ages looking at them.

'She's old,' Davey said, 'but she's fit—' pointing '—tits.' The way he said 'tits' – like a drumstick landing on a cymbal.

Other schools in the area must have been shutting down already, because a couple of months in, coaches started to come, to drop kids off from other places. We stayed separate in the classrooms, though they were all mixed up in other ways. Age, mostly – five-year-olds and twelve-year-olds sitting, standing, messing around with the same teacher. A boy got lost once, somewhere between the classroom and the coach. There were signs for a while, home-made printouts with his face on, pinned to trees in plastic pouches. I don't remember his name, just that the spray from the tide made the ink on his face run.

I remember Ma and JD talking about what I was learning. He'd come to pick me up while she was at the Pearl.

'Honestly, it's fucked up, Ma. They doin' this thing called Life Class. Tell her, Cha.'

'It's quite fun to be fair,' I started.

'It's all about ways they're gonna die. Mate, she's like eight.'

He'd started calling Ma 'mate', mostly because it pissed her off. He was right though, Life Class was extreme. A bit of it was about 'How to Live Within Means', making a bag of beans last a week, stuff like that, but most of it was how to tell different types of chemical attacks from what they did to people's skin or eyes. How to wash our hands right. Our best options for escaping a shooter. Run, hide, tell.

'Don't tell though, obviously,' Davey said, 'that's for narks.' We sat next to each other in class. I did the work, and he was rude to the teachers, but we sat close enough for the older kids to flick our arms and say we were funny, and say it to both of us.

I never got bored of him, which is one of the rarest things that can happen between two people. It was something about the way he said things, the way his eyebrows bounced around like he thought each word was ridiculous. He made me laugh even when he didn't mean to. He was clever, even if he didn't mean to be.

Davey and JD liked each other too. 'He's alright your boyfriend,' JD said. They would show off for each other in this weird way. JD was still nearly double our height, but that was maybe the age our minds met in the middle, from the questions he asked, from the way he expected us, five years younger than him, to know the answer.

Every Tuesday, Davey and I would go to an after-school club that was run by a man called Caleb. He used to have a book-shop in Broadstairs, and he said what was happening to the kids was criminal, and so he opened up his house. A nice big Victorian one round the back of Hawley Square. Davey said Caleb was just a poncey DFL, a Down from Londoner, and that his belt was too big for him, and the way the end of it stuck out looked rude.

'He has a whole cupboard full of whisky though,' I told Davey.

'Aaaand off we go,' he said. 'Don't drag those sausage feet.'

At the time, Caleb had a big belly and a big white beard. Sailory, rather than Santa-ry, with a moustache spiky enough for food to get caught. 'Protein,' he said, rather than hello. 'Protein for the brain.' And there would be snacks – slices of omelette, tuna sandwiches – on broad white plates all along his table.

When summer came, our second summer there, it was hotter than it had ever been. They called it a pyro-heatwave – the first one hot enough for presenters on TV to say it was best to stay inside. Ma heard that, over on the Isle of Wight, one day tipped 50 degrees.

Caleb had a friend who used to work at the tourist board. That was how he got the key to the main brick building of Dreamland, so we'd have somewhere big to be in the shade. I'd never been inside before. I'd only ever peered into the outside bit from a high-up flat we'd once stayed in, in a road round the back. When we got to the front door, the D-lock linking the handles was as thick as Davey's wrists. Caleb finagled it open, we stepped over a dead pigeon on the floor and wandered in.

Everything seemed massive. The empty shelves of the gift shop, the echo, the space. Davey made these kind of 'ooh-ooh' chimp noises, which flew up into the rafters of the building and bounced back to us. It was wicked in there. The pressed metal ceiling in a dome above us, the milky curves of neon tubes, dust on a million colours. We skidded around on the old roller-skating rink, and in the food court bit we found an old pizza, hard as stone, the fat of the cheese see-through, left behind in one of the ovens.

Through the back, outside, the main stage looked like it had been set on fire, then rained out. Davey leaned against the metal sheets blocking off old rides with two hands out in front of him, so I could run up his body and jump to reach the top, then pull myself up and over. I found it so easy. I had a tiny body and my mum's strong shoulders. Inside the metal cages, the arms of the Cyclone could still spin. It

36

squeaked a lot, but I could push one of the carriages until it got moving and then jump in. I pulled off coloured light bulbs and brought them back so Davey and I could play catch, taking one step back each time, until they smashed.

One day that summer, when there was a strong enough breeze to push the worst of the heat away, Liam said we should hit the town. Maybe it's just the difference to now, but it seemed there were so many people, like the whole world was out. Davey was up on a roof passing tiles up to his Uncle Trevor, and we saw some of Liam's friends, too – the smiley one with the bleach-white teeth, and the one with the missing thumb Ma always said was sexy. JD held my hand on one side and Ma on the other, and Liam played on my head like a bongo drum from behind and it felt nice to be surrounded like that.

We walked all around. We watched an old couple sitting silent with butter and jam scones in a sea-facing dining room. A fishing boat out on the crest of waves far away, seagulls like white flies around it. Baseball cap brims broken upwards into halos, hair dye, people with walking sticks. Charity shops, chip shops, shut shops. Fat people, thin people, para-sols. Bedsheets on the beach. Boats sitting like toys on the sand at low tide. England flags instead of curtains. The smell of hot, sweet oil from fried doughnuts.

Liam took us to the only arcade that was still open. Flashing lights and Grab'N'Win claws, soft toys sitting on Styrofoam. JD lifted me up so I could slot coins into the machine and then dropped me down so I could see the ones

I'd won slide towards me at eye level. He showed me how to find more on the floor, by sliding his hand under the machine. He brought out a biro lid covered in carpet fluff, one of the old big brown 2ps, and a soft piece of popcorn that he pretended to eat.

Back outside, we watched kids climb the clock tower and make time go backwards on one side, then try to pull the short hand off.

'That's what I always liked about it round here,' Ma said. 'Planet Thanet. Everything's always just that little bit off.'

Back at the flat, Liam and JD would drink beer together; sometimes they smoked. They called it Man Time, and whenever they said it, Ma looked annoyed and proud at the same time, but let them use the sofa. The thing is, more and more, JD wasn't there. He was in and out, gone for days sometimes. Like I said, he'd never been good at being still – his hands, his eyes, where he wanted to be in any given second – but he'd started to put together his own world now, something separate to ours.

He shaved his head again, and this time, his stubble went in swirls. I almost expected it to move.

'Got us a new box,' he told me one night when he was back. 'Upgrade. Look at that.' My size-two shoebox had been replaced with something bigger, metal, the kind of forgettable green you find in offices.

'Where's it from?' I asked.

'The box or the money?'

38

'Both.'

'Been hanging with the copper boys,' he said. 'Stripping, melting. Y'know, thug life.'

JD took us out to show us things. The fights on Sunday. A ring of cheering people, louder if sisters or girlfriends joined in. This girl called Smile, because she'd catch her fingers in the corners of people's mouths and pretend she was going to make them split. Out and about, in the beating summer heat, he'd steer me around with his hand on my head, his fingers equally spread all the way around, like some kind of crown.

The heatwave was also the summer when we got the call about my grandparents. Ma got loads of missed calls one night but didn't want to pick up. We were out for scampi – wet and pink, melted Skips inside the batter. Even JD had 'deigned to join us', as she put it.

When the calls didn't stop, eventually she picked up. I heard the line bounce off her ear. It wasn't a voice I recognised.

'Give me the phone,' JD said, voice like a kid again, reaching to grab it off her. 'I wanna speak to Grandpa.'

'Get away, JD,' she said. Her whole body pulled away from him, and she started walking away from us down the street. 'Yes, I know what an attorney is,' we heard her say. 'Power of attorney, of course I know.'

It was a long conversation. She walked back and forth between a bench and an old phone box. Liam mimed to her – do you want anything from the shop? She nodded, he kissed her head and came back with a medium-sized bottle of cider. One of those ye olde ones.

We were on the street for a long time. I think I understood more than JD did.

'Don't make me ask,' I remember her saying, 'but I have to ask. That doesn't make sense, though. What do you mean defaults to the state? I thought that was the point of End-Life – that you did all the paperwork first?'

When she put down the phone, she walked over to us, shaking her head. 'It's okay, love,' Liam said, 'you don't have to say.'

'There's just – it's all too much.' She looked at him. 'I didn't always love them,' she said. 'But I didn't always not love them, too. Do you understand that?' He nodded. 'I never did,' she said.

JD went out that night. I listened to Ma and Liam's conversation by pushing the door to the living room more and more open the quieter they got. 'I know they don't approve,' she was saying, 'didn't approve, whatever the hell a word "approve" is to use about your own daughter, but how fucked up is that? Not to leave me anything. Not a thing, Lee.'

Liam had made his body a tight cradle around her. 'Maybe they didn't mean for that to happen?' he was saying back. 'Maybe it's just another fucking government scam?'

When JD came back, he called me into his room. 'The last time we went,' he said, 'down to Grandad's, he gave me this.' He had a watch on his wrist. 'Real gold. Hadn't worn it till tonight. But I realised. I should invest it. Thug life.'

'Stop saying thug life.'

'It is what it is.'

We found out in the days that followed that only Grandma had been approved for Nembuta, so Grandad had to do it in the garage instead. They found him with the pipe from a vacuum cleaner linking the exhaust and the passenger-door window. There wasn't going to be a funeral.

'We can't take it personally,' Ma told us.

'I'm not,' JD said.

She took a breath, tried to make her face brighten, but it looked cold underneath her skin. 'You have to see it as part of the wider thing. Some are depressed, others are just being practical,' she said. 'Too many of us around, and not enough to actually *go* around.'

She told us that when she was young, you could plot the economy on the train tracks. Every percentage point employment went down, the more jumpers. 'It's all connected,' she said.

'Dunno why they need jumpers for,' JD said, 'still hot.'

'Jumpers on the track,' she said. 'Jumpers onto the track. Y'know, bam.' She did a squelch sound.

The train service had cut down even since we'd arrived. Not because of jumpers, more because the train to London was three days of Ma's salary by then. Also, they checked your ticket before you got on now. Checked other things too, apparently. A whole row of them in black. No guns or anything, but batons.

'Jesus,' she said as we passed Station Approach. 'Not going back any time soon. Trapped here with these tramps . . .'

41

She called them war carts, the way every young girl had a pram in front of her, jostling into the crowd like a bayonet. It brought out a different side to her – a stabbiness she didn't have in other ways. She'd shake her head and sometimes literally make sounds – sounds like something gross was trapped under her tongue – about the girls who paid to top up their heating cards with handfuls of coins. The girls with 'window panes' cut into their jeans. The girls who got pregnant in pubs and stayed there after their bellies got big. 'Yes, pot kettle black or whatever,' she'd say. 'But what's the point now? Used to be a point. New baby, new bedroom. Not any more. But on they go.'

'Problem families,' she'd say. Speech marks with her fingers; speech marks every time. 'They're being sent here again, it's clear as day.' She said that for decades London used Margate as a dumping ground. They'd stopped for a while during the boom years, but now, what with the greatest recession known to man, it was back. 'Anyone undesirable? Ship 'em off to the sea. Bing bang bosh. Not like us. We paid our way.'

'We got paid,' I reminded her.

'Well whatever. Anyway, you know what it's like. It's shit for them, shit for everyone,' she said. 'You remember our hotels in London.'

I was glad we had Liam, because the hotels here were even worse. The B&Bs and HMOs and ASTs. Circles of white paint scrubbed on the inside of windows, rubbish on every windowsill, that greeny-brown smell of weed in every corridor. Me and Davey knew this boy called Kyle, and his hotel was the worst. The front garden was a graveyard for fridges, wires frizzing out the back, microwaves with broken windows, bicycles with bent frames. A sign saying ASK PRICES INSIDE. The dustbin in his front room was one of the green ones for dog waste.

My mum and Liam would egg each other on. 'You might have "paid your way",' he said to her, 'but no one else fucking is. I mean, look at them.' They'd taken me to the playground off Sanger Close. His head tilted towards my friends – the ones whose mums didn't care if they covered their heads in the sun, he said. The ones who tensed their feet because their shoes were too big. 'It's the big old Benefits Bunch,' he said. 'Taxes high as a fucking kite, higher every single year, and I'm the only one paying them.'

And the thing was, if taxes had gone up, there was nothing, it seemed – at least where we were – to show for them. 'All of it goes into paying back the "debt",' Liam said, and he made the word sound like the thing it was: a deep, black hole. 'As if we bought something decent with the money, as if we bought a nice shiny car, rather than just lost our shitting jobs.'

If anything, where we were, things got worse. School was cancelled more and more. The rubbish around bins spread out like the sea. Liam had a friend who had a stroke and they sent him home from the hospital the same day with some voice exercises written on a piece of paper. 'Honestly, his face looks like it's made of wax and someone's holding a blowtorch underneath him. I mean bloke had a stroke, and they're fobbing him off with an aspirin!' He shook his head. 'I get it. It's not their fault, not them at the hospital, there's one doctor in the whole fucking place. I'm just saying it can't last. Not unless they want a war on their hands.'

On the days when school wasn't cancelled, JD would wait outside whatever building we were in, sitting on the railings with his bike upside down so he could spin the wheel. Then he started to have more money, so the bicycle became a dirt bike, and after that, he'd lean on the open door of his new car. It was red. He didn't actually drive me home, he just wanted people to know that I was with him.

'Oi, JD!' Davey would always call to him, or he'd go over and shake his hand. It seemed to me to be so much of what life was, showing who you knew, and how well you knew them. 'Swap you Swifty for your banger,' Davey said. He pointed at JD's car.

'Oh yeah, you wanna be a boy racer?' JD asked.

Davey nodded.

'Child star.' JD dusted off Davey's shoulder. 'Alright, you two. Be good. See you later, Cha.'

'He's so cool, JD,' Davey said, when he drove away. 'Not cool, but like, he has nice things.'

Talking of Swifty, I should have said, Davey got given a horse around that time. Got given, bought. Some guy turned up outside the pub one day with three horses, two he chained up, one he only had a string halter for. The man tapped on the window and made a sign for one of us kids to come out and keep hold of the loose horse while he went in for a drink. Davey ran out, speed of light, with all the cucumber from his lunch, and mine. When the man came back out, he told Davey if he liked the horse so much, he could have her. If he liked her and sorted him out with a bottle of vodka, gin, any old clear stuff, maybe two. I remember Davey looking at Ma behind the bar, and Ma pulling this face like, 'I am definitely not old or responsible enough to make this kind of decision' – but then going downstairs and finding one of those 1.5-litre bar bottles with an upside-down label and handing it over.

The horse was a young cob called Swifty. Palomino, hard muscle haunches, Caramac back, shaggy on her belly. Davey's uncle had worked for a rich family with stables, and they agreed he could 'park' her there. On weekends when the tide was low, Davey would ride her down the beach. The wet sand, the dry sand, the clop-slap different sounds. The beach stayed big enough for long enough to do that then. A few of us would watch him. He'd pull on the reins to make her rear. Fists up, he'd say, shadow boxing. He rode her without a saddle, scrappy legs, no shoes.

All this to say, it was Davey in the end who told me what JD was doing for money. He was lying on Swifty's back, legs light on her neck like he was in a recliner. I remember Davey smiling when he said it. He made it sound like what JD was doing was a good thing. Like JD was a doctor or a soldier or something like that. It was nothing to do with copper.

'Oh,' I said. 'Okay.' I didn't know anything about drugs. I felt a little lurch lift up in my belly.

'He's nice with it though, no?' Davey said. 'Better him than a bad guy.'

Around that time, Davey brought his Uncle Trevor's razor to class. He gave the two of us tattoos, matching triangles on the backs of our hands. There was more blood than ink, and the lines weren't straight. He said we were going to stick together no matter what, and he spat into his palm to shake on it, this loose ball of saliva.

I don't know. There are so many scenes, and most of them seem frozen now. My mum, too – I'd freeze her right then if I could. After we got the news about her parents, she decided, she told us, to relax a little. Which meant go out more. There were nights where she came home with blood on her top, or no shoes on – with Liam, without him – but she was still just about on the edge of being okay then.

There were so many edges, edges everywhere. It's just you never know where exactly the edge is until you tip over it.

I was nearly eleven when Liam took a team of guys from his work over to the 'Sit In' in Ramsgate. A human wall across the A299 – a wall thick enough for tractors, tents, tea stations but, most importantly, a wall blocking all the freight from getting out of the harbour and going through to London. 'Serious about it too,' Liam told us when he came back the first time. 'It *stinks* down there.' He looked excited.

'Lovely,' Ma said.

'No, but ferocious,' he said. That smile again. It tipped off the edge of his lips. 'Fetid. Food rotting. All sorts rotting. But it's perfect if you think about it. London needs all that crap. And what can they do apart from give us what we want?'

'Run you over?' Ma said.

'You wish.'

I asked him if I could go see, and he took me down for an afternoon. It did smell, the thick kind of bad that catches in the back of your throat. People had brought blankets to make the ground softer, they were playing cards and dominoes with T-shirts tied around their faces.

'We're going for a double-whammy effect,' he told me. He'd plucked me a rose from a nearby garden and told me to hold it under my nose. 'We're blocking all the stuff they need, but we're also doing a tax strike. All of us who's paying have stopped, and they're not getting a single dime out of us till things get sorted out,' he said. 'Fist bump.'

I reached down and punched his hand. He'd lifted me up so I could see the queue of stalled trucks, the backlog of boats that couldn't leave the harbour. When someone played music over a loudspeaker, he did a weird dad dance with me high on his shoulders.

That week was one of the last times I saw him happy like that – a helium balloon making its way up to the ceiling. He said him and his friends were communicating with people up north, who were trying the same up there. 'Far up north, like "t'ut right, t'ut left",' he said. He said it felt good to be doing something as a group. Solidarity.

'There he goes,' Ma said. 'Chairman Mao of Margate.'

That's why I remember I was nearly eleven. Because it all came to a head on my birthday.

We had a party in Liam's mum's garden, and Liam took a day off from the Sit In. Socks and pillowcases blew like bunting on the clothes lines, and Ma had decided to push the boat out. There was a loaf of chocolate cake that came already sliced, and sandwiches which had been packed in a box with apples, and the taste of apples had got inside the bread. I remember Liam's opera voice when we sang happy birthday, and Ma saying, 'Fuck, Lee, stop it, you'll break our ears', but all of us laughing. It was April. Hot in the sun, but it didn't stay in the sky forever.

I met up with Davey afterwards. I wanted to bring him some cake. We went over to Cliftonville, the long way, around the cliff edge, dipping as we ran like we could slip underneath the wind from the sea.

We went to the spot we always went to. It used to be the pirate ship, the big climbing frame one in the playground by Bugsy's, but when the mast got loose, we started to go to the Winter Gardens instead – a sloped bit of the roof just above the ticket hall which faced the sea and fitted our backs like deckchairs. If Davey jumped and waved his hands in the air enough, a big bright beam of security light would come on. A sweep of white houses in a curve behind us made it feel a bit like we were in an amphitheatre, Roman style.

Davey was semi-standing, semi-kneeling in front of me in the spotlight, telling a story like it was a play, two voices, and he was facing me – inland – rather than towards the sea. That's why we saw it happen the way we did.

Slowly, from bright to nothing, Davey's face started to disappear in front of me.

His voice dropped to silent. I didn't say anything, either. Then I felt his hand rush to my arm, reaching for me.

We looked around. All around us, the lights were going off in a wave. It started from the left of the town, and it moved right. We got to our knees, our feet, the wave continued. All around the coast, in blocks, one by one, as far as we could see, the lights went off.

Normal power cuts we'd had before. But not all at once like this, not everywhere.

There hadn't been a storm. Even right at first, something felt different. We stayed standing, almost like a test, and then both of us, at once, started to climb down the scaffolding as fast as we could.

In the tiny bit of daylight that was left, we saw a man opposite come out of his house and stand in front with a spade up like a bat.

'Home,' I said, and we ran.

No one was there when I got back. Liam's flat felt like it had grown in size, or I had shrunk. Something about being a child alone makes aloneness so much bigger. Doubly, triply alone. I could hear my footsteps more than normal, so I sat still.

Ma came back from the Pearl early. I thought she'd say it was okay, but she flicked our switches a million times. She went to the window, then came to where I was on the sofa. I hugged her from the side. She was more normal then, size wise, but I still remember feeling like I couldn't get enough of her into my hug.

'Why aren't you wearing a top?' she said.

'It's my birthday.'

'So?' she said. 'No, I know. It's shit. Sorry about this. Have you seen your brother?'

I shook my head. She lit a big scented candle Liam had given her, red wax, cinnamon, dusty on top, and I read and reread the posters on his wall, all of them in different fonts. 'Life is short, lick the bowl.' 'Let's Be-Gin.' 'Women to the left, because men are always RIGHT.' And the one he had above the sink: 'SAVE WATER. Drink beer instead.' Liam only had a microwave, so we couldn't have a hot dinner. We ate crisps instead. We slept on the sofa. I stayed awake until I felt Ma's whole body go loose, and then I found a way to turn her into my pillow.

There were still no lights in the morning, nor any sign of Liam or JD. I was so hungry that my stomach made the sound of a bath being emptied, and Ma said her headache was like a helmet now. Tight and heavy and she couldn't get it off.

When Liam did come home, he was out of breath from running up the stairs. He didn't sit down once, even though Ma tried to get him to. I asked if he had anything to eat, and he said no, then gave me some chewing gum.

'I don't get it – was it you guys?' she asked him. 'Playing with boxes?'

He looked at us. 'What do you mean "playing with boxes"?'

'Messing with the wires,' she said. 'Down at the thing.'

'What, at the Sit In? No, no,' he said. 'I was back with them after the party. They were surprised as anyone when the lights went off. Whole place went quiet as a mouse.'

'Do you think it's terrorists?' she said. 'Some kind of war thing?'

'I don't know.'

'So you just stayed put in the stench?'

'Had no choice! The roads were fucked. No traffic lights.' His thumb-knuckle grated at the grey patch on his beard. 'You're right though. Something not good's happening,' he said. 'We got word from the guys up north. The whole country's down.'

On the second day, our water stopped. When I turned the tap, I could hear the sound of the valve opening, but nothing but a drip would come out. The shops were shut. The banks were shut. The ATMs had dead screens. In the dark, people tripped on stairs. A woman Liam knew started to give birth on King Street. The baby was the wrong way round, but when they got her to the hospital they said natural births only, they couldn't do C-sections – the generator had gone out. They sent her boyfriend to find clean water, anything sterile in a bottle. But the water didn't help, forceps couldn't help, nothing could help; the baby died inside her. In other rooms in the hospitals, people on life-support machines stiffened, turned blue.

'They'll send the army or something,' Ma said. 'They'll send help or something. They have to. Doesn't matter if there are fucking "tensions". It's a national emergency.'

'It's a national disgrace,' Liam said.

But still – no one came.

Day three, sometime in the morning, the sound of Liam running up the stairs again, like he was younger than he was. He was out of breath when he got to us.

'It's them,' he was saying, 'it's them. It's fucking them.'

'Who's them?' Ma said.

'Of course they didn't come.'

'Who, Liam?'

'They're the ones who did it.'

'Liam – slow . . .' Ma said. She reached for him. He tilted his body away.

'It's the government who's doing it. Who's done it. Who's turned everything off. Even though people are dying. They're dying outside.'

'Don't be an idiot. Course it's not them. It's illegal.'

'What do you mean legal, illegal? Who cares about legal?

They own the police. It's fucking Winstable himself! Even Winstable's in on it.'

'Why, though?'

'They did it to get our arses up off the road, fine . . . but now they're just—' he grabbed a mug from the table and I remember thinking, he's about to throw that at the wall, '—they're killing people, Jas. Look outside – it's madness.'

Riots started that night. Ma tried to stop him, but JD went out, looting more than anything. He came back hours later with cuts on his hands from smashed glass and a backpack full of bottles and packs of shaving razors with the chunky anti-stealing device still attached.

He was pumped up in a weird way. He kept on trying to pick me up. His top lip was sweating. His breath smelled of burning. I don't know what he'd taken. 'I met a guy,' he told us. 'Fucking wicked guy.'

'You shat on your own doorstep,' Liam said, looking at JD's stash. 'That's what you did. Prick.'

When anything worth taking was gone, it went quiet. Shop doors left hanging off one hinge; glass fronts smashed in the middle so it almost looked like the remaining shards were a frosted Christmas effect.

Not that I saw it all in person. I'd never in my life been inside so much. 'It's not that as a girl I want to treat you differently,' Ma said to me, 'Beyoncé and all that. But it's always the first thing. Even in a nightclub. Lights go out and men are like dogs. And when it's hot outside too, Jesus. Turns up the volume on all of it.'

Everything felt long, because everything's slower in the dark. School was cancelled, and not just like normal, and not just by Ma. Davey came by and said they'd already put wood over the windows. The fridge was silent. We stopped bothering to shut it.

By midday, the living room – plain south, sun from 8 a.m. – was so hot, every breath felt like a half-breath. I have this memory of Liam trying to make the hands of the fan spin with his hands, but his fingers kept getting caught in the cage around it. Liam slept on the sofa and Ma let me sleep in their bed. Whenever she woke up in the night, she pulled the sheet so tight around us it felt like we were in a hammock. She was good over that time. A proper mum, if that makes sense. I was small and she was big and I was young and she was old and she kissed my head and said she'd look after me. There was something very simple about it.

She told me that nothing stays dark for ever. The sun rises every day. We're used to the light coming back. It has to. It will.

One evening, thirteen days later, for a single second, our lights flashed on. We looked at each other like we'd each imagined it, the way you look around to check if a sound is in your ears only. It flicked on again. None of us spoke.

Then this slow, building sound. The click of filaments waking up, the purr, again, of the fridge. I looked out of the window and along the coast. There was this spreading out of light, all of it like a fern unfolding in a nature documentary.

JD said we should have a party. He mixed dregs of the bottles he'd stolen in one of our saucepans and poured in pineapple juice.

'Lee, my friend!' JD said when Liam came home, his mouth furry with booze. 'We won!'

'What do you mean, you little idiot, "we won"?' Liam said. That anger again. It made a curl of his face.

'They're back on,' JD said, 'the fucking lights! Got cold beeeeeers, Liam,' he said, opening and shutting the fridge to make a show of the light coming on inside.

'Cold beeeeeers.' Liam said, 'Oh, is that it? Fucking Ing-er-lund, eh?' He danced with his fists, the football dance. 'You know what happened, do you?' he said. 'You know what happened while we were sitting like mugs in the dark?'

'Speak for yourself, like mugs in the dark,' JD said. 'I went out. I helped myself.'

'The lights are back on, buddy, 'cos they signed all of it away. Every last little thing of it.'

I can't remember if, right at the start, there were some people who thought it was a good idea. The Localisation Act, Localisation. Whatever you want to call it. Whatever you do call it, I guess – because I'm sure you know all of this differently to me.

For me though, it was Caleb who explained it best. When Tuesday came, Ma said I could go over to his, at the normal time we had after-school club, and even though no one else turned up at his house, we sat at his table and he fried me an egg.

'I mean I get it,' I told him, 'but I don't get it,' as the yolk popped orange.

He splashed a slug of chardonnay into his mug. I thought of the other times I'd gone to see him in the morning to borrow books, how he'd been drinking then too – 'I like my coffee white in the morning,' he'd told me once or twice, 'and with no coffee in it.'

'You heard about the tax strike?' he said then. I nodded. 'Well, they called our bluff on it. Big time.'

He said the government in London claimed they were taking the protest to its logical conclusion. People wanted autonomy? Autonomy was what they'd get. But in the dark, London pushed negotiations further.

'The councils must have tried to fight back, I'm sure they did,' he said. 'But they had no lights. No leg to stand on. What could they do?'

The Localisation Act was pushed through. Local services were put in the hands of local authorities. But more than that, they'd have to pay for them.

'A decentralised system,' Caleb said. 'But a hardcore one. In a country the size of a thumb.'

'My mum was asking if de-central could be good though?' I said. 'Better than them having all the power?'

'The thing is, everything we need, we now have to pay for it with local taxes. Do you see the problem?'

I nodded. I wanted to see.

'We're poor here,' he said. 'There aren't that many jobs. Barely any industry at all. The average earning's not much – so the tax we pay? It's pocket fluff. Now though, if we want electricity, it's a free market. And who knows what they'll charge for it.' He turned around to the sound of his tap dripping and stood up to turn it off. 'And you should hear the way they're talking about it too, Chance – like it's a good thing. "Empowering." Like it's time for us to finally stand tall on our own two feet.' He put his hand up ironically to his chest as if the national anthem were playing. 'It's bullshit,' he said. 'Lipstick on a firebomb.'

In the months that came, Caleb heard from friends in richer places about what had happened for them. Businesses who'd flooded in to offer services where the councils couldn't. A chance to profit, privatise. 'Fine if you're the Cotswolds, but . . .'

He didn't need to say it. We weren't the Cotswolds. No one came for us. Or if they did, it was the worst of anyone. Slum landlords, sharks.

But anyway, all that was later. Two days after the lights came on, a guy came round to Liam's flat asking for JD. I was in the living room, so I only saw a flash. It was Ma who opened the door. All I remember seeing was this spade for a jaw and black hair in a topknot, and how tall he was, but quicker than anything, as soon as he arrived, JD zipped himself off the sofa. It was Kole.

In the first predictions of what Localisation would look like, Liam said they had it on the news that we were one of five areas that would be the hardest hit. What they meant by that, he said, was that the gap between the budget needed for basic services and what was coming in in taxes was the biggest. Rotherham, Blackpool and Stoke were the others, plus somewhere in Wales Liam could never remember so he always called it something like Lafwadunda.

For weeks there were roaming protests. It worked on rotation and they came to Margate every other Saturday. Fluorescent cardboard rectangles held above people's heads all along the seafront. 'The world is watching.' 'Localisation = death.' 'Win-UN-stable.' 'Left to sink.' 'History will condemn you.'

'Us?' I said to Ma, when we went down to see. 'History will condemn us?'

'No, it's for the reporters. They're speaking through the cameras to the government people. Look at that one,' she said. She read it out loud. 'The only good Tory is a lavatory.'

'Who are they, though?' Liam said. 'Most of them don't even live here.' He wandered over to the press side, to a guy with a huge, expensive-looking camera. 'Take this twat,' he said, close enough for the man to hear. 'Where are you from?'

'The US,' the man said. His voice sounded like cycling up and over a hill. 'Special Report.' Then his huge camera tilted down to me. 'What do you think about what's happening, young lady?'

'Dunno?' I said. 'Exciting?' Which made JD start laughing from behind me and say, right into the lens, 'I'm trying to sell her, does anyone want a kid? I'll do her fifty per cent off.'

The cameras on the streets, the donations arriving in truckloads, boxes of tinned food in towers, people telling their stories on the internet and receiving cash in online bank accounts – for a while it seemed like they might be the new normal. But as Ma often said, normal changed a lot these days, and the world didn't watch for long. Soon, the only boxes appearing on the streets were the belongings of more people leaving. And this time, leaving in a hurry, boarded-up windows popping up in a piecemeal patchwork.

'All these houses – all the fucking best ones – and of course they can go,' Liam said. 'They only bought these places with help from their parents. No personal investment so—' he threw the 'so' into the air like a ball ' — back to Belsize fucking Park they go. Cunts.'

He'd never said that word in front of me before. It's hard to explain what happened to Liam, how it happened so quickly. The grey in his hair spread, like he'd walked with his head too close to wet white paint. He started to say what my grandparents had done was a good idea. He said it right in front of my mum. He said that any time there was any hope, any time people tried to come together, it was crushed flat like a fly, and surely it was best to do the crushing yourself.

Before Liam's factory shut down for good, he started going into work drunk, getting into accidents. All his brightness went out. JD said it was like he'd been taking happy pills the whole time we knew him and suddenly stopped them. One afternoon, when I came back from Caleb's, Liam had cut his hand on a glass he'd broken and hadn't done anything to stop the blood. He was sitting on the sofa and the whole cushion underneath him was red.

Then one night, Ma got home late from work and found Liam sitting on the end of my bed, watching me sleep with a pillow in his hands. When she asked him what he was doing, he started crying. The noise he was making started to be so loud, she had to put the pillow in his mouth so he could bite on it. 'Do you understand?' she asked me later. I said I did. I didn't.

When Ma ended it with Liam, JD told us his new friend could sort us out with a place. He said it was a 'showstopper'. 'The building', he called it.

'Which one?' Ma asked him.

'That one.' He pointed. 'The one next to Dreamland.'

He meant Arlington House. All eighteen storeys of it. The building that was four times taller than everything else in town.

Floor after floor of concrete zigzag that changed as you walked around it. Coloured curtains that stayed shut all through the day. A faded blue-and-stars Europe flag left behind in one window. A Jenga frame of concrete car park at the back.

Caleb, when I told him where we were moving, said it wasn't a good idea for us to do that. He asked me what floor. He said that you couldn't get insurance if you lived anything higher than the third.

'Caleb says if there's a fire we're done,' I told JD.

'Tell him to say it to my face. I'll wreck the snobby gaylord.'

'Don't you dare say that!' Ma went for JD's head with the back of her hand.

'What?' he said back. This jabby sound.

'Snobby. Don't you dare! He's been nice to your sister.'

'Fucking last of the DFLs.'

'JD, you knobhead,' I said. '*We* came from London.'

'Yeah but he'll run off soon like the rest of them.'

'J, he was here before you—'

'Not if you count the start. I was born here,' he said. He looked at me. 'I don't know about you, but I was. Anyway – rich in't he? From the way he speaks. When we get up there, I'm gonna pick 'em all off like a sniper.'

The way JD talked about the flat before we got there – the bedrooms, the view. He said the word kings again and again – we'd live like kings – and so, even if it was ugly on the outside, I thought inside might be different.

Ma nearly cried when we opened the door and stepped into the flat. I saw it ripple through her face, this flicker across her forehead. The carpet was ripped up at the edges, and it looked like someone had beaten one of the walls with a baseball bat. But JD went out for a takeaway and some beer, he even put a few sloshes in a cup for me, and by the evening, it was a bit better. 'Kole's in the same block too, see,' he said. 'Solid lad. Solid spot.'

He pulled us into him on either side, and escorted us over to see the view. Our thin ring of windows looked out to the sea on one side, and the dregs of Dreamland on the other, knotweed pushing up and running like green veins in marble through the concrete paths. The ditch where they'd dug up the Chair-O-Plane was waterlogged and winked in the light.

'It's good to be up high,' JD said. 'Good to per-ooze the kingdom. Good that even the fattest waves can't splash us.' He'd just washed his hands, and when he said that, he flicked a fist of droplets in my face.

Kole came over on our second day in the flat. I didn't speak to him. At one point he asked questions about me and Ma, but he asked them to JD. 'How old's them two, then?' he said.

If JD was a pretty boy, this guy was an animal. Handsome, but like a jaguar or a lion – there was something big cat about his face. He moved his mouth around like he was getting something out of his teeth and was about to spit. I'd never seen a man with long hair before, tied up like that in a bun. I thought there was a necklace pendant buried under his T-shirt, but when he took his top off, it was a piercing. Right between his pecs, with scars around it, like it had shifted under the skin a few times.

JD had a set of weights that he bought from a gym that closed down and that was what they did all day. They laughed a lot, they called each other mate a lot. Mate, mate, mate. There was something nervous about JD's laugh at first, this forced thing, almost like his lungs were clapping.

At one point Ma and I went into the room to ask if they wanted toast. Kole lifted the biggest bar JD had, and stared at me. Then he lifted it again and stared at Ma.

'Did you see his arms?' Ma said to me, pulling me away into the kitchen.

'No,' I said. I had. They were huge. 'What about them?'

'Don't look at them,' she said. She spread some margarine so thick you couldn't see the bread any more, and leaned in. 'Track marks. It's like a fucking terminus on there.'

It wasn't long after Localisation that school stopped for good. Ours, anyway. Or not stopped, but moved, to a single unit shared between three towns. I went a couple of times, but they didn't do attendance, and most of the teachers were on a web link. Near us, there was still a school for special kids, but it was run by a charity, and even they pulled out soon enough.

It wasn't hard to fill the time. Me and Davey knew kids everywhere. Old school foster kids and 'looked-after kids' who didn't seem that looked after. Kids in the flats above the Liquor Locker, and the rooms above Reaperz Inc. Nayland Rock Hotel, The Dolphin. Like I said, a lot of hotels. People had left if they could, but they weren't the people we knew. Everyone our age who stuck around, we knew to nod to. Before the shopping centre got boarded up, we took it in turns to see who could take the smell of the 'by weight' charity shop the longest. And until they got dogs at Tracey's, dogs that moved on ropes attached to long chains that ran all through the building, we would sneak back in and sit in our old classrooms. The electricity was off in the building so the boards didn't work, but we wrote on them in pens. Pretend lessons, mostly about sex.

I don't think we actually ever were bored, but we talked about being bored all the time.

We did run-outs from the Polish shops, took beers, ham, chocolate. Someone reopened – not officially, they just broke open the door – the old Club Caprice, Neon Ballroom, whatever it was called by the time it shut, and put on parties. We spent long evenings drinking in our spot on the Winter Gardens roof, until it rained too hard one night and the asphalt fell in. We charged about, tops off in the sun, hoods up in the dark. Dalby Square, Trinity Square, any square.

In my memory of that time, there was always enough food if you looked for it. One night, Davey ripped the grill off an old fridge and we used it to barbecue. He blew on the fire to make the flames leap and cracked the same joke each time – that he was a long-distance dragon. The fridge grill let all this gas out, and made everything taste funny, but we ate it all anyway, and not because we had to, just because that felt part of it.

Another moment. JD pulling me into the living room, because there was more light there. He wanted us to look at each other and tell each other what we saw.

He wasn't high, or if he was, not very. It was mostly because he was vain and some girl had just dumped him. He was the vainest boy I ever knew – whenever I stole his phone, I found albums and albums of pictures he'd taken of himself – but I was happy to do it. I missed him. When Kole was around he was different. He didn't ask me any of his questions, his questions about how things worked, or whether people were good or not.

At first, JD made a brick of his jaw, I could see him tensing, and he turned his head from one side to the other so I could get the full show. Then he laughed, this champagne big thing. 'I'm being a twat, sorry,' he said. But I didn't laugh. I looked at him. I really looked. And that's why I remember that moment so clearly. His crushed earlobes, a tangle of cartilage he could never get a piercing through. His stray eyebrows. His light paper blue eyes.

'When's my turn, dickhead?' I said after that.

He laughed again. Then did the serious jaw. His eyes narrowed. 'Kole says you're sweet-looking,' he said. 'Cute.'

I looked away from him. That was not what I was expecting.

'You're a child though.' JD looked like he was working this out for himself, like it was a mathematical thing. 'That's what you are.'

'Am not,' I said.

'You are, you div.'

'Not,' I said. I tried to do a chop thing on his neck.

He held my thin little arms above my head. 'I don't mean it rude.' He shook his head at me and shook my arms with it.

'I don't! All I'm saying is, stay that way. Stay that way.' He let my arms go, and reached for a smoke. 'Promise you will, just for a while.'

I know what he meant now. I was quite clearly a child. I was twelve. My chest was concave. I'd tried to shave my legs, but the hair grew back soft or not at all.

'Although there's one thing,' he said. 'Something someone round here's got to be an adult about.'

He pulled me into the kitchen – he was always pulling me around; not roughly, it was just because I was so light and he was so heavy – and opened the door to the tumble dryer. It hadn't worked even when we arrived but it was too bulky to even imagine carrying back down the stairs. 'And for that I nominame you.'

'Nominate.'

'Yeah.'

His fingers rapped a beat on the plastic of the machine.

'I found a place for it,' he said.

'For what?'

'The money. Our money. Upgraded again. Got a new box and everything. And I'm adding to it and all that. Properly this time. I figured it was up to me now. To be a man and stuff. For real though. Do you think?'

As he talked, he opened up the door to the tumble dryer and showed me. He reached up at an angle like he was delivering a baby and I peered in after his wrist. The new money box was stuck to the top of the barrel with duct tape.

He said that he was putting money in it, money every

week, but that we must never touch it and that that was a promise. 'A promise, Cha,' he said. I nodded. We shook hands, with one hand and then the other, in this criss-cross, unbreakable. He said I was the official guardian, and that I had to watch Ma.

'Watch out for Ma, look out for her,' he said. 'You know what I mean. I just got to thinking. Way it is, we need a back-up plan.'

Every now and then, I took out the box and looked at it. I counted the notes and there was only ever more and more in there. Because that was the thing. There started to be money around. Not out in the streets, but in our flat, definitely. JD and Kole started making kem in our bathtub. Kole had a recipe he'd inherited from his dad. ('Inherited!' Ma said. 'You'd think it was a recipe for cake.') And JD, after years of what he called market research, had tips for making it better.

He explained it to me once. It was anything, really, he said, as long as it got you fucked. But for theirs, they bulked it out with the liquid that used to go into e-cigarettes, cooked down, because they could buy boxes and boxes of the stuff for no money at all. Then they added any out-of-date legal highs they could get their hands on – spice, mamba, voodoo. When I asked to help, they let me open the packets and tip them into bowls. The squeaky crackle of cellophane. 'Oi, donkey, send it to the list, will you?' JD would say, weighing powder on his scales with one hand and sliding his phone over the table to me with the other, and I'd transcribe then send out their texts. *PSA from the NHyeS – this is the party doctor! 241 on the smoke this wknd. blow your rocks off.* Things like that. They'd be laughing as they made them up.

Kole bought masks from the hardware shop, though I never saw either of them with the material bit actually over their mouth. Whenever they were working, Ma made me wait in my bedroom with the door shut and the window open, so I never saw how they actually did it. But it meant that none of us could use the shower any more, so when we wanted to wash, we had to do it in the kitchen sink.

We weren't richer in the way that I thought richer would be. We didn't move, and our flat, the dull walls and slipping-off curtains, stayed the same. There were just new things in the living room, piled in the centre or stacked up around the edge, so there was only a kind of circular walkway through the middle.

Both JD and Kole liked furniture that was black and shiny. 'Console tables', whatever that meant. At one point, we had three or four of them. And whenever either of the boys brought a new thing back, they would call the flat a bachelor pad, or the batch patch, as if Ma and I weren't living there too.

Mostly, though, they came home with groups of people. Men and girls, the age gaps always big. JD and Kole would cram together bottles of every alcohol on every table and platefuls of kem. Literally platefuls of it, on the plates we used for eating.

They told stories together, Kole sitting bac[k]
do the work, until he'd lean forward and dro[p]
He was good at it. Good at timing. The w[ay]
ments on his face would pull our reactio[ns]
strings. Normally at some point, Kole would tell a story all
alone. When I tried to tell Caleb one of them, and kept on
saying I was getting it wrong because Kole did it better, I
remember Caleb rolling his eyes. 'Tell you one thing I've
learned in life,' he said. 'All the worst people in the world?
They're brilliant at telling stories.'

Ma would sit with them. All those people. Shy at first but
then she'd get louder. I remember her sitting to the side with
all the girls one night. I remember the way she looked at
Kole. The way she chewed her lip.

'I know I've got ten years on him,' she said to the others.
They were all looking at him too. 'But fuck me, I'd like to
teach him how it's done.' She changed her voice when she
spoke to those friends. Her voice had changed full stop.
She'd sent me to bed. I'd snuck back. She didn't know I could
hear.

At very first, or at times, anyway, it was like having two JDs.
'Gone from no dads, to two dads in a way,' Ma said. 'Now
dimwit's grown up.' That was one of the problems – she
could never work out whether Kole was my dad or my
brother. All of it was all too flat. She told me that when Kole
was around she'd prefer it if I called her Jas. That I wasn't a
baby any more, and more than anything Ma, Mum, Mad, all

e words I had for her, made her sound older than she was – older than she felt. Sometimes she'd link arms with me and I'd feel her shrink herself, like she was trying to make us sisters.

There were times when we did something as a family – JD loved the thought of having a brother, he was the one who said 'family' so much – that I saw this look pass over Kole. The muscles under his skin would relax, and for a second he'd look happy, he'd look calm. I'd feel this little soar inside me then. The thought that we could make him happy, even for a single moment. I think we all felt it. That's the thing about someone who's hard to please like that, erratic. It's addictive in a way. Anything that's rare enough tricks you. It makes you want it.

Anyway, these moments of peace – his eyes shut for a second, like he could keep it in his head – they wouldn't last long. He'd drink too much. Much more than JD, more even than my mum. I'm bigger, he'd say, I need more, or he'd go out to get some stuff, and when he came back, his shoulders would be popped again, even higher than before, and we'd feel it in ours. A tension, a pushed spring, a question we asked ourselves most days, or I did anyway – what would he do next?

So, no. Not rich in a normal way. I still didn't have any socks, but when JD visited a woman in Broadstairs for the weekend, Kole got me a pair of trainers that were so expensive he said I should only wear them inside. 'Pink,' he said. 'I don't know what girls like.' He looked embarrassed, if that was possible. 'Look grateful then. Fuck's sake, give us a smile at least.'

I looked at him. When I didn't smile, because I was trying to work out what was happening, his face became angry again, almost like a wave.

He threw the shoes next to where I was sitting on the sofa, two smack-like kicks. 'They're for bests – do you hear? Oi, dipshit. Don't you dare fuck about with them on the street.'

Over the months while you were here, I never told you much about that period of my life, but throughout it all, any time I left our front door, I wanted to run, scream, do anything that would get the tightness out of my neck. I got away with stuff. Pushed it. Got brought back to the flat by what was left of the police a few times, but no one at home seemed to mind much. Davey and I got in fights with older kids. He got his arm sliced with a knife, but he thought the scar looked good so asked me to add more afterwards. He cut a Superman S into his own leg.

We were twelve, then turned thirteen. We started having sex. Not me and Davey together, though that did happen a couple of times, as a joke, maybe, more than anything. Mostly us and other people.

The first of my friends who did it was this girl Perry Beckett, with one boy, then two more on the same night.

'They said I like it rough,' she told us when she came to find us the next afternoon. She had bruises on her arms and on her neck. We crowded around. She showed us the biggest one, this purple-yellow tie-dye, so dark it looked alive, like there might be galaxies inside it, or you could stick a finger in. She asked us if it would always be like that. If they'd always do it like that.

I don't know why the bruises made us all start. I sometimes think that there's nothing childish about being a child. The opposite, almost. My first time was okay. He was only twelve or thirteen too. It was hands and pushing more than anything, no bigger than a finger anyway, this empty, soft thing. I remember the bed more than anything, the mattress looked like a big black bite had been taken out of it, a fire from a fallen cigarette. When we came out of his house, there was a group of older teenagers sitting out nearby.

'You lot have started then. Fucking bait, bruv.' They all shook the boy's hand, that handshake where you bring it in to touch each other's back. 'Nothing else to do round here, is there?' They looked at me. 'No one else to do.'

After a few months my body had greenish thumbprints all over it. When Ma asked me what was going on, I told her we were all fighting, but for fun.

Later, when I came back with a long red scratch across my neck, she threw an ice cube across the room at me. 'Jesus,' she said. 'Isn't there enough bad going on?'

*   *   *

At the time, Kole cooked most of the kem, which meant JD was the one selling on the streets. That was why JD was the one who got caught, and went to prison once, then twice. He joked that prison was the one thing that still worked – mandatory minimums with a judge who did it in batches – except the prison he went to the second time was different from the one before. The new one used to be a holding pen, he said, a 'big-ass cage for refugees'.

The second time, JD was away for a year. Eleven months, actually, February to December, which was long enough for everything with Blue to happen.

Blue was born in November. A year later, Kole got a tattoo of Blue's birthday big on the back of his calf, but he got it wrong by a day.

When JD got out of prison, he stared at the baby. Ma handed him over and JD held his tiny pale head in the palm of his hand and stared at him.

'You two?' He looked at Ma and Kole. 'Together? I never would have . . .' He shook his head. 'I never would have guessed.' Kole took Ma's hand. 'But if you're happy,' he said. He turned to me after that, 'How you doing, titch?' but it was hard for me to look at him, or say anything.

Prison wasn't good for JD that time. It wasn't good for either of us. He came back with his muscles doughy, and under his eyes looked like black-sand beaches. I looked at him and wanted to look after him, but my whole body was wound tight, like the slightest touch would send me spinning.

'Is it because I've been away so long?' he said. 'Not you too, angry with me. Please don't be. Please come sit.' He hadn't left the house since he came back. He'd barely moved from the sofa, which I'd never seen him do before. I sat down, a little gap between us at first and then, when we were alone in the flat, he pulled me into him and started crying and I had never seen him cry before and so I cried a little bit as well.

'I think I've got it too,' he said, after the longest while.

'What?'

'The thing,' he said. 'The anxiety.'

'What, like being worried?'

'No, the proper one,' he said. He looked up at me. 'What Liam had. The anxiety – you know, when he'd flex his fingers a lot 'cos it was all pins and needlesy in there. I think I've got it too now. Do you think I have?'

I told him I didn't know. When he was in jail, he said, they gave them shots in their arms, shots to calm them down.

'But I feel shit now,' he said. 'Soft, like I can't lift up. It's not good though, it's not good. It isn't good.'

'I'm sorry.'

'It's all through my head,' he said. 'All thick.'

'It's okay.'

'But do you think it's for ever?'

He asked me after that if it would get better, and I didn't know what to say.

*   *   *

On New Year's Eve, JD said he wanted to stay home to look after the baby. He said he wanted to get to know him. He smiled for the first time in ages and said he was going to teach Blue all the secrets of life. He picked him up and kissed his eyebrows. It was the first moment that he'd looked happy since he'd come back. He did this noisy little sucky sound on Blue's nose, then walked around with him, this figure of eight rocking against his chest. Baby bro, bro, bro, bro, he said.

I went out with Davey – we lit Catherine wheels made out of bike spokes in Cliftonville and they only half-worked – but I came home early.

When I opened the door to our flat, I saw JD straight away. He was sat on the floor in a right angle in the doorway to my room. I couldn't work out the image at first – that way where your brain just stops being able to process, to put together colours and shapes and make meaning. There was powder all round him, and his face – it wasn't his face.

I touched his shoulder. He didn't move. Then I shook him. I shook him again. His head hit the wood of the door frame. It slumped forward.

I touched his neck. It was hot because the room was hot but there was no pulse. I put my fingers to his mouth, I put my ear against it, nothing. I shook him again and again and I held his head, and when I realised, when I realised, when I realised . . .

I walked backwards until my shoulders were against a wall too. Blue. Where was Blue. Fear came like cold fingers round the back of my neck and picked me up. One room, no sign of him, the next room, nothing, then finally – there he was on my bed. Too small to crawl. Too small to even hold his head up. But he was okay. Okay on the bed. My hands fell over him, around him, he started crying, I picked him up. And I sat there on the bed, and I held him, and for a while I couldn't make myself go back.

The days after that passed in a blur. Like the world was moving all around me, and I was just completely still. Seeing Ma and Kole together at the funeral made it a hundred times worse. Kole was what? Twenty-three maybe, rock-hard arms and double-yoke shoulders and these stupid lines shaved into his eyebrows. He'd rented a suit and he kept on looking down at his own body and smoothing down his arms. Everyone said how good he looked. But Ma – he hadn't thought to get her anything to wear. She was wearing a summer dress even though it had rained all morning, with a black cardigan, the buttons done up wrong until halfway through the service.

We stood together, Kole, Ma, me and Blue. Blue in Ma's arms until it looked like she might drop him, and Kole took him and tucked him under his arm like a parcel. Everyone we knew was at the service. When Davey got there he kept on saying sorry. Sorry, sorry, sorry, like it was the only word he knew.

JD's casket was open. When it was my turn to put a flower in, I looked at his hands. How big they were, how safe. The bumps on his nails, the way he could lift me above his head in a single swoop. His hands on my head. His hands making a tent for us under sheets. His hands that had always tried to keep mine warm. My brother.

With Blue in my arms, I walked behind Kole and Ma on the way home. The way he guided her down the street, like she was an old lady he was helping to cross the road. But she wasn't old, I realise that now. She was thirty-eight. He made her old. Then, as soon as they'd be home, his hands would be all over her. He'd paw her into the bedroom, slap her bum and catch my eye, and the things that he said to her in there were loud enough for me to remember some of them word for word.

The first time he hit her, I remember the blood coming from her eye, but maybe the blood had been on her hand and she moved it up by covering her face. After he'd gone, even though the networks were pretty much gone by then, she made me go to someone's house to charge her phone, and then kept on checking the sound was on, in case he called her. He came back a couple of days later with flowers, and a pack of tissues. 'Soft,' he said, as if you could buy hard ones. 'I am sorry though,' he said after that. 'I am sorry. It's not me. It's a different part of me.' He looked at her. He looked at me.

Blue was the tiniest baby anyone had ever seen. He smiled early, this faraway smile, a tiny bit sad if that's possible, but clever. His nose would crinkle, I'd think he wanted to sneeze, but it would never come. He was the size of a hand – my hand and the beginning of my wrist – for a month, and then he suddenly started to grow. The way it happened so fast reminded me of a plant.

I grew too. Tall, then taller, like I was matching him inch for inch, having a race. My ankles stuck out of my trousers. The sleeves of my T-shirts started at the middle of my shoulders. If I'd stood up next to my mum, back to back, I would have, for the first time in my life, been taller than her, but I found it hard to stand next to her. I found it hard to look at her sometimes. Her and Kole together. How happy she would be, and then the sounds that she would make, curled in the corner, when he hit her and left. The way I found her scrunched up on the sofa sometimes, sick on her top.

I cut my hair myself without a mirror. I lined up the scissors with each of my collarbones. Kole told me it was better longer, so I cut it again.

When the washout happened – huge waves, waist-high water through the whole town – I felt almost numb to it. This sense that it was bound to happen, this sense of, fine, come on then, wash it all away.

Davey and I didn't know a single person with a job. There weren't any jobs. Stealing made sense. It started for fun – curiosity, boredom, the same as breaking into Tracey's – but it was easy. We were good at it. I could scale up drainpipes, make it to the top of a wall with my fingertips. He knew people who knew people through his Uncle Trevor to sell stuff on. So many houses had been left behind, it was fifty–fifty, luck of the draw, much better than that. Sometimes alarms might ring, though less and less and, even if they did, it didn't matter. No one would come.

All around us, England went right, then right, then more right, then ultra-right, then left, but no, still right – I couldn't follow it, no one could really follow it. 'Going in circles,' Caleb said, 'that's all we need to know.' When the government was bad, charity would come our way. NGOs, non-profits, go-it-aloners. When the government got worse, we'd get less – people needed what they had at home. These were the rhythms that we lived by.

I got to sixteen. A smash of freckles across my nose, and strong arms from pull-ups into windows. It had been two years since JD had died. I wore the T-shirts that he'd left behind. I'd never been in love. And that's what I was like the day you met me.

II.

The winter you arrived, we had just moved to our second flat in the building, a flat four floors up. Kole had moved us there, because he wanted to make the first one his office.

A few nights before, Kole had hit Ma again and she was stuck in bed. Blue was with Viv from two floors down. She'd take him for the morning if I brought her things. Anything silver – saltshakers, single forks. Stuff I got from the houses.

It was November, around then, but that day was the hottest in a week of hot days. The sun was like a whip. I went out to smoke, only chose roads where there were shadows.

I sat in the shade on the roof of the Flamingo for a while, used a stick to play xylophone on broken arcade light bulbs, then wandered into town. I cut through one of the shops that had run between the seafront and the high street – a headshop, abandoned now, both doors open, missing floor-boards making it feel like a bit of a tightrope walk.

Back out on the street, I heard the sound of you running before I saw you. The sound of feet hitting the pavement at almost the same time. I did a full circle to see which way it was coming from.

And bam, just like that, you flew into me. You came so fast you smacked all the air out of me, like when you clap open a bag of crisps. I almost had time to grab your arms, but almost as quickly as you bumped into me, you pushed past.

A second later, I saw why. You were being chased. Four boys. They dodged me, three on one side, one on the other. One didn't have a top on. I didn't recognise them.

It was a silent chase. That was the thing that worried me. And so I couldn't not follow. I turned around, and ran to the corner so I could see what was happening.

When I got there, the footsteps had stopped. You were walking backwards, longish blonde hair, tall body moving back towards a wall, and the boys were walking towards you. Still no one said anything. You accidentally knocked an empty bottle with your feet, the kind of sound you feel most in your spine.

I saw you looking up at a rusty metal ladder next to you. Don't, I said to you in my head. They'd pull you down by your legs.

Then the closest boy made a grab at you. The crunches as they crossed glass and rubbish to get to you. You looked up, and that must have been the first time we saw each other.

You looked terrified. And something about your eyes caught me – caught me in them like a net.

A few metres away, I heard you saying that you didn't have anything. Then them saying what you had was enough. The one with the longest hair grabbed your arm.

'Oi, stop,' I said, and they turned around.

'Who're you?' he said. 'Didn't ask for you.'

'Doesn't look like asking bothers you.'

I kept walking towards him. He leaned down and picked up the bottle you'd kicked. He held the neck of it, the base had broken into a long, sharp jag. Then he started to pull up his T-shirt over his face.

'Don't bother about that,' I said. They were younger than they looked. Fresh-shaved heads. 'What are you even doing? You're like five years old.' Then I called over their heads, said something straight to you. 'Does Kole know you're here?'

You looked confused. Started to say no.

'He does, doesn't he,' I said. I turned to the boy coming towards me with the bottle. He was almost touching distance now. I could smell his breath. Chewing gum, crisps, kem. I could have run, it might have made sense to run, but I made my body relaxed, kept my shoulders down. 'Just trying to help you, that's all. You don't want to do that . . . not with her. Not if Kole's going to find out.'

'The fuck's Kole?' he said. But his friend reached for him and pulled him back.

'He was joking,' the friend said. 'Nothing serious. She's fine, look.'

'Ohhh,' I said. 'Are you a funny man? Seems a good joke. Seems like she's cracking up there in the corner.'

'Mate, come on, let's go.' He held his friend's T-shirt. 'She's not even fit. Fuck's sake, come on. Not worth it.'

The one with the bottle turned to me again. He spat his T-shirt out of his mouth and for a second I thought he might take a jab at me, but the others pulled him away. He threw the bottle at the wall as he left.

I walked slowly over to you. You had your head down, you wouldn't look up.

'They're gone,' I said. 'The lovely gentlemen.'

You started to say something, but I couldn't hear you. I squatted down a little.

'I don't know a Kole,' you said. And that was when you looked up. And that was when our eyes met properly. With a bang is stupid to say, but it did feel like that.

A sweep of your hair fell in front of your face. You looked different close up. Some people look the same from far away but you made sense best when your face was up close. There were your eyes, there was your nose, there was your mouth, and it felt like a lock opening. I didn't think that then – it was how I thought to say it later, but that was what it felt like. When you turn a key in a padlock and the arch pops open.

I looked at your legs, your knees. Knees are supposed to be darker. Yours looked like all the other skin. Cold, too. White mixed with purple under there. I'd forgotten every-thing. If I was supposed to say something. 'Sorry, what?' I said.

'I don't know a Kole.'

These clear, clean words. A kind of buttery sound. You weren't from round here.

'That's okay,' I said. 'You don't want to, either.' I reached for your arm, but you pulled it away. 'I'm not going to bite. I mean I do . . . I can. To eat food and everything. But I won't.'

You looked up at me.

'Not unless you ask, anyway.'

And then you smiled, and it just – I don't know. It wasn't all at once. It hit me in moments.

'I'm sure you know this more than anyone,' I said, 'but you're sitting in a pile of glass. Can I help you up?'

You looked down, then you reached for my hand. I took your arm and pulled you towards me. Your knees were still a little shaky; they buckled a bit as you stood.

'Thank you,' you said. 'Thank you very much.'

No, you were definitely not from here.

'It's okay,' I said. 'My pleasure.'

Sometimes, I wonder if the way we met is the reason why we got into the situation that we did. When I helped pick you up, the weight of your arm in my hand, the cool of your skin against my fingers, I felt this little rush in my chest. A spike, a kite, I don't know. It felt like I could save you.

When you stood up, we were almost exactly the same height. Your hair was dirty blonde and white blonde mixed together; a kink in it from having dried in a ponytail maybe. I wanted to look at you, but I didn't want to be too obvious about it.

I had half a roll-up in my hand. I was almost squashing it. I'd already smoked a little bit. Never every day, and not much, but even a little bit of kem makes you feel like your heart's inside your head. There's a beating. It feels hard to be afraid of anything. I lit it again. I wondered if I should offer it to you, but I'd accidentally made it a bit strong.

'I'm guessing you don't smoke?' I said.

'No,' you said, then, 'actually, why not . . .?'

I passed it to you. 'Hey, slowly,' I said, as you took a deep drag. Then your face exploded into a cough.

'Jesus,' you said. 'Is that poison?' You opened your mouth as if your throat could escape.

'Course,' I said. 'It's our public health crisis.'

I got another good look at your face then. You looked sweet and sad at the same time. Your chin dimpled a little when you spoke. There was something long and lean about your bones, something soft about your mouth. White teeth. A tiny gold nose piercing, and I don't know, your eyes were nice. The way they flashed made me think of a candle.

'Which lot are you with, then?' I said. 'Red Cross, Humanita, or one of the go-it-aloners? Van With A Plan?' You looked at me. 'Shit,' I went on, 'please don't tell me you're making a documentary.'

'I'm not making a documentary.'

'The amount of documentaries back in the day. I'm not even joking. Look at this face. Am I famous wherever you're from? 'Cos they were here with their cameras and I never saw the films.'

'Me neither.'

'I could still be a star though.'

'I'm not making a film. But yeah. How could you possibly tell I wasn't from here?'

'Because you ironed your shorts?'

'They're not ironed.'

'Prefer it when they look smart like you, to be honest. When they look really shit, and they're offering you charity, it's like damn, things must be really bad.'

'I'll bear it in mind,' you said. The beginning of a smile, maybe.

'It's funny, 'cos other times they, like, try and dress down, so it doesn't look so like, "Oh hi, I'm in my Christian Dior, do you want some baked beans or an abortion?" '

You laughed then. So I kept going. It was a monologue more than anything. A part of me was thinking, at least until I finish my sentence, she has to stay. 'Don't even know if they still do abortions, to be fair. Do they?' I asked you. 'There were some problems with that.'

'I only just got here,' you said. 'Fresh off the boat.'

'Well, if you need one, I know a guy.'

'Need what?'

'An abortion.'

'Think you stepped in just in time.' You pointed in the direction that the boys had left. Then you looked at your hand – it was still shaking.

'Want to walk with me a bit?' I said. 'I'll make sure they've gone. Get you to wherever you need to go?'

As we walked, I asked you when you got here. 'How fresh is fresh?'

'A couple of days.'

'And you've been working since then?'

'Yeah. But today was my day off so I figured . . . you know, an assault would be nice.'

'A little chase,' I said. 'Get the heart rate up. It's good weather for it.'

'Start the week in style,' you said. Your eyes flicked over the other people on the street. A man going by with a tiny girlfriend, her walking on the pavement, him in the road, so they were closer to the same height. A woman who'd stuffed tissue paper in between her toes to stop her flip-flops from rubbing. Pulling along a pit bull with markings like moonstone that changed in the light.

I looked at you from the side, catching you in flashes. There was a little shine of sun cream on your skin.

'Want some more?' I said. I held out the kem.

'God no. My head feels like . . .' You made a gun sign with your hand and shot yourself in the temple. 'What even is it? Do I want to know?'

'Just a local delicacy. Some places have, like, their special cheese, or like a Scotch egg or something. We have this. But don't worry. It's totally artisanal, you know. Seasonal ingredients.' I touched my hand lightly on your shoulder. 'Careful of the potholes.'

I guided you round one and took us towards the harbour. Down that close to the water, it's like colour only starts from the knee up. Everywhere below where the tide reaches is covered with a yellow sludge, that dries again, gets wet again, never washes off. Years ago, they put rocks inside wire cages to break the water, but the water broke the rocks – they're tiny now, they rattle around inside there, slip out.

We walked to the sea steps. I kicked away a little of the sand, silt, kicked a dead branch to the side, so we could sit down. On the part of the step between us, someone had written 'Tom got Emma pregmant' in marker. Pregmant with an m. 'When they built these steps, the water hardly touched them,' I said. 'Only once a day or something.' It wasn't too-too high tide, but the water was a quarter of the way up the steps already. It was only afternoon but the moon was out, a little broken shell of it.

'Is that the Turner?' you said, pointing to the tall concrete body of the art gallery, the sea-smashed windows.

'Yeah,' I said. 'Mostly a shooting range now.'

'For guns?' you said. I looked at you. 'Do you have a gun?'

'Nah.' I slapped my wrist. 'Needles.'

After not long at all, the sea started creeping towards us. I wanted it to slow down. You sat with your arms around your legs. I looked out. The waves get darker on their way in. They kind of look like liquid rock, the way flint cracks in flat angles. 'It's not a choice about going,' I said. 'That shit's brutal. The last five minutes it comes up fast as this . . .' I clicked my fingers.

'I might stay a bit,' you said.

'You can swim then?' I said. 'Better be the best swimmer in the world.' I stood up. I looked down at your head. The wavy line of your parting. The bones of your shoulders. You stayed still.

'Oh, so you're tough now?' I said.

You looked up at me. 'There were four of them, there's one of you.'

'Yeah, there's only one of me. And a whole ocean.'

'Wait,' you said. You turned round as I left. 'I don't know your name.'

'That's okay,' I said. I knew most people's names; I didn't want to know yours yet.

The whole thing lasted no more than fifteen minutes. Less than that, maybe. And the thing is, no matter how many times I watch it over in my mind, I find no reason for what happened to us afterwards. We didn't make each other laugh, really. All of our words were normal words.

I didn't look at your face and think that it was a face I wanted to kiss. It wasn't till later, when I got home, or after that, that I thought about how your face would look if your eyes were closed.

I don't know why it happens. When there is no reason. When it feels like there's no reason.

It was the start of the hottest winter we'd ever had. Old ladies used umbrellas to shade themselves. I started to sweat even if I wasn't walking fast. Men rolled their T-shirts up over their bellies. That morning, I remember thinking, it can't get hotter than this.

But it didn't matter how hot it was that day. In my mind, when I walk away from you, it always feels like I'm breathing cold air into my body, and I can feel it fill every single space inside my lungs. Light. Like a light.

After I left you on the steps, I walked back home along the high street. Davey was sitting outside the Beef and Anchor with a plastic pint glass and a cup of cockles. He had no top on, and his whole back and shoulders were covered in tattoos. Most of them were stick and poke, scratchy lines and in-jokes, a lucky horseshoe on his knuckle for Swifty, but after his mum died, he'd had a big one of her done on his shoulder, almost like a photograph. Davey's hair was a bit longer than normal, long on the top. When he saw me, he ran three fingers through it, flicked it one way then the other.

I grabbed him by his neck. 'You're blond, you weirdo.' The ends of it had gone gold in the sun.

'Everyone's got to have a summer look,' he said. He gave me a hug and offered me a cockle, peering into the pot. 'Look like fannies, don't they?'

I took a sip of his beer and looked around. The Beef and Anchor was the first pub we went to when we started drinking properly – more than the quarter pints of sweet cider we'd get at the Pearl – but it had been shut for the past two years. 'Is it open just for you, or open-open?'

'Open-open,' he said. 'The ever-promised renaissance.' Davey threw a cockle up in the air and caught it in his mouth. There was a squelch, a slight crunch. 'It's Meyer, in't it.' He said it Maya. 'The new lad.'

'What lad?'

'Got a poster of him behind the bar, anyway. The one with the slick-back hair.'

I peered in. The door to the pub was wedged open with a fire extinguisher. The lighting inside was the same as it always was – the blue light bulbs that made everyone's skin look like screens.

'He was over in Ramsgate, apparently. Action Man.'

'What you going on about?' I tapped a nail against his glass. 'How many of these?'

'The grand tour, the big I am. Action Man.'

'Wait, who's Action Man?'

'Meyer,' he said again. 'I just told you. The new lad. Politician. Had them eating out of his hands, apparently. Talking about getting the docks open again, all that. Said what was happening here was an abomnity.'

Abomnity made me laugh. 'Well it is . . . an abomnity.'

'Bullshit. I mean, yes, it's true, but he's talking bullshit. Must have found more oil off the coast. Or heard our girls are pretty and wants to sell them off into slavery.' He took another huge gulp of his pint.

'We can only hope.'

'Don't worry.'

'I'm not worried. I can't wait,' I said.

'I'll buy you.'

'Sure you will,' I said. I touched his glass. 'Seriously . . . how many of these?'

'Relax,' he said. 'It's gone lunch.' He flexed his arms above his head, then tilted his head hard to one side to make his neck crack. 'Stay with me. We can get drunk and pretend we're young.'

'Davey, we're sixteen.'

'Not me. I'm seventeen. That's old, bruv.'

I lost him sometimes. Broken arms, black eyes, and he never knew what had happened. He wandered off at that moment and finger-wrote on the side of a nearby dusty lorry, 'wish my wife was this dirty'.

'Why aren't you at work?' I called over. Over the years, Davey's business had evolved. It ran side by side with mine. He fixed windows, or boarded them up, after I'd done a house. He did it with his Uncle Trevor.

'Oh, you know, same old,' he said, walking back. 'Terrible boss. No benefits. Never any holiday pay.' He drained his pint empty, a flash of sea-froth in the bottom of the glass. 'You gonna join or what?' He scratched a dry patch on his hand. His eczema came back whenever he didn't sleep enough.

'I have to get back,' I said. 'Otherwise he's alone with her.'

'The little one?' Davey said.

'Yeah, the little one.'

I reached for a cockle, took two with my fingers. He pretended to take a step after me to reclaim them, but I made my back a bow so he couldn't reach.

'Well, give him my love,' he said. 'I see you soon, right, Cha? Properly?' He pointed at his chest. He'd had a tattoo of a heart done on the wrong side, so got another one done on the right side afterwards. Two hearts. He made them move in a pec dance.

'Yes please,' I said. 'Idiot.'

As I walked home, there was something good at the back of my mind. I flicked through. It was you.

For the first time in a week, Ma was on the sofa watching TV when I got back in. 'The sofa,' I said. 'Going up in the world.' I went over and kissed her head.

'Thought I'd pull out all the stops,' she said.

She kept her eyes fixed on the screen. The break in her skin was right on the angle of her cheekbone; she couldn't get it to seal. She hated me looking at her when she had cuts on her face.

'You'll never guess,' I said, as I pulled off my shoes. 'Apparently your boyfriend was doing the rounds in Ramsgate.'

'Kole?' she said. She sat up.

'No, the politician you like. The one with the hair. Meyer.'

'Oh, him,' she said. 'Swoon.'

'Swoon? Wait, sorry, let me just go back in time . . .'

'Have you *seen* his hair, though? They've been ugly for years till him.'

'Ugly is as ugly does.'

'Well, precisely.'

'You don't make sense,' I said. 'Before I forget, guess what? The Beef and Anchor's back open. Big day around here.'

'Ha,' she said, and she shut her eyes like she'd gone off on a little daydream. 'I always liked the Beef and Anchor. That was where I met Liam.'

She had a drink in her hand. When she sipped, she pulled it through her teeth. It sounded almost tidal. She turned the TV up. Some man had come over a few weeks before with a new wire and set of adapters. He'd put some new extender thingy up on the roof, and it was working okay now.

All the English channels we could get played the same thing. Repeats from ages ago, whole series back to back in a row. Four seasons in a day. *The Simpsons*, *Friends*, *A Place in the Sun*, a lot of shows about baking. She even seemed to like the adverts, though none of them were for shops we had. She took another sip of her drink.

'Such a waste of space,' I said.

'Love you too.'

Blue was in our room, eyes shut, on his kid bed, the little plastic bed he was getting too big for. I did what I always do. I checked he'd wake up.

I found him once like that, out cold. I put my whole body weight on him and still his eyes wouldn't budge. I found my mum and screamed at her. 'He'll fucking die.' I'd shouted it right in her face. 'See how small he is? Tiny heart. Tiny lungs.' She promised she'd only given him a flake of it, she promised she'd never do it again, but—

That day though, it was okay. It looks different when someone's sleeping because their own body wants them to. His pupils pushed around under his lids. Left, right, up, down, like he was looking for something under there. I always liked that. Like he was getting on with it without us.

He was two years old, plus a couple of months, when I met you. The little cushions around his ankles had gone. But he was still a baby really. Fat wrists, thin hair. When I spoke to him with my mouth not too far from his head, the strands would move with my breath.

Above his bed was the only thing we had on any of the walls that had come from me and Ma rather than Kole. It was a photograph of a door slightly open, and light coming through it, and everything slightly pink because of the time of day. A photo my dad had taken.

I watched Blue sleep. I used to do that a lot. Then his mouth chuppa-chupped. He started to wake up.

'Go back to sleep, bubbahead,' I said.

His tiny hand landed on my arm and I could tell from the way he pushed his fingers that he wanted me to lie down too. He liked best to sleep with someone, even better

104

if it was me. Like if he was alone he was missing out on something.

'Cub too,' he said. 'Cub you cub.'

'I'm coming too. I'm right here.'

It was about a week after that that I saw you again. Sitting on the bench in the Eliot shelter, reading a book. I tried to work out what it was as I got closer to you.

'I thought you'd drowned,' I said. I realised as the words came out that I'd forgotten to take a breath. I took one then.

'Unfortunately not,' you said. 'Sorry.' Your coat-hanger shoulders lifted up in a shrug. 'Not enough stones in my pockets.'

Your eyes were green and blue. Both colours in patches, like tiny miniature versions of the world.

'Boulders next time,' I said. 'Bricks.'

I was smiling as I said it. We both were. Like we were saying words and maybe they meant something but mostly we were just pleased to see each other. You can tell that.

'How's recovery going?' I asked you. 'From the big ordeal?'

'I mean, I'll be in therapy for years to come of course, but I'm surviving.' One of your eyes was winking into the sun. 'Thank you, again.'

'Of course,' I said. 'Any time.'

I didn't know what to say after that, so I wandered over to the railings and leaned over to peek at the beach. Look, I said, and pointed at a little piece of jellyfish, which had got caught up on the sand and wobbled each time the wind blew.

'Do you like sushi?' I said. You'd come to stand next to me.

'No rice,' you said. 'So that would be sashimi. After you.'

We fell into the kind of conversation where we mentioned things out loud. I said the rocks with all those finger holes looked like skulls. And you said some of the shells, the broken ones, looked like the inside of ears. We talked about the smell of stones and fish and salt. The way the clouds that day looked like they were in two layers, and one moved faster than the other.

'Are you here alone?' I asked eventually.

'Why, aren't you?'

'Well, right now yes. But in general, I have a mum. Mum and brother. He's two. His name's Blue.'

'I like that name,' you said. I snuck a look at the book in your hand: *Understanding Populations: A Humanitarian*— and then I couldn't make out the last word because your fingers were over it.

'What do people do around here for fun?' you asked me. 'I tried to go to a park but it was—'

'Hartsdown?' I laughed. 'Yeah, no. Don't do that.'

'I nearly got eaten by a dog. Honestly, it was the size of an elephant.'

'I feel like you might be going to all the wrong places.'

'You going to show me around, then?'

'Too busy. I already have a job, thanks.'

'What do you do?'

'I'm a thief.'

'Nice,' you said. 'I'll watch my pockets.'

'Anyway, there isn't anywhere to go. And I don't know you.'

So you said your name, and your name was Francesca. 'Though people call me Franky. Sometimes Fred.'

'I never met a Fred who looked like you.' I looked at you as I said it. The whole way you held your body was not like how I held mine. Your neck was straight up like a tree. Like there were strings holding each part of you upright. My eyes started to follow the shape of you. 'Well, if you're going to keep bothering me,' I said, 'I'll have to take you somewhere. But it will be far away and I'll leave you there.'

'Sounds good to me.'

I took us down quieter streets so we didn't pass anyone I'd have to talk to. There were people I'd normally nod at, but I looked in the other direction, didn't want to have to get into a conversation.

'I hope you know your way back,' I said, pointing at the road sign by the clock tower. It said three names. Broadstairs, Canterbury, but the last place, which used to be London, was scratched off.

'Keep the sea behind me and kind of walk in that direction, right?'

'Or run,' I said, 'depending on who's around.'

We walked past a man sitting in his window with no top on. He always sat there, but I looked at him differently. I tried to see what you were seeing. The semi-muscle, the drape under his nipples. His forehead looked like sand scratched with sticks, these deep, dusty lines. On the wires between his building and the one across the street, there were sparrows perched, evenly spaced, like fairy lights.

You looked at everything like your eyes were drinking. Up and down, as if the buildings were people and you wanted to see their whole outfit. An old TV aerial hung off the gutter, looked like a sewn-up scar. Wrought-iron balconies, flint walls shiny-black as latex, moss making cushions in old drainpipes. Cars with deep boulder dents. Two men on the flat roof of an old curry restaurant, feet off the edge. They were having a fire – too bright to see the flame, but there was a thin, dusty trail of smoke. Underneath them, white paint on a wall that said, 'Cash opps? Ask for Andy'.

But your eyes were caught on something else. 'Is that from the – what did they call it? – the water rush?' you said. You

109

were pointing at the waterline from the washout. It was up to your ribs there, a powdery white thing.

'The washout?' I said. 'Don't they give you a nice little fact pack on your first day at Humanita?'

'I know some stuff.'

'Thought you were meant to brush up, make sure you don't go round triggering.'

'I know it was two years ago. Just not everything.'

I looked at the line again. 'It's just high 'cos we're on a low bit here.'

'What was it like?'

'Oh, it was great,' I said. But I looked at you, and there was space in your face for me to be serious. 'It wasn't great actually, yeah. No. I was at home. I live up high.' Blue wasn't old enough to stand or look out of the window, and we didn't hold him up, and he cried, but we couldn't let him see. 'It looked like everything had turned to toys. The waves flipped cars easy as anything. Like they were made of plastic.' We kept on walking. 'There was a home for old people right on the seafront. They'd chosen it for the views – but they lost all their windows. There were these ladies too. Used to look after babies in the side room of an old church near us. Didn't have time to get them all out. Maybe you heard about that.'

'I think so,' you said. 'Maybe.'

'I tried to go down and help, like an idiot. I had to swim across the road. I got some bread though. The food bank – your lot, maybe, I think it was the Humanita one – had just put out its loaves. They floated out into the road. The air in the plastic packing made them bob. So, whatever, I suppose. You win some, you lose some.'

'Does it last long? Did it, I mean. A huge wave like that.'

'More than one. There were lots. One after another.'

Even a year later, there were whole sections of town left abandoned. Doorways filled with nests of rubbish, sea chalk, algae that had dried till it was see-through. Half-buried clothes, caked in seabed.

'Who needs Thailand, eh?' I said. 'We got all the sun, sand and tsunamis you could want right here.'

We fell into step with each other nicely as we walked. On one stretch of pavement there were a few big rusty splashes of dried blood, the kind Davey called ketchup. I pointed up at a big brick building so you wouldn't notice. 'That used to be a library. My friend Caleb, he's old but he's my friend, he tried to buy me a bunch of the books when they shut it down. But they wouldn't let him. There was some order from London that they had to be pulped. Health and safety reasons, or whatever bullshit.'

'That's so stupid.'

'It was alright in the end,' I said. 'I just went in and stole them.' I'd stopped in front of the building. I looked up at it. 'The first time I went in, years ago, a tiny kid, I remember thinking – this is the future! Like, year 3000 shit. Books, films, music, everything for free. They even had a piano. So yeah, obviously it was the first thing they got rid of.'

The old sign was still on the door. T-shirts and blouses must be worn at all times.

'A T-shirt and blouse together,' I said. 'Should have seen me. It was a great look.'

As we walked, I wanted to ask you if you had a boyfriend. But it felt like one of those questions that makes a person sound like a child. What kind of music do you like? What do you do in your spare time? Embarrassing.

'Do you have a boyfriend?' I said.

'No.'

We carried on walking.

'Do you?' you said.

I shook my head.

There were so many seagulls that day. Huge fat ones, bald bellies covered in scars. About twenty of them chattered in the close sky above us. Sometimes they kind of looked like fighter planes, dancing in a club, drunk. 'Have you ever tried it?' I asked.

'Flying?'

'No, seagull,' I said, 'to eat.'

'Wow. I didn't realise there were quite so many local delicacies.'

'Planet Thanet,' I said. 'Give it a month. You'll love it.'

I took you up to the industrial park hidden away behind Dreamland. Used to be factories, warehouses. Glass and metal, with ceilings so high it made it feel like people used to be taller. I always liked it there and the birds and dogs always left in the end if you shouted a bit. All of the colours had changed since the first time I'd come. Green had gone gold, gold had gone green. The metal was the same colour as the brick now.

You shut one eye, and said buildings looked flat when there wasn't any glass. Your head tipped back to let your eyes lift. They changed in the light – still blue and green, but seaglass now. From the side, I watched your mouth open. 'It's beautiful,' you said.

'Inside's a bit rotten, you'll see.'

The grass was mostly glass. We picked our way through it. You stopped to look at some old cigarette butts perched on the anti-pigeon spikes. There was a sign saying 'This is a hard hat area', but someone had scratched off the word 'hat'. I saw you smiling at that, but I could mostly see you thinking – this is not a great place to bring a person.

'It's for the view,' I said. 'There's actually a great view from the top.' I shook a ladder to test it. 'You wanna go first?'

You put your hands on the metal and your foot on the first step. Your trousers were low and as you climbed ahead of me I could see the two dimples at the base of your back. I remember thinking that they were perfectly thumb-sized.

We got to the top of the ladder and I slid over next to you on a beam that was wide enough to hold our weight. We were about 30 feet in the air. I pointed out the tip of the clock tower, named some of the rides we could make out the shapes of at Dreamland, and then Arlington House.

'That's my place,' I said. 'If you ever want to visit. I mean – definitely *don't* visit. It's— '

'Is it brutalist?'

'Yeah,' I said, 'pretty brutal.'

There was a dip lower down where lots of residue from the washout had collected. There were different woods in piles – polished, unpolished, some from houses or boats.

'You find bones sometimes, too,' I said. 'Not here, but further out – where there were farms. Some of the pigs and sheep were so waterlogged that, in the end, they had to use bottles and bottles of petrol to burn them. Could smell it from here though. Smelled of butchers, bins. Something sweet in there, too.'

Your face. I don't know why I wanted to shock you, but I did.

'Davey and I came across a pair of horses once,' I went on. 'One on top of the other, their ribs all melded together like fingers holding hands.' I did a version of it with my own. 'Davey didn't speak for days afterwards. He had his own horse once, totally obsessed with it.'

'And people?' you said.

'Yeah, people. A hundred, two hundred, five hundred, I don't even know. It's not like anyone official was there to count.'

'Is that why?' you said.

'Why what?'

'Why London was crossed out before, on the road sign.'

I looked at you. 'It's not people like you. People who help. That's – I mean it's weird, but it's kind of sweet in a way. It's just no one came for days afterwards. And we're not far. I know about Localisation. I know all that. We're supposed to look after ourselves. But people were dying. And when they did come, the London people, the government or whatever, it wasn't ambulances. It wasn't to help people fix their houses. They arrested people who were stealing. Not even bad stealing. Stealing to eat.'

'I'm sorry,' you said. 'I really am.' You looked tired, and even though the sun was directly on us, you looked cold, too.

'I'm sorry too,' I said after that. 'Best not to think about it.' I wanted to make it better. 'Look, I'm going to let you in on a secret. But knowledge is power, you have to remember that . . .'

'I'll remember.'

'Come drop back to earth with me,' I said. 'I'm going to get us some chips.'

There was a guy called Serb who parked his van in different places each day – Yoakley Square, Windmill Gardens – but it was always easy enough to find him. A smell of fat in the air, and a little dingly tune every hour. He kept bags of pre-cut chips in the fridge not the freezer so they were quicker to cook, and he turned the oil off in between customers, but somehow his chips were the best. He kept his mayo in the sun, the vinegar was strong enough to feel like it stripped your whole nose, and every now and then, he threw a chip to the seagulls as an offering.

That day Serb was at the gravel car park at the end of Fort Yard, and we sat on one of the tidal barriers they'd put in the town centre. They were all broken. They'd done them cheaply. The plastic was too thin. I once saw a man snap a bit off and use the sharp edge to pick his teeth.

I used to love the feeling of hot chips in my hands. The weight and heat of the paper. I held them out for you. 'And it's healthy, you know,' I said. 'Serb's ones are.' I broke a chip in half and showed it to you, the golden yellow outer shell and the puff of soft in the middle.

'I'm not a nutritionist,' you started to say, 'but that's not—'

'It is, though. Healthy. The fat doesn't go all the way through. It's basically like a boiled potato wrapped in a crisp. Suck it for a second, suck it like it's a straw.'

You bit, then sucked. And then, like it was the first time in your life you'd ever had salt, you started eating them really fast. A circle from the box into your mouth. It made me laugh.

'Fuck, they're good,' you said, and you looked up at me, and suddenly that word in your mouth hit the back of my belly. 'Sorry I'm eating so fast. I'm genuinely eating like a beast. I can go get us some more if you like?'

'No, no, I'm okay.' I had been starving was the truth, but it had suddenly gone away. 'Go for it. Go to town. I was just worried you were burning your mouth. You have mayonnaise on your face, by the way,' I said, 'just here.' And without thinking, the bottom of my thumb found its way onto your lip.

I remember the ridge of it. How somehow lips feels different to other skin. We both stopped. For a second, we were silent. There'd been a space between us. I'd broken it.

'I should probably go soon,' you said. 'Not now, but soon.'

'It's fine, I get it,' I said. 'Same old story every week. People only want me for my chips.' I looked down at the pack. One left.

'No, no. It's just – it's work, you know.'

'It's okay.'

'I loved the chips. I liked all of it.'

The way your feet were turned towards me. I could see one half of your body wanting one thing, one half wanting the other. And then you left.

I tried to understand it, why I felt a little in knots after you'd gone. Then I tried to think about other things instead. The way the seagulls crowded round leftovers, the feathers around their heads puffed up like they'd used hair gel. A man's face as he chose what to order. How people eat too-hot chips when they're hungry, mouth clawing at the air to let cold in. I felt in the lining of my jacket to see if I could buy something to take home to Blue.

It was just as I was about to leave, that you came back.

You had your right hand in your pocket, then took it out and put your left hand in instead. 'Hey,' you said, almost too casually, and I remember thinking, *She tried out different ways of saying that on her way back.* 'Can we go somewhere?'

'We just went somewhere.'

'Somewhere else. I don't know. Only if you want to.'

My lips were dry. I said yes by standing up. I was suddenly aware of the other people around. Some boys I knew were getting browns – chips with cut-up burger on top – and one sprayed the other with ketchup so it looked like he'd been shot in the chest.

I tried to make it look like I knew where I was going. Then I had an idea, and asked you if you'd ever been to a shell grotto before.

The shell grotto was on Shell Grotto Street; people always stole the street sign. It closed down years ago, but I'd managed to get in once or twice with Davey. We'd never hung around though, because we'd gone at night and forgot to bring lights, and no matter how long we stayed our eyes couldn't get used to the dark. The locks had been replaced. Nothing too tricky. I got my cutters out. The small ones with the spiky teeth.

'Is that legal?' you said.

'Yep, these are keys,' I replied. 'No, but it's work, my work this time, so it's—' I was angling them '—very professional.'

They're good cutters. They turn metal to plasticine. The padlock fell away. After that, the wood on the second door was soft enough to push a panel out and reach through for the handle. I opened the door for you, and we wandered into the gift shop.

Daylight tumbled in through the bars covering the dusty windows. We started wandering around, touching things. The top layers of the shells for sale were smashed – sharp edges, powder – but the underneath ones were still perfect.

I held one out to you. The ink on the paper label had leaked under the Sellotape used to laminate it, but it still had 'from Africa' handwritten on it. The shell was the size of a football. Dotted, ridged. 'I mean, what the hell is that?' I said. 'Just to find on the sand.'

You walked around the room so slowly, reading all the information boards, and telling me what they said. 'Apparently there was this little boy who was playing in his garden and he found a rabbit hole—'

'And it turned out to be this,' I finished.

'There's also a theory about pirates—'

'And pagans and cults. Oh, I know. You name it, we've claimed it.'

'Let me see your shell,' you said.

As you reached for it, I pulled it away, put it behind my back again. Your hands went to follow mine then paused as they were parallel to my body.

I'm good at those moments when I don't care. If I hadn't cared, I would have moved my face closer to yours. I stepped back.

'Do you want to go down?' I said. 'Downstairs.'

You turned towards the banister. My eyes floated over you – the waist of your collarbone, those thumbprint back dimples, the way you were already falling out of your trousers – and whatever it was, it happened in a second. I was not expecting you to affect me like that. The way it pinballed through my body, up and down, hitting sides.

'Careful,' I said. 'There are no lights down there.'

You took a piece of metal, thin as a credit card, out of your pocket and turned it on – some kind of torch thing. You held it under your face, then shone it into my eyes, and it was so strong I felt my pupils shrink. I pushed past you onto the first step of the stairwell. 'Point it forward,' I said. I didn't think about the steps in front of me, or how wet the walls were. All I could think about was how closely you were following me.

It's amazing in there, but it was even better with the light. Walls made of shells, the tips of each rubbed away by the sea and hands. All these spirals.

'I always liked how it's not just special ones,' I said. 'Like these.' I ran my palm over them. 'These are just mussels. You used to be able to buy a huge bag for a pound.'

'How far does it go?' you said, then your hand on my back, so I could lead the way. I could feel each fingertip.

The air was cold, damp. My breath kept catching. 'However far you want it to.'

When the walls got tighter together, I turned around. I remember us looking all over each other's faces, really looking, like we had to go into the dark to be allowed to do that.

'I came back because I—' you said.

'Because you what?'

You took a step closer to me. When people get that close it's to fight, or do something else. I didn't want to fight you.

Our foreheads were the first things to touch. Space to breathe. I felt yours. It was hot and clean. I felt safe as soon as we knew what was happening. Our foreheads rocked together. I used to think that foreheads were flat but they're not. Our dents said hello to each other.

You moved your head back. My lips were against your jaw. I didn't kiss you. Just moved my lips slowly, slowly, less than a second, but it felt like the slowest thing, until you made a sound. A sound from the back of your throat that pushed deep into mine.

'I don't know if I should . . .' you started.

'You are, though.'

Then slowness became speed. So fast. Lips and tooth on tooth, salt from the chips on one of the corners of our mouths. Impossible to tell which.

You tucked the torch into the waistband of your trousers, then changed your mind, and put it in your pocket. The space turned dark and your pocket shone, and your hands, free, found their way under my shirt and along the outside lanes of my back. You leaned into me. I steadied myself, put my heel against the wall, felt the ridges of a limpet pushing into my ankle.

'Do you do this?' you said then. 'Bring people here?'

I shook my head. We didn't wait after that.

I'd say it like that again and again, that it happened fast and slow at the same time. Time squashed and stretched by how close our heads were. I moved so I could put myself closer into you.

There are things that fill up your brain and make your stomach do things afterwards, when you think of them. The shape and skin of your throat as your neck arched back. Parts of you becoming hard on the inside of my knuckle. The way your eyes, when they caught the light, said what you wanted. Goosebumps, bullets. And then your eyes shut.

*   *   *

There was a type of happiness when it was over. Not because it was over, but because it had happened. We rested against each other. I licked the dip in your neck and watched it dry, slowly, my head on your shoulder. The torch was still on. Every minute that passed we could see each other a little better. Your fingers from one hand found the baby hairs at the back of my neck.

'Well that,' you said, 'was interesting.'

'Good interesting?' I blew your hair out of your face.

I felt you nod against my neck. 'I've never . . .'

'Go on.'

'Done that before.'

'Done what?'

'That.'

'Say it.'

'You know what I mean.'

'I don't.'

'Fucked a girl before.'

'Been,' I said. 'Been fucked. I fucked you.'

Our eyes caught, then that caught at the back of my belly again.

Back in the shop, there was a lamp on the wall, a light bulb set inside a skin-pink conch. You put your finger on the ridges, smoothed the dust off, then pushed in to touch the bulb, and I almost felt that inside my own body. Then you moved the old fire extinguisher I'd used to wedge the handle up.

'Did you do this?'

'Good to be safe. Thieves and robbers around.' I tapped my cutters sticking out of my back pocket. I looked at the red across your cheeks, these rubbed-out clouds of it. We walked out into a strange stormy light. Like rain was about to come, and fast. You shook your head a little, like being outside made it real.

'Back to work?' I said.

'Back to work.'

And that was it. There wasn't an official goodbye. I walked away from you without the decision being made. Part of me was sure I wouldn't be able to stop myself turning back to find you again. I'd always been glad to leave before. Of it being done, of it being okay, having liked it, maybe, but never enough to want to stay. But this time my mouth was full of things to say.

When I got round the corner, I stopped and waited. I thought about what it had been like to find your skin under your clothes. Cool and hot, how soft it was. How quickly my hands got used to you, the sound you made when you touched me for the first time. Fuck, I thought again. Fuck.

All I could think of after that was a trigger. Again and again, between my legs, I felt the hammer of a gun cocking back.

I didn't run after you. I managed not to. I walked home in a kind of daze. My chest felt like it was made of tissue paper, not enough weight in it, the air finding ways to lift it. I brought my hands up to my face.

But all that disappeared, all the lightness of it disappeared, when I got back to our door. I knew before I turned the handle that Kole was back. It's the way my mum laughs. Like there's an engine in her. For a moment I thought about turning around, running down the stairs three at a time and finding you again. But then I thought about Blue.

I pushed the door open, and they were sitting on the sofa. I saw them from the back, Kole's black topknot making him look taller. Ma's curls all stiff in bits, too much mousse. She touched her head against his with each laugh then bounced away, like she couldn't trust how much of her leaning he would like.

I walked round without saying anything. Blue was huddled into Kole's chest. Kole had been blowing a raspberry into his cheek. All three of them smiled when they saw me.

'Well if it isn't Miss Chance herself,' Kole said. He slid his hand free from behind Ma's back. Rings on his fingers.

I hated that he had my name in his mouth. My lungs felt all stuck together now. 'What you done to your face?' I said. There was a long cut up from his lip, and a smudgy green bruise under one of his eyebrows.

'Be nice,' Ma said quickly. 'Don't be rude. He's a guest.'

'Not staying, then?' I looked at him. Blue was pretending to play the piano on his stubble.

Other times I could have said that and Kole would have stood up, Blue dropping off his chest, and he would have grabbed me round the neck from the side, the hardest part of his thumb pushing into my neck where an Adam's apple would be. 'You can kill someone like that in a fucking second,' was the type of thing he'd say. 'A fucking second, you crumb.'

But this time he laughed. Then, when she figured it was allowed, my mum laughed too. A second later, you could tell he was copying them, Blue joined in.

'Cheeky little bitch you've got there, Jas,' he said.

Kole sat, like he always did, his legs wide, his heavy boots making his knees higher than you'd think, the fat knot of his crotch angled towards the television. Which is where I was standing.

'Come and say hi,' he said.

'No chance.'

'Yes, Chance.'

'Fuck off.'

'Cha . . .' Ma said. She never said it like the beginning of a dance, nothing cha cha cha about it. She said it long, char, like from a burn. 'Please. It's supposed to be a good day.'

'Why? Because you've just about stopped bleeding?' The last time I'd seen Kole, ten days before, he was pushing her head into a door frame. Her cheek had been bruised black, maybe even broken. 'Because you can almost smile again? No, you're right. Let's get the whole building over and have a party.'

Kole got ready to stand.

'We're back together, Cha,' Ma said. She reached for my hand but couldn't get far enough.

'Plane,' Blue said. 'Nairoplane.' His hand pointed at the window.

All three of us turned to look, but we were too late to see it. Blue made his hand a plane and crashed it into Kole's chest. Kole silenced his fingers with a shrug. There were dents in his cheeks. Dents that looked like matches had been put out in each of his pores.

'Calm fucking down,' he said. 'Sit fucking down, will you? Do whatever you want, but stop all this whining. Can't you see your mother's happy?' His forearm landed heavily

127

on her leg. He tweaked her knee. 'Your brother.' He pushed the word at me like he was holding my face against gravel. 'Happy. Don't you want that?'

It was the way he thought he could do it each time. Worse than that. How he actually could.

'What we going to do?' I said. 'Sit here like a family, watch the telly? We know you like that.'

The time before, he'd smashed the TV with the bottom of the bottle he'd brought round. The glass got everywhere. I had to spend whole afternoons picking tiny flecks out of Blue's feet.

'Never mind all that. I got us a new one, dint I? Just sit, little Chance.'

I looked at Ma and she was smiling still. 'You look stupid,' I told her. She didn't stop. She wove her fingers into Kole's wide hands. Blue touched his dad's face like it was a toy, and no one stopped him, and so eventually I sat down, a bit away at first, but as we sat there, because that's how these things happen, and happen again, the gaps between us got softer.

The truth is, like he'd always been, Kole could be funny. He made Blue laugh by pulling dopey faces. He told Ma and me a story about his mate Nev's new haircut. He said Nev looked like he'd covered all his hair in jam and offered himself up to rats. He'd convinced the woman at the funeral flower shop to cut his hair. The punchline was, 'Well she had scissors, didn't she?' and Kole was laughing so much as he said it. Kole kept his arm on my mum's leg, and rubbed his thumb over her knee and I watched the roughness of his skin pull hers around.

'Do you want your presents now or later?' he said to her and Blue.

For Blue, there was this toy gorilla thing, with fur that looked already rubbed. For Ma, pulled from behind Kole's back, like he was some cheap magician, a bottle of green liqueur. Frosted glass, not even full, half the label missing. She hugged him and then kissed him as he used his same fat thumb – his eyes were open throughout the kiss – to take the lid off.

'We feeling like poshos who need glasses, Chancey? Or are we just gonna make like the old days and swig from the bottle?' He moved to bring me into their circle. The hard meat of his arms.

'I'm alright, actually.' I turned away from them.

'But Cha, it's apple,' Ma said. 'One of your five a day.'

'I told you. You look dumb when you grin like that.'

I picked Blue up and took him into the corner where there's an okay rug and some of his toys. He wouldn't let go of the gorilla, and kept on saying nairoplane, nairoplane. Ma and Kole came back with mugs and so I left him with them, and shut myself in my room.

It didn't take long to hear thuds. Ma saying no. I felt my heart start to beat in my neck. Her saying no again. Then the thuds became quicker, and she wasn't saying no, it was yes, and that grunt of his.

It was coming from the bedroom, not the sofa, but I went to get Blue anyway. He was in the same spot, making the gorilla walk into the wall and then fall over, doing it again and again.

'What you doing there?' I told him. 'Come in with me.'

It was better in our room, with the radio on, though I didn't put it on full volume just in case the wrong kind of noise did come.

I started to talk to Blue, but he barely looked at me. He scratched his soft little fingernail into a cigarette burn on our carpet. He had a way of doing that. Putting his finger on problems. Cuts in the sofa, chips of paint, rust. Not in a bad way, just because he found them interesting.

'Did they leave you for long, baby boy?' I said to him now.

He carried on playing. I talked to him. I talked about getting chips, and the shell I'd seen that came from Africa. 'Africa's far,' I said. 'Got zebras there.' I talked slowly and quietly and he didn't look round once. I moved off the bed and lay next to him on the other side.

'Can I ask you something?' He still didn't say anything. 'And you won't tell Ma.' He didn't look up but, from his face, I could tell he was listening. 'If I met someone – would you mind that?' He looked at me then. His eyelashes were so long. Longer than mine. 'If they were nice. Like clever and nice and everything?'

I'd just wanted to say it. Blue picked up a toy car with three wheels and started driving it in small circles.

'Earth to Blue.' I stopped his car with my hand. 'What do you think about that?'

Finally he looked up at me, and said, 'Nairoplane doh?'

I shrugged and Blue shrugged too. And then he put down his toy and nestled into me with his T-shirt half pulled up, the tiny bead necklace of his spine pressed against me.

The next day was a Thursday – the main day we did the houses. We'd picked a corner-plot sandy-brick place on Addington Street, not far from Caleb's – curved windows, arched doorway. I didn't even need to climb, it was easy enough to push out a panel in the veranda at the back. I broke the glass badly, because I wasn't concentrating on it, but no one cared. The boys had been smoking all morning.

I looked at them. Their caps and unwashed hair. Their teapot ears and sores on their hands. They were as young as me, but their frown lines were so deep they looked purple.

I left them in the living room, and padded around the house. Carpet, floorboards. I could always tell the old DFLs in a single look round a room. They were either full seaside – blue and white stripes in bathrooms, seagull ceramics, retro posters with pictures of lighthouses; whacko majacko every colour under the sun; or so minimalist I couldn't tell if they'd taken their stuff with them or not. That day was a sea one – sea things everywhere, ship ropes instead of handrails on the stairs. I looked in drawers, under the biggest bed, under the pillows, cobwebs like clouds. But that day, I didn't care about finding anything. I couldn't make myself. I couldn't stop thinking about you. Somehow I had this idea in my head that if I left right then and walked to the beach, I'd find you.

I went downstairs and poked my head into the living room. The boys were lying scrunch-backed on one of those nice curved sofas that lots of people can sit round. I told them I was going to go.

They were smoking again. They'd found an old vinyl player. They were pretending to DJ, scratching records. It was a horrible sound.

'Can't fucking leave,' Brick said. He knocked everything off a table so he'd have a smooth surface for a few lines. 'It's just starting.'

'Got you in, didn't I? Done my bit. Be good.'

It's weird as hell but sometimes two brains can just do it. Because I did know where you'd be. I saw it in my head before I got there, and it was true. You were back at the Eliot shelter, tucked into the shade in the corner. I crept up slowly. I was about to slide my hand round the back of your neck, but as my hand got close, I felt shy. Or something like shy, anyway. I wasn't used to that.

'Are you loitering around my house?' I said. 'That's very sad.'

'I know,' you said. 'It's tragic.'

'You know what I was thinking about, by the way,' I said. I slid onto the bench next to you, but far on the other end, the sunny side. Put my feet up on it. 'Why were they running after you before?'

'Sorry?'

'How did you get those boys to chase you so fast?'

'Oh. My friends.'

'Best friends,' I said. 'Were you massaging yourself with money?'

'Believe it or not, I'd just gotten out of a car,' you said. 'And they saw me.'

'The audacity. And it was a nice car, I'm guessing.'

'It was alright.' You looked at my lips. 'I've had better.'

'Well, let's not do anything as dangerous as that, shall we?'

'I don't know,' you said. 'It was pretty exciting.'

I asked if you wanted to go for a walk with me, and you said yes, and as we walked, our hands bumped. When no one was around, you reached for one of my fingers, dropped it. I felt these things at the back of my chest.

That must have been the first time I took you to the China House. We headed west past the station, the opposite direction to the harbour, past old hotels, the awnings above each window fluttering like eyelashes in the wind. We pushed on further. This is it, I said, when we turned into a new road and got to the squeaky gate.

I'd loved that house since I was a kid, but it was even better once I'd finally got inside. Red bricks on the side, a creamy milk colour painted over the front. It was one of the first windows I'd climbed through – the peg had scratched a line down the middle of my belly; I lifted my top to show you the little scar – but I'd found a full spare set of keys almost straight away, so I could even lock it up when I came and went.

I checked there was no one on the street, then turned the key in the lock. 'See that mark?' I put my finger on the writing on the door. 'It means this place has been done. So no one else bothers. It's the shape a seagull's foot makes on the sand.' I started to push the door handle. 'There's a whole system.'

I had to lean my whole body weight into the door to get it open. I'd put clothes in plastic bags along the inside of the door, in case there was a big storm, or another big wave. Shoes, too, so it's heavy enough. I'd always leave through a back window.

The hallway was pink and there were green glass lights at metre intervals. You put your hand on the walls. 'Oh my God, I love it,' you said. You turned back to me. 'Whose is it?'

'I dunno. Sometimes you find names on old letters, or photos, but . . .'

'It's actually so nice.'

'What do you mean actually?'

You peered into the front living room. 'And tidy. You don't . . . do you clean it?'

'No, course not,' I said. You were still looking at me. 'I mean, I have. Not a lot. Just sometimes.'

'Why don't you live here?'

'I couldn't,' I said.

The thought of Kole finding us. Things breaking.

On every wall in the house, there was some kind of collection. The main room had old tea flasks, red, pink and sea-foam with Chinese writing on them and pictures of black-haired women, smiling. 'Hence the name,' I said. On the opposite wall there were jars and jars and jars of old spices. I'd always liked the idea of a collection. The idea that you could have more than one of a thing – loads of it, even.

You moved in your wandering way, touching things. A finger over the fat-thin pregnant belly of an ivory statue. A short little trill on the out-of-tune black notes of a piano. You went into a new room and tiptoed to see the highest shelf of an open cabinet.

'These are super-expensive,' you said about some plates, turning them over to see the back. Your voice went up a notch or two, then you brought it back down again. 'Rich people *love* this stuff.' You made the word love really roll in your throat. 'Old stuff like this.'

'I always found that funny,' I said. 'When you're rich, you want old things. When you're poor, you want everything new.'

We went back to the kitchen, and you opened the tea containers one by one, inhaling deeply each time. 'This one, no?' you said. 'It still smells good. Of something, anyway.'

In a way, we had afternoon tea. I found jam in a cupboard, a clean pop when it opened, and because we didn't have bread, we ate it off teaspoons. We sat on the sofa in the living room. Velvet cushions had sucked up the dust from the rest of the air. They made grey clouds as we settled into them, sticky teaspoons on our knees.

I used to think that after the first kiss, all other kisses had already been said yes to. But I felt that new thing as we sat there – I felt nervous. You blew into your cup. It was full enough to blow a wave of it over onto the saucer.

'Two women lived here, I think,' I said. I pointed to the photos in frames on the marble mantelpiece.

'Sisters?'

'No, like . . .'

'Right.' You smiled. Looked back down at your cup.

I laughed. 'This is like some Jane Austen shit.'

'What do you mean?'

'Like, I don't know. 'More tea, Richard.'

'Who's Richard?' It was your turn to laugh then. 'It's "more tea, vicar." '

As our tea cooled down, we warmed up I guess. 'I love that one,' you said about the photograph above the fireplace. It was of a girl with long red hair sitting up at a Formica counter. A slice of sunlight beaming over her hand, a rolled-up dollar bill in it. 'Pre-Raphaelite, but in a motel,' you said.

'My dad is a photographer,' I said then. 'Or, like, he took photos? I don't know what the difference is really. Never had the chance to ask.'

'Are you in touch?' you said, but in this kind of breezy way, like you didn't want to knock anything over.

'Nah, he's back in Sweden now. He had to go back. Actually before my mum knew she was pregnant with me, he left. She sent him a picture of me. He wrote back. Said he was going to come back. But he didn't have enough money in his bank account. He was like twenty or something. I don't know.' The first few were sentences I'd said so many times when I was growing up, that in my head, as I finished one, the next lined up. 'So maybe more of a kid who took photographs than a photographer?' I said. 'He's good, though. We have one on our wall at home.'

'Do you know his name?' Again, your light-touch caution thing. It made my shoulders feel tight.

'Do I know my own dad's name? Yeah. Linus. My mum was with him a whole two years. Which is like massive for her. Said he had a nose that won't quit, and that he put loads of tobacco bags up in his gums. But that he was really nice to her,' I said. I shrugged. 'And that's me out.'

'That's a lot cooler than my parents,' you said.

'What do yours do?'

'My mum's a doctor.'

'Fancy,' I said. The knot in my shoulders pulled tighter, I tried to push it back down. 'Any chance she's going to visit?'

'I don't think so.'

'We could do with a doctor.'

'More of a desk doctor,' you said. 'Academic. Shaky hands.'

'Sold,' I said. 'We'll take her.' I told you how Davey's mum, before she died, had a lump on her leg. 'Here, just above the knee.' I showed you on mine. 'She had to go to some witch doctor thing over in Herne Bay. Like, an actual witch doctor in a wooden shed. He took it out with a fucking spoon.'

'God . . .'

'Some spoon he'd heated up.'

You looked at the spoon on your lap.

'And it got infected, of course. And there were other things. So yeah, any old desk doctor – sign us up.'

When we took our cups back to the kitchen, I told you I only kept the ones I loved.

'Girls?' you said.

'No, houses. And not keep them. Keep them safe.' I tried to open a stiff cupboard to look for washing-up liquid, and at that moment, the handle came off in my hand. You started laughing and came up behind me. With one hand first, and then the other, you found the edge of my waist. My hands were still resting on the cupboard. I looked over my shoulder at you. Your lips, your eyes. Your skin. Your veins were close to the surface. A faint blue line on your forehead.

'I couldn't not touch you,' you said. 'You lifted up your arms and your back was there and it felt like I couldn't not.'

'Okay,' I said.

At first, I didn't move. Your hands found the space between my jeans and my top, and made it bigger. Your fingers felt like they were writing. Each touch the lightest thing, some kind of map.

When your hands moved away, my back pushed after you. Then your hands landed on top of my own, pinning them against the kitchen top. Your fingers made my hands look dark. I remember hoping you didn't think they were dirty. We still hadn't kissed yet.

You touched one side of me, so I'd turn around. I asked if you were sure.

Then, just like that, just like people say it should be, like magnets kept apart and then suddenly let go, we were together. I don't know if somehow you lifted me up, or I got there myself, but suddenly I was sitting on the kitchen surface and almost a second later, you were on my lap with your legs either side of me, one arm round my neck, the other holding the cupboard for balance.

Bedroom was the only word I heard you say, and I remember following you up the stairs. It was knowing what was going to happen. Seeing you. Never in my life had I wanted someone that much.

Upstairs, no lights to turn on, I made you stand and I got to my knees in front of you. I'd never wanted to be gentle before but I did then. I kissed you to the left, to the right, got closer, cleared a path. Left then right again, my mouth more open now. Gentle bristles, brush, pleasure in that. And you pushing back, trying to see where I was going and get there first. My hands finding the back of your knees. It's stupid, but the word home came to me. Then no words. You buckled, leaned over me, leaned away when it was too much, pulled me back.

I stayed there for enough time that it felt like all the time and also no time at all. No push. Slick, snug, a mouth around my fingers.

Afterwards was the first time I saw you naked in the light. Your arms and face were tanned but the rest of your skin looked like rice paper. Like I could put a finger through it. Like it would melt against my tongue.

I looked at it all. The skin between your hip bones, the way it scooped like a skate-ramp. The small little nest between your legs, ingredients for a fire. It was the fact that we were in a bed that got me. The fact that we were staying there.

'You do realise you're staring at me,' you said.

'Not true,' I said. 'I was staring into the middle distance.'

Your mosquito bites were raised. For a second, they shifted in my brain to snake bites. I wanted to suck the poison out. I wanted to protect you. It rushed into me, that feeling. You pushed your forehead into my arm. The tip of your nose was cooler than the rest of you.

You asked me about the first time I'd ever been with a girl. I told you about Rugi Thomas, who I'd known liked girls for ever.

'But how did you know that?' you said.

'She was a bit boyish. You know. She'd start to undo her flies before she opened the door to go into the toilet. That kind of thing.'

You laughed. 'Okay, Sherlock Holmes.'

'You know what I mean, though. A tomboy, or something. The way she held herself. The way she walked. She wore big T-shirts. Everyone knew she was.'

'And did they know that you were?'

'Were what? I'm not.'

'It doesn't sound like anyone knew anything.'

'She asked me if I liked boys and girls. Boys or girls.'

'And you said.'

'Wouldn't she like to know.'

'Well, obviously.'

'It was weird and I wasn't drunk but kind of drunk and I remember looking at her hands and arms more than I'd ever looked at anyone's hands and arms before.' I looked at you now. 'So I said she could try it on with me if she liked but it would never work. And she said okay.'

'Then what did she do?'

'She walked off! Walked right away. Didn't speak to me. I watched her. I tried to talk to other people but I watched her. Obviously. I couldn't stop. Later I went to find her, and speak to her, and I said, "I thought you were supposed to be trying it on with me." And she said, "Didn't it work?" '

'Right.'

'And then she took me back to her home, and she lived alone, and I didn't really think about it.'

'You can't just finish the story like that.'

'It felt fine.'

'There's no way it just felt fine.'

'Good. Or fine. No, good. I felt filled up with it.'

'Do you think about her?' you said. Said it softly. I couldn't read your eyes. What that little flicker meant. Whether you wanted to be made jealous or not. I shook my head. You'd taken my hand, unbent my fingers, and took one in your mouth.

'What about you?' I said.

'Do I think about Rugi Thomas?'

'No.'

'Don't, 'cos I already told you,' you said. I remember you shutting your eyes. Your eyelids like tissue paper.

'I want to hear it again.'

You nodded and then you turned in the bed so your face was buried in the sheets.

'I can't hear you,' I said.

'It was my first time,' you said again, your mouth muffled by cotton. Your eyes flicked up at me.

'Well you're a natural.'

'You're being cruel.'

'No, honestly,' I said. 'Like a duck to water.'

There was a plastic cover over the bed. We'd left it where it was, but now you peeled it back and slipped under the covers. The sheets were ironed. Ironed lemons and the smell of years and years of not being slept on.

'Why didn't the owners come back?' you asked me, stretching your body out into a small star. 'If I had this bed, I would come back here.'

'I think lots of people thought they were just leaving for a while, until things settled. Then no one could sell.'

Crick in my neck. I pushed at it with my knuckles until your hands took over. Our heads poked out from the duvet, and our arms, too, thick clouds of white under our elbows.

'I had a brother,' I said then. I wasn't even thinking about saying that. It just came out. Maybe it was talking about people leaving. The thought of you leaving.

'You told me. Blue like the colour, or for a different thing?'

'A different brother. Older than me.' It caught in my chest.

'Is he . . .?' You turned back to me. That breeziness again. 'Oh right. Where is he?'

This time, I tried to say it lightly too. Because each time I said it, it did it again. Like a tiny fragment of him stayed alive and each time someone said he was dead, it cut a little bit more away. 'Drugs or whatever. Nothing special.'

It wasn't the right time to tell you. I don't know why I did it. Maybe it had been so nice that I wanted to make it bad somehow. I do that. I missed out the middle and told you the end. JD's big back to the wall. The mess where his nose was. His nostrils one circle, his septum a little pink stub, his eyes even worse. The colour of the pupils had burst its banks.

You were frowning. Your forehead didn't look used to that.

'We still don't really know what had happened,' I said. 'In the end, I had to get people from the building to help get his body down.'

I didn't say that they had dropped him a few times on the stairs. How much I'd hated that.

'Did he mean to?' you said.

'JD?' I shook my head. 'He was a million fucking dumb things, but he'd never have done that. Never wanted to do that.'

Kole said it was a bad batch, a batch with all these other things added in. He said that it had come from London, down on the county lines. He said he knew where the guy was staying, he said he'd go round that night. Kole said it was nothing to do with him. Nothing to do with him again and again, until Ma believed him.

We were still naked, and as hot as we'd been, that's how cold we'd become. Salt and goosebumps.

'What about you?' I said.

Our ankles were jigsawed underneath the covers. I looked at your nipples, the pinker skin like a mountain range.

'What's wrong?' you said.

'Nothing.'

'Well, something. You just pulled your body away from me.'

'Nothing. It's just I just told you about how my brother . . .'

'I know.'

'No, but, I don't . . .'

'What?'

'I mean, you're a stranger. I don't even know what you're doing here.'

'What do you think I'm doing here?' Your hand padded over the bed, looking for mine. Couldn't find it. 'We just . . . And it was . . .' You semi-shut your eyes and did this dancing smile.

'Not that. I know that.' I looked at you. Your hair was splashed onto the pillows. There was a word in the air between us. I didn't want to say it.

Pity. It was the only word I could think of. Was that why you'd come here? That was the only reason people like you came here. But if that was what it was, where would that leave us? I wouldn't know my way back from that.

'Then don't be silly,' you said.

You pushed yourself into me. My hand found itself against the side of your belly. It was the softest skin I'd ever touched. Softer, even, than Blue's. So soft I wondered if there would be some kind of powder on my fingers when I pulled them away.

The next evening, I was lying on the floor reading when Kole came into my room, his tank top on awkwardly and his hair down, Ma just behind him, her cheeks pink and her grey tooth making a shadow in her smile.

'You kiddies coming or what?' he said.

'Not a kid.'

'Don't start.'

'Where, though?' Blue was asleep. I had my hand on his hair. Ink on my fingers. Before his nap, we'd been drawing.

'To the old Town Hall museum thing. Nev just called.'

Ma came over and picked up Blue. She could barely get him up to her waist sometimes.

'Free drinks down there, Cha,' she said. 'Some party thing. Nev said.'

'What do you mean free drinks?' I said. 'Fucking last thing you need.'

'Look at her,' Ma said to Kole. 'I've created a monster.' She shook her head, turned back to me. 'Don't be rude. Kole thought we could go down together. Like a family.'

'What a lovely family,' I said. 'But is it actually for kids or what? Blue's tired.'

But Kole was in a big, happy mood, knocking on downstairs doors to pass the invite on, then coming back and doing this kind of dance thing like he was shaking dice in his hand and then letting them out in a throw. Ma was wearing eyeliner and when she walked past me she smelled of wood and bubble gum. Another present.

'Jesus,' I said.

'What?'

'You smell like eight different prostitutes.'

'Don't be a—'

'All of them trapped in one car.'

'Bitch.' She tried to hit me but I ducked away.

Outside, on the stairs, we bumped into Viv and her son Bob, as well as Lace and Aran and Tom. Lots of other people from the building were going, too. Viv picked up Blue and rocked him like he was on a swing. 'Helloboyhelloboyhelloboy,' she said, fast, like it was all one sound. 'I've missed this hot little head.'

Once we were out, it felt good, everyone walking together like that. It was a big group. Male legs making their owners stride to the front, women a bit behind, some wearing high heels that crunched over shells and old sand.

People were dressed up. Clean T-shirts, short skirts. Jewellery, and big stuff, too. Lace had a gold ring on nearly every one of his fingers, and when Kole shook his hand he said, 'Got your clichés on, mate. It's good to see!'

The tide was high – we could hear the wet smacking of the water hitting the first sea barrier – so we walked the back way, over and out through the car park. Quickly, too, and I remember thinking, it's funny how fast people will walk towards something, especially when they don't know what it is.

When we got to the town square, in front of the main building there was already a big crowd waiting to get in. There was a queue, but it wasn't a line, it was a mash of people, with kids sheltering between legs like door frames in a storm.

I thought of you – I wondered if you'd heard about it. I looked for a flash of blonde among all the heads.

'Tell them not to run out of beer, faggot!' Kole shouted to a guy he knew up the front. I think it was Jase Jackson who used to hang out with JD and Kole back in the day. He always used to tag the s's in his name as dollar signs. Jase gave Kole the finger, but nicely. Being with Kole, we could have gone straight to the front of the queue, but we stayed back, Kole shouting hellos at people he knew, shaking hands, rough-patting backs.

Kole came back from talking to someone who was just leaving. 'What happens is, they give you these little token things, few each, and when you get inside you swap one for a beer – or something soft if you're a kid – and that's it. Free as the day.'

Ma looked happy. She found a pillow in Kole's shoulder.

'Why, though?' I said.

'Nev said it's the government.'

'What do you mean, the government?'

'That new lad. Meyer. I don't know. People who want to help, anyway.'

'Who want to help throw a party?' I said.

'Yeah?' Kole said.

' "Yeah," ' I copied his voice, 'but why? That's fucking weird.'

'Don't look at me like I'm stupid.'

At the door, we got given our tokens. Grey for the adults, orange for Blue. We wandered in, went upstairs. The main bit of the party was happening in the old council chamber, with these tall arched windows. Some kind of ceremonial dock was being used as a bar. There were a few hundred people inside. Maybe more. Some type of silky music running through the air, nothing you'd play at home.

Kole saw Nev and shouted over lots of heads till he came to join us. We were in the queue for the bar.

'Your hair, Nev . . .' Ma said. She was sucking in her cheeks so she didn't laugh. Nev scratched at one side of it – it really did looked chewed. 'It looks good, Nev. New, I'd say. A new kind of style. A lewk.' She squeezed me on the leg. Soft nails.

150

'You're a lovely person, Jas. Don't know why you put up with this bag of rocks.' Nev did a knock-knock on Kole's pecs, then slipped Kole five or six more tokens and told him there was more where that came from.

'Is he coming, then?' Ma asked Nev. 'Someone said he might be.'

'Is who coming?' Nev said.

'Meyer,' Kole cut in. 'Look at her face. The suspense!'

'Haha, I don't know, mate,' Nev said. 'But this lot seem alright though, honestly. I was put in touch 'cos they were looking for liaisons. Told 'em beer would be a good idea, if they wanted to make friends.' They cheersed, this soft plastic clink. 'I know what you're thinking,' he said. 'London men, the cuntiest that come. But these lot seem different. Talking about reconciliation. Reparations.'

'Six syllables, Nev!' I said.

'Well I dunno,' he said. 'But anything's better than how it's been.'

'What do you mean liaisons?' Kole cut in. 'Like a hooker?'

'No, no,' Nev said again. 'Not scabs or nothing, more power than that. Giving advice more. "Community links." ' He did the speech marks and rolled his eyes. 'Oh, you know. Good money. Easy work.' He winked then in a way that made him look nervous. 'I can hook you up, mate, if you're interested. If you wanna . . .' Nev said to Kole. 'I could do that.'

It always got me how big men, men with scars on their knuckles and necks, would offer Kole things, even if he wasn't asking. Kole ruffled Nev's hair, then pretended to kick him, so he scuttled away.

We drank from plastic bottles with screw-tops. They came from a fridge, but they hadn't been in there long. I pushed mine against my arm – it was only a tiny bit colder than my skin. Kole took a swig of Blue's bottle and handed it back to him. They both drank the same way, with the entire screwy bit of the bottle in their mouth.

'I can feel that on my teeth. Phwwwoo. Kid's gonna be walking up the walls,' Kole laughed, and took Ma's waist like they were about to go dancing. 'Fun, this,' he said. 'Even if it's for narks.'

The beer went to my head quickly. It wasn't very fizzy. The sound of cheers, people knocking together plastic bottles. The kids were still winding through adults' legs. It made it feel like there were two worlds operating at different heights. There was one fight, but it was broken in half quickly, and soon the two men were chatting again.

There weren't many people there my age. A few of the girls from Manston got there later. We nodded at each other and that was it. I thought about you. I stood on my tiptoes, then when I didn't see you, I asked a couple of people if they'd seen Davey. No one had.

I stood about a metre away from Kole, Ma and Blue. Kole was lairy but in a good mood, Blue was holding his leg. Kole was saying things into Ma's ear and she was laughing.

She wasn't steady on her feet and she looked very young and very old at the same time.

'Have you looked at the signs?' I asked them.

'Ain't come here to read,' Kole said.

'Only 'cos you can't.'

'Yes, I fucking can. LandSave,' he said, reading from one of the posters on the wall. 'Easy.' He crushed his empty bottle, and burped at the same time. 'Fuck knows what dumb shit it is, though.'

Ma's eyes had started to glaze, look milky. It happened more quickly than usual. The music got louder, the lights picked up pace a bit.

Everyone was moving through into the next room. There was a first-floor passageway between the two buildings, no glass in any of the windows. I looked out. Loads of people were trying to get in. Someone stood on a friend's shoulders and a bunch of people pulled him in through a missing pane. It was funny walking with Kole. People would smile at me, see Kole, their faces would drop, then they'd try to smile at him too.

I'd never been inside the Town Hall before. In the second room, there were more of the signs everywhere. It smelled of fresh paint, that chemical cut grass smell, and there was a weird stage at the front, bouncer types standing on either side. Even Kole said they were big lads.

I don't know how long we were in there for before the show started. It had all got a bit foggy since just before then.

But I remember feeling Kole's hand grab my jumper. He left Ma to the side and pulled me forward.

It's broken-up pictures more than anything. There were some dancers. Some fat guy who told jokes. Kole got us two more rounds of the plastic beers, then more, then more. It was colder now. It made the top of my mouth feel dry and my heart feel bigger, somehow. Even more, I thought about you. I asked Nev if everyone in town was invited, even new people.

'New people?' he said. One of his eyelids was starting to dip. 'Why would any fucker choose to come here?'

I wondered if you were here already, or if you'd be here soon, and suddenly I would feel a hand on my back, and we would be able to go somewhere together. I thought about the last time we'd been alone and my stomach did these flips. Perfect circles, getting bigger each time.

But like I said, it got blurry. I hate myself for that. The beer made my eyes feel like pinhole cameras. But when I pulled Blue up onto my hip, his pupils looked like the hugest things, wet black ink. A man walked onto the stage, and a screen lit up behind him. He was wearing a suit. I hadn't seen one of those in ages.

I tapped my mum's arm. 'Is that Meyer?' I asked her.

'No, no, I told you – Meyer's *fit*,' she said.

'Fuck's sake,' one of Nev's friends shouted out at the same time, 'it's not a wedding, is it?' and you could see who'd said it because the people around him leaned back in laughter.

The man on stage continued without looking up. There were sunspots on the bald parts of his head. 'A lot of you have been frustrated for a long time,' he said. 'But tonight? Tonight is the opposite of that. Tonight is a celebration.' He paused, took a breath. His chest swelled. 'We're asking you to take a step. A step with us. A step closer to a brighter future.' Between each of his sentences there was a gap big enough for a cheer. It started coming. Because, in a way, it doesn't really matter what's being said. You can make anything sound good by speaking slowly like that.

I looked over at Kole and my mum. He was pretending to slap her face, doing a hard run at it, then only tapping her cheek lightly.

'LandSave is going to change this country,' the man said. 'LandSave will change all of your lives.'

The cheering went crazy after that. I couldn't see the stage now, because everyone's hands were in the air. I pushed forward to get a look. And then the crowd surged forward even more. I held still and it felt like standing against a wave. How drunk I was, it hit me when all those people did. I couldn't stay there. I didn't say goodbye to anyone, and the worst thing was, I was so out of it I didn't even look for Blue, I just turned around, and pushed through the forest of bodies.

I vaguely remember a hand on my shoulder, a voice from behind me. 'There you are. Is it rubbish in there or what?'

It was Davey. He was covered in sawdust from work. He blew matte hair out of his eyes. I can't remember everything

I said, just that it was slurred. I remember my tongue feeling too big for my mouth.

'You alright?' he asked. I could see him looking at all the different parts of my face like he would be able to work out what I wanted to say.

'Fine,' I said. 'Just have to – might be sick.'

'Chance . . .' he said, and he started to follow me.

'Just a moment on my own, Davey,' I said. 'On my own.'

Outside, empty bottles were blowing in bumps along the cobbles. A group of young teenagers sat around sharing cigarettes or drink or kem. They made a tent over it.

I remember I couldn't walk straight. I remember my eyes watering. I wiped my eyes on the back of my wrists. I could taste the salt in them. It was warm out. The type of thick air that makes people fight. I made my way towards a bench.

And from then on, it's black.

I woke up when it was already morning. I'd slept on a bench.

The sun was shining hard at itself in the sea. The clouds looked cleaner than usual. No wind. Everything felt so still, but in a way that felt wrong, like someone had pressed pause on all of it. I wondered if I'd died.

I ran my hands over my body, to check my clothes were there, and feel if any of me was hurt when I touched it. I sat up. Eyes wake up quickly when you don't know where you are, but behind it, my head felt shaken up. My feet found the floor. Cold. I looked down. Water.

Water everywhere. Enough to surround the soles of my shoes. A crisp packet floated away from me. My eyes flicked right away to our building, then moved up to the thin line of our flat. What had I slept through? Why the fuck had I slept on a bench? Fuck, I said out loud, fuck.

As soon as I spoke, it felt like acid poured into my head. Or like I had water in my brain, and that an electric cable was being dipped into it, each time my heart beat. I had to get home. I started walking. Everything was shut. Even the shops that were sometimes still open were shut. No one else on the street. I started to walk faster.

I took the high roads, ran back to the building with cold feet sloshing in my shoes. I was out of breath when I arrived. Then I walked up the stairs slowly, this stir starting in my stomach. It's the stairs until around the tenth floor, then it's our stairs. The first had pools of water, smelled strongly of the sea; three was graffiti and boxes; eight has families on. Had. I got closer and closer.

At first, when I got to our door, it was worse than I thought. The door was open. Not all the way but enough. One of Ma's shoes was outside. An image of them flashed into my head. Face down on the ground, pools of blood for pillows. I imagine this a lot. I can always see it.

When I went through the door, I half expected to feel something heavy break through my shoulder blades. I kept flinching. Then, 'Is that you, Cha? Fucking hell.' Ma's voice. It sounded like she was talking through bread. 'Go check it's her.'

The sound of heavy feet landing on the floor. Kole opened the door to the bedroom in boxers, an old towel as a kind of shawl.

'It's her!' he called back behind him. 'Where you been you little shit-show? You worried your mum, Cha. Shouldn't do that.'

158

He pointed through the doorway, to where she was in bed. Her hair was all messy; she flattened it with her hands.

'Where's Blue, though?' I said.

Kole reached forward for my head. His fingers went over my parting and caught me from behind. 'Always so fucking aggy. What goes on in that little head?'

'Where is he?'

'Don't be a little bitch.'

'Stop calling me little.'

'Come see.'

They had all been in her bed, and even though it didn't have any sheets on – the sheets were on a pile to the left; I'd washed them for her weeks ago – it was a picture. It was a picture. Because they were not dead. None of them were dead.

'The sheets, Ma,' I said.

'Shut up about the sheets. Where you been?'

'Did you see the fucking wave, Cha – ride it!' Kole did this weird, shaky-kneed surfer thing.

'Where were you?' Ma said again.

'Out shagging,' Kole said. He reached for my head again. I shrugged away and made my hand a quick fist, and Ma put out a finger for me to stop that.

'It's been ages, babe, is all.' She only ever called me babe when Kole was around. 'We were worried. The high tide and everything.'

'You weren't worried. You're not even up.'

She flattened down her hair again. I still had her shoe in my hand.

'Is it true, then?' Ma turned to me. 'Have you been shagging?' She looked quite happy about it.

'Go on,' Kole said. 'Tell us, then. Boy or girl?' He'd always ask that. 'Look at this,' he'd once said, his zipper taut to the side. 'Packed tight in there, look! You still got it, kid.' I couldn't even be bothered to tell him he was disgusting.

'You're gross. Both of you. When did you get back? What happened? I wasn't shagging. Who says shagging, anyway? You're supposed to be an adult.' I looked at them. Why were these my adults? Kole was actually rolling on the bed laughing. He had two types of hangover. Laugh, laugh, but this mad laugh, or anger waiting just behind his eyes, getting closer to his pupils each time he blinked. 'What happened,' I said again, 'to you lot? After the party. At the party. We got separated.'

'Give a shit. Everyone was fucked.'

'I was just wondering what time the water came. If it was last night or . . .'

'Jesus, you must have really been driving down on the fella,' Kole laughed again. 'Anyway, it was mental. No wonder Meyer's knocking on our door.'

'But what is it, exactly?' Ma said. 'His LandSave thing? I couldn't hear from where I was.'

'Couldn't hear? You couldn't fucking see. You pounded into those beers, you daft old . . .' Kole wandered over and started doing pull-ups on a bar he'd put in the bedroom door frame. 'Getting jobs back. Making things work around here again. Turning the dimmer-switch down on the sun. All the flag things at the party.' He spat with his p. I saw it.

'Thought you said the posters were dumb,' I said.

'Whatever. So they done a bit of branding, made it look nice. Why's that wrong? Could be good what they're offering.' He let go of the metal and went back to standing.

'Which is what, though?' I said.

'All these fucking questions. Making it better round here, that's what they said.'

''Cos they've been pretty good at doing that, haven't they?' I said. 'Pretty reliable.'

'Fuck's sake,' he said, 'if there was ever anyone to piss on people's chips, it's you, Chance.' He reached for the pull-up bar again. 'Such an endless shit-blanket.'

Blue had been counting his fingers and making explosions on the surface of the duvet. It was only then I noticed a little patch of rust under his nose.

'His nose has been bleeding,' Ma said.

'I can see that.'

I looked at Kole for a second too long.

'Don't you fucking dare. I'll blow a nut, I swear, Cha. I swear it.'

Blue put his hands over his ears. Not even his hands, his whole arms. I hated that it was something he knew to do.

'He didn't do a thing,' Ma said. 'It's bleeding for no reason. Some of the other kids in the building too. Di came over for tissues. It's the air pressure, she reckons.'

'Not a fucking finger,' Kole said. 'I didn't lay a finger on the boy.'

'We're high up. It's the pressure.'

'We're hardly on a mountain.'

'And even if I did, who the fuck are you?' Kole said. 'You're not a policeman. Stick around if you care, don't just run off, fucking who-knows-who wherever you were.'

I walked over and kneeled next to the bed. 'You okay then, little bean?'

He nodded. He had a heat rash on his arms. I kissed it, tried to think what we might have in the cupboard for that.

'It was nice with you gone,' Kole went on. 'Always coming here with your problems.'

'I live here.'

'Well, be nice. This is a family. If you don't like it, you can run back off to lover boy.'

'Why are you still talking?' I said. I got in the bed next to Blue.

'This is how we used to sleep.' That was Ma. Her voice had softened again. Kole had moved to a chair now, his big boots up on the windowsill. I watched the big muscles in his arms relax. 'When – yeah,' she said, and I could see in her eyes she was thinking about JD rather than Kole. 'All of us in a bed. Like a raft.'

Her eyes closed and I could almost see her take the picture of JD and put him to one side.

Blue crawled onto my chest and belly. I took deep breaths so he moved up and down. It made him laugh when I did that. He grabbed at my earlobes.

This raft, I thought. How long can it stay floating?

*   *   *

When the tide was low again, I went downstairs and left the building. Thought just a little bit of kem might lift away the worst of the headache. A freak tide like that always leaves everything messy. I picked a path through seaweed, fishing net, a pair of underwear, a washed-up face-mask, worn thin as a leaf. I was licking my teeth, wondering how many days of life were on them, when I saw you. The back of you.

You were kind of peeking round a corner, stepping tentatively. I felt this smile cut through my cheeks. I straightened it out.

'They can smell it, you know,' I said. 'The fear.'

You looked up, then smiled. 'Who exactly?' you said.

'Whoever you're scared of. Local hoodlums.'

'I smell kinda good, actually.' You tilted your head so you could smell your own arm.

'Don't tell me you've got hot – running – water?' I said those three words like I was doing the voiceover of an ad – luxury, chocolate, cake.

'Well, it's, like, warm. Think it's the sun more than anything.'

'Do I not get an invite?'

'But we're so close to yours.'

'You're not going up there for love nor money.'

'Well then, the Chinese House?'

'China House.' I looked at you. 'I'm not sure. I can't give you want you want today.'

'And what's that?'

'I don't know. Sex, probably. I'm just so tired.'

You started laughing.

'Honestly I can't do it any more, I'll have to retire,' I said.

'Do what? Sex?'

'Party.'

'Oh, is that right?'

'Yeah, last night.'

'Well, thanks a lot for the invite. Anyway, I only wanted a kiss, but no worries, I'll find someone else.'

'Sure.'

'I'm very open-minded.' You folded your arms and my eyes fell down your body.

'Oh, really?' I said. 'Okay, just one kiss maybe.'

'Don't worry, I'm busy now,' you said, walking away.

'I've changed my mind—'

I followed you round a corner, to where it was cool, dark. Standing in front of you, I watched your pupils dilate. I felt my whole body do the same. Then you walked back slowly until your shoulders were against a wall. 'Just one,' I said again. Your mouth felt hungry and I wanted that hunger. Your mouth on mine, and the mess of it, and even if it was just for a minute, how all through my body, it felt like doors were being opened.

Blue's nose bled again that evening, then the next morning too. Not a lot, but enough to turn a tissue red, and it was still bleeding when Davey came over.

'Noooo, kiddo,' he said, seeing Blue. He grabbed him under the arms and spun him round, before he realised that

that was a bad idea, and then he laid him back gentle as anything, like something ironed he didn't want to crease.

'He started early,' Davey said.

'What?'

Davey did a quick double sniff. 'On the old drugs.'

'You're an idiot,' I said. 'Come, though,' and we wandered upstairs to the landing above so we could talk. We'd sat like that for years. Backs to different walls, feet meeting in the middle, kicking at each other sometimes.

'Weird party,' he said. 'Weird all of it. Kinda fun. By the time I got in there it was proper carnage. Full-grown men on the floor, kids dancing, crying. Hell's after-party in there. Got some though. Found a girl who looked a bit lost and not too—' he used his hand to mess up his face '—ugly. Not like pretty-pretty, but not *ugly*-ugly either.'

'And they say romance is dead.'

His details of the party weren't the sharpest, either. Blurry at the edges, blurry in the middle. I remember him calling patches in memories burn holes once. Me saying they were more like bruises. Never in perfect shape, never the worst pain, but they hurt if you touched them.

'LandSave,' he said. 'What kind of shitpie name is that anyway?'

'Could have done with a bit more land to be fair, when the sea was sloshing round my ankles this morning.'

'Yeah, well, it always goes back down, dunnit. We don't need them. It saves itself.'

After that, Davey did what he always did – listed everything he'd seen and done. Not in his whole life, though it felt like it. Just in the past few days, but no difference in intonation for if the thing was big or small. He could tell me about a pin that got stuck in his shoe and make it last an hour. It was still true that somehow he never bored me, but that day, I found my thoughts wandering elsewhere. You know how normally, if someone asks where the middle of you is, it's your chest. Your heart. Somewhere up there.

But that day, ever since I kissed you, I felt like I was right between my legs. I couldn't stop zooming in on little bits of you, a flick book of skin. Every time I thought of a new thing, the front wall of my stomach would go like a xylophone. A stick ran down it.

'Why you being weird for? Oi.' Davey pushed me. 'Being quiet and weird. You been fucking too?'

'No.'

'I know that look. Chancey, you put your fingers up to your mouth!' He laughed. 'Out of control.'

'I haven't.'

'You know I don't care,' he said. 'It's just when you don't tell me.'

'David . . .'

'Don't David me. Why are you my favourite person and you're also the worst?' he said. 'You're a total ding. The absolute biggest.'

The groups of men were the first things I noticed.

I didn't realise what they were waiting there for until Davey told me. They stood along the railings on the seafront, little gangs, unofficially arranged by colour of their skin. A few black guys by an old phone box, a group of Bangladeshis not far from them by a burned-out van. White English people in the biggest huddle, closest to everything. Some did press-ups. Stood on each other's toes so they could do sit-ups. Pull-ups on old scuffed scaffolding. Ups, ups, ups. Dry knuckles, shirts off.

The vans came at low tide. Four, five, six vans. White ones, different sizes.

'That's where they're picking them up for work,' Davey told me. 'For the LandSave stuff. Taking them off to the building sites.'

'The dream,' I said. 'Building what?'

'Dunno. Same as always. Cheap shitty housing. A land-mark youth centre.' He did his little eyebrow dance. 'Anything to keep the louts busy.'

We watched it once or twice. The men in the vans leaned out of their windows and pointed at the men they wanted. 'The ones who looked strongest, in't it,' Davey said. 'Even if they're proper porktown or whatever, but their arms look good.'

A couple of guys had dishcloths tucked under their caps to cover the backs of their necks. One pulled his off as he said goodbye to his mate, chucked him the bottle of water as a parting gift, and jumped in the back of a van. He was the last in, slammed the door behind him. The van sped off.

'Look at them!' Davey laughed. 'Proper going places. And look at us. Look what we got.' A stray cat, fleas circling its neck, had wandered over and was pushing its forehead into Davey's ankle. 'Never matter, come here, you prince.' And the cat scratched himself so fast, his ears or his paws made the sound of a bird's wings flapping.

Davey was joking about the going places, going up in the world, but it was true, things did seem to kick into action quicker than all the other times. I thought about the years-old graffiti at the bottom of the building. 'Talkin' bout re-generation', it said. Someone had put a big X over it, and written, GO HOME SCUM.

But this time, LandSave, whatever it was, seemed to get things moving faster than before. It wasn't just the Beef and

Anchor that was open again. Lots of pubs were reopening. It started to happen all over town. One or two near the front, a couple on the high street, even a few over in Cliftonville.

People were on the streets again, with blurry beer eyes, talking louder. White plastic chairs, garden chairs, appeared in little crowds outside each pub. The same everywhere, the cheap ones that split and pinch your back when you lean into them. 'Can't say fairer than al fresco,' Ma said, when she came out for a walk with me and Blue. 'Al fresho. Well, al hotto.' She fanned her cheeks with her hand. The signs outside the pubs – vodka and splash specials, Ale's and Cider's, white pen on fake chalkboard – had been rubbed out and rewritten with new, lower prices. She craned her neck. 'Al *very* cheapo.'

Viv came round to say she couldn't look after Blue any more. Her son Bob was going to open his pound shop back up again. She said he was getting sponsored. 'So I'm going to help him. Just like the old days. Which means that I won't be able to look after the little dibble any more.' She pointed at Blue.

'Dibble?' Ma pulled a face. 'Hope you didn't call him that a lot. And what do you mean sponsored?'

'Micro-thingy,' Viv said. She put her hand up like she was waiting for a sneeze. 'Micro-investment. Grant-y type things like they did before – stimulus. Long words, but the forms weren't bad actually. They weren't wearing suits or anything dodgy like that.'

'I'm almost embarrassed,' I told you next time we were at the China House together. 'You've arrived at a real high point. Honestly, it's normally a lot more rubbish than this. Don't tell your people – they'll stop all the charity.'

'Don't worry,' you said. 'I'll keep it quiet.'

'What's it like down at the food bank though? Meyer putting you out of business?'

'Not yet. It's been busy. Look at this, by the way.' You held out your hand and there were dents on your fingertips. 'You grind your teeth in the night, you know. It's awful. Makes the sound of heavy machinery.'

'That wasn't the night.'

'Well, when you sleep then. Open your mouth. Just here—' your thumb against my molars '—flat at the back. That side's the worst. I had to put my finger in there to stop you. And you bit me so hard.'

'Do people like him in London?' I said. I spoke with my mouth full, then kind of spat your finger out.

'The way you say that word . . .'

'How do you want me to say it?' I said. 'Lahn-don? Lon-dahn?'

'It's just – I don't know. A city isn't one place. Lots of people are still really upset about what happened.'

'Crying oceans sitting in their penthouse palaces . . .'

'Or trying to help?'

'Okay,' I said, 'point taken. And these people, they like Meyer?'

'Yeah,' you said.

'You don't sound sure.'

'Well it's never simple, is it?'

'Kole . . .' I said. 'Kole's drinking the Meyer Kool-Aid like it's a beer keg, fucking deep throat.' I opened my mouth, stuck my tongue out. 'My mum, too. It's like my friend Davey says – there's a mug in every cupboard. In my case, two.'

'And what do you think?' you said.

'I'm kind of like come, go, it's always the same old empty shit-all with these people.'

'I don't know,' you said, shrugging. 'People say he's clever. That he, like, gets things done.'

'Action Man,' I said.

'Exactly.'

'It's a dumb nickname.'

'Honestly, Chance, you going to kiss these broken fingers or what?'

Later that afternoon, I saw Davey using a janky-looking scaffolding to replace a window above a cafe, one of the old ones, think it was Beano's.

'Glass!' I said. 'Not even chipboard. Look at you go, boyyo. High roller.' He had the pane in his hands, finger smudges on it that caught in the sun. He looked through it at me. It was heavy and even though his arms were strong, the tension in them made them vibrate as he held it above his head. He laid down the glass as carefully as if it were a baby. I asked where Trev was. They normally worked together. 'Didn't you hear?' he said. 'He's over at the Pearl.'

'The Pearl's reopened too?'

'He was the last one who had the keys. The LandSave lot came round and offered him to open it back up.' Davey lowered himself down to me on a rope he had wrapped round in a reef knot. 'It's happening all over. Where you been hiding? Hello,' he said, because he hadn't said that yet. He hugged me. Stepped back. 'He's back on the juice in a big way. Trev, I mean. Like loads. Not that it's bad,' he said. He was biting on one of his cuticles. 'It's just life. Living. But I found him yesterday on the floor behind the bar. Lying on the floor. Cracked open his eyebrow like it was an egg. I mean, it was the size of an egg when I found him. All swolled up.'

'Swelled. Swollen.'

'Yeah. Not that I mind. It's cool, you understand. I'm happy for him. It's just a bit sad.'

Davey could say one thing and then the opposite in the same sentence, but I always understood what he meant. The black and the white to get to the grey, which is always the hardest thing to say. He spat out the little bit of cuticle he'd bitten off and then he looked up and worked out whether he could leave the window he was working on. 'Walk with me for a sec?' he said. 'Come see?'

We went up Dane Hill.

'You wanna be careful out, by the way, when you're off at work,' Davey said. 'The LandSave lot also brought a whole raft of forcies in. Saw a couple of boys proper bashed about. Like, not strung up exactly, but left for show.'

'Anyone we know?'

'Fuck knows by the time I saw them. But no, don't think so. Westgate boys, I reckon,' he said. He burped and blew it out in a thin stream. 'Coming here, stealing our opportunities.'

'The Westgate boys or the LandSave lot?'

'Both, I suppose. Tough times. Fucking hell!' he shouted. 'Look at that!' And his eyes darted up to just behind my shoulder.

'What?' I said and I turned, and that was when Davey made a grab for my boob, and I spun round and knocked his cap off.

'Honestly, you're on fire today,' I said. 'Idiot. Wish you were actually on fire.'

'What did I tell you? I should have been on TV. I coulda been a contender.' He made his cheeks puffy.

'A pretender.'

'A total bender. One can but hope. All these lives we'll never have, eh, Chancey.' And he licked the line of a crisp white Rizla.

We'd just got to the Pearl. The windows were open. The sound of voices, softened by carpets, fell out onto the streets. Looking through the windows I could see us there as kids – Davey smashing up a packet of scampi fries with the bottom of his glass so he could pour it into his mouth like powder.

'All this talk,' he said. 'Do you want a drink or what?'

When we stepped inside, Trevor welcomed us in, and pulled us behind the bar so we could serve ourselves. He had sores on his face, and his nose was so red it looked a little angry. Still, he himself seemed happy as anything. At one point, he even played air guitar. He took us downstairs into the cellar and showed us the kit he'd been given.

'Got these nozzle things,' Trevor said. 'Add them to the pumps to make the beer go further. Means we got a sea of the stuff.'

'Like I told you, a sea he's taking as a personal challenge,' Davey finished.

Before the pubs had shut the last time, they'd all been so quiet. In those days, people made a pint last hours. But that day, the Pearl was packed. It reminded me of the short time someone found a patch of oil not far from the coast. They did a real cowboy job on it – noticed a patch of black sea and used normal construction stuff to crack open the hole until it spurted – but suddenly a few guys had had mad amounts of money, until the patch of sea was sold off whole.

But this was a different crowd. In the main bar, Davey was the only young guy. Everyone else was older, or a girl like me.

'They saying it's alright then, Trev?' I asked. 'The boys down at the LandSave sites? Seems like everyone and his brother's down there, apart from slacker Davey.'

'Alright I think,' Trev said. 'From what I heard, they're staying out there mostly. Hence this mob squad of oldies propping up the bar.' He gestured to the two guys closest to him. 'Mob for mobility vehicle.'

'All tussling for it, these young ones,' one of the old men said. 'Getting all fit. But you've seen the vans. Looks random enough how they're picking. More like whether lady luck's looking at you.'

'Think she's got cataracts, my one,' his friend said, then accidentally burped as he laughed.

There were LandSave beermats along the length of the bar. Davey had scratched half the letters off his, so it said 'd ave'.

'It's sick in a way,' he said. 'Buying everyone back with party time.' He took a chunky gulp of his pint.

'Mate, the way you open your gullet . . .' I said.

'Austerity to Faliraki – over-fucking-night! It's fucked up.'

'Yeah,' I said. 'Fucked up. Also a *tiny* bit fun.' I raised my glass. 'Like a centimetre or something.'

It was a funny night. There was a good feeling in there. That was the evening I was supposed to come and meet you, and didn't. A few drinks in, someone put a paper full of kem on the table. I don't know who from, but no one was asking for money.

It's the first second of it, when you can't work out if you're falling or flying. Good, though. It does feel good. I took some, took more, chased that feeling and forgot all the things I was supposed to do. But I didn't do it because I was sad. I did it because I was happy. That happens too sometimes.

After that, though, when I got home, the other stuff I told you about why I couldn't see you that night, that was true.

Kole was just as wasted when he got back. He slammed the door so hard a bit of the lock detached from the wood. I only noticed that in the morning. 'Open your eyes,' he said when he saw me passed out on the sofa. He slapped me awake. Hard fingers. He shook his head. 'Always a fucking mess.'

I managed to get my hands up over my face. He kicked the sofa. Reached for my cheek, then my ear, then my neck. Normal stuff. When he pulled me off the sofa with one hand, I tried to tell him not to. I put my arms around myself.

'Don't what?' He grabbed me by my top, brought my face next to his mouth. 'Don't fucking what? You'd be lucky.' He dropped me back down again. 'You always got inside my head.' I could taste his breath. 'Did it on purpose. I know you did.' I had my eyes tight shut.

'No self-control,' he said then. 'Shitty little tease.' I heard him spit, and I felt it land wet and solid on my chest.

So yeah, when I came to the China House the day after that, you weren't angry as soon as you saw what I looked like.

You kept touching me, didn't realise at first all the places I was hurt. You said sorry all these times, one for each kiss you gave me as you took off my clothes to see what had happened. I realise now how much I felt that word – sorry, even though you hadn't done anything. I'd said it so many times, but I'd barely ever heard it before.

'I don't want to go home,' I told you. 'Not if he's coming back.'

'I don't want to go home, either,' you said, and so that was the first time we got lost. It wasn't like the other ways I'd been lost before. Where I was in a room with someone and we drank and did stuff and days passed and I didn't remember them. It was different to that. In bed, we folded around each other in all these ways. Felt the thing that maybe everybody feels – that no two bodies had ever fit together like that.

In the morning, when I woke up, you were reading in bed. You had a pair of glasses on. Black frames, a little bit too big for your face. They kept slipping down your nose and you kept pushing them back up.

'Found them in a drawer,' you said, when you noticed I was awake. 'Whole bunch of them. We have at least three pairs each.' You wiggled your nose. 'We could start an optician's.'

In that moment, I suddenly saw myself from a distance. The island of it somehow – island after island, in our bodies, in the bed, all the doors between us and the world. My thoughts divided in two like a river going round a rock: I couldn't believe I was there and I wasn't; and yet I could, I could, and I was.

'What are you reading?' I asked.

You turned the cover to me. *The Great Gatsby*. 'I found it on the shelf. I always forget how good it is.'

I copied your voice and said the same thing.

'Why, have you read it?' you said.

I looked more at the cover. There was a man with a monocle on it. 'Not really my thing. I only read about people with twenty–twenty vision.' I looked at you. 'People who've visited your new optician's.' It was easier to be silly, make a hard surface, let your beams bounce back off me.

'Do you read?' you asked after that.

'What do you mean do I read? That's a rude question.'

'Just a question.'

The thing was, I'd never talked about books with anyone but Caleb before.

'All the time,' I said. 'But hard ones, you know.' I thought of the ones I'd taken for Blue. *Guess How Much I Love You. Peppa Pig.* All the classics. Anyway. I didn't mean to interrupt.'

'You're not interrupting.'

'Make yourself at home, of course.'

I lay back. You read for a page or so more, then turned onto your side so you were facing me. The thumb of the hand that was holding the book found my belly button, circled it. You shifted on the bed, then reached down further. 'I am making a home,' you said. A sea, a river, cave, salt. 'Making a home right here.'

Soon, your book was on the floor, and your glasses too. I remember how quickly I came, and how I felt I could look at you when I did, and that it was the first time I'd ever done that, and how it made me want to cry, and how afterwards, it felt like there were stars inside my hands, and that I barely had the strength to hold them.

Later, face down on the pillow, you kissed it and said you loved this bed, and I asked you what your bed was like at home.

'Just a normal bed,' you said.

'Except gold sheets,' I said.

'Cold sheets.'

'And you think it's crap here, right?' I said, kind of out of nowhere. My thoughts split round the same rock again: I wanted to hear you say it was, I wanted to hear you say it wasn't.

'Well, I've never seen a place that changed more in the weather, that's for sure,' you said. You looked at me. 'Or a face. Hey, what's wrong?' You reached for my cheek.

'Nothing's wrong.'

'Then why are you looking like that? I like it here,' you said. 'Where did that come from? I was just saying how much I like this bed.'

That night, when I went to the bathroom as you slept, I came back and your body was so warm it felt like you'd been lying in the sun.

I got back into bed next to you, and in the mostly dark, I remember looking at each section of your face, trying to take it in in these squares, like that would let me see you more clearly.

'What's happening here?' I said, but it barely made a noise. 'How long are you going to stay?'

I wanted to ask you out loud, I was scared to ask you. I wanted to, I was scared. I pushed into your sun instead. I lay there, lay back, kept lying.

When I got home, there were letters waiting in a pile at the bottom of the stairs to our building. It was just after high tide and the bottom ones were almost paste. No stamps on them, no names. Just said *To the Occupant*. I picked one up, from the top of the pile so it was still crisp. The LandSave symbol was on the corner of the envelope. The up-and-down line of a wave, and a circle like a sun just above it.

'What's that in your hands?' Ma asked as I walked in.

'Dunno yet,' I said.

'What do you mean dunno? Why are the young so aggy? Open it.'

I gave it to her instead. She ran her thumbnail along the edge. Zip sound. 'Come sit then,' and I moved over on the sofa so she could sit next to me.

It had two bits of paper in it. Thin paper, almost see-through. A page that was dense with text, looked like an old mobile phone contract. All these clauses and brackets. The other had barely anything on it. Those symbol things for the people who can't read. There were line drawings of waves, stick people, swirls, Xs.

'Never got these. I mean what's *that* supposed to be when it's at home?' She pointed at an arrow that was also a circle that was also a sad face. 'Whole thing tires your eyes.' She put the papers down on the side of the sofa. 'Speaking of which, you got any stuff?' she asked.

'We're supposed to be being responsible adults,' I said. But I felt in my pocket, and I did, and we did it.

When I was a bit high, I read the letter again. I don't know why I'd wanted to avoid it so much. Something about it reminded me of the letters she used to get from the bank when I was a kid. She'd intentionally bury them, or use them as drink coasters, so I'd be scared to open them too. Don't be a dick, I said to myself now, and I pulled the letter out in full.

It wasn't about money. Though like the bills, it was half in red. It was about the tide. There was a list of times it had come higher than normal, with dates next to them. A graph showing the change, and then a graph showing what they thought would happen next. It was a steep curve. They'd drawn a line through it. I followed it with my finger back to the key. It said 'Fatality Point'.

Ma's eyes opened a little. 'Go on then,' she said. 'Break the news.'

'It's about the sea,' I said. There was a whole paragraph about Clean-up, Containment, C-protections. All the Cs were capital. 'C-protections. I don't know.' I was leaning against her. 'Stop moving so much. I'm trying to concentrate.'

We showed the letters to Kole when he came back. Me and Ma had fallen asleep together again and woke up feeling a bit sloppy.

'Yeah,' he said. 'Obviously I know about that. They got posters too. Got them in all the pubs. I didn't keep track of the dates myself but seems about right. Good they're taking it seriously. On a normal day it never used to get high as the park, or flood that old mattress shop down the way, did it?'

He avoided my eye. Couldn't look at me properly since he'd kicked me in my sleep. Got like that whenever he did something like that. The time he tried to come into my room in the middle of the night, even when nothing happened, even if he just stood there and looked.

It was late afternoon, maybe later, and he'd brought back a whole fried fish and a lot of chips.

'Bottom feeder, but it's not bad. Come on all you. Sit.'

He did look at me then, then double-nodded at the food, Kole's kind of 'sorry'. He spread out the wrapper on the floor and we had a picnic on the carpet. He tossed a loaf of bread into the middle too, and Blue spent a while trying to open the packet before making these tiny, squashy chip sandwiches.

'C-protection,' Ma said. 'Am I the only one not getting it?'

'C-Protection, sea protection,' Kole said. ''Cos of the floods and all that.'

'Oh, right,' she said.

'Brain of a newt,' Kole said. 'It's like trying to teach a badger to count. Anyway, I don't know all the plans they got, but it's crazy what they can do now. To sort it out. Push the sea back. It'll be something like what they done with Dover. That metal cage-fence out round the way.'

'That doesn't *stop* the water,' I said. 'That lets the water through. Just stops the people off boats swimming up. Idiot.'

'Why you being so rude for? Stop looking blue,' he said. 'Not him. Glum face, I mean. You. Why you doing that? Makes you look about forty. Can't you see we're celebrating?'

'Celebrating what?'

'Fucking change!' he said. He threw one of the letters in the air. 'I, for one, have decided to do the honourable thing.'

'Nice,' I said. 'Kill yourself?'

'Ha fucking ha. Get involved,' he said.

'What do you mean, get involved? You gonna stand by the railings and show off your balls to get in the back of some van?'

'You always think this big.' He made the gap between his fingers the size of a pea. 'Better than that of course. I told 'em who I was.'

'Big man,' I said.

'Shut up, stupid. I'll be facilitating,' he said. He said it slow like it meant something sexual. He winked at Ma. The way his eyelid squashed, the way he squashed everything. The chips were cold and soft by now, but he dangled a handful of three into his mouth. I took a bit of fish, some of Blue's bread, and went over to the window.

'Is lover boy out building with LandSave then, Chancey?' he said. 'Nice big arms for you? Bit of wedge in the bank?' I could hear him chewing with his mouth open. 'Oi, Cha. You deaf or what?'

The next time you and I saw each other was the time I'd promised to bring Blue.

'Hello,' you said, when you saw us crossing the road to the Eliot shelter. You bent over as if you were going to shake his hand. 'Hello, tiny potato.'

That was a new one. There were new names all the time. Something about someone that small makes people use all kinds of words.

Your body moved straight to his. I remember how he wouldn't look you in the eye at first. It worried me a little, because he was always good at choosing people to like. Some people, he'd see through a window and reach out like he thought his arm could go far enough to touch them. Other people, his face would squeeze the colour of lipstick.

'This is him,' I said, even though that was obvious. I had that feeling where my legs couldn't get comfortable. In a nice way though, just that it felt important. You reached into the pram and put your finger on his nose, and he turned his head away and looked at you, really looked, but sideways.

'He looks like you,' you said. 'It's really sweet.'

'What?' I said. 'That little fat thing? Charming.' But I squatted down next to the pram too. I pulled faces – fishpops with my mouth, and then sad eyes and an upside-down smile and he copied them exactly.

I showed you how my mum used to push the pram, back wheels only. She had this rhyme – look into the sky, aim high. Blue had one of JD's old bucket hats on. I pushed the front brim up so he could just about peek out, but it was massive on him.

'You're good with him,' you said. 'Do you want kids?'

'I don't know.' I felt my face turn hot. 'Maybe. Someday.'

I let him out of the pram when we got to the patch of flat where Mannings seafood shack used to park, and I remember him plodding over to your leg, like a sailor on a boat, tottering side to side. I've often thought about what adult legs must look like to young kids, like trees or something. He turned to look at me and see if it was okay. I nodded. Then he reached up and tugged at your shorts until they slipped down an inch and you had to catch them.

As we walked through town, you asked me why everyone looked at me on the street.

'Why?' I said. 'Do you want me in a burka, or something?'

'No,' you smiled. 'I like it.'

'It's him. Who wouldn't look at him?' I looked at him now. 'Mr Squidge.'

'Well he's down there, and you're up here, and they're definitely looking at you.'

'It's just that they know me. And when I was a kid, I don't know . . . I was just a bit of a mad little bandit.'

"Cos you're good now, right? A saint. With your massive secateur things coming out your pocket.'

'No, but the things I did. I used to climb up buildings, and jump between them. Properly jump between buildings. And not little pussy things like this bollard to that one. I'd do it six floors up.'

'Why?' you said.

It's funny. No one had ever really asked me that before. 'I don't actually know,' I said. 'I could never work out if I felt like nothing could kill me, or that I didn't care if I died?' I shrugged. 'Something not quite right up there.' And I moved my eyes as if I was looking into my own brain.

That was also the day we ran into Davey at the Pearl. As we arrived, he was shaking hands with Tommy Deen's brother, the one with an eyebrow piercing that went from left to right. When he saw us, he used his other hand to tap Tommy's brother twice and get him to go. Davey nodded hello at us both, deep at me, light at you. 'Davey, Franky,' I said. He wouldn't look at you. 'What you doing?'

'Oh, nothing,' he said. Then his smile cracked like an egg. He leaned towards me. 'Kem . . .' he said. 'Mate, it's so cheap at the moment. It's a joke.' Davey leaned into the pram. 'Hello, little scally,' he said. I watched Blue look at the little bag of rough, brown-white powder swinging from Davey's fingertips.

'You're such an idiot,' I said, and I pulled down the hood of the pram so Blue couldn't see any of us.

'I'm only kidding,' he said. He slid the kem into his pocket. 'You know you're my favourite humpty dumpto in the world, don't you?' he said to Blue, peeling back the hood of the pram, getting down on his knees and pretending to take a little nibble on Blue's nose.

As Davey went in to get us drinks, we found space on some of the new benches, the type of plastic that sticks to skin when it's hot. I put Blue's brakes on. Davey came back with three glasses. You reached in your pocket as if you were looking for money, but Davey wishy-washed your hand away. 'It's my uncle's place. Forget it.' He still wouldn't look at you.

It was strange to see you both sitting next to each other. Davey's inked arms, your milk ones. Davey had broken a tooth 'trying to jump on his friend's car from behind', whatever that meant, and he pulled my left hand towards his face so I could feel how sharp it was. He was playing up because he didn't know you. When a girl he did know sat down, talking to her sister on a wall nearby, Davey pulled Blue out of his pram, made him sit on one of his shoulders, like a parrot, and then paraded over to see her.

It was the first time you and I had ever had a drink together. You moved your tongue against the roof of your mouth as if you were testing how thick the liquid was. When Davey came back, he let Blue down onto my lap.

'What do you chicks reckon about all this LandSave rubbish, then?' he said, spitting out his gum in a high volley before he sat down. 'I been lonely. Everyone else is off down at the sites picking up change . . .'

'Like I said, if you're lonely, then go.'

'I'm joking. It's only young girls and old fuckers around. Been having a fine time actually.' That egg-crack smile again.

'Lovely,' I said.

'What's Kole say about it?' Davey asked. 'Has he been over to the sites yet? Seen what they're doing? I heard he was doing a bit of the hiring, firing.'

I shrugged. 'He said logistics, whatever that means.'

'Sweet gig if you can get it. Better than the grunt work.'

I didn't want to talk about Kole. I didn't want to think about Kole. The clouds moved fast behind Davey. I looked at those instead.

'Where you from, then?' Davey said to you, but he looked like he already knew the answer and all he was thinking about was what to say next.

'London. North London – but I . . .'

'Little day trip, is it?' he said. 'How nice. Must be good to be from there. Must be liberating.'

'Davey . . .' I said.

'I hear in London you can get a lovely little tumour

191

whenever you like. Have it whipped out with a nice clean snip.'

'Davey, leave it. She's not like that. Anyway—' I took a loud sip of my drink like I could swallow everything else too '—I was just telling her about when we used to jump,' I said. 'How I was like a cat.'

'Not a cat,' he said. 'A tree rat.' He tipped his anger into a laugh. 'Kami-*Cha*-zi . . . *Cha*-rtful Dodger.'

'Such a freak.' I turned to you. 'No one ever called me that.'

'It was like you wanted to jump on top of a jump and just fly through the sky right out of here,' he said.

'Something like that.' That was back when JD was in prison. It wasn't a good time for me.

'I liked you then,' Davey said. 'You're a bit of a pancake now.' He turned to you. 'I hope you scrape her off the pan from time to time,' he said. 'Flip her over. Make sure she's done on both sides.'

'Where did you pick blondey up?' Davey said when you got up to go to the toilet.

'On the beach.'

'On the beach!' He laughed. 'She crawl out the sea or what?'

'Exactly. Scales from the waist down.'

'You trying to upgrade?' His eyebrows did their dumb dance. 'No girl round here good enough for you? Speak to me in your Shakespeare and all that?'

'Mate, Latin. Only Latin. Just fucking runs off the tongue.'

'Who is she, anyway?'

'A friend.'

'Oh a friend! Sure. She's, like, looking at you with all glitter eyes.'

'A friend of Christ's? One of the Christians. Not actually a Christian, I don't think, but you know. Here to help.' I did prayer hands.

'Hope you're letting her do her confessions.'

'Every night.'

'Kinda sexy in some way,' he said. 'Got a gravelly little voice, but fucking bee stings for tits, man.' He ran his hand over his chest. He liked girls who pushed their lips out, girls other boys would punch him over. 'Tell me then.' He tipped his chair back as if he could see through the wall to where you were.

'What?'

'What you see in her.'

'How's it even like that? How's it something you can see?'

'That's what I'm saying!'

'She's—' I shook my head '—I don't know, it's gentle.' It was a strange word that came to me, but it was true. All my other relationships, I had to fight in them. But here, with you, if we fought, I'd win. And we didn't have to fight. 'I don't know if gentle's the word,' I said.

'Christ.' He shut his eyes. 'I'm getting images.'

'Not like that. Just like, I'm not going to wake up with her holding a knife over me.'

'Pfff,' he said. 'Watch out. It's always the quiet ones.'

'Gross, Davey. You've got it all over your face.'

'What?' he said. He rubbed his lips, trying to get any food off.

'Jealousy, you prick.'

When you came back out, we finished our drinks and didn't stay much longer. You pushed the pram ahead, which meant Davey had the chance to catch me by the arm and pull me back to him.

'That whole wash-the-feet-of-the-poor type saviour thing – don't you think it's creepy?'

'Dude, it's not creepy.'

'Yeah, it's like . . . get off my feet.' He started to laugh, but I couldn't tell if he was joking. I wasn't sure if he could tell, either.

'No one wants to touch your feet, Davey. Look, she's harmless. And she'll be gone soon, anyway. Move on to the next disaster zone.'

'Isn't harmless though,' he said. He shook his head, then finished the drink you'd left on the table. 'Not if you like her.'

After we left, I let Blue out of the pram again and we walked with him slowly. It's funny how walking that slowly makes everyone have to concentrate more. We didn't talk. We just watched his head, the sloppy pit-pat of his feet, the way his rubber soles slapped the pavement, how he looked up to see if he was doing it right. You leaned over and squeezed my hand as he did that. Other things he did too. We walked through sun and shade. I remember you kissing the back of my neck. How it ran down my spine. I don't know if I'd ever been kissed there before.

At one point Blue lifted up a traffic cone and carried it in a hug.

'Is that heavy?' I asked him.

'No,' he said.

'Are you sure?'

'No,' he said.

And I remember you laughing and I remember you holding my hand tighter.

I did my work faster than ever before. I flew through doors, dashed round floors, so I could meet you between your shifts. On a couple of low-down streets, the bottoms of some wooden doors were getting so soft with seawater I could smack out the area round a cat flap just by kicking. The routine was always the same. I'd choose the house, and the way we got in. After that, a couple of young guys would do the basics – sweep up the obvious places, mantelpieces and show cabinets, swoop up any booze, pouring different dregs into one big bottle so it was easier to take with us. I'd go upstairs and look for things that were hidden. 'Hidden.' Most people are stupid. Crazy how many actually tuck things under mattresses. Envelopes behind heavy mirrors. Jewellery on the top of tall wardrobes.

Most of my team stayed the same, but a couple of older boys who worked with us from time to time had quit for a while to go down to work at the sites. Most must have thought it was decent, because they were going back day after day, but one guy – I can't remember his proper name now, Kent, he went by – came back and asked if he could work with us again. He said he'd had to hitchhike.

'It's shit. I mean, if you're a clunky fucker, go for it, but it's all concrete bollocks,' he told us. 'At the site things. Fucking heavy shit. Foundations. A reservoir. Don't even care if it's a hospital or whatever. I'm not doing that. I thought they had robots for that kind of rubbish these days,' he said, reaching for the kem someone was smoking, 'or at least trucks or something. They're always talking about the future but it felt like medieval days. Fucking worse than that. Iron Age.'

I remember someone called him a pussy, but anyway, it didn't matter. Still every day, more and more vans full of men left.

There were three main food banks I knew of at the time. The small Christian one which had taken over the old Nisa in Cliftonville, the tiny one Davey called the Povshop, and Humanita, which was in the small church on Union Crescent. It was Humanita you'd said you worked for, so I pushed the door open one day. The squeak of the hinge. The wood smell of church mixed with the smell of overripe fruit, sweet bananas, a bit of sweat.

Jesus. I might have even said it out loud. It was almost empty.

There was a time just after Localisation when it was overflowing with donations. There'd be boxes outside, piled up like a new edge to the building. Some evenings they did the cooking themselves. I remember a paella once – enormous, bright-orange rice, chicken thighs. Liam used to joke it was the best restaurant in town. But it was empty now. My footstep shot an echo up to the ceiling. Then another sound. I looked up.

There was a woman sitting on one of the pews crying, and three other people were leaning in around her. None of them were you, though – they were all a lot older. The woman was crying into a dishcloth or a towel or a sheet, not sure what, but it was huge. Then one of the women saw me and half walked over. 'Sorry, love,' she said, 'she's got a panic attack.'

'No, no, sorry, my fault. Totally fine,' I said, backing out. 'Don't worry about me.' The woman on the pew started crying louder, and it filled the whole church, which made it seem even emptier, somehow.

It was as I opened the door to go out that I saw the sign.

It was handwritten in biro, but with the Humanita stamp at the bottom. The word LandSave had been written but then crossed out with a big black X. And underneath it, it said – block capitals – 'MEYER MUST BE STOPPED'.

198

'It was Humanita, you said, wasn't it?' I asked you later.

'Yeah,' you said. Your finger was tracing the bridge of my nose, still feeling for the bump I'd told you had come from a childhood break.

'I went near there today. The church, I mean. Fuck me, the paella days are over.'

'Like I told you,' you said, 'very much still in business.'

'Then why are they against the LandSave stuff?'

'What do you mean? Did you go in?' Your finger paused.

'There was a big fuck-off sign on the door. Said Meyer must be stopped.'

'Why did you go though? If you're hungry I can help.'

'Not hungry. I came to see you, you numpty. Wanted to see you in action.'

'Isn't it weird to go without asking?'

'How's it weird?'

'I don't turn up to your job.'

'It's just I thought you said Meyer was good?' I said. 'So that's all I'm asking, why don't they like him? Is it because he's a bit "England for the English", all that? I mean, most of them are.'

'I don't know,' you said. 'I mean, maybe it wasn't even Humanita who put the sign there? Maybe it was just someone who stuck it to the door?'

But it had a Humanita stamp on it, I wanted to say. I didn't want to fight though. It was like I told Davey. There were enough fights everywhere else. I changed the angle of my body. 'Might have also wanted to check in on you, too,' I said. 'See if you look good when you do it. Like a sexy Mother Teresa or something.' You looked at me. 'See if they have crushes on you,' I went on, 'the people you help.'

'No,' you said. 'Don't worry.'

'Oh no, I'd like it. Tell me about one, at least. Some dude with no teeth.'

'Barry doesn't need teeth,' you said. 'It's the way he looks at me.'

'I'll kill him.'

'Seriously, though,' you said, 'you're not hungry or anything?'

'Me? I'm out at five-star restaurants all the time. Got great nutrition,' I said. 'I mean, look at me. I'm completely fine.' I started twitching.

You laughed then and I looked at you, and I felt it all. It was the edges of your eyes. It was your mouth when you smiled. I did not expect this. To feel this. I'd never felt like this.

I looked down at the floor. I could tell from the way the box of sunlight slid in through the windows in a slant like that, that it was nearly time. 'Let me just check the tide,' I said. I peered out of the front door, then came back. 'Okay, we're good,' I said. 'Come with me a sec.'

I took your hand, held your finger, took your hand again, and led you down the empty street, dry sand at the kerb, red-brick buildings lining the path down to a little set of steps. And then, there it was. The beach out towards Westgate. It stretched out ahead of us – a thin, sandy bay, hidden from the main town. The sea was low, the beach looked like bright white dust. Further out, little alleys of black seaweed made their way back to the water.

'What's it called?' you asked, as we found a spot to sit down.

'My beach.'

'Is that the official name?'

'Course. What do you expect? It's got the best sand. And yeah, it's good 'cos . . .' I looked behind me. 'I can't see my flat just staring down at me.'

'Right,' you said. You nodded. 'Does your mum get the binoculars out?'

'Oh yeah, a proper telescope. Long lens. My number-one protector.' I shook my head. 'No, not at all. I just don't want to see it. Prefer to see that,' I said. I pointed in the other direction, along the length of the sand towards the sun, which was starting to go down. The sky was this bright, burning gold, a bursting cloud of it, like it was reaching forwards towards us. 'It's mad light here,' I said, leaning back. 'It's got all these colours you wouldn't expect – like it shouldn't make sense, but it does make sense? If that makes sense. I mean, look at it.'

'The sky's so much bigger than in London. I've noticed that a lot.'

'Like, I don't believe in God, but sometimes it's like he just kind of licks his finger and points magic at us.'

'Didn't know God was a finger licker . . .'

'You know what I mean, though. And those green parakeets.' One bopped past us from the roof of one of the beach huts behind us. 'Fucking funny, like little tennis balls just whopping through the sky. Anyway, what I'm trying to say is. Things can be rubbish, but then you see a sky like that and it's like – I have that. That's mine. Which is why I wanna look in that direction,' I said. 'Not behind me.'

You picked up some sand. You rubbed it between your fingers and your thumb, grains falling slowly enough that you could almost count them.

'Okay, honest question,' I said. It was time to ask. 'Are you planning to stick around here? Just for a little bit?'

'Here?' you said. 'Right here, right now?'

'Just 'cos I wanted to give you this.'

It was a key. I held it out in my palm.

'It's to here. There, I mean.' My head tilted towards the China House. Heat burned a hole in my cheeks. 'Just 'cos it's easy,' I said. 'Easier.'

'Just 'cos it's easy,' you said.

'Just 'cos it's easy.'

I think that I'd never understood a bed until meeting you. Not properly. All of the things a bed allows to happen.

It was the smallest things that made me feel the most. Watching you drop something on the floor and not be able to pick it up. A tiny scar across your collarbone, only in some lights. Your back. You bending over. The two of us like snakes on the bed.

You cancelled everything else out. And when we weren't together, I could sit there, and just think about you. Not for a short amount of time. A lot of time could pass. Same as any other drug. I thought about your body as I walked, I thought about your body as I was supposed to be having a conversation with someone else.

I would lie in bed, my back to Blue so it didn't feel weird, and try to imagine every inch of you. I had you stand in front of me and turn slowly. I wanted to do things I'd never done with anyone. I wanted to put my whole fist in your mouth.

It wasn't soft like people say it's soft. We crashed into each other. I took handfuls of you. We never wanted to stop. And for days that turned into weeks, we didn't.

Then, one day, I was walking away from the China House, was maybe a hundred metres away, when a hand slammed into the back of my neck. For a second I thought it was you, then the fingers clenched. So hard I thought my own skin would choke me. It was Kole.

He pulled me by my neck into a doorway. The door opened. I tried to hook my foot round the edge to stop him from pulling me into the building, but I missed. We clattered into a small space. It was full of boxes.

'What the fuck are you doing?' I said. I had to cough so I could breathe again.

'I saw you,' he said. 'Don't think I don't know. I saw you with her.'

'Saw me with who? Get off me.' I tried to dip low to shake him off.

'And don't you fucking lie to me, I know exactly what you're doing to her.'

'What's wrong with you? Stop it.' I'd managed to duck out of his grip but he'd grabbed my T-shirt instead. 'What's it to you, you freak? I can do what I like.'

'Not her,' he said. 'Not her, you can't.' He slapped me. A fucking wallop, so hard I heard the sound as if it came from somewhere else. 'Why would you try and fuck it up like that?'

'What are you talking about, fuck it up? How's it your business?'

'This whole thing is business, Chance. I got money in this. There's money.'

'What money?'

'And I know you'll fuck it up for me. Spread your poison about me. I know.'

'What money?' I shouted at him. 'There's no fucking money in food banks.' I'd managed to yank away from him.

'Food banks?' he said. 'What do you mean food banks?'

'She works at a food bank.'

'What?'

'She works at a food bank, for fuck's sake. Humanita.'

He looked at me. 'You've been in there, have you? Seen her doling out beans?'

'Shut up.'

'Fucking stupid.' But then his face changed. He took a step back. 'Wait,' he said. 'Fucking hell, wait. Do you actually really not know?' And then he laughed. He was holding my arms so I couldn't hit him. I tried to spit but it didn't get far enough. 'Everyone says you're clever but you're thicker than pig shit,' he said. I got a hand free and went for his head again. He was holding me at arm's length, properly laughing now.

'Know what, you dick?' I said. 'Fucking say it.'

'Your girl,' he said.

'What about her?'

'She doesn't work in a food bank. She works for LandSave.'

'No, she doesn't,' I said.

'She works for LandSave, you fucking idiot. High up.'

'You're a liar, Kole. You don't know shit.'

'Not a fucking liar. And if you fuck her, you'll fuck it all up. You'll fuck it for me. You'll say your shit about me.' As he said that the anger came back. He was holding me really tightly then. 'You always have. You always do.'

He said some other things, then his hands let go of me, both at the same time. I stumbled back, and my back slid down against the wall. He walked out.

I sat down on the floor in the small hot room after he left.

Kole had told me if I touched you again he'd crush my hands. Make them bones of yours dust, he'd said. See how she likes you then. I brought my hands to my chest, curled around them, curled up tighter. I coughed, then I couldn't stop coughing, and when I looked at my hands, there was blood in my palms, a bright spray of it.

I didn't stay there all night. Eventually I picked myself up and took myself to the China House. It was there at the back of my eyes whenever I shut them. It was there at the back of my throat. Kole I didn't care about. Kole would calm down. Kole was just jealous.

But you. You. If Kole was telling the truth, why had you lied to me?

*   *   *

When I got to the China House, I lay on the sofa. I tried to find a position where my body didn't hurt. After an hour or so, I heard your key in the door.

'Hey,' you called from the hallway. 'Hello?' you said again when you walked into the room. But I didn't get up, didn't say anything, couldn't look at you. 'Hey – are you okay?' you said again, your hand reaching for me.

It was your voice, suddenly. I heard it like the first time again. The cool-water poshness of it.

'Why are you just lying there?' you said when I didn't move.

'How's it going down at Humanita? You like it?'

'What?'

'Help people a lot, do you?'

'I . . .'

'I don't get it,' I said. 'Does it feel like a joke or something?'

'I don't know what you're talking about.'

'LandSave,' I said. 'Fucking LandSave.'

'Chance . . .' you said, but I watched your face go red around the edges. I watched it spread.

'And you know who had to tell me?' I didn't even have to say his name. The crack in my voice.

'But what did he say, though? Because I am working at Humanita, I am doing work with them.'

'What are you even talking about?'

'I wasn't lying to you,' you said. 'He's right, I'm here with LandSave, but I am based at Humanita most days – I wasn't lying. I wouldn't lie to you, Chance . . .'

'How is it both? What are you doing at Humanita if you're LandSave?'

'It's research. Interviews, sometimes. We're just trying to build a picture of the population. It's menial, admin – data inputting more than anything.'

'Bullshit, menial. Kole said you were high up.'

'Well, he's wrong. I'm a year and a half older than you, Chance, you know that. I'm just an intern.'

'What the fuck is an intern? Interning doing what?'

'Places like Humanita, they were the only ones to keep any kind of record after Localisation. For years, information was missing on our side—'

'Everything was fucking missing,' I said. 'Help was missing.'

'But now we can only work out the needs of the area, if we build a picture of the population—'

'Stop saying population, it's not about population, we're people.'

'That's what I mean. If we can understand how we can help people.'

'So fucking understanding.'

'But I wasn't lying to you, Chance. You asked if I was help-ing. And I am. I am here to help. We are helping. That's what we're doing.'

'Even when I asked you – I asked you what you thought of Meyer.'

'I told you! What was I supposed to do? You're always going on about how much you hate people in London, how you didn't trust Meyer's Kool-Aid or whatever – so I . . .' You got down onto your knees beside me. 'I don't know.'

'Always going on about helping. But helping how? Helping do what?' You started to speak and I remembered a new thing. 'Fucking soup,' I said. 'I swear you even said some shit about serving soup.' It cut sharp as a knife, the feeling of being an idiot.

'I don't know what to say. The situation the country's in now, it's . . .' And then you just stopped. Looked at your hands, looked at the window.

'Oh, and now you're lost for words. Oh, that's excellent. Really good.'

'I'm not lost for words, but it can't go on. You know that. It's not sustainable. That's what I'm trying to say. Sea levels are changing. Houses are being lost. England has to work out how to deal with it. We all have to do our bit.'

'After years of fucking us over, you want our help—'

'No, let me finish. I'm saying we all have to come together. All of us. That's why we need to get things moving again. Reverse years of separation.'

'Stop speaking like this—'

'But I'm saying that's on us. It's on us to fix it.'

'Why did you come here? And not these people. Not LandSave. You.'

'I told you. Because I wanted to help.'

'Well, it doesn't sound like you're doing much with your

admin data research or whatever, so why did you come here?' I said again.

'It's not about me. It's about the broader thing, I wanted to go somewhere where I could make an impact.'

'Who uses that word? Uses it about themselves?'

'I was curious too. Is that what this is? Is that what you want to hear?'

'No.'

'I know it sounds gross. I know I'm not supposed to say that, but that was part of it.'

'Why are you smiling like that?'

'I'm not smiling, it's just . . .'

'Just what?'

'It's just I'm an idiot. I should have said. I should have said straight away. But I liked you enough to say anything. I like you enough. I would have said anything.'

'Well, could you not?'

'I didn't want to lose this.' You were still on your knees next to my chair.

'And what's this?'

'Don't be like that, Chance, you know what this is. Will you please let me not be so far away,' you said.

'You're close enough.'

'I want to be closer.'

'But why would I want that?'

'I don't know. Just please.'

'For what reason?'

'Because.'

'Because what?'

'Even just sitting here,' you said. 'Just being this close to you.'

'Finish your sentences.'

You took my hand and stood up.

Then you undid the buttons of your trousers and pulled my hand inside your underwear.

The flash it sent through the body felt almost spiky. Tops of my arms. Places I wouldn't expect. 'I'm sorry,' you said. 'It was dumb of me not to say. It was stupid, but that's all. And you know now. And I'm here now. Nothing has changed. We're both here.'

You pulled me onto the floor so we were below the line of the window. Mouth against my ear, you said I could do anything to you I wanted, and when the time came, I did.

It feels strange to think of now, the madness of fucking. The things you end up saying. The softness afterwards, just as hard in the opposite direction. Tangles you can't find your way into otherwise.

Afterwards, you lay there, your heart making the skin on your chest bounce, fear making your pupils wide, and you asked me to hold your hands. I thought it was because I'd still felt far away, or because my own hands had crept to your throat at one point, but it wasn't that. Your hands had frozen.

'I can't move them,' you said. 'Look.'

Your fingertips were together, as if you wanted to make your hand a flower, but a flower before it opened. 'I don't know what it is. It's never happened before.' You tried to use my hands to stretch out yours. I took your fingers and tried to push them open. It felt like teaching someone to walk again. 'I'm sorry,' you said.

'For what?'

'For all of it.' You pushed your face into mine so I couldn't look at you. I held still, I wanted to hold that coldness for a second, make you feel it, but I couldn't. Your hands were nearly back to normal, but you stretched them out once more against me, fingers spread.

It was the vulnerability that got me. Got me again. The fact I could make you feel that. I bit lightly into your head, moved my teeth against your hair. The feeling filled me just like it had before. It seems so stupid now. But I wanted to protect you and protect you and never stop protecting you, I really did.

In the morning, before you woke up, I went into the other bedroom. There was a jewellery box I'd hidden in a cupboard, wrapped in jumpers and some bedsheets. My hand pushed in slowly. The sudden fear that somehow someone had taken it, then the relief of finding it hard under my fingers.

I had promised I'd never touch it. But it was either that or JD's money box, so I pulled it out. Wood like tiger's eye. Swirling, golden. A padlock. I used a heavy stone bowl from the mantelpiece to smash it open. I had never broken anything in that house before and I said sorry out loud even though no one could hear.

There were four little trays inside. One full of silver, one full of gold, one for things. Notes folded up, a pen, a pin, a stone, a photo. That was folded, too, a crease line between two faces. The necklaces were knotted. All of it felt heavy and cool, like it'd been kept in a fridge, and I took everything that was gold, rings mostly, and slipped it in my pocket.

'Oi,' I said, standing over you and nudging you awake with my feet. 'So tell me then. What's this research that you need?'

I remember watching you wake up, your eyes adjusting to the light, adjusting to seeing me. And I remember wondering if you were scared of me, if you liked me really, if I would ever see you again, if you loved me maybe, a million ifs crowded into a split second.

'You don't have to look so worried,' I said after that. 'I'm just saying, if you like, we could go on a little school trip.'

After you agreed, kissed me, left, I went straight to Davey's warehouse. I hadn't seen him since the day at the pub.

'You,' he said, in this mixed way, when I knocked on the open door. The tide was low now, but he had piles of rags and plastic sheeting ready by the door to keep the water out. I stepped over it, wiped my feet, and he continued hammering something. 'What you saying?'

'Saying hello? Why you being strange?'

'No, it's just. Where you been? Like ships in the night. Chips in the nightclub. I keep on looking for you but you're nowhere. I thought they might be taking girls at the sites suddenly. Might have been worried,' he said. 'Might not have been.' He had a petrol-stained cloth around his neck and he used it to wipe some little drops of sweat off his temple. He'd shaved his head. Not clean to the bone, but a three all over. He kept on running his hands over it, which made him look nervous. He saw me looking, smiled then. 'Touch it,' he said. 'Weirdest thing.'

'Very kind, but . . .'

'You'll like it!'

'I've touched heads before.'

'Mad, though. How your own body can shock you.'

I knew that feeling – it made me think of you. His new haircut made his head look smaller. He was trying to grow a beard but the hairs had a wiriness to them. Little antennas, almost, reaching out in different directions. I told him he looked good. Then, before he could ask why I was saying something nice, I told him I needed a bike.

I could see in his eyes that he wanted to ask me why. His smoky eyes, his happy-sad smile. Instead he said, 'What kind?'

'Fast.'

'Do you even know how to ride?'

'JD had one,' I said. Which was true, though he'd never let me ride it. I'd only been allowed to sit on the back. I'd never liked it. JD would make the engine roar whenever he passed a girl he liked, which was every girl. 'I'll bring it back. It's just for the day. I wouldn't want it for free. I know that.'

I passed him one of the rings I had in my pocket. It looked smaller in his hand. He slipped it onto the tip of his little finger.

'Look nice with my hair, won't it,' he said. He handed the ring back to me. 'Don't be dumb with your ring. I don't need that. Come out back and have a look.'

I always loved the repair shop as a kid. There were so many places to hide. Panels and scraps of plywood propped against the walls, the window frames we'd jump in and out of when we were little. Trevor's old certificates for hygiene at the pub, a wall of them, the latest one back in 2012.

Davey took me into the next room and pulled back a blue tarp. He had a couple of pedal bikes, one for a kid, pink, with tangled tassels coming out of the handlebars, and then he had three motorbikes with proper engines. He told me he was halfway through fixing the smallest one, so I'd have to take the middle. He helped me onto it and my feet barely touched the floor.

'I feel like I'm on a horse,' I said.

'Well we're fucked then, woman. Because you were always shit on those.'

It was the first time he'd ever called me woman. He didn't mean it in a bad way, but I noticed it. I got off so Davey could get the motor going. He blew dust off the seat. He told me it was a nice one. He kept on touching his hair still. I said thank you a lot of times – so many that he probably didn't think they counted for much.

I was halfway out the shop when he called me again. I turned around and he'd taken off his leather jacket. He threw it at me, said, 'It's hot but – safer,' and I caught it, put it on. The shoulders fell halfway down my arms. I pushed up the sleeves so I could see my fingers.

'I like that jacket,' he said. 'Bring it back in one piece.'

* * *

217

Riding a motorbike is easier than you'd think, if you go fast enough. I went in starts, and stops. The weight of it, the rattle, the beat. I pulled back on the throttle, then let it spin out of my grip completely, wished it wasn't so loud. You were waiting on the corner where I told you to.

'Where's your helmet?' you said. 'More to the point, where's mine?'

'You'll have to put your hands up over your head, won't you? Make a barrier.'

'Is this even yours?' You touched the matte leather of the seat, the bit Davey had blown clean.

'I'm on it, aren't I?'

A smile grew in your cheeks. Your leg swung round behind me.

'Just don't lean out to look,' I said.

Your arm slid around my waist. 'Why?'

'Just not right now.'

'Why?'

'Because this is my first time.'

And then I just drove. You sat so close to me, it almost felt like we had the same body. I could feel you against my tailbone, your legs as wide as they could go. Just before we got to the edge of Dreamland, I realised I hadn't asked Davey about petrol. But I just kept on going. I didn't care. Your arms were wrapped around me. I didn't care. We sped down roads I hadn't been on in years.

My palms stung a little from gripping the handlebars so tightly. Your hands found their way under my T-shirt. Then you let go, and I could see from our shadow that you had put your arms out, flying.

I made up the names of places I didn't know. On some stretches of road, the 'For Sale' signs on the buildings were rained into curls. Doors were open, low windows were broken. It looked like if you wanted the house you could just take it.

'Do people live here?' you said. You made your chin tense and used it to massage a bit of my shoulder. 'Sometimes I just think fuck it all – I'd like to.'

'Live here?' I nearly turned around to look back at you. 'Madder than me.'

'I don't know. Something about windows. Any window.'

But face forward, I was smiling. I felt it too – that I could live here with you. That I would live anywhere with you.

You nudged me again with your chin. 'You can go, you know.'

I'd stopped at a traffic light before we realised it was just broken, and the red was only paint put on top. You had a scarf wrapped round your shoulders so you wouldn't burn. Either side of us, the cabbage and cauliflower fields were burned dark on either side. When I went faster, you held me tighter. I went as fast as I could.

At an old phone tower, we tipped the bike on its side and decided to climb up. All around it, seagulls were making nests along the length of the old cables, these stretched-out stick cities. I started the climb up, two rungs at a time. We went higher, then higher still, until we could see the sea round the coast like a knife-thin stretch of silver.

I took you to Ramsgate because I'd always loved it. I hadn't been for years. All the grass around the bandstand on Wellington Crescent was burned yellow. The salt in the rain had knocked little holes into all the white paint of the houses. Half of the pillars holding up second-floor terraces had given way, which made the crescent look like a ship capsizing. Outdoor tables had slid off and stayed where they'd fallen. A lot of the palm trees were massive now. Some had melted into huge dead octopuses, but others must not have minded the heat. All along the front, these enormous high flowers, furry leaves, Ma used to call them bee towers, reaching for I don't know what.

I tried to work out if people were still living in the houses facing the sea. We whipped round the curve of the Albion Hotel. There were MDF boards over half the windows. After that, the road dipped through a fake quarry – boxy boulders, a little waterfall – until it came out onto Harbour Parade. It was low tide. The topsy-turvy masts of one or two submerged yachts grew like plants out of the water. On the right, there was a row of red-brick marina arches, a curve of them, like decoration round a cake. The sun washed over all of it.

'It's beautiful,' you said.

'Of course! It's one of the five royal ports. Cinque Ports, in French,' I said. 'Sank ports now.' I looked out. 'Still, though. Pretty fucking glorious.'

The harbour stretched out like a hug – two road-thick piers pushing out into the sea and wrapping round like arms. The bike felt good between my legs, but it was stupid to do it. The path along the pier was slick with algae, and the morning's tide. And the water was already coming back up. I could see it hitting the walls and champagne-ing up white at the end of the harbour arm, where the old restaurant was.

'Fuck it,' I said. 'Let's go. Love a little race against tide, don't you?'

The wheels of the bike slipped and skidded along the wet stone of the pier. It felt like we were driving straight into the sea. All the street lamps along the edge were bent inland, smacked down into a bow by the waves. The wheels crunched over crab shells; I wove round rugs of seaweed.

When we got to the restaurant, I kicked down the stand of the motorbike and turned around in my seat so I could face you. The smiles of our knees were touching.

'There're still dining tables in here!' you said, looking over my shoulder, making your voice loud enough to rise above the whipped wind bouncing off the waves from the sea. 'It's so cool,' you said.

'Cool is one word,' I said back. 'One word I wouldn't use for you.' I used your arm to point at the red-brick arches back behind us on the mainland. 'See all the way along at the end – that's the Sailors' Church.'

I told you about the summer some boat people had taken asylum there. 'Or whatever it is when you hide in a church.'

'Sanctuary.'

'There were loads of them. Big boat. Caleb made us come over here. Me, Davey and some other kid from after-school. We came down to the church and slept there with all them so the police couldn't kick them out.'

'Was it scary?' you said.

'Why scary?' I said back. 'Don't put that in your notes. No, they were the scared ones. A lot of them wouldn't stop shaking. Wasn't so fun for anyone, actually. Apart from Davey. He loved it. Tried to teach them words of English. Rude words, of course. He was quiet about it when we got back. I know he was being an idiot when you met him but he's always been like that . . .'

'Like what?'

'Nice, I mean. Even if it's the dumbest timing, or there's no point in it, he's always liked to help people. It's like a disease. He can't stop himself.'

Above us, the sky had split exactly in two. Behind the painted seafront houses, the sky was orange; over the water, gunmetal clouds made their way towards us. It was starting to get dark. Apart from a few curtain twitches, and some kids messing with sticks by the car park, we'd barely seen anyone about. As we pulled out of Ramsgate, the sun from one side burned into windows that weren't broken and turned them the colour of a lit match.

The next day – or maybe it was two days after we went to Ramsgate, everything went so quickly after that – I was home, lying on the floor, lifting Blue up and down above my head like dumb-bells, and he was laughing, I just remember his face laughing, when Kole burst in through the front door.

'Get up,' he shouted. 'Fucking get up.' He kicked one of my feet. 'You're coming with me right now.'

'What've I done?'

'Get up, I said.' He lifted Blue out of my arms – he treated him like a cat sometimes, scruff of the neck – and dropped him on Ma, who was dozing on the sofa. 'Jas, you stay with the shrimp. And Chancey—' he stepped over my legs and dipped in and out of the kitchen '—get off the fucking floor. You're coming with me.'

He pulled me to the door.

'I'm not going till you tell me why,' I said.

'Why don't you ask your fucking girlfriend?' he shot back.

He didn't need to drag me after that. I followed, two steps behind him, lighter on my feet, but my legs less long. Our footsteps threw echoes into the stairwell, so did his hand – his palm was pounding the banister. An old safety sign a few inches away clattered to the floor. And then a flash of metal caught my eye. It was the sharpest knife we owned. He'd taken it from the kitchen.

'Kole, stop now.' I grabbed his arm. 'Serious now. Tell me what's happening.'

'LandSave. It's your fucking LandSave thing.'

'How's it *my* thing?'

'No one's being paid, first off. Working like fucking dogs and no one's had a dime yet.'

'What's that got to do with me?'

'Your bitch, though.'

'I spoke to her. She's an intern, Kole. Something low down she said. What's she supposed to do about people being paid?'

'You think that's bad,' Kole went on. 'It's not even that at all.'

'Then what?'

'It's the things that they're building at the sites.'

'What about them?'

'They're not fucking houses. Not fucking shopping things.' The knife flipped in his hand. 'It's not buildings, Chance.'

I looked at him.

224

'Don't you fucking look at me like you don't know,' he said. He pointed at me with the knife. 'Don't do that.'

'But I *don't* know,' I said, and he must have seen from the way my face was that it was true.

'There are no windows, Chance,' he said. 'It's not buildings.'

'Then what the fuck is it?'

His pupils were black in the dim of the stairwell. 'It's a wall,' he said.

He pushed past me. I ran after him. 'You can't just say that,' I said. 'A wall to do what?' I tried to turn him round. 'Fucking stop, Kole.'

'I don't know yet. But it's not fucking good, is it?' He looked at me. He looked at his knife. We both looked down at that. 'We can't look like we stand for it. Not you, not me. I been making money, maybe the only one getting paid, so this isn't messing around now, Chance. Nev's had his head kicked in 'cos he was helping out. Not me, though. No one's going to crucify me.' I followed him out of the front door of the building. 'The LandSave lot are all living at the Sands,' he said. 'The posh old hotel. But you probably know that, don't you.'

I shook my head. 'I've never visited her,' I said. I could taste blood so strongly in my mouth, I ran my tongue over my teeth to see if I'd lost one. 'Please, Kole. Whatever it is, it won't be her fault. It isn't my fault.'

'Well fucking show it then,' he said.

When we got to the Sands, there was a crowd of people out front. The first thing I noticed was Nev. Some men were holding him by the neck against the wall. One of them was punching him in the stomach, then the ribs. Stomach, ribs, and you could hear the different sounds each punch made.

'Fuck that,' Kole said. 'I'm not ending up like him.' He pushed his way to the front. Then made this showy sound, like he wanted people to hear, as he stamped on the back of Nev's head. 'Fucking scab,' he shouted.

I looked up at the building, imagining you behind the curtains. I wanted you to be there. I wanted you to be nowhere near.

'The fuck you keep looking at?' Kole said. 'People will notice. You want me to tell 'em all what you've been up to?'

'Yeah, go on then, you idiot. Tell who?'

Then the sound of the crowd changed. Someone had come out of the building. More than one person – five. Guards.

Kole grabbed my arm and pulled me forwards into the crowd. Then a barging from behind pushed us faster still, till we ended up pressed up tight against the fence out front of the hotel. Kole put his hands on it, shook it so hard I swear I heard the metal bend.

That was the moment three of the guards stood forward at the same time. Their guns moved at the same time too, like extra limbs. Then the whole-ear sound of a rock cracking hard against a cymbal. They shot into the air.

Even Kole stumbled back. His hands went high – 'Easy,' he said – hands that calm down fighters in a pub. He made his way along the fence towards the guards, hands up still, and leaned forward. He started talking to one of them. I watched him, peace hands turning choppy then softening again. Then he turned back to the crowd.

'They're saying someone should speak!' Kole shouted out to everyone behind him. 'They say they want it one-on-one.'

Voices rushed between the groups of people standing there.

'Well, I say I do it,' Kole said. 'No one'll have one over me.'

I looked around. To the left of me, behind me. People's faces. It was impossible to stop Kole if he wanted something, but no one trusted him. He knew that.

'Objections?' he said after that. 'I'll take the girl with me if you want. Keep things civil.'

It took a second before I realised it was me he was talking about. He walked back through the crowd, and he put his hand round the back of my neck.

Almost right away, the crowd parted. I looked up, a few people tried to catch my eye, someone nodded at me – encouragement, or something like it. Kole pushed me forwards, his hand heavy under my hair. I could hear a rushing in my ears. Two men with guns made a space between two barriers. Another two men were behind them, guns pointed at our chests. 'Easy,' Kole said again, loud enough for the crowd behind us to hear. 'We're company.' My legs stiffened. Kole's grip got tighter. 'Excited to see your missus, are ya?' he said into the space between his hand and my neck.

They patted us down before they let us through the door. Not just lightly – everywhere. When they pulled the knife from the back of Kole's waistband, there were cheers from the crowd. 'What?' Kole said to the guy who took it. 'It's normal. I want that back afterwards.'

This silence as the doors shut behind us. The smell of fresh paint again. We were led through a wide doorway, two, then through to a room full of tables. The guards followed behind us. I looked back once or twice. Uniforms in patches of changing grey, camouflage shapes but for a city rather than anywhere green. When we stopped, a couple of the guards walked ahead. They made a five-man circle around us. I knew the room. It used to be a dance hall. High ceilings. Big windows. The windows were blacked out.

'Where's the one I been speaking to?' Kole said, trying to prove his in. Now the crowd couldn't see him, his manners were back. This thin surface of pallyness. My heart wouldn't settle down. I tried to cough the feeling away.

Suddenly, the door to the room started to push open and my stomach spun like a coin thinking it might be you. But no, it was a man in a suit, no tie, who walked in.

'This man I seen . . .' Kole said. 'I seen you,' he said to him. 'I seen you in the photos with the big man. Is he coming down or what? Meyer?'

The man seemed cold, bored. He didn't answer the question. 'I won't take up too much of your time,' he said, which meant we shouldn't take up much of his.

I looked at him. Salt and pepper hair, barely any wrinkles. A tiny bit shiny between his eyebrows, a scar running along his nose. He looked at both of our hands like he might shake them, then decided against it. Took a little step back instead, like he didn't want to share our air.

'This is my daughter,' Kole said. 'Chance.'

'Not your daughter.' I pulled away, but he gripped my shoulder.

'Chance,' the man said. 'What a fortunate name.'

'It's not yours though, is it?' I said. Kole's fingertips pushed harder against my skin. 'And it seems I don't have much luck.'

Kole laughed then, his take-up space laugh. One of his teeth was so chipped, it looked like a saw. He was smiling though, doing sweetness and light. 'Be nice,' Kole said to me. I wasn't used to him playing any kind of long game. He turned to the man in the suit. 'Got stuff to deal with, you see,' he said to him. 'Money for one, then I want to know more about this – this . . . thing you lot are building.'

'People were saying it was flats, a new hospital,' I said. 'Something good.'

'I hear they're calling it a wall outside,' the man said. 'Which is all very well if you're in pursuit of drama. Sorry to be prosaic, but it's sea protection. And it's been in the pipeline for many years. Every single person was informed.'

'No, they weren't,' I said. I stared at him.

'There were letters.'

The letter I'd taken so long to open. The letter I'd read high. C-protection. Containment. 'Well they didn't say where your barrier things would be.'

'What did you imagine, may I ask?' the man went on. 'A large concrete monstrosity between you and the sea?'

Kole seemed to find that funny.

'A significant sea wall has been in the pipeline for years,' the man said again.

'Maybe in rich parts of the country,' I said. 'But not here.'

'Well,' he said. He did this quick little exhale. 'We have a duty to protect the country. Let's put it this way. It's got bad enough for the money to be found.'

'Hold on for a sec,' Kole said. 'I'm not trying to be thick, but can you not see a problem with us being here, and the sea protection being way over there inland?'

The man's face was static, his eyes almost bored. Some people are happy to leave silences. He let us do the work. We waited.

'Go on then, mate, spit it out,' Kole said.

'Why do you think my team is here?' he said finally. 'People have been leaving for years. In a sense, they've gone ahead. But we're here to—' his eyes flitted across the room for how to say it '—bring up the rearguard, as it were.'

'The who?' Kole said.

'The less socially mobile, shall we say.' He shrugged with his mouth. 'We're here to negotiate the relocations.'

Kole looked at me as if I'd tell him what that meant.

'To redistribute those in social housing,' the man finished.

'What do you mean redistribute?' I said. 'Redistribute us where?'

'Inland,' he said. 'As you say. Away to safety.'

It hit me then, all through my chest, this tugging from nowhere. 'But what if we don't want to?' I said.

'What do you mean?' he said.

'What if we don't want to go? What if we want to stay here?' I said. Then the thought of you – how had it happened again? How had you not told me any of this?

'I don't have to tell you about the sea,' he went on. 'You live here. But what's happening now. The tidal surge the other night. The floods two years ago.'

'The washout.'

'That was nothing.'

'It wasn't nothing.'

'Believe me,' he said, 'in comparison, your "washout" will be nothing.'

'Sure,' I said. 'If you leave us in the mud again.'

'It's going to get much, much worse,' the man said.

'You – or the sea?'

He looked at me.

'Listen to the man,' Kole said.

'Don't you start . . .'

'LandSave is a once-in-a-generation project,' the man said. 'It stands to change everything.'

'Good for you,' I said.

'It will save lives,' he said. 'Lives that need to be saved. Isn't that what you want? People will drown otherwise.'

'Why did you want to talk to us?' I said. 'I still don't understand what you're asking for.'

'Just your support,' he said. He smiled for the first time. Gently, a soft-light-bulb smile. I imagined the ways it must have worked for him. 'Kind words in the right places. People don't like change, you see. Particularly if it feels . . . I don't know, thrust upon them.'

'By someone like you.' I looked at him. The open collar of his crisp white shirt. The snick of a fixed hare lip. His watch that was gold.

'Well, exactly,' he said. 'Which is why we need allies. People who are known in the community. People who are liked.' He said this looking at me.

'She'll do it,' Kole waded in. 'When you say relocate, what does that mean? Like a new start? A fresh start somewhere else?'

The man nodded.

'And you making it worth our while when we get there?' Kole said. 'And I mean that. I want good stuff. All of it.'

The man nodded again.

Kole took hold of my shoulder. 'If I say so, she'll do it. We both will. Whoever you want us to speak to, we'll do it.'

Kole grabbed my arm as soon as we got outside.

'Still at it then?' he said. 'You off to find her? By the way, if you ever wanna mix it up. Get a bit of D involved . . .' He pushed his thumb into the belt loop closest to his flies.

I didn't say anything; I just ran. He called after me, called me a bitch, idiot, same old. I ran as hard as I could. It felt like my lungs had been put through a cheese grater after. When I got to the China House, you were inside, sitting midway up the staircase. The look on your face. Like you were the one who had a right to be upset.

'Get up,' I said. 'Like some fucking crying kid for Childline. Get up.'

I walked into the living room, didn't look back to see where you were. I lay down straight away across the sofa, I made no space for you. I pushed the knuckle of my thumb into my forehead. The muscle felt trapped in all these tiny bumps.

'Chance . . .'

'No, really, don't.'

'I was scared. All those people outside, blocking the door . . .'

'I just don't understand,' I said. I shut my eyes and tried to think of a single colour. Caleb used to tell me to do that. It never helped. 'I mean, what is it? Do you have some mental disorder? Some fucking mental thing that forces you to lie all the time?'

'No,' you said. 'I . . .'

'Great answer.'

'Let me do that,' you tried to say, about my hands working at my forehead.

I pushed you away. 'What do you think you're trying to do?'

'Make it better.'

'How can you do that?'

We looked at each other and there was a whole world between us. How does it happen, feeling that far away? When you've been so close to someone? You looked at me. Then put out your palms like I might want to hold them.

'Aren't you going to say something? You're just going to sit there?' I looked at you. 'Pretending you know less than me. I met your boss man. Who even is he, anyway?'

'Which guy?'

'Grey hair. Wears a suit. Fucking shiny face.'

'His name's Andrew or something. I don't even know. He's not a boss.'

'And the way he fucking speaks.'

'Chance, he's no one. He's just a random guy.'

'Then tell me why was it him? Tell me why it's always someone else who has to tell me things?'

'Tell you what?'

'That it's a wall they're building. That it's a wall.'

'Because it wasn't fixed, Chance. Because none of it was set in stone. Because there were a million options on the table. I – it's – look, it's complicated.'

'You're right, I probably wouldn't understand it. It might be really difficult for me. Best not to trouble my shit brain.'

'Chance . . .'

'You never said I'd have to leave my house.' It made my nose sting saying that.

'I . . .' You shook your head again. 'Part of me presumed you knew.'

'What?' I said.

'I suppose it's just, how could you not know? It's nothing you don't know already. What did you call it? The washout? Well, it's happening everywhere. Cliffs falling into the sea. Front doors under water. It's like the whole country is sinking.'

I started slow clapping.

'But we talked about this, Chance. This is the only way,' you said.

'The only way to what?'

'To make sure as much of the country as possible is protected.'

'He said we'd drown,' I told you. It caught in the back of my throat. 'He kept on saying we'll drown otherwise.'

'That's why they're getting you out.'

'And taking us where?'

'There are places. Places made for it.'

'Made for what?'

'For receiving people. Settling them.'

'I'm not stupid. When I was a kid. I remember all that. People from other places trying to get here. Where they put them. Dying in mud. Mud and shit. I'm not doing that.'

'It's not like that any more.'

'How do you know?'

'Because.'

'Because what?'

'We're better at these things now. No one does it like that any more. That's why they wanted a team of us to build a picture of the area, so we can give people the specific support they need—'

'Who's we?'

'Why are you fighting with me?'

'Because it matters. I have people to look after.'

'We'll go to London,' you said. 'You'll come with me to London.'

'That makes perfect sense. No, you're right, you're right. Seems like a great idea. I'll move to zone one, shall I?'

'Why do you have to make it like this?'

'I don't want to go to London. I hate London.' It sounded so childish when I said it. I shut my eyes so I didn't have to look at you. 'What could I even do there?' No empty houses in London. No one I knew, no one who knew me.

You said some things about it. I let you talk. You said how we'd go out to eat. You said you'd take me out to eat. You even named some restaurants, a bar. 'The only reason I didn't say anything was because things were changing all the time. Every day. There was talk of a hydraulic system, different ways of doing it, not leaving at all . . .'

'So you just fucked me instead.'

'But is it bad?' Your face really did look stricken then. There was this tremble in your forehead. 'That's my question. And I mean it, Chance. Is it bad if you have to leave? It's not like it's perfect here. Whereas if they do the relocations well . . .? I'm asking because I really don't know.' You were shaking your head. 'Couldn't it be good? Couldn't it be good for us?'

'Who's us?'

'You and me.'

'And what about my mum?' I said. 'Blue?' Even their names made my nose sting again. Guilt like this sharp thing. 'What about every single person I know?'

'They'll be fine. Not even fine. Better. All of it will be okay.' You shifted your body so I felt your weight, how close you were. 'I'll make sure it's okay.'

'How? As you keep saying, you're an intern. You do research. Nothing. How can you make sure it's okay?'

238

'I'll do my best, at least. We can both do that.'

'They said I should help them,' I said after that. 'Should I do that? Look at me.'

'I am looking.'

'No, look me in the eyes, properly. Is that what I have to do?'

'Look around you,' you said. 'It's the only way.'

'But why should I trust them?'

'Well, if you don't trust them, do you trust me?'

I was silent.

'Do you trust me?' you said again.

'How can you ask me that?'

'Because I'm going to need you to.'

In the morning, you brought me tea in bed.

'I opened every single tin,' you said. 'Found you the best.'

'I hope you shut them afterwards.'

'I shut them afterwards. I just wanted to say . . .' You looked down at your feet, then you looked back at me.

'What?'

'That it can be like this. That we can have all this,' you said. 'When everything's done. I do think that. If you want it,' you said. You looked at me. 'I want it.'

The curtains were open a tiny bit and exactly at that moment a cut of hot sun escaped from behind a cloud and lit up a path across your hair. I don't know how to describe these moments. I still don't know. How they felt like a different world. The softness, the safety. The way they could feel like medicine, magic, memory loss, everything.

I would have done anything to stay there. I didn't want to do anything to make myself have to leave.

'No more secrets,' you said. You said it yourself.

'No more secrets.'

More posters appeared across town. Mostly the boys who'd been paid to put them up just ran off with the staple guns and had staple fights in the street, thumbs bleeding. Still, in some places there were so many posters, all on top of each other, that they leaned off the walls in thick, peeling chunks.

The latest one was a map. Thanet, the shaky almost-circle curve of it, the three dots around the edge – Margate, Broadstairs, Ramsgate. All the major roads were drawn in blue, the forks in them looked like veins. Then there was a second map, below it. The same shape, but a red line – the sea wall – cutting it in half. England Mainland on one side. New Thanet on the other.

New Thanet. All around the edge, instead of sea, there were inward arrows. The land itself was shaded in blue, and on top they'd written EXTREME FLOOD RISK.

SIGN UP FOR RELOCATION, it said after that, all in red, repeated again and again, at the bottom of the page.

I went by the windows Davey had been working on. He wasn't there. I went to the pub. Lots of pubs. It was one of the pretty ones up on the Northdown Road where I finally found him. He was sitting on the bar when I walked in, feet up on a bar stool, his T-shirt tucked into the back pocket of his jeans. He was telling a story, making a show of it, because a small group of older men was sitting in a circle round him, calling him 'young lad'.

'What's he going on about now?' I said. 'Always loved the sound of his own voice.'

He'd do this when we were young. Sitting on the stoops of Athelstan Road. Something about the way he moved his hands, he could get anyone to listen.

'Not you too,' he said when he saw me. He jumped off the bar so he was on two feet. 'Standing there looking like everything's fine. Looking so light about it.'

'About what? Davey, I only just walked through the door.'

'Relo-fucking-cation,' he said.

'What if I'm just happy to see you?'

'I'm starting to think people round here have mud between their ears.' He looked at me, shook his head.

'Oi, what you going on about mud?' one of the oldest men cut in.

'Mate, I'm tired more than anything,' I said.

'But you've thought about what it means, have you?' he said to me. A few of the other men around him tilted their heads back with a 'not again'. 'Have you?'

'I'm thinking about it, yeah.'

'They think they can just ship us all out.'

'Least Meyer says it like it is,' one of the men piped up. 'For years they been putting plasters on it.'

'Always going on about "says it like it is",' Davey said. 'That's easy. I want someone who says it like it could be. And for that to be better. Not just leaving this place for dead. And now you with your smile.'

'I'm not even smiling,' I said.

'You are,' he said. Shouted, actually. He was shouting.

I leaned away from him. 'Davey, stop. You're spitting in my face.'

'Oh fuck off, Cha.' He turned back to the bar. 'Why do you have to make it dumb?'

'I just don't know why you're shouting.'

'Because it's my home! Because it's my work. Because it's everything I know.'

'Davey—'

'Because, unlike everybody else, I'm not fucking crazy.'

'Davey, you spent your whole childhood on the back of a horse trying to get as far away as you could. I was there, remember?'

'I remember,' he said. 'But I wasn't trying to get away. I was never trying to get away. Maybe it's fine for you. You weren't born here. You came here. Maybe it's easy for you to

243

just pack up and float away.' Eczema over the tattoos on his hands, eczema on his cheek. 'I'm serious, Cha.'

'But what if it's a good thing?' I heard your words come out of my mouth. 'Not even good, but just necessary. That's what I'm trying to say.'

'How can it be good?' The room had gone silent around us.

'No, I'm serious. What if it's a good thing for all of us?'

'What are you even talking about?' His voice had started to come from the top of his throat. 'You think it's just me, but it's Caleb too. I went to see him. He says not to trust a thing about any of these people.'

'Caleb? Davey, come on now . . . Caleb drinks all the time. There are times I've heard Caleb talk about aliens.'

It felt awful as soon as it came out of my mouth. The men around us laughed. Davey looked at me. He shook his head. He'd almost finished his pint. He two-knuckle knocked on the bar to signal for another.

'That bit you don't mind,' I said.

'What?'

'That bit's fine with you. That the booze is cheaper. That there's kem all around – that bit you can pick up and keep.'

'But why do you think they're doing that, Chance?' His eyes flicked down to the last sip in his glass. I could see he wanted to drink it. He put the glass down.

It went from funny to not funny. A few people laughing still, but they were old laughs not new ones.

'But is it not better even already?' I asked him. 'Just answer me for a second. Is it not getting better since they came?'

'You'd know. You went in,' Davey said. 'You went in and hung about with royalty.'

'They're not royalty.'

'Well, who are they?'

'What was I supposed to do? Kole made me. And the LandSave people, they're trying, at least. People have jobs. Until we go, people have places to sit and just be normal.' I pointed around me. 'They're trying to help. Don't be a fucking idiot.'

The room was silent.

' "Until we go",' Davey said. 'What the fuck even is that? They've left us to die again and again. Turned the power off. Turned hospitals off.'

'How is that them? That happened when we were eleven, Davey. It's so long ago.'

'But hospitals, Cha – on purpose. And when the washout came and kids were floating in the water, they left us again. They did it again. Why is it different now?'

'Because these people are trying to fix it.'

'Right,' he said. ''Cos leaving fixes everything, doesn't it?' He put his glass on its side, and the last of it spilled out onto the bar top. 'Enjoy yourself,' he said. He walked out.

It happened again and again on the street. People coming up to ask what the meeting was like. Asking me what I thought of LandSave, wanting to know what I'd heard about relocations.

'They're alright,' I said. 'Not alright. Good. They'll be good this time.'

The more I said it, the more I felt it. And when I thought of you, I found myself able to promise.

Soon, no matter how hard I tried, no matter how much I wanted to make myself feel it, the pinching in my stomach settled. The reasons settled too. The reasons to be okay with leaving. You, Blue, the thought of getting him somewhere with schools. It was strange how quickly that part happened. Blue at school – as soon as I'd imagined it, it was all I could think about.

And it wasn't just me. The okay-ness was everywhere. There were one or two people like Davey, but more than anything, our streets were fine with it. *Soonamy*, someone had written in pen over the top of loads of the posters, with a drawing of a wave. There were smiley faces over others. Maybe it wasn't excitement in the air, but it wasn't far from that. Nervous energy. Delicate, tight.

'I knew you'd come round,' Kole said, the first time we crossed paths again at home. 'Know where your bread's buttered. Good girl.'

'I'm not good,' I said.

'Bad little bitch, then. Is that better? Anyway. It's pretty easy maths. It's called: what do the fuckers have to lose. They've shoved 'em round before. They can hack it. Even heard one lad say it was nice to have structure.'

I started to see the sea again. I know that sounds stupid, but I started to see it as a separate creature, rather than it just being there, like furniture or a field. And it wasn't just me, either. People started looking for big waves. But it was almost like they wanted them to appear. There used to be this line of cloud that sat along the horizon of the sea, a little cushion that padded the sun and stopped the sunset. It felt like, now, almost every evening someone would point and say, there it is, that's the wave, the big one. And right before we get taken to the promised land as well.

It was the middle of winter, though winter had become the wrong word for it. It was hot as ever in the days. Sometimes even early morning and late at night as well. Hot and dark at the same time. That's what my mum said was so un-British about it. End of days, she said, but she seemed cheerful about the whole thing. 'If Kole's coming,' she said, a lot of times. 'If we're going to go as a family.'

When I wasn't with you, when I wasn't working, I started to write lists. Not on paper, but in my head. The things I could bring. I started saying goodbyes in my head. Not to people, but to places, houses. The flaky-pink tiles of the Lido. Dented street names. The walls of the China House. I'd touch things.

The Turner was the place we had to go to sign up for reloca-tion slots. A team of cleaners went in one Friday, and all of the old billboards around the building filled up with signs saying it would open the Monday after that.

'Slots, though,' I asked you the night before it opened. 'What does that mean?' We were lying on the sofa in the China House. I had my back to you with my head on your chest, your legs wrapped around me. 'Are they just going to slot us into little, what . . . slits across the country wherever there's space?'

'Yes, exactly. Tiny little holes. Can't really move your arms . . .'

'Like a lovely little grave,' I said.

'Exactly,' you laughed. 'You should get there early, though.' You rested your chin on my shoulder.

'Get the best grave.' I nudged past you and got onto my knees in front of the wooden liquor cabinet. 'Shall we?' I said. 'To mark this momentous occasion.' You scooted next to me. 'Lap-hurra-owa-igg,' I read, turning a bottle so the label faced us.

'Laphroaig. That's a nice one, actually. Bacon-y.'

'Aged fifteen years. Probably thirty by now. Nice little midlife crisis.'

We used glasses. We sniffed it, tilted. It burned the back of my throat. I felt happy. I lay back against the wide floor-boards. I felt the heat of it settle all through my back. You rifled through records in heavy clumps. You put on Aretha Franklin – the crackle of it, the fizz, before the voice – and also things I didn't recognise. You counted the rings of the record so you could play me one song in particular you loved on *Astral Weeks*. The strum at the beginning, lifting, lifting. You played it three times in a row, till I was lifted far away. I could have been on a boat. I felt like I could have lain there for ever.

'What's a day like there?' I said. 'What's a day like for you there?'

'London?'

'Yeah. I mean, personally, I'm going to get my slot *not* in London, far away from London, but say I was to visit.'

'Say you were to visit, well . . .' You tilted and turned your body so you faced me instead.

'For real, though,' I said. 'Tell me something so I'm not too shocked when I get there. By the future-future. I don't want to arrive in the big city and not know how to hang with the kids. I want slang, Franky. I need words.'

'It's funny, London's so not the future-future. There's stuff, but like, people don't really use it. Like paradises, you mean? All that weird fantasy stuff? They're dumb. Just like old men go.'

'My people.'

'Well, we can try one if you like. Rent a creepy little cubicle.'

'Or something like that, anyway,' I said. 'I could drop some dollars.' I pictured our money box in my head. I imagined JD's blessing. 'Take you out sometime.'

'Okay, cowboy.'

'But like on a date, you know.'

'I'd love a date.'

I remember the other albums we played. Steely Dan, Talking Heads. Everything older than us, like knowing time had existed before was proof that it would be there ahead of us too. I remember the order we played them in. You asked me if I thought you'd kissed me on every inch of my body yet. I said we should make sure. It seems strange to think of it now, but it was – I remember feeling it at the time, and I still feel it now – one of the best evenings I ever had.

You told me you'd never felt like this in your life. Nothing like it, you said. Nothing even close to like it. I found it so hard to get the words out, but they came eventually. Me too, I said. Maybe they are things that everyone says to everyone, but I had never heard them before. I had never said them.

The next morning, the queue was small when I got to the Turner, maybe only forty people up ahead of us. I looked down at what I was wearing. Everyone else had their smartest clothes on.

'It's like they're all going to a wedding,' I said.

'Well, it won't be based on that.' You looked at me. 'You're better, anyway. Taste of whisky.'

'Lah-furra-gah bluhblah,' I said. 'Hey, Franky, call up the boss,' I said as I walked away, 'put in a good word.'

The doors to the Turner opened not long after, and they let about half the queue in in one go. I looked around. It wasn't so different from the last times I'd been in. They'd swept up the syringes, at least. There were benches inside, made of the same cheap plastic as the ones outside all the pubs. Half the huge walls were made of glass, their edges a frame around the sea. On one of the non-sea-facing walls, there was a paper poster of a painting that had once been there. It was of our harbour. It looked like the sea was burning.

I took a seat on one of the rows. Soon, a woman in a shirt walked the row's length, stopping at different intervals. When she got close enough, I heard what she was saying. Get your papers out. If you have papers, get them in order while you wait.

I looked around. Some of the people near me had passports in their hands or in see-through plastic pouches they kept smoothing down, but I had nothing. I'd never had a job where I'd had to show anything. I'd never even held a passport. I'd never left the country.

'How did you get that?' I said to the man next to me.

'It's an old one – red one – expired now but I had it for twenty years or summin'. Son's wedding. Just the once.'

I nodded.

'S'pose we just see what they can do,' he said.

And so we waited. A halogen bulb was twitching on and off like an insect was trapped in it. As people got up, we moved along the bench. It made a squeaking sound.

Outside, the queue got longer and longer. It had to snake up the hill backwards, up towards Fort Crescent to avoid the tide. No shade. Some people came with cut-open cardboard boxes they held up to block the sun.

There was a form to fill in. There weren't many questions. How long we'd been here, what our professions were. Whether we had family in the rest of the country.

The girl on the other side of me, a tiny bit older than me – I recognised her from old parties – put her pen between the wrong fingers. 'Haven't held one of these for ages,' she said.

'It's okay,' I said, 'I'll do it.' I read her the questions, she told me the answers and I wrote them down. Always, none, no one.

Eventually we all slid to the end of the bench. A woman asked me to go to one of the processing tables. And, I don't know – I could say it all, but we both know what happened.

I sat down at the desk and said I wanted to apply for my mum and brother as well. I handed over my form, and the woman said they needed blood too. That the forms were just a formality.

I pushed my finger into a pin on her desk until a fat dot of red came out. I got given a number. And none of it – none of it at all – mattered.

I was sent to wait back at the same hard bench. Outside, some boys had brought buckets with ice and drinks to sell to the queue. A kid pressed his head up against the glass window, and the cloud of his breath made a perfect circle.

Inside, one by one, our numbers appeared on a screen. One by one, people got given a group. Priority, then group one, group two, group three.

'Wait, what does the group number mean?' I asked the girl I'd helped with the form.

'The order they're doing it in,' she said. 'The order we go.'

'What order?' I said. As the words came out, I felt my blood start to tick. 'I didn't know there was an order.'

A moment like that either sticks clean and perfect in your mind, or you make it disappear, you have to. Because when my number came up, there was no group next to it.

It never went green. It went red.

'Deferred', it said.

I found myself standing up. The girl turned to look at me. Other people turned to look too.

I went up to the desk. My legs felt empty, like my bones weren't hard any more. 'What does that mean?' I said. I pointed.

'Deferred?' the woman said without looking up. 'A later date. You'll be processed at a later date.'

'The fuck's that mean? Later, when?'

'Do I look like a magician with all the answers?' she said. 'Listen, it's not me. It's the system that works it out.'

'Why, though? What does it say?'

'I don't have access to any of the specifics.'

'Just tell me what it says on the screen then – it has to say something.'

'Can you not hear me?' she said.

I could hear the beginning of a high-pitched ringing fill my ears instead. I wanted to reach over the desk but there were guards around. 'Well, I need to speak to someone then,' I said. 'There was a man I spoke to before. I went into the Sands before.'

'You'll have to make an appointment,' she said.

'Okay, make me an appointment.'

'You'll have to go through the official channels.'

'What the fuck is this, if it's not official? You all here for fun?'

'You'll have to make an appointment,' she said again.

I looked at her. 'What are you, fucking broken?'

'Nothing we can do without an appointment,' she said one last time.

'Yeah, whatever,' I said. I started walking to the door. I couldn't take a breath that counted, could get deep enough – they all stopped before they made it past my throat. I tried to think of one moment where you hadn't left things out, where you hadn't made me walk into a situation like an idiot.

You were there, standing just outside, when I pushed the door open. I remember the sting of it, how bright your face was.

'What's wrong with you?' I said.

'What?'

'We had all night. All fucking night.'

'I don't understand . . .' There was a flower in your hand, purple, sweet, you'd picked it from the street.

'Does it feel good?' I said.

'Does what feel good?'

'You didn't tell me they were doing it in groups. All these weird different priorities.'

'I . . .' You looked behind me, back into the Turner. 'It'll be to help. They can't move a whole town at once. I don't know. Priorities, how? I didn't know about that.'

'But what does deferred mean?' I said.

'What?'

'What does deferred mean?' I said again. I said it slowly. I said it clearly.

'I don't know.' But your face. It didn't look good.

'The woman said it was the system,' I said. 'That the system works it all out. But works it all out based on what?' I looked at you.

'No,' you said. 'Definitely not. My work? No. They won't be using it like that. They aren't. They can't. But I can fix it. I can go into the system and try to fix it. I'll come to find you . . .'

It started to fill me. It should have been anger, but it was shame that came – a thick, dark clot of it. I felt ashamed more than anything. Whatever it was about me that wasn't good, wasn't good enough.

'No more,' I said. I couldn't look at you. 'No more. I'm done this time.'

I started to walk away.

'I'll find you, Chance,' you called after me as I started to walk fast. Out of body. 'I can fix it,' you shouted, 'all of it . . .', but I think by then I was already running. How far did you follow me? Some other people shouted out at me from the queue but I didn't listen. I just ran – left, right, right, left, turning corners at random – until I was on a street I hardly recognised.

I had a small square of kem in my pocket. I'd picked it up for Ma and it was meant to last her a week. All of the colour had been thumbed off the cardboard it was wrapped in. I didn't have anything to smoke it with. I crushed a crystal with the back of my thumbnail. It looked like salt, or sugar. Darker than that. I pushed it into the roof of my mouth. Didn't taste like either. It turned to heat, then burn. Fire. Felt like circles in my head. Too much. Took more.

I tried to find Davey before the world started to fade.

I remember him cutting wood when I came in. Turning off his saw, pulling up his mask. I remember his dusty eyebrows, the cut-fingernail curve of a scar on his hairline. He gave me this old, red, deep-backed armchair to sleep in. Said my eyes were more open than he'd ever seen, but that they weren't really working. 'I slapped you and everything,' he told me later, half proudly, half wanting to admit it.

When I woke up, the kem had broken everything into pieces. I wanted the pieces to be gone too. I went to his fridge. The fridge didn't work – it wasn't even plugged into the wall – but it was where he kept his drinks anyway.

'Hold it, tiger,' he said. 'You just belted yourself. Are you sure you want that?'

'Yeah. Don't look at me like that.'

And so Davey took a beer too. So I wouldn't be alone, he said. There was dirt, something brown, on the seat I'd slept in. I hoped I hadn't done that. I sat back down to cover it just in case.

'Do you want to talk about it?' Davey said.

I shook my head.

'Is it your mum, though? Trev's bad at the moment.'

'It's not her.'

'Kole, then?'

'Not him, either.' I brought the beer up to my lips. Every part of my body ached, like I'd been lifting weights in my sleep. 'Just what's happening.'

'And what's that, exactly? 'Cos all of it seems like a shambles to me.'

'I said I don't want to talk about it.'

'You can't just drink all my beer in silence. Not the whole lot of it. Not if we're not talking.'

'Fine,' I said. 'Tell me a story.'

'Okay.'

'And I'll tell you why it's shit.'

'First time you smiled,' he laughed. 'And it's 'cos you're being a bitch.'

Davey had finished his beer already. He didn't always want to start, but once he did, he went fast. He wasn't wearing a top, and he had a new tattoo down his spine. A zip. There was cling film stuck over it.

We sat in silence and sips. Davey showed me things he had around the house. Boys like to do that. Whenever your face found its way back into my mind, I found myself shaking my head. Actually shaking it. As if that would get it away. We'd moved from bottles to cans, and Davey scrunched his in his hands when he was done.

'Listen,' he said. 'I'm sorry about the last time, at the pub. They can fuck the rest of shit up, fine, but not us. Not you and me. Not us being friends.'

'Always friends,' I said. I kissed my tattoo.

'Looks drawn in pencil now,' he said. He took in a deeper breath than normal, like he'd missed one out. 'Let's go out,' he said. 'When was the last time we went out?'

'We have been going out. Haven't we been going out?'

'When was the last time you got some?' he asked.

I shook my head again. Downed my beer, rapped my nail on the neck of the empty can.

'No time,' I said. 'Never done it.'

'Let's go out, you doughnut.'

I was aware again of the dirt on the seat. I asked him if he had clothes I could borrow. I didn't know whether he'd already noticed. When I got off the chair, I put an old bit of newspaper on it.

Davey had a few pieces of girl clothes from people who'd stayed over. 'But you won't want any of this pink stuff, will you?' He came back with baggy shorts and an even bigger T-shirt instead. The shorts were stiff and smelled like soap, the T-shirt smelled like Davey – Rizlas, petrol, sawdust and, somewhere in there, apple juice.

Davey had tried to come in when I was getting changed.

260

'Just a quick look,' he laughed, 'old times' sake! Cha, don't be—'

I slammed the door onto his arm and he was still pretending to nurse it when I came out. We went to the pub at the very top of the high street. Davey's clothes changed how I walked. His shorts were low on my hips. I borrowed a cap too, also pulled that low. I felt it solid in my chest – I didn't want to be myself any more.

The pub was so full, there were gangs of people outside it too. I remember some men by the door making an arch for us to enter under. 'Proper lifers', as Davey called them – faces folded, teeth broken. There were younger teenagers in there too, eyebrows on their upper lips. But it was full and people seemed happy. Somewhere along the line, someone had told someone had told someone that relocations meant new houses. Brand-new houses. Four beds, garages. 'Not that they even have fucking cars, but,' Davey said, shaking his head, 'each to their mother-fucking own.'

When the pubs had first reopened it was just in the daytime and early evening. Now they were open into the night. I fell over a lot. A few times that didn't hurt. One that did. I remember hands surrounding me to pick or push me up, like one of those child's toys that you can't fully knock over.

By the next afternoon, my legs had bruises in places that wouldn't break a fall. Bruises from thumbs, fingers.

There's not much from that night I remember. Davey told me the next day that the pints were half the normal price, and even then, they were mostly giving them away for free.

'Why?' I'd asked Davey the first time, when he pushed away my money.

'Wasn't a time to ask why.'

'Did the guy know you?'

'Knew him a bit. Knew him to see. Don't we know everyone? Not his name. Cheers, by the way . . .'

The beer was a bit flat, maybe that was it. A little bit metal-y too, like it was from the end of the barrel. 'Still does the trick,' Davey said. His finger found its way onto a bruise above my knee, just lightly. His nails had all these white flecks in them. 'Come on then, let's get these down.'

I woke up naked with a jumper over me like a blanket. I don't think anything had happened.

Davey was on the floor in the next room, as if he'd leaped and missed the bed. He was wearing boxers, but they looked too big for him and were scrunched up. So many tattoos, he looked almost dressed.

Our days went on like that. 'Are you sure you want this?' Davey asked me that morning. 'Don't you want to check up on home?' he said the day after that. 'What about your girl? I forgot about her.'

'She's not my girl.'

We settled into what we were doing, and he didn't ask any more. He put the word out that we wanted stuff, and a couple of boys we knew came round. 'It's getting better,' Davey said. He'd take such deep drags the muscles in his neck would twitch. 'Gets better all the time.' He let out the breath. The smoke was thick as a blanket. He told me again and again how much he'd missed this. Us spending time together.

Each night, the pubs were busier and busier. The special offers got better and better. Some nights I couldn't remember paying for a single thing.

'You were being so funny last night, man,' Davey said one morning. 'Talking about everything being fucked up, getting all proper dark. Tried to take me to the Sands at one point.' He laughed. 'Looked like you wanted to start a war.'

My stomach twisted.

'Whatever,' I said. 'I was just drunk. Forget that.'

'Mate, I was fine with it – glad you're seeing the light.'

But I wanted the dark. I wanted blankness. I wanted to forget. We drank more and more, and there was always more after that. Plastic glasses made ice mountains at the edges of the streets. I remember sitting, swaying, bliss-eyed in the toilet, holding the handle of the door for balance. And whenever I caught a thought of you, or Blue, all of the things I hadn't done or couldn't do, I tried to push it as far away as possible.

It was somewhere between three or four days before I went home. It felt like no time. It also felt like forever. There were holes through all of it, dread threading in and out of them.

Our front door. The pause I always took. Scared each time of what I'd find. I'd lost my key. I had to knock.

Ma took a while but she came. She didn't ask where I'd been. 'The state of you,' was all she said. I walked straight to Blue's room. Ma followed me to the door.

'He's fine,' I said. And when I heard those words, even though I was the one who said them, my chest felt like it was collapsing.

'Course he's fine,' she repeated. 'What did you expect?'

It seems stupid to say it, but it felt like even in a few days he had grown. I kissed away a tiny web of sleep on one of his eyelashes. I promised I wouldn't miss anything else. I sat with him on his bed, until it felt like my being in his space made it dirty. I got up, said sorry. I looked at myself in the mirror. The flesh in my face was in the wrong places. I had borrowed someone else's make-up one night. It was smudged, run. It looked like I'd been crying. 'Stop now,' I said to the strange reflection. 'That's enough now,' I said again. 'Hey,' I said, knees on the floor, reaching over the bed to hold his hand, 'hey, I love you,' I said. It felt like a wave crashing in my chest. 'Hey, I love you so much, do you know that? Do you know?'

After a while, Ma called me back into the sofa room.

'Some girl came for you,' she said.

A breeze hit the back of my belly. Cold.

'Don't worry, I didn't let her in,' she said. 'She asked if you or Blue were here. Name and everything. What does she want to see Blue for?'

'What did she look like?' I said. I knew what you looked like.

'Some kind of blonde thing. Pretty. Not a big bruiser about to knock the door down or anything.'

You had been outside where I live. You had seen our stairs. You had seen my mum.

'But you didn't let her in?'

I thought about the holes in the sofa, the way you could see through to the foam. The parts of carpet that were missing. The smudges on the windows.

'Course I didn't. Said for some cash she could see him,' Ma said. 'But as a joke, of course. She didn't hang about. Do you owe her something? Money or something?'

I shook my head. 'She's the one who should have something for me,' I said.

'Well I don't know about that,' Ma said, 'but she said she'd come back.' She was talking more than usual. It seemed like she was happy to have someone to talk to. 'You didn't bring any cigs back with you, did you? Tell you what. I was happy when she said it was you she was looking for.'

'Why?'

'She looked . . . young, you know. I thought she was here for Kole, maybe. If he's been out doing that again . . .' She'd been scratching the skin around her thumbs. 'You don't think he has, do you?'

Kole hadn't been home for a few days, either, she said. I didn't think I'd seen him. I hoped I hadn't. If we'd been in the same pub, he'd have definitely come over.

'No idea,' I said.

'How does she know Blue, though? This blonde girl?'

'Doesn't everyone know him?'

She looked me up and down. 'The state of you,' she said again. She shook her head.

I went back into my room. I couldn't work out what to do. If I should wait for you here. Or if I should go and find you and tell you you'd got the wrong place. That it wasn't my mum you'd seen, that it wasn't my house. The most important thing was this, though – I couldn't leave Blue again right away.

Kole came home once or twice, a mess of beer and sweat. He slept in a star on Ma's bed, his belly rising like a hard, skin hill. He'd wake up and talk sometimes but he made no sense.

It was so hot. Day and night, a thick cloak of it. I tied sheets and clothes to the corners of the window to block out the worst of it, but Blue cried, and wouldn't stop sometimes. I tried to run water into buckets so we could put our feet in it, but our feet made the water warm up too quickly.

The air tasted like it had been breathed and breathed and breathed again. Blue asked me when it would stop. I hated not having an answer. With a child, it's not supposed to be like that.

I watched the Turner from the window. The queues were long then short, long then short, a snake with a changing tail. I didn't want to tell Ma I'd been. I didn't tell anyone. Every time I thought about it, shame slipped like a razor down my spine. Why had I been deferred? What did that even mean? My brain made fists, fought itself. Why did I have to rely on someone like you to fix it? How long would it take?

The next day, when we heard that Tessy Watts from the seventh floor was in the first priority group, and had already got all the paperwork through, Viv asked me if I wanted to come down.

'It's this badge thing,' Tessy told us when we got there. 'Been told I got forty-eight hours.'

'Forty-eight?' Viv said. 'That's practically tomorrow.'

Tess put an open packet of Jammie Dodgers out on the table, ate one and got the red sticky stuff caught on her front teeth. She showed us the badge she'd been given but she didn't let Viv hold it completely, even though, as she kept on saying, it hadn't been activated yet.

'Have they said where you're off to?' Viv asked. 'Have they given you pictures?'

'I don't really know ... I'm just ...' Tessy ate another biscuit and wiped her fingers with a drying-up cloth. 'And here was me thinking I'd never leave this place.'

'Exciting, though,' Viv said. 'To start afresh.' She looked round Tessy's walls as if there would be things to bring, but she didn't have much. Didn't have anything, really. There was a small box by the door.

'Yes,' Tessy said. 'Very exciting.'

By then, Davey was the only person I knew who thought relocation was stupid. I couldn't face going to see Caleb. The thought of questions, the thought of having to give answers.

'But just listen to them out there,' Davey said when he came by to check on me. 'You'd think they were on crack. Moving out of tsunami-land and right into Buck Pal. Yeah. Sounds about right.' He did a thumbs-up. 'Sounds realistic. Fucking dick-for-brains. Tell me you haven't been down there to the Turner, Cha?' he said after that.

'No,' I said back.

The knot in my belly got tighter. I kept on thinking about what the LandSave man at the Sands had said. I used to like the sound of the tides, the sound of the waves when they hit walls and made a smack of spray. I used to run towards it. When we were kids, we'd run towards the water then run away until our T-shirts were see-through and our hair hung wet. But now, each time the tide started to come in, or pulled out too fast, or whenever the wind whipped up and seemed to start chopping, I looked at Blue and felt a whole new fear. I could swim, I could climb. I'd be fine. But Blue. The thought of anything bad happening to him.

The only thing Ma worried about was when Kole would be back, and what state he'd be in. 'They'll come and get us when it's time,' was what she said, again and again. 'Won't they, boo?' and she nodded at Blue until he nodded too.

I remember trying to make one moment that was normal for him. Even though it had been too hot to shop, we had a few cans of beans and a huge bag of crisps in the cupboard and I decided to use everything at once. 'Do you know what a feast is?' I asked him. I dusted my hand back and forth over his head. 'A banquet?' Last Supper was probably what I meant.

For the ceremony of it, I heated it up, even though turning on the gas in the heat felt like some kind of crime. I put all the food onto one big plate for both of us. I let Blue eat with his fingers. He pushed aside some beans – I'd let them cool down so he wouldn't burn himself – and said, 'I see you, chip.' He looked up at me.

'That's not a chip, it's a crisp,' I said back before I realised he'd said a full sentence. His first one.

'Chip,' he said, and pulled it out from under the beans. It was a bit soft. He ate it anyway. 'Chip,' he said again, and his face looked like he knew he was clever. He ate with his mouth so wide open, like each time he was testing how far his jaw would go.

Terrifying to love someone like that.

'Chip,' he said again.

'That one's a mini sausage.' It was in the beans. And in his hand it looked like an extra-fat little finger. 'You're not clever yet, dummo.'

'Chip,' he said again.

'Dummo,' I said back.

When it was the two of us, we became like animals. When he got food on his face, I licked it off, because it was the easiest way and it made it feel like we didn't need anything or anyone else.

He looked at me and I looked at him. 'How do you get them cheeks?' I asked him. 'Fat boy.'

I took his hands and helped him stand up. Sometimes we danced like that. Me half bending over, him reaching up, and no music, but it was still nice. At that moment, his feet fit perfectly in the space between the beginning of my toes and the start of my ankle.

After we danced, we napped on the sofa. I couldn't work out if having the windows open made it better or worse. When I woke up, sweat fell into my eyelashes like rain. There was no way to get the leather against our backs cool.

In the heat, and with nothing more to eat, and Blue pulling at my big toe like it would make something happen, I thought about you. I played echoes of conversations. Small cuts, a little quickening when something snuck in and surprised me. We slept. 'Come, baby, let's sleep again,' I said to Blue. We slept as much as I could.

We had been told that we had fifteen days to register for relocation before the move started.

That time was nearly up.

And then two things happened in the night. In the middle of the night, one night after the other.

Kole came back late, neither night, nor morning, and instead of falling asleep in his boots, he started knocking stuff over, using the whole surface of his arms to smash things off tables, shelves.

I could hear him. He was talking under his breath, but I couldn't work out what he was saying. I just heard him get closer to my bedroom, the one I shared with Blue. I had my mouth on Blue's forehead. Then Blue rolled over on the sheets. I was worried he would wake up, make a sound. Catch Kole's attention. I slipped my arm out from underneath him as carefully as possible, and moved to the door so I could slide the bolt as quietly as I could. Then I pushed my back hard against the wood.

I could hear Kole speaking now. He was saying he needed money.

Then I heard Ma's voice too. Please don't, I remember thinking, please don't. Please stay in bed.

'Kole, no,' I heard her say. 'It's for the future.'

'What future? What fucking future?'

'I don't know, but Kole—'

'And don't think for half a fucking minute your little bitch doesn't know what's about to happen.'

Then the creak of the broken tumble dryer. It had taken me and Davey nearly three hours to lug it up the stairs when we moved.

'No—' I said, accidentally out loud. Kole was going for JD's money box. Our box. I started to hear a pleading in her voice. I imagined her tugging his clothes. There was a second of struggle, then the sound of a fist and a skull connecting, two things that don't want to give in. Again and again.

I opened the door in time to see him using the metal cash-box to smash her legs. I ran across the room, tried to put myself in between them, but he knocked me to the floor with a single hand.

Silence. One second of it. Ma pushed her face into her hands, to stem blood, I think. Kole stood over us, bigger than I had ever seen him. If Blue had made a noise, I think Kole would have gone in for him. But nothing – no sound or person strong enough – got in the way of Kole leaving. Leaving with all the money JD had left us. Still, even on the worst of days, we had hardly touched it.

Ma's legs, when I turned the light on. I'd never seen a knee like that. Knees are supposed to be hard, bone, like a dome. Her knee was like a soft-boiled egg, cracked flat. I tried to bend her leg the right way. I watched it. It was like ink spreading.

'How did he know it was there?' I heard my voice say.

'I saw you look at it,' she said, 'I saw you check it. Just once. And I only told him once, just once.' We looked at her knee and watched it turn purple right in front of our eyes. 'I'm going to be sick,' she said.

Kole had left the front door wide open. All that we'd saved. Even the rings I'd taken from the China House. Every last bit of it was gone.

The next day I told Ma the sounds we could hear were fireworks.

Told her, even though she could barely hear me. She was pretty much out cold. I'd had someone bring her something for the pain. Grey pills with a red dot on each one, which the guy crushed up with the back of a fork and said worked quicker if we used one of these. He passed me a needle. It looked like it had been washed, but it had already been used so many times the numbers on the side had rubbed off.

Blue tried to stroke Ma's knee but his hand always landed flat – looked more like it was hitting – so I put him higher on the bed, closer up to her head. He played with her hair, gave her kisses. He couldn't do them properly either. It was an open mouth, a popping sound.

Someone must have told Viv what had happened, because she brought round bread and some soup she'd made. I asked her what was going on outside.

'Protesting,' she said. 'Protesting the move. Something about getting deferred? I don't know. Normal faces, normal rubbish.'

'Do you know where?' Still my first thought was you. You being okay.

'Never had much focus, have they? Not that lot,' Viv said. 'Not their thing. Smashing up who knows what.' My face must have fallen because she told me not to worry. 'Oh, don't!' she said. 'Not you too. Chin up. Don't it always pass? We'll ride it out. Look at us,' she said. 'We're doing alright.'

Which made us both laugh, and she held my hands so tight I felt the bones slide around in there.

That night, I left Blue in bed with Ma, and tried to get some rest on the sofa, with my cutters in my hand in case Kole came back. I was half-asleep, half-awake, when there was another hammering at the door. At first it knocked its way into my dream. I made sense of it there. And then I woke up.

I was sure it was him. But then, behind each beat, a voice started to come through the door. Slowly, it became clearer. It wasn't strong enough to push through the wood. It was your voice. My body stopped.

I walked to the door. I didn't open it right away. I found myself with my hands and head pressed against it. Perhaps just a second or two but it felt like so much longer.

276

When I finally opened it, the fist you'd been knocking with almost came through onto me. Our eyes met. I went to shut the door again, and you put your foot in the way. You were wearing the grey camouflage.

'Why are you dressed like that?'

'It's so they know who we are. I ran away from everyone to get here. I shouldn't be here,' you said. 'I shouldn't be here.'

I noticed how dark it was in the stairwell. Normally at least a few of the light bulbs would flicker on if someone moved. But nothing. The light from our corridor bounced off your face. You were out of breath.

'The lift, it . . .'

'It hasn't for ages.'

I stood in the door so you couldn't see into the flat behind me. It couldn't have mattered less in that moment but I was suddenly conscious of whether it had a smell. I turned off the light behind me so you couldn't see inside and went out into the corridor with you, my eyes adjusting by then.

'I don't know how to say this,' you started, 'but something is happening and it's happening right now.'

'What thing? What do you mean, something?'

'I think it's going to get bad. They said they're closing everything by the morning. And I don't know what to do. They never said it would be like this.'

'Closing what?'

You looked at me. 'I tried to say they couldn't. I tried to say, Chance. I tried to stop them but . . .'

'Tried to stop what? Speak properly.'

'All I know is they're taking us out now.'

'Who's "us"? Taking you where? Have you done it – did you fix it for me?'

'I – it's on a ledger – there's no way of changing it. I tried everything – I didn't know that that was . . . I didn't know.'

You looked down the stairs like someone might have been following you. 'But they'll come back for us?' I said. I thought of the way my mum had said it, how sure she was. I looked at you, watched this red spreading through your cheeks, I could see it even in the semi-darkness. 'So now you're going to just go?' The space behind my eyes stung.

'I don't have a choice.'

'You do have a choice.'

'Chance, please—'

'You always have a choice. People like you always have a choice.'

I moved to go back into the flat. I tried to shut the door again, and again your leg blocked it.

'No, wait,' you said. 'You have to wait. There's something else.'

'What?'

'I can take him.'

I didn't say anything. I just looked at you.

'Blue. I can take him,' you said. 'How old is he?'

'What are you even saying?' I tried to push you away harder.

'Listen to me. Just listen. Stop trying to shut the door. He's not on the records. He's too young.'

'You're crazy.' I looked at you. 'You must be crazy.' I must have been crying by then. I hated myself for that.

'It's only if I go,' you said, 'that I have any chance to fix this. I'll keep him safe. I'll come back. I can come back. You know I can.'

'How can you?'

'My dad is—'

'What do you even mean "my dad is"?' But you didn't need to answer. Those three words already said everything. Where you start, where you end up.

I think you tried to kiss me, touch my face, at least, because I pushed you harder than I meant to. You stumbled back. 'If you're going, then just go,' I said. Pride. Pride again. There instead of a backbone. I was wearing one of JD's old T-shirts. I felt tiny in it. I pulled it around me.

'I can't leave you like this . . .' you started.

But I had pulled the door behind me. I walked away through our corridor. Your hand was landing flat on the door again. You must have slammed against the wood harder and harder as I walked away because the sound stayed the same as I walked into Ma's bedroom.

Her leg was up higher than her heart, propped on some more of JD's old clothes, because each time she moved, it would start bleeding again. Around her mouth was wet, because of the new stuff she was on. The second time, I'd had to give it to her. Find a vein that was close enough to the surface. And because there was no one else to help with Blue, he'd watched. I'd watched him watch. The shame of that.

The sounds from the street flared up again. My eyes landed on pieces of our life in the flat. The brown halo of smoke and oil above the cooker. The fridge I knew was empty.

The change felt as light as turning the page. I went back to the door. I opened it, and left it open.

'Wait,' I said.

When I got to him, he was asleep in a curl. I took him in my arms. His back curved, his thumb in his mouth. And then I started walking. I walked down the corridor to our front door. I pulled it wide.

When I put him in your arms, I almost hoped he'd wake up. Notice that he was no longer touching me. But he stayed asleep.

'I'll get some stuff,' I said.

'There'll be other clothes there.'

I stopped. 'It's not that.'

I came back with a small bag of kem.

'In case he cries, and cries and doesn't stop crying and his face . . .' I couldn't look at you. 'I tried to stop her. She said she only did it once. But just in case. I don't know. If he doesn't look right. Just the tiniest bit.' I knew people who had died coming off it, when they'd come off it just like that, and I didn't know how much Ma used to give him.

'You have to stay here,' you said. 'Please listen. I'll come back for you. We'll come back. I promise.'

Tears were burning paths down my cheeks. Yours too, maybe. I can't remember now.

'Look at me,' you said after that. 'Don't follow me. Don't go up to anyone in a uniform. Don't even look them in the eye. They're under orders to shoot. They won't even have to do paperwork. Please.' You had one arm round Blue, the other arm was holding my wrist. 'Promise you won't.'

'Did you know?' I said. 'Did you know they were going to do this?'

'No,' you said. 'No.' You were shaking your head. 'I don't know. I knew something. Not everything. Not this. Not this. I had no idea it was this.' You reached for my chest. You put your hand on my chest. I stood back from you. 'I've been such an idiot,' you said. 'I've been the worst idiot. But I'll come back. I'll come back for you. I promise you I'll do that. I'm sorry.'

You did not want to take the first step away from me, so I told you I'd take you down. It wasn't for you, it was for Blue. Before we left our floor, I kissed him everywhere on his head – his scalp was hot, his hair was cold, feathers – and he was still mostly sleeping so he didn't know, I was glad he didn't know, that he was leaving.

The three of us stood on the step as this happened, which meant your face was there so I did kiss you too once. There might have been love inside it, and hate, but maybe love. I don't know. We'd never even said that word.

In the end I just said: 'Please be okay. Please look after him.'

You nodded. Blue was sleeping still. I could see you were beginning to find him heavy. His head pushed into your chest.

It was how trusting he was that got me. Tiny, trusting boy. The way he always thought he was safe.

When I think back now, the thing I can't believe most is that I didn't tell you. It was on the tip of my tongue, it was at the back of my throat, it was a rock in my chest. Not that I loved you. Not that I loved you. That's nothing.

On the landing, four floors from the bottom, that's when I should have said it. When your hand went up to stop me coming any further. When you carried on without me. His head. I watched it leave and all I could think about was how hot it always was.

He was mine. That's what I would have told you.

I knew him first. He was mine. He is mine.

Tiny, trusting boy. He didn't show when he was inside me at all. He came out when I went to the toilet. Which makes it sound dirty but it wasn't like that. It was strange. Easy. Honestly, he just fell from me. I was small, but he was smaller. This wet, pink bundle. I would have thought I was dying, thought I was mad, but I remembered my periods hadn't come for months. I hadn't cared, it was better like that, but my breasts had felt like there was wood trapped in them. I hadn't been able to run.

Whatever way I say it will be wrong. I was thirteen, but it wasn't my first time. And I had been kissing Kole, doing other things too. We'd ended up in the same pub as him. JD was in prison, Kole kept buying us all these drinks. Davey was jealous, excited at the same time. We were both excited. Kole knew everyone. Everyone in the room would look at him. Energy whirlpooled around him. I don't remember everything. Just that it hurt when he did it a second time, and a third.

I wasn't at home when I had him, but I wasn't far. I ran water over the baby in the sink. The baby because he wasn't Blue yet. I took him back with hand towels around him, everything still attached. Him and me, I mean. The cord was purple, looked chewed up.

Ma had to prise him out of my hands. The paper was soaked in blood, fell apart in her fingers. Viv was good at things like that, she came to cut. So she knew. She was younger then – I remember her face as it was that day. Hair black, mouth terrified. She cried before Ma did. Ma asked me who'd done it to me. I wouldn't say. She asked me again. It went on like that. Viv kept saying how small he was, he's tiny, too small, like a bird he's tiny. She said we had to keep him warm. They held him by the oven, with the heat on low and the oven door open, and I lay near them, silent, normal, maybe not normal, but silent, unsure of what had just happened.

It came out eventually. It's not that Ma wasn't angry at first. She slapped Kole round the face, and punched him in the head too when he came round. Asked what was wrong with him, said I was half his size, all of that. Said he couldn't come into the flat. Said she'd get the police. What police? he said.

He asked if we'd already told JD, and Ma said of course not, because he'd only go and kill us all when he got out. Kill Kole, kill me, kill her for letting it happen. After that, though, some other time she did let him in. She said she wanted to let him explain. They got drunk together. He'd brought bottles and bottles round.

They told me their plan in the morning, like it would fix everything, and even though it wasn't like they were asking me, I said yes. They started sleeping in the same bed, and that was it.

It didn't feel like I was lying when I called him my brother. After time and time and time, it could feel true.

But imagine, then, watching you carry him down the stairs. These circles, your shoulder coming into view, the top of your heads, the sound of your feet taking him away.

I don't remember walking back up the stairs. I leaned over the banister and saw a man in a bullet-proof vest burst into the stairwell. He had some kind of gun. He shouted up to me: 'Stay back. Do you understand me? Stay back, whoever you are.' All in black. His voice bounced back off every step. I dropped to my knees.

I don't know if that man was with you. There to protect you, or whether they'd put someone at the bottom of the building to keep us in. But he seemed to know you. He put his arm around your back to protect you. Escorted you out. I took one last look.

When you disappeared, my throat closed. Felt like a walnut for the first time, the feeling that would always come back. Small, hard, messy. Like if I could put my tongue against it, it would dry my mouth instantly.

I couldn't trust my legs. When I got back to the flat I found myself going to the window to see if I could see you. I don't know if it was you I saw, or someone else. It looked like there were other people running. It wasn't long before there were gunshots. The heart reacts to sounds like that, it tries to match them. Bullets like hard flicks, skittering. I shut the window. The noise dulled. I was shaking. But if my body was standing in our flat, I was somewhere else. My arms were still in the way they'd been to hold Blue.

I found my way to his bed, and my head was filled with the same sentence again and again. What have you done? What have you done? What have you done?

There were those star stickers on his ceiling. The ones that are meant to glow and look faraway and go kind of green when you turn the light off. The edges of the points were peeling off, which made them look like they were about to fall. He used to go to sleep counting them, because he'd forget where he started, and he didn't know many numbers anyway.

I tried to feel the shape of exactly where he'd sleep. I imagined it warm, imagined I could keep it that way.

The bulb in his room had blown a while ago. The stars did not light up that night.

III.

When I woke up, I felt in the bed for him.

That first moment where more than one thing is still possible. Then it came back in a rush. Your face as you felt for the right way to hold him, the way his hair was starting to curl, his eyes pressed shut, his fingers. I felt like I was drowning.

There were sounds. They were not good sounds – sirens, shouts, a scream, the shaky rumbles of small explosions. For a second, I wondered if they were only in my head. I put my fingers in my ears to check. Quieter, but the noises were still everywhere. My body felt too heavy to sit up. I did everything slowly.

I went to the window. It couldn't have been much after seven. The sky was pink, the cold kind. I always expected fighting to happen in the night, but that morning, when I looked out of the window, I felt this sinking.

Cars were burning. Three, four, more. Whole streets lit up orange. Above us, the whipping sound of a helicopter. Maybe more than one. I couldn't see them – I only saw the tracking lights, faint because it was morning, scooting over rooftops.

I pulled the curtains shut. How had I slept? How could I have slept?

Straight away, I went to block our door. Dragged the big armchair over so it was in the way, propped up an empty gas bottle to keep the handle blocked. I looked in our cupboards to see what food we had. I pulled everything out onto the sideboard. Two already opened packets of rice. A tin of tomato sauce. A can of sardines that Kole had half cracked then wrapped up in a plastic bag.

Lessons from school came back to me. I filled up empty pots and pans with the water from the tap. I filled the bath, too. The tap spat and spluttered and for a moment I worried it was too loud. That people would hear we were inside. I turned it off, then turned it on again. Didn't matter. Something comforting about the sound of the water.

There started to be enough people running up and down the building for the stairs to shake. Voices, too – I could only make out bits of what they were saying. I kneeled on the armchair, pressed my ear against the door. Was that Lace's voice? Could I get down to Viv? Should I tell them not to go out? But I stayed stone still. With my face against my hands, I could hear a beat in my fingers.

The saliva in my mouth felt too thin, I kept on having to

spit it out. There was a blast that was big enough to make a photo of JD slide off a shelf and smash.

Ma didn't wake up and I didn't want to wake her. There was too much to explain. And how would I ever say it? I looked into her room, but I couldn't look directly at her. Her open knee, her open mouth, the sores around it. All of the rubbish – plates, bottles, bras – that had piled up on her bedside table.

Each time I went and checked her breathing, all I could think was, you don't know yet. You don't know anything yet, and I was jealous.

Then she called for me.

'You but,' she said, when I went into her room. 'But where's?' She patted the bed around her body. 'Where's?'

'Where's what?' I said. 'What do you want?'

She started coughing, then not being able to breathe. This rough sound, sandpaper.

'He isn't here,' I said. It felt like the worst thing I'd ever said.

She looked at me like she was scared. And then she started making this new sound. The beginning of a scream, getting louder.

'Stop it,' I said. 'Shut up.' I sat on the bed close to her, on top of one of her hands. The noise she was making got louder. Too loud. I could feel her trying to move away from me. I tried to put a hand over her mouth, not in a bad way at first. 'You'll get us killed,' I said.

But then I realised what she was looking around for. The way her hand landed flat on the bed. She wasn't looking for Blue. She was looking for packets of kem that weren't empty.

That was the first time I hit her. Not even hit her but pushed her face into the pillow with the hard bit of my hand. It made a sound. The shock in her eyes. I hadn't meant to do that.

'It's your fault,' I said. 'You. You were the one who was supposed to protect us. And it was you who . . .' It was seeing her, it had been seeing her, broken on the bed, that had changed my mind.

'You.' I looked at her again. Then no more words. After that, I ran to the sink in the kitchen and vomited water.

She mostly slept. Or she would wake up and make no sense. It's hard to look at someone crying and not feel a thing. But I felt nothing. Less than that. Neither of us seemed human to me.

'I remember Kole,' she said, early the second day, 'and then I remember – I don't remember.'

She'd spent so much of her life pretending that she didn't forget, it was hard for her to admit that.

'Just sleep,' I said.

I sat by the half-open curtains, and looked out across the town like you might both still be there. There were no more helicopters, those sounds had stopped, but windows kept smashing. Mostly it was silent though, which was almost worse. Silent apart from dogs barking. Blue, Blue, Blue, Blue, Blue. His name fell like rain in my head.

Behind me, Ma tossed, turned, scratched at the mattress. The surface looked like it was satin but it made this harsh sound. And if it wasn't the empty packets, it was Kole not Blue she cried for, when she was shaking and scratching at her skin like she was allergic to it, and I was pouring water into her mouth and it stayed dry. It was Kole's name she said, teeth clenched, teeth clenched so hard one broke as I was in front of her. Her elbows were thicker than the parts of her arm on either side. Her legs were joints and stretched skin. When she was quiet, when she was still, I looked at her and thought, where did you go? How did you just disappear like that?

I made us something to eat, but over halfway through the day as best as I could judge it, like waiting made it count for something. Two plates. We had individual gas and still had a full bottle, plus the dregs in the bottle against the door, at this point. I made rice. A tiny bit of the tomato sauce, such a small amount it didn't even turn the rice pink. Somewhere in the back of our lukewarm fridge, I found a single egg, don't know from how long ago, but I used that too. Mixed it in, yolk in stringy clumps. I threw a spoon onto her bed, but when I came back in she was pushing handfuls of it into her mouth, then stopped and said she had no appetite. When she didn't touch it for another hour, I ate it for her. That also made me cry. Not there, with her, and not in her way. Mostly I made no noise.

Eventually, she asked me what was happening. She sat up, and started to lean forward, like she'd be able to reach to open her curtains. They were shower curtains. Plastic, shiny, with cartoon fish on. Kole had got them for free.

'What's happening?' she said again, her voice full of brakes. She moved her leg, and pain cut through her face.

'We're waiting,' I said.

'For what?' Her voice was still slurry, the side of her jaw was so swollen.

'Drink the water I got you. Don't look at me, just drink it.' She drank like a child, two hands around the glass. Some of it dripped down one side of her chin.

I watched the water fall. 'Don't you notice?' I asked her. I couldn't bear it any more. 'Why haven't you said anything?'

She looked at me. I looked at her. Each time he smacked her face like that it broke the other scars loose.

'It's quiet,' she said. 'It's gone quiet now.'

'You're not retarded,' I said. 'Speak properly. Who's not here?'

'Yes I know but—'

'Blue's not here,' I said.

'Viv . . .' she said after that. 'Is it Viv I gave him to?' She looked at me again. I could see fear heat her eyes. 'It's Viv, isn't it? Is that what I did?'

She started to cry. She had thought it was her fault.

I couldn't say anything. I should have. I didn't. I watched her eyes shut and then open again. 'I can't always see,' she said. This fogginess now. My eyes had water across them too.

294

'But he'll be back?' she said.

'Yes,' I said, 'we'll get him back.'

Earlier, I'd found a pack of cigarettes tucked in a dusty drawer, hidden from one of the times she'd tried to give up. I brought them into the bedroom. We smoked one lying on the bed, sharing her empty lunch plate as an ashtray. The cigarette had dried out and tasted like lead, but we finished it.

She shut her eyes and I could see her trying to let it take her somewhere else. I shut my eyes too, and tried to go with her.

So this is it, I thought. Until you come back, this is it. I made myself check the words you'd said, and then I let myself hear you say it. You said you'd come back. You promised.

Just before I drifted off again, I heard the sound of footsteps on the stairs. They came closer. Came to the door. 'Wait,' I said, as if she was going anywhere. And then there was a knock.

Davey's knock. I was almost sure of it – the one we'd made up as kids, the beat from a rap song we liked. Still, I picked up a frying pan on the way to the door.

'Who is it?' I said through the door. My throat felt unused to speaking, my ears weren't used to the sound of my voice.

'Who do you think?' he said, voice spaced out by the door. 'It's a badman robber.' He paused. 'Course it's me. Why you being weird for? Open up.'

I pushed away some of the barricade I'd made and got the door open a crack. Davey was trying to look serious, but he broke into the biggest smile when the gap was big enough for us to be able to see each other. He had chocolate bars in his hands. He held them out to me.

'Why you been hiding?' he said. 'It's alright out there. Or – not so bad. They've mostly gone now.'

He squeezed in, his snake hips sideways so I didn't have to move so much of the furniture, and he walked into the living room. 'Mother of God,' he said. 'You made it like a fortress.' He looked me up and down and I realised what I was wearing. The same T-shirt still, his T-shirt, and a pair of old shell-suit trousers that crinkled when I walked. He laughed when he saw the frying pan. 'Well, fuckin' hello!' he said. 'Don't I get a hug?'

There was a cut on his arm and he'd covered it up with silver duct tape. He poked his head through into Ma's room. 'Hello, Mrs Jas. Little fella around? Was thinking he must have been scared.'

'Not right now,' I said. 'Someone's looking after him. Is that chocolate?'

'Yeah.'

'Well you gonna open it or what?'

Davey fell back onto the sofa. He threw the chocolate into my lap, and pushed at his thigh to get rid of the acid feeling in his legs from the walk up the stairs, and was about to speak.

'Davey, before you . . .' It was just looking at him. Seeing him right there in front of me. 'I thought maybe you had . . .'

'What, died?' he said. 'Nah. Hey, don't do that! It's okay. Don't be silly. You're not supposed to be soft like that. Please don't.'

But I'd brought my knees up to my forehead, and when he put his arms around me too, the tears fell hot and bigger than I'd ever seen my tears before.

He sat with me for an hour. Fed me chocolate. Kept saying I was an idiot. I kept saying I was an idiot too, and that he was. I don't know why we said that to each other so much all through our lives. Maybe because we both always knew we weren't. Somehow he managed to make me laugh too. We both laughed. I can't remember what about. Fear, euphoria – they're weirdly close together sometimes.

Davey said it kicked off like this. That all the people at the Sands had started to leave in the middle of the night, that a whole string of blacked-out trucks had come for them. This must have been who you'd run away from to find me. But someone had given a tip-off, or the news got out somehow, and a group of men tried to block the convoy. 'Stood across the road,' Davey said. 'Kole was there. Did a good job, apparently. I don't know all the names, but I heard Dane Chambers, Leroy Fox. That lot.'

'How did they know to stop them?'

'Because it's not normal to do that. None of it's normal. Run like that. If those jokers are gonna up and leave, it should be us who's running them out. "Relocate." Fuck that. Like we're these little plastic pieces they can just sweep up. If anyone's gonna relocate, it should be us relocating them.'

Davey said our lot had their faces wrapped – balaclavas, bats – but it wasn't rough at first. But then someone from behind threw a bottle at the window of the official vehicle and that's when the others started shooting. Into the air at first, or at ankles, but when the boys didn't run away—'

'We didn't shoot, did we?' Your faces flashed into my mind. I kept trying to work out timings.

'What you going on about?' He looked at me. 'Why does it matter if we did? They came back with fucking helicopters after that. Them droney things.' He broke off a large hunk of chocolate, started sucking on it. 'Heard a head got chopped off. One of our lot getting their lot, I mean. Apparently he had to go at the guy for hours.' Davey did a sawing motion, smiling. 'Ten minutes, at least. Stamina! But no, we didn't shoot. Who round here has a piece? Not lying around, anyway.'

'Your teeth,' I said. Chocolate was blacking half of them out. I felt the sugar lift at the corners of my chest. Not a lot, but a little. He bent over and wiped his front teeth on the arm of the sofa.

'Happy now?'

It was hard to tell from Davey what it had really been like. One minute he was doing gun hands – the sounds too – the next, he was using his elbow to press down on his thigh because it had a nervous kind of twitch in it.

The first day of fighting, he said, was when the army was still there. The convoy had got out, but sent the army back. Dressed like the army, anyway. Uniforms, machine guns high to their chests. Not just in Margate, but in Broadstairs and Ramsgate, too, all through Thanet. He said they'd blocked off the roads leaving town. Huge concrete blocks, the ones they used to stop lorry attacks. That was when it had gone suddenly quiet.

'Our guys flared up a bit,' he said. 'Banged their chests a bit but then everyone went home.'

'But the sounds kept on. Sounded like World War Six.'

'Oh yeah, but that was just—' he laughed for real this time '—what do they call it? Pillaging.' He said the word like he was folding it. 'Where do you think I got this chocolate from?'

Davey told me he'd run into 'Nosey McWhatserface' on the way up and said we could go down and see her.

'Viv,' I said – my voice scooped up. 'Ma, though.' I pointed through to her tumbled-up body in the bedroom. She was lying half under, half out of the sheet. Her twiglet legs, empty hips. I'd try to clean her once or twice, but she was still in the same clothes she'd been wearing when Kole beat her.

'She's hardly going to wander off. Just come.'

Davey dragged the armchair more out of the way and opened the door for me. The staircase looked okay. A floor down, an open suitcase filled the landing, clothes scattered everywhere. For the first time in days, I stepped out of our front door.

'Wait,' I said. I thought about leaving you a note in case you came back, but how could I do that in front of Davey?

'It's not for long,' he said. 'Stop being a shaky little jitterbug.'

Viv had never hugged me before, but she did that day, so quickly she trapped both my arms in it. She grabbed the tops of my shoulders. 'We knocked!' she said. 'On the door. We thought you'd. Dunno what I thought.' She turned back inside. 'Robert! Look who it is.'

Bob was sitting on a wicker chair in the corner, reading an old magazine, no cover left. He didn't have a top on. His stomach looked like dough, had that same kind of stretch mark. I wanted to hug him too.

Viv gave us tea with no milk, even apologised for that. 'I think maybe we all done the same thing. Thought it was best to stay schtum.' She sipped. 'Put, I mean. What a fucking shit show all for nothing.' She looked over at her fridge.

'I got food if you need it, Viv,' Davey said.

'Not food, relocations. The number thingy.' Her letter was on the fridge, stuck down with a Seaworld magnet. 'Only show-off Tessy got to go. The priority lot went like that.' She clicked her fingers. 'No one else. Didn't matter if you had group one, group two. I found out what it was, by the way. The way they were doing the groupings.'

'Hardly matters now,' Bob said from the other side of the room.

'The priority lot were key workers,' Viv said.

'What, even Tessy?' I couldn't imagine her with a job.

'Used to be a carer. For some rich old bloke. So no wonder they thought she was "useful",' Viv said, pulling a face. 'Anyway. Number-one black mark against you was if you'd ever taken benefits.'

Davey laughed. 'Fuck off,' he said.

'Back in the day before Localisation, I mean. They looked at family lines and everything. If you'd taken too much social housing or disability or whatever.'

A teaspoon began to stir my belly. 'What do you mean, looked at family lines?' I said.

'Like, the history, I guess. The stats. Stuff like that. I don't know,' she said. Second, she said, was if you had a criminal record. 'Standard, I guess,' she shrugged. 'And third, if you'd never left. If you hadn't travelled round much, I mean.'

'If you didn't have a passport,' I said.

'Yeah.' She nodded. 'Some rubbish about not being ready for it, psychotically.'

'Psychologically,' I said. But the word barely came out. I'd started to feel sick.

'Like it would make you kooky in the head or something.'

This twisting through my body – was this what they'd done with your work?

Davey looked at me, then crossed his eyes. 'Glad we didn't waste our time then, eh, Chancey? We both tick pretty much every single box.'

'Let's go,' I said, tipping my head at him, not long after that. I needed to stop thinking about it. Until you could explain, I needed to shut my mind, shut it like a box. We went back upstairs to check on Ma. She was awake and Davey helped me lift her over to the sofa, so we could all sit together. He pulled another chocolate bar out of his pocket. This one was not so good. It had melted then reset, had that white fossilised look to it. We ate it slowly at first, then as there got less of it, we ate it faster and faster. I remember Davey touching Ma on the rounded bone of her shoulder, on a bit of skin that didn't have a bruise on it. 'I've given her all the goss, young Jas, so make sure she fills you in.'

After that, he carried Ma back to the bed in his arms, her hands wrapped around his neck. He put her down in a different position because he had noticed the bedsores all down the left side of her back.

'I'm sorry,' he said to me afterwards, 'about all that. That Kole did that. He's such a fuck-up. I always meant to say. If he ever tries again, I'll . . .'

'You'll what?'

'I would, though.'

'Thanks a lot,' I said. 'Now that he's gone.' But I was smiling.

Davey pulled at my T-shirt. 'Come on,' he said. 'Change that. You and me are going out. Smells like the menopause in here. Come. Outside. Into the world.'

*   *   *

Davey walked a tiny bit ahead, like some kind of tour guide. When we got out of the building he pulled off his shirt to show me his back. It had been so hot, he said, half his skin had fallen off. He rubbed at a bit now, and it came off in stretchy flakes, like the glue we used to let dry on our hands at school.

The sun after days inside felt like a shock. It burned so hard, the shadows it cut were the neatest lines. I could feel the light hit the back of my eyes. There was a tipped-over pram, seaweed on top of it, and up in buildings around us bashed-in windows, but the sea had carried most of the mess from the fighting away. It was so quiet, I felt braced for sudden sound. It's hard to walk normally, talk normally when you're doing that.

'Stop stepping weird,' Davey said, draping his T-shirt round his neck like a boxer's towel. 'It's only thieves about. And you're the worst of them.' He looked back for me. I was standing by a shoe, the laces caught on a bus-stop pole. He dropped back. 'Honestly, don't be wet. No one's going to touch you. You're Kole's girl.'

'You saw her knee. He left.'

'Maybe. But these fishes don't know that.'

The tide was low. The sand was the colour of dark cement. We walked along the parade.

'Feels like a ghost town,' I said.

'Exactly,' he said. 'Got the run of the place.'

All along the seafront were the barriers that had gone up while you were here. More rocks in wire cages. Barbed wire, too, on the parts that were dangerous to climb over. It wound and looped, looked like the ripples of a whip. The plastic bags tangled up in it looked like flags.

I stood there with Davey, and saw so many of the places I'd been with you. The Eliot shelter, the dipped, rusty roof of the Flamingo. I kept looking back at the building. Now everything had calmed down, I got it into my head you might be back at any minute.

The wind blew around us in a circle. The clouds were gold that day. And behind the clouds, this bright, milky blue, the colour of eyes you can't help but mention afterwards.

'On a good day . . .' Davey kept saying, his hands up around his temples like a frame. I'd heard people say those words so many times. On a good day, on a good day, on a good day. That on a good day, there's no place better in the world. 'On a good day,' he said again, and shook his head, holding his face up to the sun. 'More than that, old days again.' It looked like he might reach for my hand. 'Independence Day. For real this time.'

He crouched down and started to draw something in between a circle and a heart in the sand. Actually it was more like a skull. Hypnotic watching his finger cut a path through the sand.

'I can't stay,' I said. 'Can't stay out long.'

'Okay, but let's go see Caleb,' he said. 'Caleb at least. It would be rude not to.'

* * *

The green paint on Caleb's door he'd topped up so many times. I thought about my hand knocking when I was a child after school, Davey scuffling behind me and saying the snacks better be good today. We didn't want to ring the bell, so we tapped on the window instead. Silence.

Then, ear to the glass, the sound of someone getting off the sofa. After a moment, a hand moved the curtain back a sliver.

'Oh, it's you kids,' he said. The curtain fell. We waited for the door to open. He came to the door, opened it thin as an inch. 'You alone?' he said.

'Oh, don't you be a fruit too,' Davey replied.

When Caleb opened the door wider, there was a rifle in his hand.

'Fucking hell!' Davey said. He half got the giggles. 'The fuck is that?'

'It's sawn off.'

'I can see that.'

'Let me look.'

'Get off.'

The edges of the barrel were silver, rough cut. They snagged at the light. As Caleb shovelled us into his hall, Davey saw the rest of the barrel lying on the dining table. He walked straight through and picked it up.

'Can I have this bit, then?' He swung it in the air. 'Souvenir. Fucking heavy.'

'Why do you think I chopped it off?'

''Cos you're an OG,' Davey said. He did his MC at a rave voice: 'H'original gangsta.'

'Only problem is, you start to lose range. So when I shoot you with one of these,' Caleb said, 'I'll have to do it right up close.' He put the gun down on the table, his hand still firmly over it.

'Bet that bounces back like a bitch,' Davey said. 'Honestly, I'm impressed.'

'I was in the navy, you little twat,' Caleb said, 'don't be impressed with me.' I was laughing too by that point. 'Well, come and sit down then,' he said. 'Make yourself useful.'

Caleb opened wine. Didn't open it, it was already open. But he poured us glasses. Empties clustered round the bin like a stained-glass window. 'I couldn't get to the end of the street at first,' he said. 'Felt like being in the trenches. So go on then – what was all that about?'

'Oh mannn,' Davey said, taking a big gulp. 'Another regeneration down the pan. We're like Teflon. Just repel 'em off.'

'Teflon doesn't repel people,' Caleb said, grumpy but in a nice way, because it was part of the thing they always played – good teacher, bad student. 'An example of Teflon is a frying pan.' Caleb turned away; he turned to me. 'You okay, Chance?' he said. 'You seem quieter than usual.'

'Yeah, I'm alright. I'm okay, actually. I'll be fine.'

But the truth is, I felt more than alright. Somehow I'd started to feel good. I remember, even with the first sip, this feeling of relief, a warm cool wash. Glad to be alive. Glad Davey and Caleb were alive. Glad – I had started to feel glad again – for you.

I don't know how to explain it. Possibility was what I felt. Could it be possible? Possible it would all be okay. That I could still have you. That I would soon have Blue.

I realised later that perhaps if Caleb had poured me a second glass that full I would have told them. Not everything. But I'd have told them to be ready. In case somebody came back for us. Just in case, I would have said. Just in total case. But it would have felt good. I didn't say a word.

Caleb may have had his gun out, but when more and more people started coming out of their homes, no one was killing each other for a piece of bread. None of it was like that at all.

At first, the electricity was on pretty steady. Shaky-steady, but that was normal. Only foreign channels on the TV, but the lights were fine for weeks, actually.

On our way back from Caleb's, more than anything it felt like everyone on the street was smiling at each other, saying, How you doing? How's it going for you? Got what you need? Even strangers.

'Look at them all. They're nice,' Davey said, 'and here you are being all shy on the street. It's weird.'

'It's nothing,' I said. 'Just I feel bad.'

''Cos you said it was good? LandSave and everything?'

I couldn't look at him.

'Well, whatever,' he said. 'Don't sweat it, it's fine. It's like what Caleb was saying. It's just a power trick. The Black-Out Round 2. 'Cept this time we still have our fridges on. So it's winner winner chicken dinner.'

'Yeah,' I said.

'And how were you to know, anyway? All that matters is we're here. We're here aren't we?'

'We're here,' I said.

'Ain't no one going to make us leave.'

But when I got home, I packed a bag. Just for me at first. Underwear, random stuff. Then I repacked a bigger bag for Ma too, and some of Kole's clothes for Davey. I unfolded little scenes in my head then I folded them back up again. I thought about how you might come. By car, by convoy. I thought about Blue's face when he saw me again. I practised how I'd be with you. Unsure at first, then, when we were alone . . .

Even Davey. I was sure I could convince him to come with me in the end.

The only problem was how to say things until you got there. Particularly when Davey asked where Blue was, when we met the next day.

We were up on the train tracks behind the building. Half a boat had washed up there, or been dumped, and it was angled just right to give us shade. I was picking off ivy leaves that had started to grow inside it, seeing how many times I could bend them before they broke.

'Seriously,' he asked. 'If he wasn't with Viv that time?'

'Just with a friend, I said. I told you. Friend of my mum's.' My chest burned. I was fine at lying. Just terrible at lying to Davey.

Which is why it felt like a relief when suddenly we saw the planes. Heard them rather than saw them. That sucking sound, the way planes pull at the sky. We stopped talking. Then there they were: white, with bits of red on them, high enough and fast enough for us not to be able to read the letters on the side.

'Bloody hell,' Davey said. 'A royal flyover.'

When the planes were nearly above us, their underbellies opened. Two objects the size of cars dropped out. We both stood up. A second later, two parachutes unfolded with a clap. For a second, it looked as if whatever it was would head back into the clouds. Davey's body jerked as if he'd be able to reach it. Then the weight tugged at the string and the cargo started to fall again, in a diagonal direction towards us. The parachutes were satiny. They swelled up then sank small, like jellyfish, or skirts catching in the wind.

Then, about 100 feet up, some kind of netting burst open to set lots of small individual packages free. They blew apart from each other. I didn't even know what it was, but I knew I wanted it. We tried to predict where they would land. Davey and I split up. I found mine further down towards the water. Whoever was sending it must have worked out the tide wrong, because I saw a lot of packages bobbing in the sea. Still, both Davey and I got one each. He'd rescued his from someone's garden. We waited until we had found each other again before we opened them.

Each package was the size of a shoebox, red, edged with plastic popper wrap. 'So if it lands on your head!' Davey said, chucking his up in the air between us and almost heade-ring it, before taking out his flick knife and handing it to me. 'You go first,' he said, but there was no need for a knife. The box was sealed with Velcro. My hand pushed in past cello-phane, past the coolness of plastics and metal – you could tell how high up the plane had been from that.

'There's no note,' I said, and I couldn't hide the sadness in my voice. It's so stupid, but in my head, I was sure it had come from you.

'Why would there be a note?' Davey said. 'Give it here.'

He pulled out slices of white bread. Plastic sachets, crunchy to the touch. We broke a piece in half and shared it. There were packets of other things too. Pale raisins in one, mints in another, some sachets of powder which said ADD TO WATER. Two tins of paste-stuff. One had a fish symbol on it, the other had three different animals on it. Sheep, pig, chicken.

'What's that say?' Davey showed me the label.

'Farm spread,' I read off the side. 'Does not contain meat.' I pulled a question mark face.

We opened them both. Different colours of brown. One of them had a greenish tinge to the surface.

'Fucking hell. Has it come to this?' Davey said, but his smile was face-wide. He plunged a finger in, brought it up to his mouth.

312

I waited until he was about to swallow. 'Wonderful way to poison people,' I said.

'Yeah.' He pretended to spit. Licked his lips. 'That is what they'd do though, isn't it? Make it like a game. Make us fight for it.' He scooped up the last of the tin. 'Tasty, though. Not bad for a goodbye present.'

'It's not a goodbye,' I started, but—

'You missed it,' he said. 'Flat to the side.'

He pulled out a piece of paper. I froze. 'Let me see,' I said.

But he opened it away from me. He looked at it a while then started shaking his head. 'Such fuckers,' he said. 'It's not even them. The government, I mean. The LandSave lot. That's a cross, innit?' He handed over the paper. 'More bloody Christians.'

It had a red border. There was a cross, and there was a passage from Psalms in italic in the middle. I read the first bit out loud. 'For he will deliver the needy who cry out, the afflicted who have no one to help . . . Gross,' I said. I read the second bit in my head. *He will take pity on the weak and the needy and save the needy from death . . . for precious is their blood in his sight.* 'Yeah, Christians,' I said.

'What's the bit in red?' he asked.

'*Dios te bendiga*. It's a foreign language. Dunno how to say it.'

'Foreign where from, though?'

'I said I don't know. Italy. Spain. I dunno what that flag at the bottom is.'

'Fuck, man,' he laughed. 'You know it's bad if Spain is sending help.'

As he said that, a pair of older men walked by. They were ripping each packet open and jamming whatever it was into their mouths. We looked at them, then we looked at each other, and both of us knew what that look meant.

'We've got to get organised,' he said. And until I could include him in mine, I was glad I was included in his 'we'.

After the planes, a boy we all called Mac the Kid scooted round the concrete blocks and went as far as Monkton and back on his dirt bike. He never wore a helmet, just a backwards cap done up two further than the tightest ring because his head was so small, and when he came back, he said he'd seen what the sites had been building.

There was a group around him. Davey pushed into it.

'It's big boy, mate,' Mac told us. 'Three of you,' he said to Davey. 'Fuckin' eight of me.'

'You're a madman,' Davey replied. 'What if they'd had guns still?'

'I kept my distance,' Mac said. 'Snuck up, stayed far. Kind of like that spy way,' he said. 'But it wasn't even that what made it weird.' He made this sound, like the back of his throat was itchy and he was trying to scratch it. 'Do you know if they had them dig? Our boys down there? Do you know if they made them dig much?'

Because on our side of the wall, Mac said, it had been dug out. It was muddy, but more than that, it was deep. All along the wall, and that the water was only going to get deeper. He'd gone at low tide. I thought about what that boy Kent had said about the sites. That it was grunt work; foundations, a reservoir.

'That's mad,' Davey said, as we walked away. 'That's fucking mad. I knew it, though.'

'Knew what?'

'What I drew in the sand.'

'The skull thing?'

'It's not a skull thing. It's us. Here,' Davey said. 'What we'll be here.'

I looked at him. Dead was what I thought.

'Think about it,' he said. 'It isn't just a wall.'

'Sea wall,' I said. 'Sea protections.'

'Well, whatever you call it. It's not just a wall.' He looked at me. 'They've made a channel. They've dug the channel back.'

'What channel?'

'Don't you remember history?' he said. 'Roman days. Isle of Thanet.' He threw a pebble in the air and kicked it like it was a football. 'It's an island. We're going to be an island again.'

I don't know how many people Mac told, or if other people worked it out at the same time, but that night, the first yachts that could still float started to leave the harbour in Ramsgate. The people taking them weren't the people who owned them.

'A boat's a fucking boat, but take it where?' Davey said, feet up on our sofa. 'Where they gonna go? Bet they headed straight for Calais, the chumps.'

'That won't be good,' Ma said. 'Not after what we did to them.'

'You and me, Jas, we'd head to a deserted beach,' he said. He made the beach with his hand, fingers spread to be the sand. 'Hawaii, somewhere. Not that I'm leaving. Leave all this?' He looked at me. Then he put his arm around me, but it didn't land in the right places. 'No chance. No, Chance, right? This is home.'

And if I remember right, despite the packed bags under the sofa, I nodded.

It's the only way I understand it now. I thought the situation would end at any moment. Sometimes it grew inside me like a plant. This feeling of hope, the thought of you coming back, Blue in your arms. I slipped off to secret passages in my head. I'll come back for you. Wasn't that what you'd said?

But then a week passed, two. I tried to imagine instead what might be stopping you. I imagined you arguing with people. Arms blocking you. Doors being locked. And then, within the same second, I'd see you sitting back, playing with Blue, or worse, him nowhere near, and you not thinking about him, either. His teeth. I kept on thinking about how small they were, how he would get new ones. His head. Pushing my nose or my eye into his forehead. How he would hold things, the grip of all his fingers around one of mine.

Where were you now? What were you doing? Because the only scene I could play was you coming back. When I tried to imagine where you were, if that was London, I couldn't do it. I couldn't make up a room or a window or a day where you were, because I had no idea what they would be like there.

Davey and I started working in a mathematical way to get as many tins and cans as we could from the houses that were left. But it wasn't just us now. Everyone was doing it. Still, we'd had practice; we did it better, faster, more. All across my shoulders I had these tiny dots of blood, skin-prints from heavy bags.

'Stockpile,' Davey said, halfway up the stairs of the building one day. 'Stock market. We'll start a stock exchange. Oi, didn't you used to live in this one?' He nudged his foot against a front door.

'That one,' I said. I pointed across the way. 'Kole's HQ. Kem shop. Move, though. My fingers will drop off if I have to hold these any longer.'

I jogged the next few stairs so the pain would be over faster, and Davey stared at the door as we curved past it, so hard he nearly tripped on a step.

'Where is he?' Davey said then.

For a second I was certain he was talking about Blue. 'Who?'

'Kole. For real. It's been a while now. People been asking. And I heard a bunch of different stuff. That he was living in that castle on North Foreland. That some plane came for him. Jokers. Serious, though, do you know if he's dead or what?'

'I don't care if he's dead.'

'I know you don't care but it's shady, Cha. You're like a fucking lampshade sometimes.'

'Just leave it, I said.'

'Fucking dark, man.'

'Just stop for once. When I ask you sometimes.'

'I mean, it's a lot of things. Like where's Blue at?'

319

'Stop, Davey.'

'Why you looking like that? You don't have to make it weird. Just tell me where he is.'

'Shut up, Davey.' It broke in my throat. I sat down on the stairs.

'Chance,' he said. 'Get up.'

The bag with the cans tipped over. The metal clattered down the stairs. My heart felt like it did the same.

'Stop messing about,' he said. 'Say it, Chance, whatever it is. Scaring me now.'

How do you tell someone? How do you tell someone something like that? I said it quietly, made even quieter by it having to pass through the wall I'd made with my arms around my face.

'He isn't here,' I said.

'What do you mean he isn't here?'

'Someone took him.' That was how I said it.

'What?'

'Someone took him,' I said again. Davey was trying to peel my arms away so he could see me.

'What do you mean, someone? Who, Chance? Who, for fuck's sake?'

'It was night. It was the middle of the night.'

'What difference does that make!'

'They said they were saving him.'

'You're joking. Tell me you're joking.'

'It was when the fighting was starting. I didn't know what to do.'

320

'What do you mean, you didn't know what to do. Who? Who? Saving him how? Where were they going?'

'To someone in the thing,' I said. 'Someone who'd be safe.'

'The girl?' he said. 'The fucking girl?'

'She's going to come back.'

'You don't just let . . . You don't just let. Fuck's sake, Cha. Why would you do that?' The light changed. He'd walked away from me.

When I did look up, all the blood had left his face. Then he walked away further and punched a wall. Raised a fist and brought it down like a hammer. I'd never seen him like that. Both hands were up against the wall and he roared at it. He came back with a bleeding hand, then he put it to his mouth, and bit a small bit of flesh around it, to distract himself from the first pain.

He sat down next to me, this heavy body. He was silent for a long time, then he said sorry. Sorry he'd done that. Sorry for everything. His forehead found my arm. It's not your fault, he said, which was the thing that made it worse. We'll fix it, he said. We can fix it. Together we can fix anything.

The days after that passed slow and thick, ants in my legs, everywhere. Davey stayed with us for a few days, but he would barely speak. I saw him holding one of Blue's toy cars, pushing at it with his thumb and then putting it in his pocket. I wasn't supposed to notice.

He sent a kid who was hovering in the stairwell to pick up drugs. 'I don't give a fuck what you bring,' Davey told him, 'but bring something.'

'You've never been like this before,' I told him.

'It's you that's fucking weird. How were you being normal?'

'Because nothing's normal.'

'How come you didn't say?' he asked me.

Say what? That it was my fault? That it was okay, because I believed you'd be back?

'You're the one who doesn't make sense,' he said after that.

'And you do? What the fuck's that in your hand? You got some janky crack pipe now?'

'Honestly, whatever, Cha,' he said.

'Look at me a sec—'

'Just quiet,' he said, 'just for one moment as I take this.' He turned a quarter of the way away from me, and then he turned his whole back, and the one thing I heard was the rough-scratch spin of a lighter stone.

A second wave of people tried to leave by boat. It took less than a week for Ramsgate's harbour to empty. To empty completely this time, apart from the boats with holes in, though people were soon trying to fix those. We heard there were fights. People falling between boats and getting crushed, ribs poking through T-shirts, backwards knees, hulls stuck hard on the Goodwin Sands.

Back in Margate, from our window, I watched a family, kids in their arms, try to leave in a small blow-up dinghy they stole from one of the old tourist shops. They tried six. Half of them didn't blow up at all, and with the other half, the glue must have dried to powder. They fell apart in the water. The youngest kid had armbands, the other kid was holding onto a big, empty bottle.

'The one with the armbands was crying,' I said when I told Davey.

'What the fuck? Why didn't you stop them? Why didn't you wake me up?'

323

I told him they got 100 metres off the shore and then started to throw their bags out, as the boat started to fill with water. Eventually they kicked back to the beach, dragging what they could with them.

'Their feet were bleeding,' I said.

'Why are you saying it like that? You can't just sit here.'

'You're sitting here.'

'Stop letting people leave. What's wrong with you?'

'I couldn't leave you—'

'And kids too – are you a psychopath? Suddenly you don't give a fuck about anyone?'

'I was looking after you,' I said. But it sounded weak in my mouth, weak in the air between us. Yes, at moments, I'd kept water by his side, but apart from that I hadn't done much.

He was right. There was this block in my head. The flat dinghies. Ripped shoulders pulling their way back up the beach. It felt like I was watching a film. And it was the same when we started to hear about people leaving the other way too. Viv said someone got the concrete blocks off the main A-road out of town with a forklift truck. She said that one of the minibuses that used to be The Loop had started to make the journey up to the border.

'Apparently it's like a campsite,' Viv said, 'but if you were there for a holiday, you'd shoot yourself in the head.'

'Why the fuck are they trying to leave for then?' Davey asked Viv. It was what he kept on saying. 'What's wrong with it here? Why are they ruining it?'

'Shit overflowing from buckets,' Viv went on, 'rats with big fat tails like worms. Do you remember Misha? She went with her kids. Took a tent, but the ground's too soft to even bash the pegs in. Shantytown,' she said. 'Lots of Ramsgate lot there. Broadstairs lot. Our lot. Like refugees, but everyone white. I heard they shot at people trying to cross.'

'You heard or it's true?' I said.

'I heard and it's true,' she said.

But still still still I couldn't make the reality of it reach me. Not in the way it should have done. Part of it was because I was in two places at the same time. Here, the real here, but mostly there, far away with you and Blue. This escape I'd made in my head.

When anger came, when fear walked circles inside me, I would go to the China House. I would look at the music we listened to. I would lie in our bed. I would shut my eyes so hard that I heard white noise, and I would do that until the adrenaline fell out of my body and onto the sheets.

I thought about watching you sleep. How you made shapes with your fingers in the night, like you were conducting orchestras, but slowly, or putting your hands out to stop cars. Soft movements, deliberate. Your fingers long, not quite straight. How I kissed your hair away from your mouth. How you had actually been there.

I tried to remember what you tasted like. Clean, warm, moss, pink. Whenever I thought about something new, it could still whip through me.

And then, as soon as it did, the adrenaline would crawl back up, take over, feel worse, feel bigger, feel like my blood had turned against me.

My blood, my boy. His toys were still scattered around the flat. It was like there were force fields around them. I edged past. We all did.

I'd told Ma what had happened with Blue after I told Davey. She'd just nodded, kept on nodding. The relief, I think, of knowing it wasn't her fault.

'Aren't you going to ask me questions?' I said. At first I was angry. A fire growing at the back of my chest.

'But I trust you,' she said.

'How can you trust me?'

'Because look at me, Chance. My God I trust you more than I trust myself.'

'What do you think he's doing?' I asked her one day when the silence built back up again. 'My one,' I said. I tried to take her with me. 'Our one.'

She didn't say anything for a while, then 'Evacuee', she said. 'That's what they used to call it. I was trying to think of it for ages.'

'So you do . . .?' I said. Blanket of pain behind my eyes. Behind my whole face. 'You do think about him?'

'All the time.'

Salt, heat, tightness, in a rush as the tears came. I turned so she couldn't see.

'For what it's worth.' She touched the small of my back. I liked that that was the way to say it. I wanted to feel smaller than her for a second. 'I don't think you did the wrong thing.' Her thumb moved, then her little finger moved too, this soft one-two tapping. 'The thing that I always think is, you lot would have been better without me.'

It was the way she said 'you lot' that got me, that there had been more than just me. That there had been JD.

'So,' she said. 'You know.'

'Don't say that.'

'But it's different for you. It is – it should be. Because you were good.'

'Was I?' I asked. She'd never said that before.

'So good it made me jealous sometimes. Which is so dumb, isn't it.'

It hit me then. The unfurling again, like the light coming back on. If you were coming back, if you'd bring him back, if Blue would come back here, we had to make it decent. We had to make it good.

'I'm going to the roof,' I said.

'Don't you even think about it,' she said.

'Not to jump.'

'I'll kill you.'

'Not just yet, anyway.'

I set off up the stairs. At the very top, there was a window with a single fist punched through it, around it a rusty frame. I reached through, careful of the inside of my wrist,

327

and undid a bolt. I pushed it open and, foot perched on the handle of someone's door, I pulled myself up into the sky.

The wind caught in my T-shirt. Something about knowing how high up I was made my legs feel funny too, like I could trip up on air alone.

I was right. They were still there. For a while, when I was a kid, a woman in the building had built a garden on the roof. She'd been dead for years but the wooden planters were still there. And all around them, it looked like it had snowed – the whole roof was white with dried seagull shit.

I wanted Ma to see it. I went down to get her.

'Air's good for you,' I said. I put her arm round my shoulder to get her up the stairs, and this time, I propped the emergency escape ladder against the Velux.

'But my knee,' she said.

'Yeah well, it'll never heal right if you don't use it. Off you trot.'

' "Trot." Not a horse. Don't be rude.'

'I'll push you from behind.'

'Does it look straight to you?' she said, when we eventually made it. One side of the building, the one with all the rigged-up TV aerials, looked higher than the other.

'Leaning tower of Margate,' I said. 'But don't you see?'

'I see a dead penguin.'

'What?'

'I mean seagull. Whatever they're called. Hope it's nothing to do with that thing.'

'No, nothing to do with that.' I went over and lifted the dead seagull up by a big loose wing, then tossed it off the edge of the building. It fell in this slow circle. I turned back to the roof. It was about half the size of a football field. 'It's essentially a sea of shit up here,' I said. 'Which is perfect.'

'Right,' she said, sea legs swaying. 'Perfect for what?'

'Vegetables. Davey and I have been doing cans. But we need fresh stuff. For gangrene. To avoid gangrene.'

'The one where your legs fall off?'

'Yeah.'

'Scurvy.' She looked down at her tangled knee. 'Well I can hardly afford that, can I?'

'So are you going to help or what?' I said.

'Why are you being nice to me?' she said. 'You haven't been nice to me since you were about seven.'

''Cos I'm trying to get free labour.'

And so I started. I used a saucepan to get up as much of the shit as I could and get it into the planters. Funny what sticks from childhood. Caleb had told us about guano, using bird shit as compost, and I remembered because Davey always called it Guantanamo. Said Margate was Guantanamo Bay.

Even on that first day, before I'd really started, all these fantasies sprang up – you arriving and seeing green, having something good to give Blue to eat, that I could handle things, that I was strong, that I had something good, that I had something to give.

That night, I asked Davey if he wanted to help. His back straightened. He sat up, then asked, like I was a supermarket, 'Do you do carrots?'

'What do you mean, do I do carrots? I only went up there this morning.'

'Can you, though?' he said. 'Do carrots?'

'I don't know,' I told him, 'I can try.'

The next day, Davey came back with a bag of food scraps.

'Yes I know it smells,' he said. 'I went through bins for that.'

'Well, it's definitely organic.' I peered into the bag, saw a parsnip top, and an apple wrinkled to the size of an apricot.

'Dunno how you do it, so I got both,' he said. He threw what looked like playing cards at me. They made a maracas sound. Seeds. 'They went off about five years ago but I won't tell if you don't.'

'You're amazing.'

'Yeah, I know. But even superman's gotta have a break. You want?' His kem was rolled thumb-thick.

Ma was asleep so I said yes. 'Fucking hell, it's strong.'

'Yeah, it's not bang on, is it?' he said.

'What do you mean bang on?'

'I gotta go. I'll be back, though. Tell you what we're missing, and I need it, Chance, I really do . . .'

'What?'

330

He turned his mouth into a trumpet so he could do his posh voice, 'Purple sprouting broccoli.'

From abandoned flats below, I stole men's shirts for me and Ma.

'Gardening gear,' I told her. In white cotton, with the too-long sleeves rolled up to her wrists, she looked like a painter again.

I worked in bursts because of the heat. I watered all the time from the cracked-open fire hydrant at the foot of the building. There was pleasure in the pain of it. Carrying buckets heavy as rocks up all those stairs, my fingers squashing thin under the plastic, turning yellow with all the blood trapped in the tips.

Up top, I'd go to the edge and watch the waves. I'd watch them go white, go whiter, go even higher, break. Sometimes it felt like a siege, these crests of white, like rows of soldiers. I'd do the calculations. If I was on the beach for that, would I try to dive through it? Would I run?

'If it wasn't full of rubbish,' Ma said, deckchair tilting so she could see, 'you could probably surf one like that.'

'I'd like to see you try.'

'Do you remember that thing Thanet Earth?' she said. 'Nothing to do with the waves, just I was thinking. Biggest greenhouse in Europe or something, like a city. All for cucumbers.'

'JD took me there on his bike once, I think,' I said. 'Weren't there guards? Swear they nearly shot when we got close.'

331

'It's the light I remember,' she said. 'Spent an evening in Canterbury once. Not sure how I got there. One of those. But anyway, the guy was driving me back, and at one point he refused to go on. There was this orange light on the horizon, crazy big. I remember, he was like: "Fuck that. I'm not driving towards the apocalypse." But it was just Thanet Earth. They kept the heat lamps on all night.'

'This is what I mean,' I said. 'People'll do anything for vegetables.'

She nodded. She tucked her feet under her, so they were out of the sun. 'I like it up here,' she said. 'Thanks for this.'

'My pleasure.'

'In a way, it's like therapy.'

'Course it is if you're reclining in your chair with a parasol.'

'It's my leg!' she said.

But she was right, it was nice. Nice to have her there even if she didn't help much. Her knee was healing with all these cracks, like an egg stuck back together, but something about her was softening again. And not in that sloppy way. Tender for being tender, not because she wanted something.

In the evenings, when we got back to the flat, she'd kiss my head, tell me it smelled of olives and cooking, nice things. And up on the roof, it was easier to speak to each other than it had been for years. Something about our hands being busy, our backs facing each other.

One afternoon, I just came out with it. I asked her why it had got so bad. There was silence at first.

332

'Not in a mean way,' I said.

'No, I know,' she said. 'I'm thinking.'

I waited. Pushed the earth tighter into a pot.

'Because it starts as fun,' she said. 'It starts as living. It started as all this life, Chance. Does that make sense? When it feels big in your chest?'

I had my back to her. I nodded.

'Some people do it 'cos they're depressed. I thought I was different. I did actually feel happy. I do think I did. It's just the line,' she said. 'It always got a little rubbed out for me.'

'And Kole?' I said. Again, it was only because I had my back to her. 'I never got it. You stood up to Liam. When he got weird and everything, you left him.'

'I did.'

'Then Kole . . .'

I heard her breathe out. 'They say there's a person for everyone,' she started.

I was about to turn round. I couldn't bear for her to say that still.

'It's true. There's a person for everyone who will completely break them. He was that person for me. I could never say no to him. No matter what. No matter what. I never could.'

I nodded.

'I'm so glad that's never happened to you,' she said.

I nodded again. But that's exactly what had happened. That was exactly what it had been like with you. I still

333

couldn't understand it. How our bodies could know something is wrong for us and do it anyway. Do it, and do it, and do it again.

Up on the roof, the sun was strong and we used shower curtains to cover the patches when it stormed. Gradually, something started happening: it wasn't too long before we had the beginning green of new leaves.

Then one day, a little kid pushed his way up onto the roof. A runner.

'The lady said you was here,' he said.

'Who's the lady? Who are you?'

'What you got here?' the boy said, looking round the roof, eyes wide. 'This is mad, fam.'

'Oi, don't touch. What do you want?'

'You know a Caleb? Said he wants to see you.'

'Is he alright?'

'You live up high, man, you got anything extra? Long,' he said. 'Long to get up here.'

'Is he alright, though?' I said. 'Oi, stop, is he hurt?' I shouted after him, but he just shrugged as he ran off.

The water was high as I made my way to Caleb's. When I got there, the door was open.

335

'Finally,' he said, when he saw me.

'You're alive!' I said back.

'I've been trying to work it out,' he said. I followed him into the kitchen. He'd been drinking. There was a cloud of booze in his wake. 'The point of it all,' he said.

'The point of what?' I said. 'Life?' My hands were covered in dirt. I made my way to his sink. 'You look thin. Not boylimic are you? Eating okay? Can tell you're drink—'

'LandSave,' he said. 'The LandSave people. Who they were, why they were here.'

I turned back from the tap.

'I had it all in front of me all along,' he said.

'Do you remember a man called Rex Winstable?' Caleb asked me.

I found myself nodding. I did know that name.

'Hugely powerful at one time,' Caleb said. 'Classic upperclass Nazi sympathiser.'

'My grandad liked him,' I said. I thought back. 'It was him that paid for us to come here. Or not him but his – I don't know what they call it . . .'

'His foundation?'

'Some money thing, yeah.'

'Right. Well, every year, the think-tank arm of it used to do this essay competition. Sounds pointless, but it was big. Controversial, high profile, huge prize money, launched careers. Anyway, follow me—'

Caleb pushed past me, and went upstairs. I'd only ever

been upstairs at his house once or twice. Up on the first floor, the walls were lined with even more books than down below, floor to ceiling in thin, different-coloured slices. He led me into a room. There was a table in the middle of it.

There were three books on the table, each one a different colour. A simple embossed title, *The Right is Revolutionary Essay Competition*, volumes I, II and III, and under that, the year each one was published.

Caleb put his finger on one. 'Guess who won in this particular year?' he said, tapping on the date.

'How am I supposed to do that?'

'A young man called Edwin,' he said. 'Edwin Meyer.'

I reached for the book. 'Let me see.'

'Wait. I need to explain first. I always followed Winstable. Found him interesting. Don't know if you ever saw him on TV, but he was bald, charmless, kind of thumping, you know? Edwin Meyer on the other hand . . . he had something else. Ease,' he said. 'This ease. Everything Winstable didn't have.'

'So they fought?' I said. 'After this prize thing?'

'The opposite. Winstable made him his protégé. But it wasn't long before Meyer was calling the shots.'

'Okay . . .' I said. 'What do you mean, though? Protégé like how?'

'It set a whole different thing in motion. I'm convinced Meyer was the one who got Winstable to push for Localisation. And it worked. It was kryptonite. It cleared the path for Meyer to take over.' Caleb was speaking really fast. There were patches of gluey stuff on the corners of his mouth.

'Meyer's policies were even worse. Toxic. But the way he said them . . . The man could sell a new son to God.'

'But my mum liked him,' I said. 'Lots of people did. My mum's not racist, she's not anything like that.'

'I'm sure she's not. He's just one of those people. Nothing sticks. Anything that's bad, he'd say was a joke. He got away with everything. Topped lists of people you're not supposed to find attractive but do. All this call-me-by-my-first-name, I'll-drink-a-pint-with-you man of the people bullshit.'

'Action Man,' I said.

'Exactly. Because he says things and then does them. Or, in this case, he does things without saying them.' Caleb had the book in his hand. 'This edition is incredibly rare. That's why I kept it. Meyer tried to get it out of print. He had every single copy he could find pulped. He said it was just an intel- lectual exercise – that he was extremely young. Pushing extrapolation to its limit. All this rubbish. But if you look at what's happening now, it's all here, I swear to God. It's the blueprint for what they've done.'

'What does it say?'

'He pitched it as an ethical ideal. Moral, environmental, you name it. Every kind of ideal.'

'Pitched what, Caleb?'

'Population cutback,' he said. 'Extreme population cutback. Too many people. Too many migrants. Too many everyone. He suggested countries took matters into their own hands. You remember that guy in Japan, who gassed a whole load of kids?'

'A bit,' I said. 'Not a lot.'

'In this essay, he calls that "a landmark undertaking". In other words, a good start.'

I felt suddenly like I was watching myself from above. Like I was this small thing tucked against the ceiling. I imagined the tops of our heads.

'And if he has power now . . .' Caleb said.

'We know he has power now.'

'That's his thing. Reduce populations. Make sure only the "best" survive. They're academics, the people at the very top. He's pals with Nobel Prize winners. They don't have the manpower, but they think they're clever. They *are* clever. I mean, who built the wall?'

'We did,' I said. 'They got us to finish it ourselves.'

'If you think about it, it's a masterpiece,' Caleb said. 'Send all your undesirables to the edge of the country. Then get them to dig like animals until it becomes an island again.'

'But someone will stop it,' I said. 'They have to.'

'Who? The government? He *is* the government. The rest of us left here? We're under clear instructions right now. What we're supposed to do now is die.'

'But I don't want to die,' I said. My voice sounded like the smallest thing.

'Well, neither do I. But the whole thing's set up against us. To look like our fault. When we die, it's their proof. That we were just deadweight all along. I mean, just look at this bullshit.' He opened the book to the title page of the essay.

'Countering Dysgenics to Save the Planet,' he read. 'The Radical Next Battles of the "IQ" War.'

'Dys-what?' I said.

'Dysgenics. Opposite of eugenics. Opposite of natural selection. It's about the population getting – quote-unquote – worse.'

Caleb started reading from the opening paragraph. Suddenly, I was no longer up on the ceiling. It was like the walls and the whole house above me were all falling into me at the same time. I pulled the book away.

'Can I just think please?' I said. 'Leave me a moment. I want to read it for myself.'

I sat with the book, my back to the wall, the spines of other books pressing into mine. There were italics at first. A footnote said it was from his acceptance speech.

There's a conversation happening as we sit here today. You've heard it yourself. You've had it yourself. Today, as I accept this prize, it is clearer to me than ever we have no choice but to make our voice louder. These conversations must emerge from darkened rooms. They deserve the light. They are, after all, the only thing that will save us.

By now, it is clear to scientific communities at large that we are far too many, and thus, our days remaining on this planet too few. But what can be done, they ask? What actions can be considered 'humane'? Who, they ask, has a right to play God?

They are making a mistake: It is not a right. It is a duty.

I turned the page. I read the essay in bursts, my finger following the lines.

We stand in a world facing a catastrophe the likes of which history has never seen. Lacerating, unpredictable weather patterns due to climate change. Food shortages across the Americas reminiscent of the dust bowl. Africa's growing desert shifting the patterns of human settlement that have existed for millennia. The ever-hovering threat of more, and more deadly, pandemics; social unrest, or even war due to dwindling resources. The public demand for solutions has never been more acute.

And yet politicians stand idle. The failure to respond is down to our refusal to look, with clear eyes, at the root cause of the problem: devastating overpopulation and, most importantly, its culprit.

Many of us have understood this crisis, and acted accordingly. In the past 20 years, birth rates among educated Britons have dropped by an estimated 41 per cent. Foster and adoption rates are on the rise. The picture of a British family has changed drastically in many parts of the country – we have taken action.

Some brave leaders have gone even further, pushing forward the politically sensitive but ultimately necessary decision to make it easier for those nearing the end of their lives to choose their departure from the earth. The work of End-Life has made impressive progress in making it possible for people to give the gift of the last few years of their lives, and the resources they would consume, to future generations.

But it is not enough.

Those economically active citizens among us who have made countless sacrifices – perhaps the large family they'd imagined as a child, a single infant of their own, or the last few years with a grandparent – continue to fall prey to the poor decisions of some segments of society. These segments of society ignore the research, refuse the family-planning services offered by our government and, ultimately, put the future of humanity at risk.

Let me paint a picture of this segment of society that I'm describing. Offered a free and comprehensive education by the state, they fail to make use of it; pregnant with or 'fathering' their first child at sixteen, with no plan, no income and no stability, they choose to see the pregnancy to term. Thus begins the process of generational dependence on the state. Offered the open arms of our NHS and the gift of free education, they take without giving – and teach their children to do the same.

We can no longer afford to be hamstrung by the Marxist demand to accept, embrace and support all ways of life. In the past, we may have felt pity for the segment of society that I've just described. Indeed, over the years 'pity' has elicited increasingly elaborate fiscal responses. But, if anything, what initial governmental responses to SARS-CoV-2, for example, made clearer than ever is that a profligate welfare state is merely a recipe for self-destruction

– a recipe for increased reliance, pitch-black apathy and a soaring debt shouldered by the rest of us.

These matters are, as we know too well, interconnected. Population density puts us all at greater risk. And yet, this selfish behaviour continues unabated.

This blinkers-on approach which has defined public policy for years is no longer morally acceptable. Ultimately, our responsibility is to our own children, and to our children's children – should there still be a world left for them. It's time for bold thinking and the courage to act in the best interests of humanity as a whole. We can see what the problem is – we now have a moral obligation to solve it.

I therefore propose the following steps to immediately and significantly address the crisis of overpopulation:

1. Differentiate segments of society to enable targeted policy responses. This is not a question of class, or wealth, but of decisions: are these citizens making decisions in the best interests of society as a whole, or are they making decisions based on their immediate personal interest? Technology allows us to look at predictors of family size. Such assessments should be used to identify high-risk households for population contribution and dependence on shared resources. This would give us a unique opportunity to offer heightened medical measures, such as selected sterilisations and alternatives, in anticipation.

2. Remove the state support that enables high-risk segments of the population to reproduce unabated. Regarding the previous statement, in incarceration zones, for example, sexual neutralisation programmes would likely have myriad positive effects.

3. Empower at the earliest opportunity local management of resources. People will only make decisions in the best interests of their communities when the consequences of their actions are felt. Today, London and the home counties provide tax wealth that is distributed throughout the country. Those on the outer edges of society reap the benefits, without contributing in a meaningful way to the financial cost. A locally managed tax system would allow people to be more directly involved in the political decisions that affect their lives.

4. Take steps to protect those who have the best interests of society at heart. Ambitious social organisation programmes, identification systems and new infrastructure protecting our principal cities can help pave our return to the order which correctly dominated previous societies for millennia: natural selection favouring intelligence, talent, aspiration, character.

There was more and more and more. I turned the page to the last paragraph.

It can no longer remain the 'un-sayable'. It must no longer be the 'un-doable'. It is, in fact, a unique opportunity. Both to save the ecosystems we live in, and in doing so, reverse the cognitive decline which has held our planet and its societies to ransom for too long. Measures must be taken to eliminate the spiralling reproduction of those who contribute the least to society, yet take the most from it. They must be taken without delay.

I wondered if I would be sick. As I read it, I felt a finger pressing at the back of my throat. I thought about what the man at the Sands had said. 'It will save lives. Lives that need to be saved.'

I took the book back downstairs to the living room, where Caleb was. 'Can I take this?' I said, and as I said it, the book fell open in my hand to the back page.

Meyer's author photo. He was much younger, wearing a crewneck jumper. He was smiling, and even though it was black and white you could tell he was standing in front of a sunset.

Edwin Meyer PhD MSc Oxon was educated at Harrow, Oxford, and Columbia, where he graduated summa cum laude, and received the Nelson-Wright Prize for Excellence. A regular contributor to various acclaimed publications, he lives in London, with his wife, fellow academic Dr Jane Meyer, and their young daughter Francesca.

It took a moment to understand. I read the last sentence twice.

I looked at his picture again. It was his nose, it was something in his eyes. It was his confidence.

Francesca. Their young daughter Francesca.

'No,' I said. The word fell out of me, it spread like ink in water. You'd said your mum was a doctor. 'My dad is . . .' you'd said. 'My dad is . . .' I should have let you say it. I saw it now.

'He has a daughter,' I said. 'He has a daughter. I think I know her,' I said. 'She was here.'

It happened when I walked outside of Caleb's front door that day. Just like that, the film lifted. Film like cinema. Film like a layer in front of my eyes. I let myself see. I saw it all.

I'd told people LandSave was a good thing. When Davey had wanted to fight, I'd made people stop. I'd done that because of you. I'd done it all because of you.

All these things started to come together, then fall apart. The car you'd arrived in, the reason those boys chased you. Meyer had been in Ramsgate that day. You must have been with him just before you met me. The boys Davey had seen beaten on the street – were they the same boys? Had you found a way to make them pay?

All of it – the cheap booze, the sudden money, the distraction. And how long ago this had all started. With Localisation, but even before then – with records of who had taken benefits, who had never left. And later, your part in that. What you had done. Your research, your data, whatever it was you'd been doing. More and more kept coming – JD, the shots he'd been given that had made him soft, made him—

The pain in my chest felt like a hammer landing.

Blue, Blue, Blue, Blue, Blue. Where had you taken him? Why had you taken him?

More unbearable still – how could I have let you?

Back at the flat, the sun beat at our windows so hard I was sure it would crack the glass. The fight beat harder in my head. It was all the time now. My eyes were closed, and I did rings with you in the dark. I broke open old conversations, shouted questions I should have asked.

I could finally imagine your house. It didn't matter what it looked like. Just a big house and you there. I imagined seeing you from behind and putting my arm around your neck and stopping you breathing till you told me where he was. I imagined holding your head against the floor, forehead making sounds against marble, until you said sorry. Asking you how much you'd known, again and again, until you told me everything. The scenes I made got worse and worse. I'd wake up with blood under my fingernails, from scratching at my head, my arms, my legs.

At home, I fought with everything. Fought with you, fought with guilt, fought with my mum again. I even fought with Davey when he said I'd had enough kem.

'I think it, Jas thinks it,' Davey said. 'Sitting there looking like a proper mong, Cha.'

'You can talk. You did this for weeks.'

'Yeah but you're a girl. It looks shit on a girl.'

I sat up.

'See – that woke you.'

'Idiot.'

'You like my shoes?' he said. They were brown, leather, new looking. The tip of both toes pointed in the same direction. 'Both of them are left feet! Nice, though,' he said. He did a little tap dance. 'Guess how much?' He didn't wait for me to answer. 'For free, motherfucker!'

He told me stuff was washing up on the beach. More than usual, and not just driftwood. Boxes that must have fallen from ships. 'Bananas today,' he said. He pointed to the cluster of yellow on the table. 'Brought that back, look. It's properly mad.'

My stomach turned like a wave. I thought about the super-tide warning signs they'd put on the posters. Water rushing away from us. Open pockmarks in the sand. Changes in the tide.

'Come down to the beach,' Davey said. 'Just a little day trip to the sea.'

'I can't.'

'Oh yeah, 'cos you're running a Footsy 500 company up here, aren't you.'

'Shut up.'

'I'll carry you, you idiot. I'll do whatever, just eat one and come.' He grabbed two bananas from the bunch of yellow on the table and handed them to me still attached at the husky stem. Salt had got inside the skin. Still. The feeling of peeling them open. Soft against teeth.

'Look at that,' he said, chewing his own with his mouth open. 'You can't even hide it.'

'What?'

'You're grinning. It's like you're going to explode with happiness.'

'I'm not,' I said, but it was true, he had made me smile even a tiny bit, for the first time in days. 'You seem perky,' I said.

'Yeah, 'cos I got my friend back. Got her eyes open, at least.'

'Idiot.'

'You got nice eyes.'

On the way to the beach, we vaulted the leaking plastic flood blocks.

The tide was out, and he was right – boxes were tumbled all along the empty sand. The cluster closest to us was plywood crates. As Davey prised one open, I walked over to some smaller squares of damp cardboard. All the ink had washed off the side. I scratched off loose Sellotape, pushed a side open with my knuckles, and pulled out one of the small objects inside.

It was a baby's bottle I ended up holding. There must have been twenty, thirty in the box, the same shape and colour as the one that we'd had for Blue. Ma used to fill ours with powdered milk. She said it would be weird if I fed him myself. I'd tried to anyway, just once, when we were alone one time, but it had hurt so much.

As I held it, the bottom of my belly felt like it was being scraped in some way. This emptiness.

'What's that face for?' Davey said, then he looked down at what I was holding. 'Okay, so bad luck on box one, but – hey.' He reached for my waist, then squeezed my earlobe when we were face to face. 'I've got something for that. You know I do. Got tons of the stuff.'

'I can't,' I said. 'And I can't pay. I don't have any money to pay. I told you that before.'

'You don't have to pay. It's me. When have I ever asked you for anything?'

But it wasn't that. It wasn't that at all.

What was I doing? What had I been doing? There was only one thing that was important. It didn't matter why you'd taken him, it didn't matter if you'd wanted to help, if you were good or bad, if you'd known what your dad was doing. Only one thing mattered – I had to get Blue back.

'I have to go,' I said, and I meant it in every way.

Davey looked at me. 'You've heard then, have you?' he said.

'Heard what?'

'You'll hear from someone soon, anyway.'

'What?'

'Some lads have arrived,' he said. 'They reckon they can get people out.' I looked at him, and he looked at me. 'Don't do it, Chancey,' he said. 'I swear down it's a trap.'

352

A couple of them sounded like they were from other countries, but they always had at least one person with them who spoke English. I didn't see them all. One lot said they had boats parked up in Pegwell Bay – speedboats, lifejackets, the whole works. Another came with a coach. A shitty coach with broken headlights, and a driver with a twisted body, his torso two-thirds of him, vodka on the dashboard.

The whole scene looked desperate. I suppose it had spread out everywhere we couldn't. Desperation, I mean. It moves through walls. It's the kind of thing you can smell across the sea.

'What people?' Ma said when I told her about the men who'd come.

'Not official people. Smugglers. I don't know. Gangs.'

'From where?'

'Dunno, I said. The other side of the wall.'

'Well, how are they getting here, if we can't get there?'

'I'd guess that's their whole marketing plan.' I found myself taking a breath. 'Listen,' I said, 'serious for a second. If we could, would you want to?'

'I thought you said Blue was coming back here?'

'Well, I think the plan might have changed.'

All I needed to know was that it was safe. It had to be better than waiting. What Caleb had said played again and again through my head. What we're supposed to do now is die. But I couldn't just die. I refused.

The first person I knew who left was Lace. Lace, no rings on his fingers now, said it was a lot cheaper if you didn't bring anything with you, and he left without even a backpack. I asked him to find a way to tell me if it was safe.

'Yeah,' he said, 'but how?'

'Just please,' I asked him, 'if you can.'

I tried to speak to one guy, stacked, not an inch of fat, and asked if we could pay when we got there. He laughed at me. Then he looked at me.

'Other ways to pay,' he said. Underneath his eyes was as yellow as smokers' fingers. They looked rubbed with Vaseline.

'For how many people?' I said.

'How many people you bring?' he said. 'Or how many people I bring?'

I didn't say anything.

'Don't you be worry,' he said, after that. 'Water warm if you fall in.'

I walked away and was stopped by Davey.

'Were you talking to him?' he said.

'No, we were just standing in front of each other in silence. What do you think? Why are you following me?'

'Were you talking to him?' he said again.

'You're not my dad.'

'Tell me not you,' he said. 'Please tell me not you too. I know you said before but I thought you were joking.'

'I don't have any money,' I said. I couldn't look at him.

He reached for my cheek. Made it so I was facing him. 'If you see anyone else who's leaving, you tell them to stop. Please, Cha. You promise me that.'

'Why, Davey? Why won't you stop? All this fucking Planet Thanet till I die thing – it isn't working.'

'It's not that,' he said. 'It's not even that this time. It's just that all this "get you out" shit – it's a fucking lie. No way it isn't lies. Have you heard what these people are saying? That they're going to step off the coach and straight into a job. Spoke to one woman. She had a fucking child with her.'

'She's hardly gonna leave her child behind.'

'She said their lorry had a metal-lined box in the back for them to sit in. To check there's not too much breathing. Checks at the border or something like that.'

'Good if they're being careful.'

'It's not careful! It's not about care. It's just so they die quicker. They'll be dead before an hour's up. Don't you see, mate? They're paying to die.'

'Why you calling me mate?'

' "Smugglers" got some clout to it. Sounds piratey, decent. But this lot are basic fucking crims. Look at them. Where the hell do they have to take people?'

But I didn't care what Davey said. If I could balance the risk right, I should take it. I was sure, right then, that this is what the money from our money box was supposed to have been for. I pictured it in my head, remembered counting the money, tried to remember how much there'd been, planned what we'd have done with it.

Sometimes it felt so simple. It hit me clean, like a clear bar of light. Go on and fuck the guy, fuck whoever you need to, just fucking go.

But the day I decided to do it, they found Lace on the beach. His skin was white, looked loose, like a case around his body that was too big for him. There were open cuts across the side of his head, this roundness to them, like they'd come from a blunt instrument.

And it wasn't just Lace. Other bodies started washing up on the beach too. Bodies we recognised, others we didn't. There was even one that had papers from Iceland on it, in a waterproof pouch strapped round the waist. He was grey on the sea steps, others were spread heaps on the sand. It didn't matter if you could see it, you'd know when one was close. The smell of bad fruit, rotten flower water, meat, shit, but so much worse that it filled up your whole mouth.

One day, the morning after a big storm, another body washed up. Even if this body was curled up in a heap at first, this body turned onto all fours and coughed a lot. There was water, sand, blood in the cough – but this person was alive.

A group of men made a circle around him as he came round. He was black, his skin was dark on the wet concrete sand. When the man could talk, he shouted. It wasn't English. That was when one of the men closest to him punched him in the head. His lip split open and a tooth came loose, more blood in the sand.

I was with Davey on the beach that day. When we saw what was happening, we ran. Davey got there faster than me. He pushed his way into the middle of all of it. The man was bleeding in these long strings from the mouth, and his face was almost too swollen to speak.

'What d'you fucking want here?' one of the men circling him was shouting. He had a piece of driftwood in his hand. It was covered in bent nails. 'He's Jamaican or something, int'he?' He was going to hit the man on the sand with the wood when Davey pulled him out of the way.

'What you going on about, Jamaican?' I said. 'They speak fucking English in Jamaica.'

'African cunt, then.'

'You're a fucking idiot,' Davey put his body between the two men. The man on the beach was on his knees, his hands in a prayer in front of him. He carried on speaking.

'He's speaking French maybe,' I said. 'Something like that. I don't know.'

'If he's speaking about me . . .' the man with the wood said.

'It's not about you,' Davey started. 'He doesn't give a shit about you. No one gives a shit about you.'

'I'll slice his fucking heart out.'

Davey got to his knees beside the man. 'Listen, I don't know what you're saying,' he made a cross over his mouth with his hands. 'We don't understand. No comprendo? I don't know.' He turned to me. 'You sure it's French, Cha? Does Caleb do French?'

The man started to look like he was allergic to his own skin, like he might pull it off. A white, dry rash was all across his stomach. He'd been in the water for so long his skin looked like a thumbprint. Parts of it starting to rise up in patchy welts.

'What's he asking for? What's he saying?' the man with the plank in his hand said.

'Don't be dumb, I'm sure he wants to get the water off him. He wants a fucking shower.' Davey looked at him, looked at the wood. 'What's wrong with you? Don't you know anyone who left?'

'Yeah – got a cousin who went. Cousin and her kid. Paid for it myself, din't I?'

'And what did you want? What were you hoping for when they got somewhere?' Davey helped the man on the beach stand up; he had the man's arm across the back of his neck now and was holding him up like that. 'If you see anyone out there who needs help, we should be charging out into the water to get them.'

We took the man to Caleb's house, each of his arms over one of our shoulders. He was all bones, not heavy at all, sometimes his feet walked, sometimes they stopped and we carried him.

I remember not knowing what to say, and saying stupid things like, 'Caleb's really nice, so don't worry.' 'You're okay now, buddy, you're okay,' Davey said at the same time.

When he got to the door, Caleb looked thin too, even thinner than last time. He'd put string through his belt loops.

'What are you doing?' he asked us.

'He came up on the beach. Some dickheads found him. Do you speak French?'

'I did.'

'Well, is this French?'

Davey gestured that the man should talk. When he didn't say anything, Caleb said: 'Français? Vous parlez Français?'

'Français, oui, oui, oui.' The man took Caleb's hand. 'Mais pas de France.'

The man was shivering.

'You need a bath,' Caleb said. 'Bain, pour laver?'

The man nodded. Then he turned to us and started almost crying.

'What's he saying?'

'He's saying thank you,' Caleb said. 'I'll get him water. I'll make sure he eats. Leave him here. I have space. I'll get him fixed up.' Then he turned to me: 'Where have you been? I've been worried.'

'I've been—'

'She's been bad but she's getting better,' Davey said. 'We'll get her better.'

On the way home, Davey said the bodies on the beach were proof that what had happened to us was happening every-where. That we were right to have stayed. 'Gotta run and drop something off, but I'll come by for dinner,' he said.

'What dinner?'

'Not fussy, you know me. A carrot or two will do.'

'You heard the storm last night. It's fucked the garden for weeks.'

The wind was so loud, had branches in it, bins, constant smashes of sand, that Ma had suggested we each slept in a different door frame in our flat. In the morning, some of the wind turbines out at sea had lost propellers. They looked like daisies with their petals ripped off.

'I'll bring something then,' he said.

'Nothing fancy,' I said. 'Just a starter, main and dessert.'

'Dude paid with this,' Davey said that evening when he arrived at our flat.

'Who did? Paid for what?'

Davey slapped something hard and wet, wrapped in cling film, onto the table. It was a red colour, fleshy. 'Whale!' he said, like he'd made it himself.

'So dumb,' I said. 'Literally the stupidest man I ever met.'

'Shit you not. Huge one washed up in Westgate. Maybe not a whale-whale, but big enough. People were carving shapes in its side. Kind of like graffiti. Smelled bad.'

'Delicious.'

'It'll be like tuna! Whack it in a pan. Chicken of the sea.'

It shrank and tasted like tyres when we cooked it, but we ate it straight from the pan, nothing else on the side.

'Here,' Davey said, after we'd nearly finished, when Ma went to the loo. 'If you want your meal to be balanced.' And he unwrapped his second parcel – a huge mountain of kem.

Sometimes you look at someone – you look into their face – and, like a Rubik's cube, it all falls into place. 'What did you mean before?' I said. '"Dude paid with this"?'

He shrugged. But I knew.

It was our old flat – our first one, four floors down – where Davey had been spending his time. The flat where JD and Kole had started their business. That was the reason why he'd been sleeping on our sofa so much. All that kem he had, he'd been making it himself. In the old bathtub, with their pots and their pipes.

'It's not like you don't have some,' he said, 'if it's there.'

'Yeah, but to make it. To make more. To sell it to people.'

'Oh, whatever. Stop though.'

'How, even?' I said.

''Cos it's a ghost, mate, the stuff you need to make it. It's like Casper. Moves through any old wall.'

'Don't smile like that. It's what happened to JD, to my mum.'

'Stop,' he said again. 'You're being too much now.'

'It's not too much.'

'It is, though. The way you're looking at me.'

That night, in the pitch-black semi-cool, Davey moved all Kole's equipment back to his old glazing workshop.

I told him not to. I tried to block him in the door. 'Stay the night. Please Davey, come see Caleb with me in the morning.'

'It's not just you,' he said. His cheeks were red. 'I been thinking, too. I've cared what you think too long, and where does it get me? I'm trying to do good, and you're making me feel bad.'

'But Davey—'

'You do it too much,' he said.

'Has he left too?' Ma asked in the morning.

'He did,' I said, 'but he'll be back. Just being a boy. Hey, I've got a second before the tide,' I said.

I got into her bed next to her. I felt sad. Sad about Davey. Sad about everything. I wanted to hear the sound of her breathing, feel a warmth that was human not sun. 'I'm off out,' I said. 'Can I pick you up anything from the shops?' She laughed, pulled my hand to her cheek to make it a quick pillow and told me to be safe. 'Thank you,' I said.

By then, one in every three tides came up around and beyond the building. Up into Dreamland, which always filled first, then up and over into the park. At highest tide, it could get up to the first floor. In a storm, like the storm we'd just had, it smacked up to the second.

I made my way to Caleb's. 'You came back,' he said, when he opened the door.

'Don't sound surprised.'

'Well, you kept me waiting several decades last time, didn't you?'

'I was working stuff out.'

'Did you, then?' he said. 'Did you know his daughter?' But just then there was a creak of the floorboards at the top of the stairs.

It was the man from the beach. He had a white towel around his waist, and one of Caleb's T-shirts on, and he came down the stairs, gentle on his feet, and Caleb pulled out a seat for him. 'Hiya,' I said.

'This is Drissa,' Caleb said. Drissa took my hand and he shook it, and I remember how cool his hands were on a day that was so hot.

'Yesterday evening, he wouldn't speak,' Caleb said. 'And last night I woke up to him screaming. Saying words, but I couldn't put any of it together really. Pas bon, mon français,' he said to Drissa. 'Très rusty.'

'Non, ça va,' Drissa said.

'But today it was good. We worked out some stuff.'

There was a map on the table.

'It fits with what we thought,' Caleb said to me. 'It's just it's bigger than we thought. What's happening here, it really is happening everywhere.'

Caleb told me Drissa was from Mali, but had come through Niger to Libya, then across the water into Greece. Albania after that, then Italy. Drissa's finger traced the map.

'I think he's blocked out a lot of it,' Caleb said. He looked at Drissa. 'Anyone would. And again, maybe I didn't understand everything, but from what I think he's saying, in all these places—' I looked at Drissa's hand on the map, Caleb's right next to it '—they'd built – or were starting to build – big walls round major cities.'

'Carry on,' I said. 'I'm listening.'

'Beyond that, everywhere else was fucked,' Caleb went on. 'Drissa was trying to get to Paris. Paris,' he said to Drissa in a French accent. 'He had family there. But there were walls there, too. The suburbs were burned out. Burned black.'

A stone sunk to the bottom of my stomach. I thought of you and Blue in London. Fires burning around you.

'But inside?' I turned to Drissa. 'What's it like inside?' My hands were moving, but I was shit at miming. 'Inside they are safe, the people?'

'Qui?' Drissa said.

'The rich people,' I said. 'The ones inside the cities.'

'Je sais pas. Y'a des attaques suicidaires,' Drissa said. 'Comment ça se dit?' he said. He looked at Caleb. Drissa started to mime back, explosions with his arms.

'Suicide bombs,' Caleb said. 'People trying to protest, get back in, I don't know. Listen, whoever's powerful in the world, they'll have just roped off what they can. As soon as one person goes, "Fuck it, we're saving ourselves," everyone does. It's human nature.' He finished his drink. 'Fucking humans. There's something better about a wave, don't you think?'

Then, as if he'd swallowed the wrong way, he coughed and couldn't stop coughing. When he looked in the tissue, he flinched at what was in there.

'You should get that looked at,' I said.

'Yeah, I'll nip to the doc's.'

'No, I'm serious.'

'I just need rest,' he said.

'Well, then, I should go,' I said.

'You're always welcome, Chance,' he said. 'Always.'

He walked me to the door. 'Thank you, Caleb.'

'It's nice,' he said, tilting his head back to where Drissa was, 'to have company.'

'I'm sorry that I didn't come back for a while.'

'In more important news, guess what?' Caleb said, like he'd been waiting to say it. 'Drissa had a husband before. Or a boyfriend anyway.' His face broke into a smile, before it crumpled into a cough again. 'He's like me.'

'I mean try and play it cool at least,' I said.

'I am, I am,' he said. 'Of course. He's not in a good way. Like I said, he screamed all through the night.'

'Jesus – what did you do to him?'

And we laughed, and it was stupid and not even funny, but it was real and it was nice to see Caleb happy, and so I felt happy too for a moment as I walked home.

I expected Davey to be back on my sofa when I got there. But he wasn't, and he didn't come back that night, or the next night, or any of the nights after that.

'Where is he?' Ma asked.

'I don't know,' I said.

'What is it about us that the men always leave?'

Davey started to send boys up to the building instead, with bits of extra food, small bags of kem. At first I said no. 'Where is he, though?' I said. 'Tell him to come himself.'

'Busy.' The boy shuffled from foot to foot. Scuffed arms, thin legs.

'How old are you?'

'Just take it,' he said, and dropped the packet on the ground by my feet.

Time passed. Fell forwards like one of those toys that climb down stairs. People came to our door to sell things. All of it was stolen. Except the things that came were sadder, and we were less sad to see them.

I tried to find new houses, but there were hardly any left.

They'd all been done so badly. Doors kicked in, windows smashed the wrong way, glass everywhere. I'd still find the occasional box of pasta, or bottle of rum with a dusty neck, the labels falling off. Cellars were good places to look, even if they'd been flooded. I found a wedding dress once, folded up and hidden in a deep freeze, the silk stone cold. I picked off a couple of pearls, let them roll around in my palm, then felt bad and put them back on top of the dress.

The water that ran from our taps looked like it had dandruff, and got worse and worse. Huge white flakes floating in it now. We drank from mugs so we could see it less.

Rain came and pecked at the plastic covering what was left of the vegetables. Then, worse, our gas ran out, and when I tried to get more, there was nothing I could swap for even the smallest amount.

A man in Market Square hacked wooden tables to bits that he could sell for firewood. It was the only way to cook. From behind closed doors, there was this thick, sweet, poison smell of varnish in the air as they burned. A little boy came all the way up to our flat just trying to sell us something. 'Keys,' he said.

'I don't need your keys,' Ma said. 'What you going on about? Keys to where?'

But it was a bundle of piano keys he had behind his back.

Outside, on the days I went outside, the streets were deserted, felt like triggers about to be pulled. The last of the smugglers left. Even I could see that the last options were not good ones. The vans had slack wheels, I saw one guy smack the window with a cricket bat when a woman leaned out to say goodbye. Instead of leaving the building, I tried to go into flats that were empty on other floors instead. One day, I found an old lady in a bath. I didn't recognise her. Hard to say, though, her cheeks scooped away like that. Maybe she'd drowned, but everything was dry now. Her clothes were folded up and placed on the sink. She'd been there so long it didn't even smell. Maybe if it had, I'd have felt something. But I felt nothing, and when I got back home, it was days later that I thought to mention it to Ma.

I went to see Caleb and it could be nice there, but once or twice he was coughing too much to really speak properly, and said I should come back when he felt better. Drissa stayed with him. I couldn't always understand the words they were saying, but they laughed a lot when they were together. Their house smelled of food. I always wanted to stay longer than it felt right to.

Weeks passed. When loneliness finally got too much, I went to find Davey.

'Thought you were too good for me,' he said.

'I never said that.' I looked at him. 'Not once.'

He was sitting on his big red chair when I got there and he had a computer game controller in his hand, even though it wasn't connected to anything. He pressed the buttons and said it was to stop him from scratching. His arms were bright red. I'd never seen them that bad.

This time, I was the one who made him go outside. I wanted to see him see it, the place we'd grown up, hear him still try to say it was okay to stay.

There was no one on the street, apart from dogs. When the big ones lay down, they looked melted in the heat, flat to the ground like spilled water. Some had sunburn, I think. We walked to a park. We kicked away some rubbish and lay in uncut grass near a burned-out black spot where a fire had been. Crushed cans nearby, crisp packets, a bright curve of orange peel. I picked what looked like a feather out of the ash. A feather or a dandelion. I blew it. A fragment of bone was left in my fingers.

'What do you reckon?' I asked. Looked like a dog bone to me. 'Some terrier? One of the little yappy ones?'

'Don't talk like that,' he said. 'You know I hate that. And what you're doing right now. You're doing it still. I've never done that to you.'

'What, Davey?' It was true though. I'd never seen him smoke that much in one go. He didn't even seem high.

'Judging,' he said. 'I know you're doing that.'

'I'm not.'

'I have to go,' he said. 'It's you. You make me want to go.'

'Where?' I said. 'Look at me. There's nowhere to go.' But he was already walking away.

The next time I went to see Caleb, it was the first time he told me I couldn't come in. He told me to come back in a few days, said we'd have lunch, pretend to be civilised, but it didn't happen like that.

Thinking back, Caleb was probably ill from the first day Davey and I went to find him after the LandSave people left. That beginning of a cough, the way his T-shirt seemed stretched for a stomach that no longer existed. But it got worse. Soon, it wasn't just his belly that was gone, it was his hair. It was so thin it looked like new hair rather than old hair.

Davey said maybe he'd got ill the gay way, but he didn't say it meanly. And when I went to visit Caleb, Davey had sent over food and something for the pain.

I was at home one afternoon when a boy came for me to say that Caleb was finding it hard to breathe. I told the boy to go send word to Davey, too. When I got there, I brought up a chair next to Drissa's, by Caleb's bed, and I put my hands on the edge of the mattress, and when Davey got there, we talked to him and talked to him, until long after he could hear us.

When he was gone, I remember staring at Caleb's wrist. His watch was too big for it now. I couldn't stop looking. The space between the leather and the bone. All the empty space.

After we carried Caleb out of his house, Davey went straight back inside, and straight to Caleb's bedside drawer. It was where Caleb kept his gun. I didn't know what to say.

But then Davey wrapped it in one of Caleb's silk scarves and handed it to Drissa. It was the way he held it out with both hands. Davey nodded a lot. 'Whatever you need,' he told Drissa. 'Just ask for Davey, okay? Whatever you need. Davey, okay?'

'Poor fucker,' he said, when we left long after dark. 'Be alone at a time like this. Be not from here at a time like this. Needs all the help he can get.'

Davey slapped a mosquito that had landed on the back of his neck. There were mosquitoes everywhere. I had bites all over me, they changed the shape of my body. I noticed them most when I wanted to sleep. I realised I didn't want to sleep alone. 'You coming up then?' I said, when we were outside the building. 'You coming back?'

'I mean I'd like to, but . . .' he said. 'Probably not a good idea.' He looked at me; I watched him catch himself. 'How's it going, anyway? Your plans.'

'What plans?'

'The Great Escape. You still building your tunnel?' I saw them fight in him then: curiosity, anger, tenderness.

I didn't say anything.

'I saw that film once,' he said. He tried to say it lightly. 'They shot the blind man.'

I was scared of them that night, the mosquitoes. The whining clouds, loop-the-loops, getting closer. Maybe something bad in a bite was what had happened to Caleb. That was what Mac the Kid said had made him ill, anyway, but there were needles around too, and lots of them. All these thin faces. Mac said his teeth felt loose in his gums. Like when he coughed he could feel them moving. And it wasn't just the mosquitoes or the needles, all that really needed to go wrong was the water. It did. It was everywhere. It didn't have to be waves. The toilets stopped flushing.

Viv stopped having people over. When I went down to ask her if her taps were running brown too, she had to undo three locks to let me in. The whole building was emptier. The weight of it had changed, like the loose teeth. The noises it made got worse. Beating sun, beating water. And so many flats were missing windows now, that there was also this sort of whistle. It wasn't a whistle. It could sound like screaming sometimes.

Davey made his kem cheaper and cheaper. Maybe he could make too much for the number of people left. Maybe he just wanted people to do it with. More cheeks hollowed out. Tendons in necks so close to the skin it was easy to see the ridges. Blue forks of lightning on the insides of people's arms, on their calves. When I was a kid, I used to think bits of Ma's red nail varnish had chipped off onto her cheek, but I realised that they were just veins that had burst. Small and oblong. They shone. She had more and more of them.

When my period came, I used old T-shirts, and then it stopped coming at all. No one knocked on our door any more. No one had the energy to get up to the eleventh floor, and no one had anything to sell, anyway. Davey's boys still came, but less regularly. He sent food from time to time, but not a lot. Silence spread out like a blanket.

When the sea was all the way in, the roads it filled were silver. The sky changed. The heat made a haze that hardly ever lifted. The air waved back and forth in silky, shifting stripes. Our windows were hot, sticky, the outside scuffed by sand. It had become impossible to see a way out.

If I needed to get anything I had to go out before the sun came up. Four, five, six in the morning. It was too hot after that. We ate hardly anything. We made a bag of rice last more than a week. We slept when it got dark, before it got dark. We slept a lot.

Somewhere along the way, I forgot the details of what you look like. Worse, I lost Blue's face, too. I found my arms moving into the position of how I'd hold him, even though he'd be too big now. He'd be three, he'd be four, I didn't even know. I tried to imagine how much he must have grown, the ways his face might have changed, but that made me lose him even more.

I've changed too. I look at the back of my hand, and see all these different triangles. When I touch my body it feels hard in places it wasn't hard before. When I walk past mirrors or windows I try not to look in them.

You said you would come back. How long had I waited now?

Mornings still came when the sky was a perfect blue, and the sea was like a show, diamonds coming up to the surface. On a good day, on a good day. But it was almost harder to look at it when it was like that. It hits you one way when you're happy, smacks you another when you're sad. Because even if the sea shone, and the sky could look like a postcard, the good days had no good in them any more.

I'd waited so long, it felt like too late. Too late, too late. It shot ripples through my head.

At night, I dreamed about a wave. I dreamed that it would pick me up. I dreamed that I was somersaulting under water. That it would feel like being held. I dreamed that it would be slow. I dreamed it would be rushing. I dreamed that it would crush me. I dreamed that it would come.

IV.

Instead, the day came when I saw the man pull his son out from the sea, and the night came when there was a knock on the door. Two heavy, dull beats, the gap between them slightly too long.

'That's not Davey,' Ma said. She turned to me. 'It isn't Davey, is it?'

I shook my head. We were on the sofa. It felt like we hadn't spoken in so long. And then it happened: the sound of a key sliding into the lock.

My body tensed. She froze too. We both turned to the door.

His face was in a tunnel.

Around it, the brim of a cap and a hoodie, despite the heat. He pushed both off.

He stood in the doorway to the living room, filling it, a shaven head now. It was Kole. Alive, with new scars, standing there like he thought we would run to him and hug him.

Ma did, though. She ran to him, ran as best she could, and hugged him. Straight away she started to cry, and then, when he finally put his arms around her, she turned her hands into these kind of cartoon fists and started beating on his chest. It made a sound but didn't look like it hurt. She said his name again and again. For a while, he let her do it, then he grabbed her wrists. He stared at me the whole time.

'Why's her voice funny?' he said.

'You beat her half to death,' I said. 'That close.' I was standing by then. The floor unsteady under my feet. I'd stood up too fast.

'Stop that.'

'Where have you been?' Ma said. Her skirt had ridden up. I don't know what had bruised her like that, all down her thigh.

'Why are you here?' I said. My fists were clenched too. I could feel my heart beat in my palms. 'Why didn't you come back before?'

''Cos what the fuck is here, Chance? What the fuck is left here?' I wanted him to let go of her wrists. 'I've been fighting,' he said. 'We been out there. Doing things.'

'Who's we?' Ma said.

He brought one of her fists up to his mouth and kissed it. This rough kind of kiss.

'Is there someone else?' she asked. 'Is that what it is, Kole?'

'Stop it,' I said. 'He beat you, took everything. Walked out. And now you—'

I'd forgotten how quickly Kole could cross a room. He dropped Ma's hands, pushed past her and came at me. Grabbed my head.

'You don't know the things I've seen.' His breath was hot. I remember it smelled of metal. 'You don't know shit, Cha.'

The muscles in his arm were twitching in that way they do when you hold a press-up. But I couldn't not look at him. The rosebud on his neck from a broken bottle. I'd always shut my eyes when he'd come to see me in the night, pretend to be asleep. But I looked at him now.

Ma came from behind and hugged Kole like he was a mountain. She shut her eyes and, for the quickest second, it was like years and years were scrubbed off her face. She was saying things into his shoulder blades I couldn't hear. But also, you're back now, you're back now.

He pulled her round so he was facing both of us. Squiggles of veins pushed out the skin above his ears. It almost looked like writing.

'You're not getting it. Neither of you.' We looked at him. 'I got there. I fucking been there.'

'Where's there?'

'London. Anywhere I want.'

We stared at him. 'Like shit,' I said. And nearly at the same time, Ma said, 'Cha – don't.'

'But why did I bother to come back? For this shit. For you two's rubbish.'

'Exactly. If you got there, you never would've come back.'
I looked around at the flat like that was proof. It was proof.
I'd been sleeping on the sofa. The sheet looked like it had
been stained with tea. You could see the shape of my body.
Tidemarks.

Kole pulled a small square of plastic out of his pocket.

'What's that then, you little shit?' he said.

He handed it to me. Ma was still hugging him. I wanted to
pull her off. Have us stand together, not need to lean on him.
This energy she had, though. Where did it come from? Why
hadn't she had it for me?

Kole's small square looked like an old credit card, but
with a third cut off. There was a smaller square inside it that
looked like glass, a hologram, rainbow thing, dancing inside
it. There was a photo on it too.

'That's not you,' I said. 'And your name's not Adebayo
Akinto . . .' It was a long name.

He snatched it back. 'They don't look, they just scan it.
It's a bar square, isn't it? It's the future. What's wrong with
you?'

'You haven't been to London. I know you haven't,' I said.
Kole shrugged Ma off. 'You just stole it from some dead
guy's pocket, or even dumber, you paid money for it.'

'Shut it, Cha.'

'Paid for it like an idiot.' I kept going. I couldn't stop. I
hadn't spoken to anyone else but Ma for days. 'So don't come
back here playing the big man.'

'Say that again and I'll fucking break your neck.'

380

'I'll break yours—' I got halfway through the sentence before the skin between his thumb and finger hit my windpipe. His other hand went low and I thought he was going to grab between my legs, but he took a handful of material, the zip of my jeans, the button, and picked me up. I was so thin by then – I'd had to cut new holes on my belt – the only strain in his face was about making his grip tighter and tighter around my voice box. He pushed me up against the wall. The seam of my jeans cut a deep line in between my legs. My feet were off the floor.

Ma was saying, Don't Kole, don't Kole, but she wasn't doing much about it.

He roared in my face. His metal breath was hotter still and sour and it hit the back of my open mouth. All the oxygen was gone from it. Then suddenly he let go, both hands at once, and I bent in half, crumpled to the floor. 'It's not you I came for,' he said. 'You look like shit now, anyway. Where's my boy?' Kole walked in the direction of his room, and Ma ran round, to stand in the way.

'We need to talk to you,' she said. 'That's why I wanted to talk.'

He pushed her over, too. He disappeared into Blue's room. 'Come out, kiddo,' he said. We could hear him opening cupboards. We heard him lift the bed. Wood breaking. He shouted again. The sound of his palm slamming down on a wall.

When he came back into the living room, it was Ma he got to first. He shouted in her face – she tried to turn away but it made the sound worse, right in her ear – 'Where is he?' he shouted. I managed to make it to my feet. It felt like my throat was concave, that he'd pushed it in on itself. Like the top layers of flesh had been scraped away with a blade. Kole put the crook of his arm round her neck.

'I will kill her, you know. I'll break every one of her matchstick bones. Tell me where he is.'

Ma was saying she didn't know, and begging Kole, and her foot was kicking out, flicking up and down. She couldn't breathe.

'It wasn't her,' I said. 'It was nothing even to do with her.' It was hard to get the words out. They came half in coughs at first. 'I did it,' I said. I put a hand out like I might be able to block him. The veins around his pupils looked like they'd spread, multiplied. Redness like a web.

And then he leaped. Kole pushed my face into the carpet to stop me from breathing. Dust filled my mouth. I tried to spit and my teeth hit the hard of the floor underneath. This is it, I thought. And suddenly I felt okay with that. Better Blue is there than here. Wherever he is, it must be better. Better that he doesn't have to see this. In my head, I told him I loved him.

And then I felt the full force of Kole's body land on me. Huge lead weight. That broke one of my back teeth. Then his body was rolling off me. He lurched back, took his arms off me and I turned around to see him reaching behind himself, reaching towards his back. He made this sound. Awful sound. Then he started to slump onto his side, and fell backwards which was the thing that finished him off. It was Ma who had done it. Ma who'd got the knife. Ma who saved me. She did this time.

I looked at Kole. He was sitting up now. His T-shirt had ridden up and the tip of the knife poked through his tummy, just above his belly button. His back was a little arched. He looked at us. He tried to reach either side of him.

'What have you done?' he said. 'What the fuck did you do?' His blood poured into his hands like water. After that, for a moment, his hands moved, like he was making fists, then letting them go, and then the whole of him went still. His eyes were open.

'I couldn't pull it out,' Ma said. 'I can't.' Her hands fell off the handle and into her lap.

She made this tiny sound at first, and then was silent, which was worse.

She'd used a serrated knife, one of the ones for bread. In the whole time we'd lived here, we'd never used that knife before. It was in the flat when we got here. Both of our hands were on the handle, trying to pull it out. I thought of the cuts of beef the chef would get at the Pearl – these fibres running through it, like rope, never easy to cut.

His blood continued to bubble out. Some of it was thin and fast, but there were heavier bits too that held their shape.

Ma came back from Blue's room with his blanket. I shook my head. She took my sheet from the sofa instead. All of this happened without either of us saying a word.

*   *   *

Afterwards, when we'd got our breath back, Ma looked through the bag Kole had left by the door. Her feet were in the same place they were when she was hugging him, but then her back slipped down against the door frame. She threw some things in my direction – a protein bar that looked trodden on, a broken compass. She put a spare T-shirt in her pile, between her legs. She held it up to her face to smell it before she did that. She walked to the sofa and lay down.

'Do you think he did?' was the only thing she said to me.

'Get there?' I said.

'No,' she said. 'Do you think he did love me? Ever once?' She looked up at me. 'Or did he stay all that time for you?'

Kole lay there in our living room for the rest of the morning. We'd pushed all the sheets we had in the house under his body to soak up the blood. He almost looked like he was on a cloud. Or in bed. Like he might wake up at any moment. Ma tried to shut his eyes, but they kept coming back open, or at least one of them did. That made her cry. It was hard to wash our hands without soap, so we had to use our nails. Our skin stayed red from the rubbing.

When we heard creaking in the stairwell, I wondered if anyone had known Kole was coming to see us, but no one came to the door. It wasn't hotter than any other day, but we noticed it more, and it wasn't long before the smell of blood was thick in the air. Iron, these dense waves of it. It was when the flies came, not many at first, then more and more, finding places on his body to settle, that we knew we had to get rid of him.

We waited until it was getting dark and the tide was high, until it hit, then filled, the bottom of the building. He was too heavy to lift, even with both of us trying. We could get him off the floor, but not high enough to go out of the window. In the end, we had to get him up on a table first, legs and arms hanging off. I had to hit the window with a hammer five times to break it, and with each smack, Ma flinched like she was the one being hit.

'Can you stop that?' I said. 'Please.'

I realised what it was when I went to turn him over. Face down, Kole's shoulders made me think of JD, and I was suddenly filled with, I didn't mean to be, but I was suddenly filled with . . . it wasn't affection. It wasn't that, but – his shoulder, his arm. I used to know you, I thought. It was as simple as that. You used to be alive.

The pane had a sheet of plastic over it on the outside, so it didn't smash. I kicked it out. It hung there, half off, like a plaster with only one side sticking. We started to roll Kole out. We'd tried to wrap him up in all of the sheets, but we didn't have anything to tie it up with so parts of him kept slipping out.

Ma tried to hold him back at the last minute, but her fingers weren't strong enough. The water was deep enough for him to splash, but he also hit, with a muffled thud, the road beneath. Ma didn't look, but I did. I looked out to see if anyone else was watching in the half-dark.

It was an hour after that that she started crying again and shaking and saying things about whose fault it was, and me. I played with a shard of glass from the window and accidentally cut myself. I looked for something to hold the blood in but we'd used every scrap of material we had in the house.

Ma had Kole's T-shirt on her lap, and she continued to put it up to her face every few minutes. I pulled his bag over and opened it. There was a can of beans, with writing that had dots over the o's. There was a plastic pack of frankfurter sausages. He'd eaten two of them, but the last four were rolled inside the packaging, sealed with a hairband. I ate half of one. Put the other half next to Ma's hands. It tasted okay.

Kole didn't have much, but at the bottom of his bag, wrapped in a different T-shirt, I found a gun.

I'd never held one before. Not even Caleb's. It was black metal that had been in the sun, near sweat, the steel underneath was coming through the paint. There was cross-hatching over the handle. I scratched my nail over it.

I turned it from one side to the other. The weight of it surprised me – it was heavy as a brick. How the fuck was I supposed to use this thing? I held it out in front of me. I put it down. I put a cushion over it for a second. I picked it up again.

It was loaded, brass inside the black. It smelled of empty tins. I moved the cylinder around. Clicking sound. The safety lock looked like it had been hit off with a hammer. The things it must have done.

*   *   *

After Kole was gone, for the rest of the day, and for days after that, the smell of everything upset me. I could smell milk. Old milk that had gone dry around the bottle top. I could smell it everywhere. Bile flushed into my mouth, and I spat it out of the broken window. I kept on feeling the weight of his flesh around the knife.

I told Ma I was going to bed, and took Blue's blanket back to our old room. I hadn't been in there for a while. At first I went in all the time. Every morning, every afternoon. But I missed a day, then two, then felt so bad, I just stopped.

I curled under Blue's blanket. I kept my feet off the bed so I didn't make stains. My soles were black, and one toe was bleeding too, from all the broken glass from the window. Blue had left a toy in the bed, a plastic train that had been stuck back together with Sellotape. I felt its edges. Felt them so hard I hoped they'd break my skin.

Where are you now? I said that out loud into the room. How many times had I asked that. Where are you?

I pushed my face into the pillow. I wanted to find Blue somewhere there. But the bad milk smell was everywhere. There's something about lying still enough for long enough. At some point, I fell into a hot, cold, dreamless sleep.

I've often wondered since if I knew in some way, deeper than skin, deeper than brain, what I would wake up to. The next morning, when I woke up and walked into the living room, she was lying on the sofa, and she had found a good position. Her head looked comfortable. Her back was straight, her legs were over the edge of the sofa's arm. Her bad leg had a cushion underneath it.

There were small plastic bags all over the table, and they were empty. And there were bits of folded card on what would have been her lap, if she'd been able to sit up.

Her gums were burned with it, and there was a needle on the floor next to her, the tip bent. I don't know if she'd used needles on her own before. I don't know if she'd used them right. There were red-black dots on the middle of her forearm, the place she'd told me, as a kid, was the right place to apply perfume. Higher up than you'd think. I touched her, and she was cold as clay.

It did not feel real. People say that. All these things people say. But we say them because they're true. It did not feel real.

I tried to say her name but it stopped somewhere before it got to my mouth. I dropped to my knees next to her. I pushed her forehead out of a frown. I touched her hair. Apart from the very ends, it was her natural colour again. I looked at it against my fingers. Her hair. How could she not be there?

What do I do now? I asked her. I tried to see if I could read anything in her face. Anything. I said it again. What do I do now?

I could hear the sound of rushing water. I can't just leave you here, I said out loud. I pressed my face against the cloth of the sofa. I did that for a long time. Part of me wanted to be angry with her. But that didn't come at first. I stayed on my knees and tried to make her hand hold mine. I told her stories from when I was young. Her ones. Stories where she'd made me laugh, ran instead of walking, when her eyes burned bright, and her dimples were deep and dark, and she needed earth wires, and had no idea of where she would end up.

It was easy to pack. I just looked at Kole's blood, spread in circles on the floor from when I'd tried to clean it, and at Ma, who still looked asleep but who could not get warm in the sun that filled the room. I knew I could not stay there. It was clear now. Clearer than anything. Nothing would stop me this time. I had to find you, I had to get my boy.

I put on trousers with pockets. I did my belt up one more notch. I repacked Kole's bag. Underneath the gun, there were bullets, kept in an old ice-cream tub, to keep them dry. It felt strange to see that – I had never known Kole to be organised, but the person who had packed that bag had wrapped everything tightly. I wondered what he'd been doing. What he'd done. I took the gun from his T-shirt and re-wrapped it in one of my own.

By her bed, I found Ma's notebooks. They were full of drawings. They weren't good if good means like a photograph. They were mostly lines, a single line she followed across a whole page, but with each one I could see what she meant. I lifted her neck as carefully as I could and undid the clasp of her necklace. It used to have lots of different pendants on it, but she'd sold them one by one apart from one she'd had since a child, a St Christopher in a tiny circle. I took it off, and put it around my own neck. Her hair was caught in the clasp and I left it there.

I pulled the photo that my dad had taken off the wall. The picture of the door, hope, escape – I took it out of the frame, rolled it up and slid it in my bag.

In the real-life doorway, my hand on it because I couldn't stop feeling like I'd stood up too fast, I looked at the flat. I thought of the first time JD brought us to the building – the tears, the takeaway. And when Kole brought us 'up' to this place. The plans Ma made to change the carpet, put in a new kitchen. I'm not saying it got better, over our time here. Just that we made it bigger, by being here.

For a long time, I could not leave her. I kept going back into the room. It was strange, because I had been making decisions for us for months now but as soon as she was gone, I realised I had all these questions I wanted to ask her.

I didn't know whether to lock the door so no one would disturb her or to leave it open, just in case. In case. But in case what? At the last moment, I went back and kissed her again. Cold forehead, soft forehead, her hairline. I remembered climbing into her bed before, when her body was hot and she took my hand as a pillow.

I told her I was scared. It was true. I hadn't been out of the building for weeks by then. Not all the way, anyway. There was a man down on the third floor who still had all this powdered soup and I'd been to see him a few times, but that was it. Got food from him, or Davey's boys. Davey. I hadn't seen him in weeks.

I looked out of our window. The tide was low, and getting lower, but the concrete was still wet. I had two hours max before the water would be back.

I made my bag as small as possible. Then smaller again. My pockets were heavy enough for me to have to make a second belt. I pulled the string from Ma's old duffel coat. Tied it tightly. I wanted to look like I was just out for a couple of hours to see what I could find. That I'd be heading home as soon as the water started coming up. Because if you look like you're leaving, people think you have somewhere to go.

I touched the walls as I walked down the stairs. Just a finger against the brick. I walked quietly. Wondered if I should have the gun in a place where I could reach it. Wondered if maybe we were the last people left. At Viv's door, locked, no postcard on the door any more, I wrote a note, slid it under. *It's me*, it said. *i had to go. i hope you're okay. Check on Ma, maybe. Sorry. i am sorry. And thank you, Viv, thank you for everything.* On one of the lower floors, there was a pot plant in a plastic urn that it looked like someone was still watering. I walked faster, started to run. I didn't want to surprise anyone, but no doors opened – apart from the ones that had been open for years, the ones that had holes in the doors instead of locks.

In what used to be the lobby, instead of carpets, there were mountains of damp sand. Broken shells and rubbish, all the colours faded. Seaweed. The glass of the front door was gone, but the wire meshing was still there. I climbed over the sand and tried to look out. It was like looking through a tennis racket. I pushed out onto the flat, wet street. Even though I was at sea level, I felt like I was higher than I've ever been in my life, like I was looking over an edge, and I would fall over it, and never stop falling. The door creaked open even though I pushed it slowly, then it spanked shut. Hard enough for my body to shrink into a crouch.

No one will ever understand how hard it was to walk forward. I wanted to go back for her. Never think I didn't. I wanted to check on her one last time. I imagined her waking up. I imagined what would happen to her if she was alone. The open window. The open door.

There was no one on the streets near the building. I could hear the high-pitched battle of seagulls. They came closer, got further away again. I could hear the washing and sucking of the water. The only way that I could keep on walking was by not looking back.

I only broke that rule once, when I was almost round the corner. I turned round and the building was bright gold. The window we'd broken was the only place that didn't catch the sun.

Davey was not in the main workshop. He was upstairs, in an empty room, with two guys I didn't recognise. They raised their heads like they knew me, so maybe I knew them once. But they were men now and their faces had changed, cheekbones like Vs. They were burning something, sniffing it to see if it was ready.

Davey looked surprised to see me, but there was something quiet about it, like not all of the parts of his face were working still. He asked if I wanted to join them. He said it was new. He said I could help them come up with a name for it. I asked if he'd come outside with me.

His cheeks looked like putty, like if you pushed at them they would hold the shape. His hair was closer-shaved than the last time I'd seen him, but he must have done it with a blunt razor because he had cuts drying brown on the bits where his head was bumpy. He pulled on a T-shirt and while it was going over his head, my eyes caught on the downwards smile of his belly button. That made me want to cry.

It felt like longer than weeks since we'd seen each other. You look well, he told me, and I said you too, because what else can you say? Davey kept looking back into the room like he was worried the boys would try whatever it was without him. He kept on trying to scratch his back, a bit of it he couldn't reach.

I pushed him round the corner so the boys couldn't see us and I said I'd scratch his back for him. He faced the wall and I lifted up his T-shirt – his back was black with tattoos, and muscled and bruised and also red from being dry – and I rubbed him with my halfway knuckles so my nails wouldn't take his skin off.

He hunched forward and his spine showed. Then he arched back until his shoulder blades looked almost like wings. He turned his head to the side to make his neck crack. 'That's good,' he said. 'Thank you.'

My fingertips paused.

'I'm sorry,' he said. 'That I disappeared, you know?'

'It's okay,' I said. 'I did too.'

'I know but – normally I . . .' He coughed and his back felt like empty bones.

'Are you sure you're okay?' I said. I stopped scratching him. It came in a wave, this throat-closing feeling. I didn't kiss the top of his back, I just put my face against it.

'You're not going too, are you,' he said. He didn't say it like a question. I stayed still. 'Are you going to leave here?' His breath turned sharp. Neither of us wanted to look at each other. That stinging that happens.

'What about your mum?' He was almost whispering. We could hear the boys shout and laugh in the other room. Davey's voice fell between the cracks. Hard to hear him. I tried to scratch him again but he shrugged away, said I didn't have to.

'She's not coming,' I said and I shook my head against his back, and when I didn't stop shaking my head, I think he understood.

We stood like that for a second or two but it felt like longer. Then Davey turned around and held my head to his shoulder. The way he did it, my face was tight against him and I could taste his T-shirt and I couldn't breathe, but I didn't mind.

'Where are you going to go?' he asked, and I just said, 'Please don't tell anyone.'

'Who is there to tell?'

The boys next door put on music – it was a tinny sound, with a fast beat. They shouted over it. Davey turned towards the door, and straightened his T-shirt. 'So you just came to say goodbye?'

I nodded. I could feel the weight of Kole's gun in my bag.

'So-bye-then,' he said. He pushed my shoulder. He tried to smile.

'Davey,' I said, 'you can come if you want.' But I mostly said it because I knew that he wouldn't.

He shook his head, but his smile seemed more real after that. He pushed me away one last time and then went back into the room with the boys and the music. Before the door shut, I saw one of the boys flexing his arm and pumping his hand to get the blood going. The other boy had a syringe between his teeth, a rollie behind his ear. He took the syringe out, flicked it and blew the tip. 'For after,' he said to Davey.

*   *   *

I couldn't look. I started down the stairs, but by the time I was at the bottom, Davey had followed me. He'd shut the door behind him and was shouting after me to wait. He ran down the stairs and found me. His eyes looked less cloudy. He blew whatever they'd been smoking out through his teeth, then he coughed again. He asked me to come with him for a second, and then he took me through to the garage.

'You have to understand that I can't leave because I'm here. I mean, I'm from here. I've made a life here.' He almost pointed in the direction of whatever was going on in the other room, but stopped himself. 'I mean, I've thought about it. I have, Cha, seriously . . .'

'Then why, Davey?'

''Cos it's lots of things. I feel a fear in me sometimes,' he said, 'when I think about going far.' His fingertips were on his collarbone. 'Like a cloud right here,' he said. 'Sounds dumb, but you know what you know, if you know what I mean.'

I nodded.

'And I always imagined it, since I was a kid, that we'd be old here. You and me. Other people. Together or something. Since I was a kid,' he said again. 'Not a very good imagination, I know.'

'It's a good imagination,' I said.

'And my mum too. She's right here. I visit her. She died here, I'll die here too. I'm okay with that. That's how it works.'

'It doesn't have to be how it works.'

'I don't know why I grabbed you again, but I just wanted to give you something. I don't even know what you need.' He laughed then. 'Is there anything that you need?'

He picked up a screwdriver but then put it down. He offered a set of bolts, then pulled a face and said, 'Probably not these.' We went around the room, and honestly, everything he had he wanted to give it to me. In the end I left with a padlock and a penknife and some matches, because, as Davey kept saying, you never know.

'Stop now,' I said. 'So heavy it's going to break.' I smiled too and it was the first time I'd smiled in ages. Davey looked at me for so long, and I looked back.

'You look pretty,' he said. Kept looking. 'Don't do that.'

He told me I should cut my hair. I asked him to do it for me, and my hair fell off my shoulders onto the floor.

'Keep it like that,' he said. He handed me scissors which I put in my bag. In a way, he said, flashing his eyes at where my breasts should be, it was good I'd got so thin.

And then, before I left, Davey asked if I would stay with him. He said he would look after me.

'I wanted to do it better than he did. That was the whole thing. I wanted to be able to look after you better than he did,' he said. 'It was the only thing I wanted. Do you understand that?'

'Davey.'

'But I was just the same.' His chest was itchy now, or maybe he was just rubbing his heart. 'I'm sorry for that.' He was rubbing at his breastbone, anyway. 'You know that I ...' he looked very hard into my eyes. 'You know I always have, right?'

When I left Davey's, the sea had already changed direction. It was coming fast now. Still, I tried to walk lightly, like each step was one I could undo. Davey had written some place names down on a bit of paper. I had the paper in my hand. I couldn't read all of them – Davey's handwriting was like a pile of twigs, and already, the words he'd said were slipping away.

I thought about Davey and I thought about Davey. In those last minutes, his face had become his own again. He'd drawn me a map I didn't understand, he used a pen to show me where to go. I listened, but I couldn't hear. 'Do you know what I mean when I say that?' he kept asking.

I tried to play what he'd said in my head again now, but the words felt slippery, kept shifting.

'Don't go to Westwood,' he'd said. 'It's a fucking war zone. Everything gone. Not even just the good stuff. All of it's gone. And they're still fighting.'

'Who are?' I asked. 'Fighting who?' But he continued talking. He told me to head towards Manston, but not to go anywhere near the old airstrips.

'This is what I've heard,' he said, 'you go Nash, Manston, Hengist, Stonelees. Are you listening to me? Nash. Manston. Hengist. Stonelees.' Those are the words he wrote down. 'But that was what everyone was trying, so you've got to . . .' He looked at me and he sniffed hard because his nose had started bleeding. He put a finger to a nostril and sucked the blood off, saying sorry. 'You think of it as "the wall", but it's not just one. You cross that wall and there'll be more. It's not like you'll be home free after that. It's not like the hard bit will be done. The stuff I've heard, Cha. It's not good. It's so fucking far from being that.'

'How do you know this stuff?'

'Because I sell. Because people talk? I dunno. And really, I don't know. So don't be dumb about any of this.'

'What happens at Stonelees?' I asked him. But he just stared at the map he had drawn and started marking Xs in red for places I should avoid. There were Xs everywhere.

I put the map back in my pocket now, half-folded, half-scrumpled. It was the wrong shape and made no sense. He'd crossed out street names and written them in new places, but I wanted it anyway.

* * *

The only cars that were left in the streets were at odd angles. Most had been burned black. Their hoods popped, their doors wrenched off, their headlights smashed out. Dead eyes. Like I said, I tried to walk lightly, but I couldn't get any of the lightness to reach my face.

You are just going to get something. I tried to let that sentence change the way I held myself. You are just going to get something and bring it back.

How many people were still in town by then? That day, it looked like no one. There were only one or two dogs, ribs pushing at their skin like fingers.

As I got to the edge of town, the bits I knew less and less and then not at all, I sped up. Hard to explain the feeling in my chest. The spinning fear of leaving everything. At one point I thought I heard a 'hey' from up high, a voice that sounded young and fast, and I sprinted until my lungs were needles and rested with my back against the wall. I waited but I heard no footsteps. My heart sounded like a finger beating against the wood of a guitar, except faster than a finger can go.

I got to the first roadblocks, and it was the first time I'd seen them. I vaulted over them and anger filled my chest. How had I never got this far before? How had I stayed so still, for so long? You used to be light all the time, you used to run, you used to be afraid of nothing. Me, I mean.

As I left the only town I'd ever really known, I let myself, maybe for the first time, see what Kole had done to me. What he had taken. How he'd found space in me for fear, and left it there. But how he was gone now, how he was floating, how he would sink.

I walked faster. The sign for the Queen Elizabeth hospital was bent in a way that looked like a car had driven into it. The metal was twisted. I walked past a row of Portaloos, pushed onto their sides, doors open. When I got to the car wash, I tried the taps. One spurted on with a shaky splutter. The water ran brown for a moment, then seemed okay. I tasted it with my tongue. Thought fuck it, put my mouth over the hose. It was better than the other option. The verge of the road was full of fizzy drinks bottles, full of piss like dark yellow lemonade.

I had to get off the road. I needed to keep the road in sight but stick to fields, stay hidden. As I walked, it got slowly greener. Not that there was more green, just that it was a different colour. The green that grew where the sea got to was brown, sucked thin, salted looking. This green felt fresher.

The grass had grown so tall here, I had to lift my legs high to walk and keep my head down at the same time. I wished I could push up the grass behind me so no one could follow. I realised how all sounds seem louder when it's your own body that's making them.

I started to turn each step into a word or a number. The sun had burned away the morning clouds. Its beam was so strong it felt solid. The sky was bigger.

The fact that you were both under it, both also under it somewhere, started to feel more real.

I imagined kissing you. I imagined killing you. More than anything, I thought about Blue. Each step I took brought me closer.

That first day, I barely came across anyone. A scattering of people – an old man cleaning a car without tyres, his wife at the upstairs window who told him to come inside as soon as she saw me. Everyone I saw seemed to avoid me even more than I avoided them. Soon, even before an hour had passed, one of my knees started clicking. Making the noise a small branch does when it's thrown in a fire. I wasn't used to walking long distances. One of my toenails broke against the tip of my shoe. I found the bit that had come off and it was soft. Brittle too, almost like chalk. I rolled it back and forth between my fingers and wondered if all my bones had become like that.

In a field where the grass was long enough to fold around me when I sat down, I stopped to eat one of Kole's sausages. It had sweated in my pocket. It was softer than before, but it left my lips salty, and that was nice. I lay back for a while – I thought that if I let what I'd eaten go down slower, I would take more from it. I pressed my eyes until I saw tie-dye.

It was nearly dark when I woke up. However hot it was, the sun wasn't sticking around for long. I touched my tummy and there was dew on my T-shirt, beads of it, that looked like they'd picked up the colour of the material. I put my lip to one. It tasted sour. The sky above me was dark blue, bruised looking. The clouds looked like they were about to buckle. Then the first drop landed.

I ran as fast as I could. Kole's bag, heavy with the gun, banged against my hip and left a cut there. The drops started, felt more like balls, heavy when they hit my head.

That was when I saw a sign saying HOLIDAYS. Next to it, a child's swing, chains hanging rusty, the seat missing. Behind them, caravans. I caught my breath under a tree. I held Kole's bag so it wouldn't bang against me and make noise. As I got closer to the caravans, glass crunched under my feet, the wind whistled through broken windows. The first one I came to was dark inside and out. Someone had torched it and the plastic almost looked like it had turned to wood. There was a huge hole in the ceiling of a second, from a fallen tree branch, but a third looked okay. My hand found the cold of Kole's gun. The handle was stiff; it took me a moment to open the door. When I did, I pointed the gun in both ways as quickly as I could then I realised I wasn't even looking. The sudden quiet, relatively, away from the rain.

The door locked from the inside. I slid the bolt across. A small kitchen sink, full of dust. There was a jam jar next to the tap with four toothbrushes in it – two big, two small. Insects had turned to powder in the lightshade, but you could still see the little lines of their legs. I opened all the cupboards. There were brown coffee cups, handles missing. In a biscuit tin, a yellow plastic pot of rust-red iodine tablets. I turned the tap and no water ran. There was an empty crisp packet on the floor. My fingers scooted around it and scooped up the leftover salt. Deep in the back of one cupboard I found a can of mushy peas.

I ate in the toilet because it felt better to have two doors between me and the outside, and I sat there until the rattling patter of rain on the roof dimmed to a drip, then turned off. By then, it was pitch-black.

I felt my way to bunk beds. I chose the top one so if someone came in the night they wouldn't see me straight away. I slept with the gun in my hand, my hand tucked under a small pillow that threw up a storm of grey dust whenever I moved my head. My dreams were a mess. You were there, kissing my knees. Then you kissed the inside of my arms. You whispered into my ear that it would all be okay, and then, the way that happens in dreams, your face became Meyer's face, and then Kole's, and my eyes snapped open. The dreams only got worse after that.

In the morning, it felt like my skin had shrunk. I made my way to the mirror in the bathroom. My neck was bright, electric red. Sunburn. I peeled off my thin T-shirt, flinching as the seams hit.

All of the ideas my mum would have had to fix it ran through my head. Cold showers, sunflower oil. None of them had ever worked. I didn't care. All I wanted was for her to be there.

I decided to spend one more day at the caravan park and leave at the crack of dawn the next morning. My toe that had lost the nail was still bleeding, and there were cuts all across the back of my ankles too. I'd worn my shoes in the water and when they'd dried, the salt had turned them rock hard.

I washed my trainers in a stream, and while they were drying, I made food. Under the sink in a different caravan, I'd found a bag of open pasta. There were some bugs inside the top layer, dead now, but I put each piece of pasta in my mouth like a flute and blew them out. One of the cookers still had gas so I dragged the heavy blue bottle back to my place. I found water in one of the kettles. There were lily pads of mould on the surface of the water but I dragged them off with the back of a spoon. The first bowl of pasta I cooked too quickly, the second too long, but I ate the whole bag in almost one go and then vomited white water.

Outside, the day was bright. The sun made stars as it came through the cracks in the window. I found some moisturiser, almost empty, and cut it open to get the last little bit out and put it on my neck, and when my shoes were dry, I walked to try to get a better sense of where I was. Kole's compass was broken. I could point it the same way, and it would show me N, then E then S.

Somewhere not too far from the caravans, I found berries. Further on, I found a bus, flipped on its side a few hundred metres after a stop. The pole at the bus stop had been turned into a flag with a T-shirt and someone had painted some place names in white paint on the road. None of the names were on Davey's map.

It was at the furthest point in the walk that I saw Westwood Cross, the old shopping centre, in the distance.

From up where I was, half a mile away, on a hill, it looked like a series of old and open boxes. There were huge hangars in the centre, and grids of unfinished toy houses round the edge. Years ago, someone had taken the sign from Debenhams and rearranged it so it said DAM HENS – but all the letters were gone now. After what Davey said, I would have thought I'd be able to see fighting from a distance. But there was no noise and I couldn't see a single person there.

I put another berry into my mouth and I remember thinking, did we just invent this? Did we stay inside our houses and think we weren't allowed to leave but actually it was all just in our heads?

But that was when the music started. The squeak of a speaker system. The highest sound. Then something like cellos, but also a thumping beat. All of it coming from

Westwood. And that was when I accidentally squashed all the berries that were left in my hand, and ran in the opposite direction.

When I got back to the caravans, I went to get a bottle of whisky I'd found that morning. I'd found it together with a pack of cigarettes tucked up on a ridge underneath one of the trailers. One cigarette was missing but, apart from that, neither had been touched. They were in a plastic bag bought from a petrol station. I imagined the dad who'd probably brought it back here, planned to enjoy away from his wife and kids. The receipt was still in the bag. It had the brand names written out on it, prices. The magic of that.

I sat on a deckchair under a parasol with broken spokes. The seal on the bottle broke with a crack. I told myself I'd have a quick sip, then pack up, get going again.

The problem was, I kept on thinking about the music from Westwood. I thought about it more and more. The whisky made my veins less stiff; it felt like hope, or something close to it, and in a cloud of madness, it seemed to make sense that I should go back there.

I woke up in the same deckchair with the bottle in my lap, only a few inches of it left. The cigarettes were nearly finished too, and I'd folded the pack into some sort of origami. I didn't remember doing that. I just about had time to think what an idiot I was, when I leaned out of the chair and vomited again

– brown milk now. I wondered if I was actually ill. Like Mac had been, or Caleb.

Home. My stomach clenched again. Like a fist, tighter than that. I cleaned my chin. I packed up my stuff. But still, the music was the only thing I could think of. I thought about how they used to play music at the train station and at bus stops because it made people calmer. Music was a good thing. Maybe it was still playing.

I climbed back up the shallow hill. The music had stopped, but I could see people in one of the car parks now. I made a frame around my eyes with my fingers so I could focus more. Green had cracked through the tarmac but you could still see some of the car park markings, faded white rectangles. The people were sitting on the roofs of cars with their feet where the engine would be. I heard the sound of a laugh. Their bodies looked big, that was one of the first things I noticed. Like they had enough to eat. Then I heard another laugh.

This sudden feeling of hope again. What if it was nice there? What if there was someone in charge? What if they were cooking meals? Not food but meals. I couldn't get my body to move away. I was imagining eating. I wondered if they were planning how to get across, if maybe it would be easier if we were all together.

I think I was about to stand up and start walking towards them when suddenly I heard a noise in the bushes behind me. I jerked round but couldn't see anyone. Then a twig or a stone landed in the grass next to me. I reached for the gun, but the T-shirt was too tight around it. I flinched, expecting to feel something heavy and hard against the back of my head. But the only thing that came was a voice.

'Don't do it,' the voice said, and before I could unwrap the gun, I turned and saw the person the voice came from. It was a woman. A woman with a dirty face and white hair in a ponytail on top of her head. 'I know what you're thinking of doing, but you shouldn't.' I stared at her. 'Don't mind that,' she said, pointing to the mud on her face, 'I put that there.'

The mud sat dark in her wrinkles. She told me her name – quickly, like doing that would be the thing that would stop us hurting each other.

'You're too young for me to let you go there and get killed,' she said. 'Don't do it. Those men are no good. I promise you that.'

She noticed me looking at her arms and told me not to worry, she just bruised easily. It's funny. She didn't look like my mum at all, not really, but when I looked at her all I could think was – my mum won't get a chance to do that, to get old like that.

'I have a place,' I found myself saying. 'A place where I'm staying. If you like we could sit there. We could talk for a bit.'

When we got to the caravan park, she said she'd been there before, but she didn't know when, because she kept accidentally going in circles. She had a bag. It was lots of plastic carrier bags, one inside the other, but over time, holes had rubbed through the outer bags so you could see flashes of different plastics. She pulled out something that looked like an abacus. There was silvery flesh on the grid of it. She pulled a piece off and started to chew.

She told me it was water-bird meat, dried in the sun, and told me how they tasted fatty, but almost like fish. She offered me some and I tried it in the end. I let it sit in my mouth, and it melted – this soft, acidy melting – so slowly it was almost comforting.

She told me she was looking for her daughter, and asked if I'd seen her. She said that apart from the birds, there were water plants I could eat too. Sea cabbage, something like that. She said I'd have to remember the way she described these things because she didn't have the energy to walk with me to find them.

I let her take a look at Davey's map, and she spread out the soft material over her knee in a way that made me think of a pirate. 'Monstan?' she said.

'Manston.'

'Not a writer, your friend.' She looked at me. She looked at the map again. 'Where do you reckon we are on this?'

I pointed. She shook her head, and drew a new map on top of Davey's with her shaky fingers. She saw it all differently.

'What about the wall?' I said. 'Have you been there yet?'

'Wall?' she said. 'I don't know any wall.' She got a little bit of the dried bird meat out of her teeth with her middle finger-nail. 'I must have left before all that.'

I asked her what was wrong with Westwood, and she told me that it was only men, and that nothing is good when it's only men, because it's the easiest way to get rid of evolution. She kept on falling asleep. Eventually, she told me she was tired and asked if she could stay the night.

'It's not like it's mine,' I said.

'Still, good to be polite.'

She stood a little closer to me and asked if she was allowed to hug me and I said okay and she didn't smell that good or that bad either and we both shut our eyes and pretended the other was another person, I think.

'I'm looking for someone too,' I said. 'My brother and my son.' My throat closed. 'It's the same person. And a girl. Another girl.'

I had to tell someone. I wanted to tell someone. Her heartbeat was slow, steady, I felt it.

'We'll find them,' she said.

They came for us in a car. When I heard the sound of the engine, the sound of wheels against the gravel, the sound of shouting, I should have tried to run, I should have tried to hide and get the old woman to come with me.

I had no idea what was happening though, and she was asleep. Asleep on the chair, her cheek resting on a jumper she'd found. She twitched as she slept – I'd watched her for a while before I'd fallen asleep too.

It must have been four or five, early morning, when they came. A little bit of light outside, but only just starting to come through the windows. I remember the sound of car doors slamming almost at the same time. I watched her eyes open wide. My eyes were already like that. The whites of our eyes shone at each other.

There were four of them at first. I didn't have time to jump down from the bunk bed. Their bodies seemed to bang into all of the walls at the same time. They had guns or bats in their hands. Both. Whatever it was, they were dark, and by the time they left, all of the glass was broken.

She was the one they went for. They crowded round her. Then I saw what they were doing through a gap between two bodies and I saw them hold her face back by her hair and cut her throat. Sideways, but lengthways too, so in the middle, where an Adam's apple would be there was a cross.

No one saw me at first. No one had seen me. I tried to pull my body far back in the bunk and deep down into the mattress, so deep I'd disappear.

It was another man, a man who walked in on his own, who spotted me.

'Jesus,' I heard him say, when he saw her neck. He stumbled backwards closer to where I was. He was shorter than the other men. He had a crowbar in his hand.

As he got closer, I prayed he wouldn't turn around. I tried not to breathe. Then, as I turned to put my head sideways, even more out of sight, our eyes caught in the mirror.

He spun around. I was seeing everything out of the corner of my eye. It looked like his arm was long, but it was just a metal bar he was raising into the air.

It was as the bar was coming down – I watched it coming, it was going to break any part of me it landed on – that I recognised him. It took me a moment to understand.

Liam. It was Liam.

414

He had a beard now, but I was sure it was him. It was Liam. All of this flooded together at once. His arm froze, and just in time, just before it hit me, the angle of his swing changed. It hit the wood of the bunk bed instead.

'Oi, what was that?' one of the men called through an eggshell-thin wall.

'Fuck all,' Liam shouted back. 'Just rooting round for supplies.'

His eyes were locked on me the whole time. I could hardly move, but I tried to nod. He hadn't seen me for years. I wanted him to be sure it was me. His finger went to his lips. 'Don't say a word,' he mouthed.

I could hear the sound of feet scuffling in the next room. One spat. 'Done now,' the other man said, 'we're headin' out, Lee,' and he slammed the door so hard on his way out it bounced back open. Liam looked through into the other room to make sure they'd all gone.

'Chance,' he said. And then the way he held his body changed completely. His face softened. He stepped onto the bottom bunk so he could see me properly. 'Fucking hell, Chance . . .'

I started to say something. He covered my mouth.

'No, if they hear you, if they see you – fuck.'

'Why did they do that?' I said. My throat wasn't working.

'Because she was stealing from us,' he said. 'I think. I don't know. I don't even know any more. Your mum,' he said. 'How's your mum?'

I shook my head.

'You have to get away from here. As fast as you can, as far as you can. Get away from them, okay? Are you listening to me?'

I nodded.

'Lee!' one of the men shouted from outside.

'Take this,' Liam said. He put his crowbar down next to me on the bed. 'I'm going to get them away.' He looked out of the window again then turned back to the bunk. 'You don't move till they've gone, do you understand? You stay still as a fucking plank. You have to look after yourself, Chance.'

He walked away from me. He opened the door of the caravan.

'Fucking took your time,' one of the others shouted at him. 'Something good in there or what?'

'Fucking nothing. Empty-handed, aren't I?'

'Left your iron in there, mate,' the guy said. 'I'll go get it.'

'Don't,' Liam said. But he'd said it too quickly.

I tried to watch through the windows. The second man was taller, wider. He moved to go past Liam.

'Just don't, I said,' Liam said again.

'Are you touching me?'

'Yeah, I'm touching you. It fucking snapped clean in two, din't it?' Liam said. 'Useless now.'

There was a silence.

'You've done enough in there,' I heard Liam say. 'So now let's all fuck off, shall we?'

416

I shut my eyes. I expected to hear the sound of the door opening.

Instead, I heard the doors slamming at slightly different times again. The sound of their engine. Wheels against the gravel. Skids. Shouts getting smaller as they sped away.

My eyes stayed shut, but the images I could see against the inside of my eyelids seemed so real I could feel my face crush in on itself again and again, trying to push them away.

When I made myself look at the woman, there was still blood coming out of her neck. It was drying in layers, the bottom ones darker, the fresh ones almost pink.

I held my sleeve over my mouth. I shut her eyes with my fingers. Her eyelids didn't fight like I thought they would. Not like Kole's had. Something about her skin was so soft it reminded me of the driest leaves, the ones that crumble in your fingers. I took the blanket from the bed and put it over her. Then I grabbed whatever else I could see that was useful and put it all into Kole's canvas bag.

I left the caravan park behind me, and did exactly what

Liam had said – I ran as fast and as low as I could, in the opposite direction to the shopping centre.

There was countryside for miles. A colour-by-numbers book, but with only half filled in. Some plants liking the sun, others shrinking in it. Rough dry bushes with pink feather flowers, spongy swells of ground figs. Then different patches charred black.

Telephone pylons had been tipped over. Some had tarps over them, been tents maybe. From a distance, they looked like corpses, covered to keep them decent. I peeled back a tarp, a smaller one, and tied it to my bag strap in case it rained again.

Along the train tracks, all the old signal boxes had been axed open. There were all these butterflies. Bright red, black and blue. The brushwood and purple clouds. Names my mum taught me as a kid. Beet fields and sundogs. Then all these flashes – the gaping splits on the woman's neck, Kole's thick and bleeding back, the bodies on the beaches – that slid into one other like a flick book.

In the middle of the day, when there was no choice but to find shade, I looked at my body, because if I looked at a small single place, it was easier not to think about other things. The hair on some parts had stopped growing. One leg had more hair on it than the other. I'd fallen onto my knee at one point and lost all my skin. The scraped-away place had a shine now, constantly wet. I tried to scrape the dirt out of it with my fingernail, but that was dirty too.

I had no food, no water. I had to go faster.

*   *   *

419

I walked and I walked and I walked. I passed a home with boarded-up windows and superglue in all the locks. No roof. I tried to use Davey's map, but more than anything, I chose whatever path the shade made, and tried to navigate north, away from the coast, away from the sun.

For a while, a dirty dry-mud slope ran alongside the road. I figured I'd be able to see further from the top, see where I was, where I should go. My feet kept slipping in the dust as I tried to climb it. I put my hands to the earth, and scrambled like that instead. When I got to the top, I teetered on the dusty, crumbling edge. Beyond it was a steep drop into a ditch. My eyes skipped like stones across it. A colourful mess of rags, a suitcase, the stuttering of a rat, but more than anything – a terrible smell of rotting.

I slid back down the bank away from it all, then held leaves to my face and breathed into those to get the smell away. My stomach felt like knives. I prayed I would find food soon. Even my skin felt thinner. As I walked on, I found myself saying things out loud rather than in my head. People's names. The ends of sentences.

I was wearing a coat I'd taken from the caravan. A thin red coat because it had a hood for the sun. There were things in the pockets. Old bus tickets, balled in the corners of the pockets. There was also a packet of sugar on the left side. One of the small ones they used to give away with a coffee. It said Saint-Louis on it. I held it while I walked. It was stiff at first, but turned soft, to silk.

I felt that while I still had it I would be okay. I thought about what having the crystals on my tongue would feel like, how they'd melt, crunch under my teeth. How my headache might stop.

And as I walked, each step became a beat, some kind of 'if'. The thinness of that word, how much it can mean.

The water started slowly, and then it was everywhere.

Up until then, the ground had been logged and soggy at points, but the water had run into little rivers. It wound through rushes. Everywhere else, it had been dry enough. Walkable. The sun had baked some roads to cracks. This was different. I looked up. The clouds looked like falling dust that had been paused. Then I looked down. The same clouds, reflected. Ahead, the fields were like glass, doubling the sky.

There was no way round the water, so I started to walk slowly through it. Harder patches of ground, then sudden sinkholes, impossible to predict. I wasn't wearing the right shoes. Kole's boots had been nearly to the knees, with a drawstring at the top to keep them tight. We'd pushed him out of the window in them without thinking. However big they'd be, I wished I had them now. The path seemed to slope downwards. Within a few steps, the water fell into my shoes in a rush. Through the holes for laces, over and under the tongue.

It felt like each step I took would push the ground deeper. Sink the whole thing. Like I was treading on some kind of water lily that wouldn't take my weight.

The clouds lowered, and they didn't feel cool, they felt hot. Smoke. This dirtiness to them. My skin was peeling again. It came off on my fingers whenever I touched my face. I put a piece on my tongue, to see if it tasted of anything.

I could only see a few metres ahead of me. I tried to imagine seeing myself from above instead. Like a dot. Like that would help.

I struck a bit of harder ground. Then, suddenly, a breeze. The clouds fell back.

And there it was. A river. Silver as eels, throwing back light from the other side.

And behind it, at last, the wall.

It was made of breeze blocks. They were waterlogged to grey. They faded evenly as my eyes moved up them. There were dents in the concrete, from gunshots, thrown rocks maybe.

High up on one side, it looked like a couple of blocks were missing. I tried to judge from the hole how thick the wall was. But nothing. It looked like it might be hollow. Something about the whole thing looked cheaply built, quickly built.

But here it was. The thing we'd made with our own hands. It was huge. It felt like it stretched on for ever, its edges tapering into the mist. Weren't there meant to be roads? A bridge? A gate? Anything. I thought of the stories we'd heard – the tent villages, the soldiers who shot. But there were no signs of any of that.

I couldn't understand. The gangs, at least – the smugglers had driven truckloads of people away. I'd seen that with my own eyes. I'd seen them drive off in old coaches. Coaches with cracked windows and luggage holds with missing doors. The coaches had come back time and time again. People had paid to go.

I walked slowly along the edge of the water. I nudged my foot at the silt as if I'd find something underneath. And then it came in drips. Drips of cold along the back of my neck.

The ditches a few miles back. The ditches with their mess and smell. The rags, the suitcase. The rags were clothes. They'd been bodies. The people who'd tried to leave, who'd tried to get across. The people who'd been told there'd be jobs where they were going. Were the ditches where they'd ended up?

My stomach, the muscles of it, folded in half. I started to retch, but there was nothing inside me that could possibly come out. I started to see their faces, faces that pressed against glass, mouths that made the shape of goodbye. It was all I could see.

My headache started to feel like someone unknotting my brain. On the high enough ground in front of the river I lay down in the half-shade of a huge, tangled digger tyre. The sun felt like a hand pressing down on me. My legs folded underneath me, the way an animal's legs buckle to sit. I put down the tarp and spread my body flat to even out the weight. I was so thirsty it became a different feeling altogether. There was water everywhere, but it was thick with mud.

As I lay there, I held the pass that Kole had said had got him across, got him into London. The lamination caught the light and I saw parts of my face in the reflection, then behind it, sharing the space, the man from the photo. He must have been over fifty, he was black, he had a shaven head.

'Do I look like you?' I think I said, out loud again maybe, because I almost laughed.

And that was when I must have passed out. It happened gently. Because I remember thinking: it does feel like a pass, one hand passing me to another, passing me on, passing me back and forth, passing me out.

I looked at the sun just before that happened. Middle of the sky. Hotter than anything. It must have been just before midday when the world disappeared.

When I woke, the edges around my vision were dark, cloudy. I tried to blink the fuzziness away.

I scrambled to a sitting position. How could I have fallen asleep here?

But when I sat up, here had changed. The water had sunk back down. There was a channel still ahead, thick and deep, but at my feet there was a wide beach of dark, wet silt – the top layer loose with the last of the water, the occasional pock of a bubble popping.

Land again, or something like it. I started to walk. Parallel to the channel, parallel to the wall.

With the water low, now there were signs that a few people had made it this far. The people who'd gone on their own, maybe, right at the start. Here and there, I could make out tent poles dug into the ground, visible now, leaning at odd angles. A rucksack, some kind of bag, anyway, caught in the skeleton branches of a tree.

Mostly, I kept my eyes on the wall. There didn't seem to be movement anywhere near, but it was hard to see. Hard to see anywhere. Low clouds kept blocking it, appearing, then peeling back again. In the short moments where the wall was clear in my vision, the one or two watchtowers looked deserted. Watchtowers is too big a word. They stood out tall at certain intervals, but all of the glass in every window was smashed. It all looked abandoned.

And then a clot of cloud cleared, and in front of me, about a hundred steps away, I saw a patch of darkness at the edge of the water.

It was a figure, or two figures maybe. Too high and too big to be one person. I felt for the gun.

The sun had got inside my head, and made everything burned there. Bleached. Blank, anyhow. The gun was in my hand. It tugged at my wrist. I kept on walking towards the dark shape.

I was getting closer and closer. This strange calm. I knew it was wrong to feel it. Only ten feet away now, the clouds were so thick, soon it would be reaching distance. Arms out, gunmetal hot. I turned my head away, as if that would make it not count.

The gun started shaking in my hand. It was too heavy to hold out like that. I turned back.

428

And then I saw it was a horse. At first, I thought maybe I was dreaming. Start in Dreamland, end up there, too. Never escape.

But it was real. Standing, tussling, head high, next to – that was surely a body lying on the ground.

The head was covered loosely with a black plastic bag. The dirty clouds had left dust over it. I got closer.

The horse shuffled, then settled again.

Three. My teeth started a beat . . . Three, then two, then one.

I pulled back the covering.

I didn't mean to cry when I saw him. But again, that's just what happened.

His lean, inky body. The line of muscle either side of his belly button. This little crust on his eyelashes. Davey. I found myself on my knees next to him. I touched his neck and it pushed back against my fingers. A pulse. But it was weak, barely a fraction of a beat. The cracks in his lips were so deep. I had the smallest bit of water left in my bag. I took the sugar from my pocket, opened it and tipped it in. Anything to bring him back to life. I shook the bottle, and started to pour it into his mouth, my fingers around his face catching the drops. He coughed. But he coughed. I never loved a cough more. And when he came to, he jolted away, and put his forearms up against his body, until he realised it was me.

I fell back, flat-backed and, for a moment, we were silent.

Then on Davey's face. Not a smile, but. Another cough, wet this time.

'It's you,' he said.

His eyes were red, like he hadn't breathed, and couldn't.

'What are you doing here?' I said. I kept on saying, 'What are you doing?'

'There isn't anyone here,' he said.

I was scared his eyes were going to close again. I shifted next to him to keep him sitting up.

'Not a fucking soul,' he said. 'I even shouted.'

'Don't,' I said. 'Just . . .'

'No one came.'

I touched his temple and it felt like there were more dips in his skull than there should be. I looked across at the rest of his body. And that was when I realised he was wearing a welding outfit. Unzipped to the waist but, still. He even had a mask too, hanging from his neck.

'Good, isn't it?' he said. He took a breath and it sounded like water running over stones. 'Back to the future.' When he coughed again, I felt it through his whole back.

'What the hell, Davey?' I pointed at the horse.

'You know this guy. Gal. Sorry.' He pushed his forehead against her, spoke into her coat.

I put my hands on Davey's face. I moved, was on my knees in front of him now.

I had to do something to get him more water. I filled one bottle from the cleanest pool I could find, then, next to him, close to him, I poured it from one to the other, slowly, with my spare T-shirt stretched over the top like a filter. My hands were shaking.

'Are you going to do that now?' he said.

'When was the last time you had something to drink?'

'If you mean water . . .' he said. 'Actual water?' His voice was weak but he laughed. 'I don't know. Maybe last year?'

As I poured, my mouth made the shapes it makes when it's concentrating. It was watering too. The weave of this T-shirt was tight. The drips fell slowly. It made me think of time, the whole of it. The way it drips like that. From one place to another, with things stripped from it.

'I'm sorry it's taking so long,' I said.

It was so hot but Davey was shaking like it was cold. Whatever he had taken leaving his body, maybe, I don't know. I put in one of the iodine pills I'd taken from the caravan.

'Where did you get that?' he said.

'Look. It turns it pink.'

I gave the bottle a shake. It made a soft fizzing sound, and it made the water taste how heaters smell, when someone first turns them on.

'Like burning,' Davey said, when I gave him the first sip.

'I know. Just drink it.'

I wanted him to have the whole bottle, and I realised that sometimes the thing that can save you more than anything else is having someone to look after.

'I went to your house,' he said.

'You don't have to say anything. Have some water first—'

'I saw her,' he said. 'I'm sorry.'

Still. This peace, being with him.

'It isn't still . . .?' In that moment, I forgot the name of Davey's horse he'd had when we were kids. 'I thought you had to sell it.'

'Not "it", you sadist. Her,' he said. 'I got her back, didn't I.' I reached out, gave her a little scruffle too. A powder-thin cloud rubbed free from her coat. 'The family who bought her kept her in this field,' he said. 'I'd visit. Watch her at least. But one day, I saw they were packing up to leave. So I went back in the night. Got her out.' He smiled then. 'She was a lamb though. Easy as peach.'

'And after that?'

'Kept her in some old music studio.'

'Made her a pop star.'

'Nah, but soundproof walls, everything. Abandoned.' He coughed again and his face did this crumple thing. 'And grazing not far. But that was why—' he took a jagged, broken breath '—I wanted the vegetables. Bit of why. Lives off air, this one. But every queen's gotta have her carrots.'

Davey told me he had got here quickly, too quickly. Stupidly quickly. He said he didn't even remember deciding. He'd gone to my house to check if I'd left for real. And then he saw Ma. And after that, he and the horse had just flown here.

'Like just so fast. Dumb, really. Rode through the heat. Even at midday. And I got here before you. So I've been waiting,' he said. 'Out here in this fucking nightmare.'

I nodded.

'For you.'

'I know.'

'It was because of the goodbye.'

I looked at the sky. The clouds looked like they'd come from far away.

'I didn't want to say goodbye.'

I think what I found hardest, what I'd always found hardest, was him being kind to me.

'Because I'm an idiot sometimes,' he said. 'Because I didn't realise. And then I did. I realised you had gone to get him back. The little feller.'

'Davey, I—'

'I have to tell you something.' We both said it at the same time. Davey pushed forwards with his. 'I never wanted to ask. I'm not gonna ask now. But I know some things. I know he's not your mum's.'

'Davey.'

'I know that because ... we were young and everything but I was there. I was looking. Always looking at you. Looking out for you.'

'I know.'

'And you and me, we. At that time. Sometimes. It was the way he always touched things. Blue, I mean. Interested. Like I am. It's stupid. I know that doesn't mean anything.'

434

'Davey.' His name. I don't know how many times I said it.

'And he liked me. He did, didn't he? Don't say anything. I don't want you to. That's not what I'm asking for. Even if it's this much—' he made a space between his thumb and his finger; it was tiny, kept closing because his hands were shaking '—that's fine,' he said. 'That's all I need. And it doesn't matter either way. I'd still want to come.'

'But I don't even know what I'm going to do, though,' I said. 'From here on. This is as far as I thought.'

I looked at him. Now he was looking away I felt safe to, and I looked at him. I couldn't stop looking at him. He stood up for the first time, using the horse for balance.

'I'm sorry I'm making you do this,' I told him.

'I'm sorry I made you stay so long,' he said back.

The channel was connected to the tide, because it was still sinking down and more. Things had started showing up on the riverbed now. A sleeping bag pinned down by a huge rock. A lifejacket with a cut in it. Davey was shaky on his feet at first, but shook his head and blew blood, dried and not dry, out of his nose. We got our things together. I tried to take one of Davey's bags. It was heavy enough to jolt my shoulder.

'Good of you to bring rocks,' I said.

'Scaffolding,' he replied, without even looking back.

Davey had brought pulleys and ropes he had left over from the window business. He said he'd just grabbed it, thrown stuff in a bag. But we'd be able to make do. He said we could ride the horse over to the edge of the wall, depending on how high the water was. 'She can take it. Fed her better than myself all these years. I mean, look at her,' he said, tipping his head back to admire her, as if he'd made her himself. 'She's a leggy bird.'

I asked Davey if he'd seen anyone on the way here, anyone at all.

'One guy. Old guy. No teeth,' he said.

'The dream.'

'Shagged him, course.' He reached into his bag. 'I brought this, by the way. Been saving it for the right occasion.' He let it roll off his palm. 'Proper three-pack.' This thud as it hit the ground. Three tins of tuna, still wrapped in plastic. The plastic was a bit yellow, had come loose. 'It's no whale but . . . You can do the honours,' he said.

I cracked it, and a little bit of oil came out of the hole. I put my tongue on it straight away. I kept on looking up at him. Like a child I looked up. Salt, slip, the thick taste of fish. I couldn't stop smiling. The oil was hot. It was almost sweet too. I peeled back the metal. Even just the colour of the meat. We ate with our fingers. I chewed each mouthful then I would suck it, suck it, suck it for every drop. Chew, then suck. It got caught in my teeth. I ran my tongue around my mouth. We ate two of the three cans, and kept on saying 'what?' to each other because neither of us could stop smiling, and then we licked our fingers and licked them again and could not stop licking our fingers.

After we ate, we sat legs out, hands behind us. I noticed Davey looking at Kole's gun. It was next to me. 'Hope that thing's got the child lock on it,' he said. 'Can I?' He took it in his hands. Then he unpopped the cylinder in a smooth, creamy click. 'What?' he said. 'I'm a boy, it's in my blood.'

'You're a twat's what you are,' I said, and he laughed.

He let a few of the bullets fall out onto his palm. 'The fuck are these?' he said. He tilted his hand from side to side so they rolled back and forth.

'It's Kole's,' I said. 'All of it's Kole's.'

'You had a gun this whole time?'

'No,' I said.

'I thought all that North Foreland stuff, the stuff about him being king of the castle there . . . I thought it was just a rumour you started. I thought he was dead.'

'No,' I stopped. 'Or yeah. Yes, now.'

He saw there was more. He also saw there would be time for me to tell it.

'Anyway, what that fucker's done,' he said, 'is slice the top of these.' He showed me the tip of each bullet. A cross was cut into each one. It went quite deep. 'Just a little nick with a Stanley knife. But it makes them the worst. Explode on contact. The exit wound is . . .' He didn't mean to, but the tips of his lips lifted. 'Done a nice job on them, though,' he said, and he slotted the bullets back, one by one, into the gun. 'R', he said, 'I', he said, 'P'.

As we waited for the water to sink to its lowest point, we spoke about a lot of things and also not much. We sat there for a while. We talked about people we had both known. The names, we used their whole names, they filled us up in some way. I still couldn't work out if all this was a hello or goodbye. Davey held my hands and touched my face and we kissed each other a lot of times and I put my head on him and they felt like the right things to do.

'I don't think it will get any lower than that,' Davey said at a certain point. The colour of the silt. It looked like freshly poured concrete. The type we'd try to find as kids so we could write in it.

We looked at the shape of the waves to see if the water would head out even more, but they kept changing and it didn't matter. It was time to go.

'Stop saying the horse,' he said to me. 'She has a name.' I nodded. 'Swifty,' he said. 'Swifty! You're stone cold,' he said, shaking his head at me. 'The stone coldest. Stop being rude and check her feet with me.' The way she lifted each ankle for him, one by one, all he had to do was touch it. 'She hates it when stones are stuck.'

After that, I held Kole's gun tucked in my armpit as I did up my jacket, and it nearly dropped into the sludge.

'I'll take that,' Davey said, as he slid the barrel deep into his leather belt.

He had me stand on his knee to mount. Old days. Davey's body as a climbing frame. There was no saddle, just like there was always no saddle. He led her forward, looking down to see how her hooves would take to the ground.

He spoke into her neck, and shut his eyes when he was talking, and then there we were.

We waded, this ramshackle trio, into the water.

Swifty went easy through the water. Her legs made tiny slivers of waves that pushed away from us. I weighed so little by this point that she didn't even seem to know I was on her back. I put my hand behind me and stroked her hip, and there was flesh on the bone – more flesh than I had.

We had almost got halfway across – Davey still on his feet, water to his thigh now, me high on Swifty's back – when we heard the first of the sounds.

The wind sharpened. This high-pitched noise at first, then low. Getting louder. It was coming from the other side. Davey turned to me. His eyes. He went on his tiptoes like that would help. 'Fuck,' he said. 'Oh fuck.' He turned back then forward again. Fast one way, then the other. Swifty started to do the same. 'Can you see what it is?' he said.

I put my hands up to shield the sun so I could see. The noise got louder and louder. And then I saw it.

'Davey,' I said. 'It's a plane.'

We were clear as day for them to see. Swifty's white back in the middle of the brown flood plain. The coat I'd stolen from the house was red. We stopped. Davey looked straight up. We both did. It wasn't like the planes that had dropped food packages. It looked military, but low, light. I felt sure in that moment that it would fire if it saw us.

And then Davey placed the reins over the horse's neck, so I could take them, and he pulled Kole's gun out from his belt.

His shoulders were shaking. He gripped the gun with both hands.

For a second I couldn't speak. The plane got nearer. It got lower, too. Davey moved his arms in time with its path.

'I'll do it,' he said. 'I can do it, maybe. It just has to get a tiny bit closer.'

Davey's arms weren't shaking from fear, just from how tightly he was holding the gun. It was when I saw the slightest shift in his body, and I knew he was about to pull the trigger, that I shouted for him to stop.

'What, Chance?' he said.

'What if . . .' The thought that it could be you in there. Somehow, my first thought was still always you. You being okay.

'If what, Chance? What? Just say it.'

I couldn't. But he looked at me like he could see everything.

'How many chances? You give them every chance,' he said. 'Every chance. And when is it . . .'

There were tears running down my face. His hands dropped.

'Even for a maybe,' he said.

The plane was nearly directly above us now.

'You're an idiot,' he said. He looked right at me. 'You always have been. You're so dumb about this stuff,' he said. 'You're so stupid.'

But I looked at him, and he was crying too.

We braced for them to shoot. Davey's arms were up over Swifty's side and I held them. I could feel it. I could feel it, everything ending. I could feel it between the bones in my spine. At least I'd got this far. At least I tried. That thought washed through me.

But then the plane flew high again. It flew over us – then it flew on.

I switched between looking up, and shutting my eyes so tightly I saw colours rather than black. Neither of us could say anything. As it passed over us, our heads followed it. As it got further away, the sound seemed to snag in the air behind it. But it kept going, it kept going, it kept going.

In the panic, Davey had turned us back around. We were facing home again. The colour in his face. Anything left of it had gone. 'Do you want to go back?' he said. 'Should we just?' He looked at me. 'We know it there.'

'No,' I said.

'Or I can go back? I can go back if you want me to. If that's what you want, Chance.'

But I shook my head. We shook our heads at the same time, actually.

'I suppose we're here now, aren't we?' he said. 'Better get on with it.'

And so we waded on, Davey, Swifty and me, in the direction of the wall. Rolls and rolls of barbed wire had fallen from where they had originally been placed, and caught the light, in jagged flashes, in the water. We'd decided on the place with the missing rectangles of breeze block. Figured it could be a foothold, handhold, eyehole, something. Adrenaline doesn't leave the body quickly. Mine swirled with it. I could feel it under my collarbone.

Sometimes one of Swifty's legs sank and left us off balance, but she'd only take a second to right herself. Stayed easy as anything, even as the water got higher and higher.

We were getting closer. It was fifteen foot tall. Twenty. Mac was right. Three of Davey, maybe four. Taller as we got near. Davey got there first. Looked back at us. Then we both put our hands against it. Up close, the breeze block was rough cut, almost had a kind of sparkle to it. Some parts had been painted with that sticky, slick anti-climb paint, but it was done so roughly. Random smears, easy to avoid. I rubbed my finger against the mortar between two low-down bricks, and a few grains of it came away so easily.

And that was when I looked at the wall, and looked at it, and saw that it wasn't really a wall made for water. Not in any real way. The blocks were turning dark with damp already. The mortar was normal mortar, made of sand. It wasn't a wall to stop water. It was a wall to stop us.

But not this person, I thought. Not this person any more.

We tied one of Davey's ropes to the crowbar. The plan was to throw the bar through the hole in the breeze block, and hope it would jam on the other side, so we could use the rope to pull ourselves up. Twice I missed. Hard to throw from sitting down. We dragged the crowbar back to us through the muddy water.

'Let it steam out your hand like a fucking javelin,' Davey said, and the third time, I made it. It flew through the hole. I tugged the rope. It held tight. We looked at each other.

'I'm going first,' Davey said, "cos you're about eight times better at climbing than me and I'm not getting stuck here.'

He turned to Swifty and took her heavy soft head in his arms. He kissed the front of her nose, then pressed his forehead against it and took the deepest inhale as if he could make the smell stay there. He kissed her one more time, then he turned away quickly, like a second longer would have stopped him leaving. He pulled at the rope, then, without looking at me, he started to walk up the wall.

His feet moved easy against the grey. He used the rope as a kind of banister. 'Can you see through?' I shouted up when he made it to the hole.

He said something about it being green, green on the other side.

'What?' I said.

'Greener on the other side. It's a joke. I can't see a thing yet. Hollow inside.'

With his feet standing in the hole, he could reach to the top of the wall. His wrists went white as he pulled himself up. I watched his back – so vulnerable like that, with his hands above his head. But he gave this grunt thing and then he hauled himself up. I looked up too. His head was in front of the sun and it flared either side of him. He was sitting on the edge of the wall, right at the top of it.

'Okay then, spiv,' he said, flexing blood back into his wrists. 'You coming up or what?'

I got the rest of the bags up to him, one by one. Pulleys and carabiners. Reef knots. Knots I hadn't used for so long.

With my hand on Swifty's blaze for luck, I said thank you, then started to climb. Hands on the rope, feet on the wall. All my blood in my fingertips. The ease of it, though. The space that seemed to spring between my feet and the water. This lifting in my chest.

'You're right,' I shouted up. 'I'm fucking great at this.' He laughed at me.

People must have done this before. Surely they must have. Davey dropped down a second rope for me, and just as I swung from one to the other, I saw a handprint of blood about a metre and a half to the side of my head.

'What?' he said.

'Nothing.' Looked dry, at least.

As Davey pulled me up, my coat came open and I cut my belly on the brick. I lifted up my T-shirt. Four hot red stripes.

'Jesus,' Davey said, pulling his trainer free from some rusty razor wire. 'Look at it.'

The top of the wall was just about thick enough to walk along. There were cigarette packets and food packets strewn along it, so heavily rained-on that the cardboard had unfolded into its blue print, melted into the grain of the concrete. A little drone of some sort, broken, like a toy without batteries. A helmet too, left out like a bowl. It seemed like no one had been there for a while.

The watchtowers were every hundred metres or so. Like the rest of the wall, they looked like they'd been made somewhere else. Thrown up quickly here. The screws that had held the sheets of metal together had come loose. Further on, a couple of the towers were tipping off. We walked along to the next one. The remnants of a fire on the floor. Wet ash and chewed meat bones.

'Who do you think they were, the people here?' I said.

'Here up here, or here down there?'

'Both.'

'Just normal people,' he said.

Swifty wouldn't stop following us. She was walking alongside the wall at the same pace, but the water was getting higher now. High over her belly, her tail in it. She was starting to get unsettled.

'Go!' Davey said. He even made the sound of a whip, tongue against teeth. 'Please.' But still she stood there, like she wouldn't leave without him. I could see him sucking his top lip into his mouth. He had tears in his eyes again.

'Hey,' I said. 'You wanna take that?' I pointed down to the crowbar and the rope.

'No. Fuck this wall. Fuck all these shitty made-up things.' He said he wanted to leave it for someone else to find it. Someone who needed it. Someone like us.

'What if there are more of them?'

'Walls? We'll find a way. Don't you think? Spidergirl. Didn't we always say that?'

He reached out and offered his hand to me, and in his hand I saw the whole story. Our tiny-boned bodies when we met at the Pearl, our naked chests as we ran through the darkness. All the other hands we had reached for, all the other hands that had reached for us.

'We're gonna mash our ankles doing this,' he said. He looked down at the ground. His eyebrows moved in that way they did when we were kids. His pupils in the sunlight looked almost purple.

Strange creatures. Davey in his welding suit, me in a stolen red coat. I looked out for the first time at the way ahead. Open, broken fields. You, Blue.

'Davey?' Fear came back. Fear like a flash of black. 'What if there's nothing? What if it's worse than that?'

But he didn't say a word. The tattoos on our hands, the nearly-nothing that was left of them, were touching. We stood tall on the breaking point between two worlds.

And then we jumped.

AUTHOR'S NOTE

This book is fiction, but it builds on events and policies that are occurring today. Much of the following is well-documented and well-known, but since *Dreamland* is set in a close future, close to home – and today's political landscape can seem at times hard to believe – I wanted to be clear about which elements are based on fact.

Housing

Over the last several decades, London councils have paid millions of pounds to move families in social housing to the outskirts of the capital, or to other areas of Britain. This happens in various ways. Sometimes, tenants are sent a letter from a 'decant officer', offering cash in exchange for leaving their homes and moving across the country. More often, this pushing-out-of-borough happens when a family loses their home – a situation made increasingly likely by a punitive combination of rising rents in the capital and severe benefits caps – and the only option they are given is to move far from the area in which they live.

If a family becomes homeless, the council has a duty to offer emergency or temporary accommodation. In theory, the Housing Act 1996 demands that councils house tenants within their borough 'so far as reasonably practicable', but the definition of reasonable has become increasingly elastic. In 2016, for example, an average of 500 families a week were sent out-of-borough this way, and thousands of families have been forced out of London altogether – sometimes given as little as twenty-four hours to accept new accommodation hundreds of miles away.

Relocation like this can be distressing and even life-threatening – being moved away from jobs, schools and support systems has led to breakdown, miscarriage and suicide attempts. In addition, the accommodation provided is frequently unsuitable: B&Bs or former hotels broken into bedsits where large families might share small, single rooms and bathrooms with other tenants; converted office blocks, carved up into units barely wider than an arm-span; or even shipping containers that are ice-cold in winter and hot enough to cause heat rash in summer. According to Shelter, at the end of June 2019, 'there were 86,130 homeless households living in temporary accommodation in England—the equivalent of the population of York, and representing an increase of 45% in just five years. This included 127,370 children.' The word 'temporary' is often deeply misleading too: such placements can last years.

This is a complex situation that councils are often strong-armed into as a result of a huge housing shortage, funding decimated by austerity, and existing real estate assets having to be sold off to keep services afloat. This has led to increased privatisation, creating a system vulnerable to abuse. There are incentives for private landlords and for-profit 'service providers' who rent to councils: not only can they be eligible for one-off financial 'sweeteners' for housing people without homes, they can often charge highly inflated 'nightly paid' rates, sometimes playing desperate councils off against each other to get the highest amount.

There are also clear incentives for London councils to move families beyond the city limits: housing outside of London is cheaper, and once relocated, families use social services in the new area instead, reducing costs to London councils even further.

When plots or buildings come up outside the capital that are suitable for development into long-term affordable housing, there have been examples of London authorities outbidding local councils to snap them up – making it all the more difficult for councils outside of London to meet the needs of their existing citizens, who can be left behind on interminable waiting lists.

Margate
The coastal town of Margate, on the Isle of Thanet in Kent, has been affected by these patterns. Beginning as early as the

1980s, like many British seaside towns it became a place where London councils relocated some of their most vulnerable populations, despite Margate offering relatively few opportunities for employment at the time, and local services already being overstretched. By 2005, at one local primary school, the transience of families being shifted in and out of town had resulted in a reported 50 per cent annual turnover in the student population.

This, though, is just one part of Margate's history of roller-coaster fortunes. Once a small, working coastal town, in the eighteenth century it became a pioneer of the British seaside resort, with novel sea-bathing machines, playhouses, Georgian squares and in-vogue sanatoriums attracting dukes and duchesses. As accessibility from London shifted from fourteen hours by stagecoach, to six and a half hours by 'steamer' boat along the Thames, to just a few hours on the railway, its popularity as a holiday destination soared over the next 200 years.

Then, in the 1970s, cheap flights and European package deals started to lure holidaymakers in a different direction. This caused a downturn that was forcefully compounded by recession in the early 1980s.

As economic opportunities diminished, Margate's former tourist lodgings found a new use as accommodation for people who had been made homeless, newly arrived immigrants, and other vulnerable groups. Large hotels were block-booked as emergency accommodation, or bought as investments by private landlords who could rely on government-assured rents. As institutional, Victorian-style asylums were shut down in London to make way for community care, patients were dispersed across the country, including to private accommodation in Margate (where the nearest specialist support was in Bexley, 70 miles away). At the turn of the millennium, when David Seabrook was writing his memoir-cum-travelogue of Thanet, *All the Devils Are Here*, he recounts Cliftonville being dubbed 'Kosoville' at the time, as a result of an influx of refugees from Eastern Europe. Other nicknames of the period included the 'Costa del Dole' – which conveys something of the employment situation facing new arrivals.

For others, the sense of being sent to the edge of the country to wait for their fate to be determined was even more literal. In the early 2000s, a number of people seeking asylum in the UK were sent on coaches from London to stay at the sea-facing Nayland Rock Hotel while they waited for decisions to be made about whether they would be allowed to stay in the country. In the years that followed, the hotel was earmarked to be used, instead, as a holding centre for 'failed' asylum seekers whose applications had been rejected. This time they would be awaiting deportation.

The situation today

Today in Margate, the tide of popularity has turned yet again. The same elements that attracted visitors in the first place – the sea, beautiful architecture, and Turner sunsets ('The skies over Thanet are the loveliest in all Europe,' the painter once said) – have combined with a buoyant arts scene and high-speed train link to London to reverse Margate's fortunes. The year 2019 saw record numbers of visitors welcomed, and millions of pounds injected into the local economy.

This has also brought with it a new complexity. The renewed surge in demand for housing (often by Londoners, themselves escaping runaway prices in the capital) has led the average house price in Margate to rocket by over 40 per cent in the last five years – more than 300 per cent the rate of central London zones one and two over the same period. Given that Margate Central and Cliftonville West still remain within the 10 per cent most-deprived areas of the UK, these spiralling prices often outpace local budgets. Equally, a strong buy-to-let and returning holiday rental market threatens the ongoing affordability for long-standing renters: landlords who banked property years ago now have new, more profitable avenues to make money.

Displacement continues in myriad forms throughout the country. In 2018 it was revealed that, as part of so-called 'reconnection policies', various councils throughout the UK had offered thousands of people without homes one-way train tickets to leave councils' areas of responsibility and, effectively, 'return to where they came from' – even though, in some cases, the people sent away didn't know anyone where they were going.

Simultaneously, the British government is experimenting with increasingly brutal methods to limit immigration. In late 2020, it emerged that the UK Home Office, hoping to deter the arrival of asylum seekers, had discussed the ideas of off-shore processing, and wave machines and marine fencing to deter incoming boats.

Meanwhile, the impact of climate change is increasingly felt in Britain and around the world. One in six people in Britain already lives at risk of flooding; in the coming decades, due to heavier rainfall plus sea-level rise, once-a-century sea-level events are predicted to become annual. In the government's 2017 National Risk Register of Civil Emergencies, coastal flood risk was second only to pandemic flu. The Environment Agency has said that 'continuing to maintain all the current coastal flood defences over the next 100 years is unsustainable', and that difficult conversations will need to be had about which areas can be protected and which can not.

Dreamland imagines what happens next.

Sources for Author's Note

For more information about temporary accommodation, as well as social tenants being displaced, shelter.org.uk is a vital resource. Shelter does extraordinary work not only supporting people, but documenting experiences and bringing out finely researched and accessible reports – if you want to read more, need help, or want to support their work, visit their website (see above). On London families being 'silently shipped out' of the city, and 'reconnection policies', there has been excellent reporting by The Independent *and* The Guardian *in particular. Alan White's 2012 essay in the* New Statesman, *'Thousands of homeless families drift to the end of the track', is a blistering overview of the Margate-specific context up until the last decade; Matthew Clayfield's 'On Margate Sands: Farage, Dreamland, and the UKIP-ification of the Tories' reaches into more recent history. Further sources for this author's note can be found below.*

'English councils breaking law in "secretly" relocating homeless people', Sarah Marsh, *The Guardian*, 1 October 2020

'London council in "social cleansing" row over bid to move tenants to Birmingham', Nadia Khomani, *The Guardian*, 6 May 2015

'Over 50,000 families shipped out of London boroughs in the past three years due to welfare cuts and soaring rents', *The Independent*, 29 Feb 2016

'Homeless families to be expelled from London by councils', Patrick Butler and Ben Ferguson, *The Guardian*, 4 November 2012

'Now scarce social housing is being flogged off at auction by councils desperate to stay afloat', Glyn Robbins, *The Independent*, 17 May 2019

'Londoners to be sent to Canterbury after council bidding war for housing', Damian Gayle, *The Guardian*, 25 May 2016

'London councils pay landlords £14m in "incentives" to house homeless people', Robert Booth, *The Guardian*, 25 March 2019

'Councils "forcing homeless families to relocate miles away"', Patrick Butler, *The Guardian*, 22 May 2016

'Bleak Houses: Tackling the crisis of family homelessness in England', Children's Commissioner, August 2019

Reports by Shelter
'Research: Temporary Accommodation in London'
'Sick and Tired – The Impact of Temporary Accommodation on the Health of Homeless Families'
'Report: Cashing in – How a shortage of social housing is fuelling a multimillion-pound temporary accommodation sector'
'Briefing: Offering Temporary Accommodation Out of Area'
'Report: Far From Alone'

'Live Margate Housing Intervention Business Plan', Kent County Council/Thanet District Council

'Margate's seaside heritage', Historic England, 2007

'As they close London's psychiatric hospitals, where's the care? Report', John Lister, COHSE, 1991

'Thousands of homeless families drift to the end of the track', Alan White, *New Statesman*, 21 November 2012

'On Margate Sands: Farage, Dreamland, and the UKIP-ification of the Tories', Matthew Clayfield originally published in the *Saturday Paper* as 'Waiting for Dreamland', 24 May 2017

'Making Towards a Promised Land, Wendy Ewald in conversation with Michael Morris', ArtAngel, 15 Jul 2005

All the Devils Are Here, David Seabrook, Granta (2002)

'Margate: will the buyers keep coming from London?', Harriet Fitch Little, *Financial Times*, 12 April 2018

'Turning the Tide: Social justice in five seaside towns', The Centre for Social Justice, 2016

'Out of Area – Vulnerable Placements Thanet District Briefing Pack', Thanet Leadership Group, 2018

'From moving migrants to Ascension Island to a wave machine in the Channel, all the leaked proposals considered by Priti Patel', Chloe Chaplain, *iNews*, 1 October 2020

'Coastal erosion: the homes lost to the sea', David Shukman, *BBC*, 14 February 2020

'Coastal floods warning in UK as sea levels rise', David Shukman, *BBC*, 14 February 2020

'Extreme sea level events "will hit once a year by 2050"', Damian Carrington, *The Guardian*, 25 September 2019

'Coastal flooding and erosion, and adaptation to climate change: Interim Report', DEFRA, 2019

'Climate change impacts and adaptation', The Environment Agency, 2018

ACKNOWLEDGEMENTS

This novel was born out of kindness from so many people. It was very difficult to write, and took a long time to write – if this list of gratitude seems long, it's that a huge amount of help was needed.

I'm very grateful for friends who offered solidarity: Erinn, Lucy, Nafkote, Nadja, Yelena, Amanda, Albert, Marie, Mary, Raoul, Lauren, Samira, Alex, among so many more. Friends who in various ways gave me a place to stay – Spencer and Sabine, Nick, Andrew, Louis and Alex, Freya, and Danny (Danny in particular for the note that read 'Rosa, don't break anything'). I'm grateful for friends who were early readers – something which is a brave and thankless job (though I hope you know how thankful I am): Leila, Anna, Natalie, Lish, Lydia, Butch, David, Nancy, Minnie, Jethro, Lauren, Laura, Leah.

Leah, you once read *Dreamland* on your phone in eight hours making corrections as you went. It isn't easy to be the partner of a writer – you do so with enormous grace, endless generosity, patience, light. Also: a truly beautiful ability to tell me when I'm being annoying, kindly. I love you, and thank you. I'm thankful for you every day. There is so much more I could say.

Louis and Steph; Ani, Sarah and Leila (again) – thank you for dear friendship, but also employment. This book wouldn't exist without you.

I'm immensely grateful to the Society of Authors for their K Blundell Trust grant.

I'm grateful, and always will be, to Shakespeare and Company and the De Groot Foundation, without whom I might have gone more directly to my true calling – an estate agent. Seriously though, Sylvia, David, Linda, Laura, Krista, Adam: there is nowhere on earth like your bookshop. You have made a harbour.

I'm grateful to Hedgebrook, Vermont Studio Center, and the Lemon Tree House for residencies that changed the shape of my life, and ripple through everything that's happened since.

Victoria Pepe, who published my first novel at Virago: this book had died when I emailed you and asked you to help edit. Thank you for punching it in the chest and bringing it back to life.

Thank you to Chris White for taking a chance on this book with such thoughtfulness, care and energy. You have been such a shining pleasure to work with. A huge thank you, too, to Kaiya Shang, Amy Fulwood, Becky McCarthy, Charlotte Chapman, and the rest of the team at Scribner. Thank you to Karolina Sutton for staying aboard during a seven-year-long roller-coaster ride/write that must have seemed painfully slow at points – thank you for helping shape this book, and taking it into the right hands. Thank you, too, to the rest of the brilliant team at Curtis Brown.

The screen print of AMAZING high up in a window on page 21, that's by Charlie Evaristo-Boyce – be sure to check out his wonderful work.

Julia Mathison, that envelope was one of the kindest things anyone has ever done for me.

Lastly, thank you to my parents for moving to Thanet. It was an unexpected move for me to follow you here, but I'm so glad I did. Thank you to my brilliant, brightly coloured mum for leading the way, in so many ways. Thank you to my kind and practical dad who read an early version of this book and said, 'It's okay, but you don't know a thing about guns' – and took me directly to a gun shop.

If you are reading this and you have not been to Thanet, come. It's beautiful – as Davey says, 'on a good day', but not only on a good day. White chalk, pink cliff flowers, huge skies, bright sand, swimming when you're brave enough. Come and see all the places like Dreamland, the Turner Contemporary, the Winter Gardens, the Shell Grotto, and all the beaches from Westgate to Pegwell. They are incredible.